after
isabella

For Alli and Annie Tibbatts
with all my love

after isabella

ROSIE FIORE

ALLEN&UNWIN

Published in trade paperback in Great Britain in 2016 by Allen & Unwin

This paperback edition published in 2017

Allen & Unwin
c/o Atlantic Books
Ormond House
26–27 Boswell Street
London WC1N 3JZ

Phone: 020 7269 1610
Fax: 020 7430 0916
Email: UK@allenandunwin.com
Web: www.allenandunwin.com/uk

A CIP catalogue record for this book is available from the British Library.

Paperback ISBN 978 1 76029 242 3
Ebook ISBN 978 1 92557 521 7

Printed in Great Britain by CPI Group (UK) Ltd, Croydon CR0 4YY

10 9 8 7 6 5 4 3 2 1

PROLOGUE

She'd been restlessly asleep for hours, her fingers plucking irregularly at the covers, her eyelids fluttering, her breathing rattly and noisy. Esther sat and watched her. She'd been told that these were all signs that the end was near. It was quite possible that she wouldn't wake again. Her breathing would slow and then stop, and that would be it. Esther leaned back in her chair. She hadn't slept for a long time and she was weary. She shut her eyes for a second, just to rest them.

The breathing stopped and Esther's eyes flew open. The face on the pillow looked awake and alert, her eyes wide open and almost amused.

'Caught you napping.'

'Sorry,' Esther said. 'Can I get you anything?'

'No thanks.' She smiled a genuinely warm, attentive and lovely smile. 'You must be knackered, sorry.'

'I'm fine,' said Esther. 'Honestly. How are you doing? Want more morphine?'

'No pain right now. But I tell you what, my feet are bloody freezing.'

'Your feet? Really?' The room was warm, and the bed was covered with a heavy, fluffy duvet.

'Yeah.'

'Can I get you some socks?'

'I don't think that'll work. I think my body's storing all the heat around what's left of my essential organs. I don't think I'm able to generate my own heat for my extremities. Maybe a hot water bottle... only I don't think I own one.'

'I don't think you do,' said Esther. She paused for a second. 'I read somewhere, although I suspect it's completely spurious, that when D. H. Lawrence was dying, he complained his feet were cold, and his wife, Frieda, put them in her bosom to warm them.'

'Her bosom?'

'I haven't got much of a bosom, but I do generate quite a bit of body heat.'

The chuckle from the bed sounded lively, not at all like the chuckle of someone dying. 'Would you? Would you do that for me?'

'For you, Millais, anything.'

Esther folded back the duvet from the bottom of the bed and lay on her side. She lifted her shirt and drew the two cold feet to her, pressing them against her stomach, then drawing her jumper and the duvet down over them. 'Better?'

'Better. Thank you. Your belly is so soft. Squidgy.' A smile, silence, and eyes that closed slowly.

Esther lay still, breathing softly and watching, until she too fell asleep for a time.

CHAPTER ONE

'The first time I saw Isabella, I was nine years old. We'd moved from Richmond to north London. It was only ten miles or so, but it might as well have been the other side of the world. I knew I'd never ever see my friends again, and that I would be alone forever.

'My mum took me for my first day at the new school, and they called Isabella to the office to take me to my classroom. The head, who was one of those touchy-feely enthusiastic types, leapt up and stood with her hands on Isabella's shoulders as she introduced us. "Isabella Millais is one of our star students!" She beamed. "She's just won a competition and had a picture published in a national magazine, fancy that!" She went on about how Isabella was a credit to her teachers, and Isabella looked straight at me. It took me a moment, but then I realized we were exactly the same height. We had the same long, straight, dark brown hair, and the same dark eyes. She had skinny legs and bumpy knees like me too. She could have been my twin sister. It was like looking in a mirror.

'I must have been staring, because she stared back. She kept her face quite still, but then she very slightly crossed her eyes so she was squinting and stuck the tiniest tip of her tongue out of the corner of her mouth. I couldn't believe her nerve. If the head had spotted her... She didn't even seem to care that my mum, who was standing next to me, could see her. And as quickly as she'd pulled the face, she stopped, and said, "Welcome to St Mary's. I'll show you where the classroom is."

'I picked up my bag and followed her, and my mum stayed behind to talk to the head. Isabella and I walked down the corridor together. She walked fast, and she held her head high. She always walked like that, looking straight ahead. She walked like that for as long as I knew her. I had to trot a bit to keep up. We got to the classroom door and she stopped and checked her watch. Then she yanked my arm so we were bent double and couldn't be seen through the glass panel of the door. She pulled me along, past the classroom and on down the corridor. We went down some stairs into the gymnasium, which was empty. She took me across the room to a huge pile of gym mats, and we sat on the floor behind them, so we couldn't be seen from the door. "It's fifteen minutes to lunchtime," she said. "We'll go back at one minute to, and then there won't be time for embarrassing introductions and making you stand up in front of the class. We can just go straight to lunch." She reached into her blazer pocket and brought out a squished chocolate bar. She broke it in two and gave me half. The bigger half. I knew then that she would be my friend for life.

'And she was. All the way through school, and through university, even though we weren't in the same city. She was always on the end of the phone, or sending me funny letters and pictures in the post, or turning up at my room in halls at eleven o'clock on a Friday night to stay for the weekend. She held my hair back the first time I got drunk enough to be sick. She was my bridesmaid when I got married, and she was godmother to my little girl, Lucie.

'When she found out she was ill, she didn't want to tell anyone. She had this idea that she could just carry on, live her life and have her treatment. She couldn't bear the idea that anyone would pity her, or whisper about her, or think of her as "the one with cancer". She didn't even tell me. I only found out when Sally rang to let me know. Isabella was so sick, she couldn't look after herself, so Sally moved in with her. Now to us, growing up, Sally was the annoying little sister, trailing after Isabella and me, wanting to join in our games – we used to hide from her, or send her on impossible errands. Sometimes we even locked her in the cellar. But when the chips were down, it was Sally Isabella needed. Sally gave up her job and looked after Isabella 24/7 for a year and a half until... Until the end.

'And here we are. The end, the end of Isabella. The most vibrant, hilarious and brilliant person I have ever known. An amazing architect, cook and friend. I know she meant something different, something special to every single one of you, or you wouldn't be here to say goodbye. It just seems... unbelievable that a light like that can have gone from the world. I know it'll take me a very long time to get used to it. I'll still expect to hear her voice on the end of the phone, to see her name popping up in my inbox with a crazy, witty message. I can't believe I won't get another one of her handmade birthday cards. I can't begin to imagine how this feels for Sally, and Isabella's mum, Joan. Our hearts are with you, Sally and Joan, and we'll all be there for you, anytime of the day or night. Rest in peace, Bells. The sister I never had. I can't believe you're gone.'

Esther held it together until she read these last words from the pages gripped in her hand. She could feel the hot tears gathering, and then they spilled over, blurring her glasses. She had somehow got into the pulpit in this church, but she wasn't sure how to get out. She turned ineffectually from side to side. She felt the priest's hand take her elbow firmly but gently and guide her down the three little steps, and she slumped back into the pew next to Stephen.

The ridiculous shiny dark brown of the coffin intruded into her peripheral vision. How could Isabella, or what was left of Isabella, be lying silent and still in that box? She couldn't look at it, hadn't looked at it through her eulogy. It made no sense.

She was thirty-nine years old and this was only the third funeral she had ever been to. It seemed like a strange and archaic ritual, but she wasn't terribly sure how it should be done differently. What are we supposed to do with dead people, she wondered. We have to put them somewhere, dispose of the bodies in a way that is safe and hygienic, assure ourselves that they really, truly are gone, and find a way of moving on. This odd agglomeration of words, music, a box and flowers seemed to be the accepted method. In this case, however, it seemed to have nothing to do with Isabella, who had been an atheist, unmusical, and rather averse to flower arrangements, preferring to decorate her home with minimalist, dramatic displays of bamboo or still lifes of sticks and stones.

The assembled people rose to sing a hymn, Psalm 23. It must have been Joan's choice. Esther hadn't sung it since primary school, and she had a vague memory, or thought she did, of last having sung it beside Isabella, who had a deep and rather gravelly voice and a tendency to sing everything in a low monotone. Esther had never known if Isabella was tone-deaf or was just taking the mick. The latter was likely. The priest began to intone prayers, and even though Esther had been to so few funerals, the words were familiar to her. From films or TV, she imagined.

And then, suddenly, it was all over. The black-coated men entered in procession and efficiently shouldered the coffin. Sally stood to follow it, her arm around Joan's plump shoulders. As they walked out, Sally glanced over and gave Esther a weak smile, nodding her thanks for the eulogy. The cremation was to be private. Esther was relieved about that – she certainly didn't feel up to watching that sleek box slide through a curtain into the furnace. Right now, all she could think of was that she would give anything, anything at all, to drink a large glass of very cold wine very quickly indeed. And then maybe another.

Luckily, everyone else was of the same mind. As soon as the funeral party arrived at the pub where the wake was to be held, Esther was handed a glass. Waiters circulated with trays, and she couldn't help noticing that even though it was just two in the afternoon, people seemed determined to drink quite a lot, quite fast. The chatter was more animated than she might have expected. There was palpable relief that the solemn and grim part of the proceedings had been concluded. She was conscious that Stephen was watching her gulp down her wine. He made no comment but called the waiter over and asked for a lime and soda. Good. So he was planning to drive. That made things easier. She took the last sip and lifted another glass off a tray as the waiter passed near her.

She looked around the room. She had been so nervous about the eulogy that she hadn't really registered who else was in the church. She recognized very few people. There were a lot of elderly women, friends of Joan's, she assumed. Then there were the well-dressed, well-groomed people – work colleagues of Isabella's probably. There was no one else from their school days, although there was a rumpled man of about her age, who she thought might be an old university boyfriend of Isabella's. He stood alone by the food table, sipping from his drink and steadily and absent-mindedly eating Scotch eggs and crumbed mushrooms. Whoever he had been in years gone by, he didn't look like Isabella's type now.

With a glass and a half of wine inside her, Esther relaxed a little. She hadn't embarrassed herself. She had given her dearest and oldest friend a decent send-off. She just had to say a few words to Joan and Sally and she could go. They had arrived a few minutes before from the crematorium and were surrounded by a group of well-meaning old biddies. She wasn't going to get near them anytime soon. She sipped her glass more slowly. She really should eat something, but going to get food meant going near the food table and the slightly desperate-looking ex-boyfriend.

'Could you possibly get me a plate of something to eat?' she said to Stephen, who was standing staring gloomily into his lime and soda. He nodded and headed for the table.

It was a mistake, because Stephen's going left her alone, and the rumpled ex-boyfriend clearly took that as a sign. He brushed crumbs from his lapels and came over to her.

'Thanks for your words,' he said, holding out a hand. 'Good to see you again.'

Esther shook his hand and smiled.

'I can't quite believe she's gone,' he continued. 'Someone like that...'

'She was uncompromisingly alive, wasn't she?'

'You always had a way with words.' He smiled at her, and she couldn't help noticing he had a tiny smear of ketchup in the corner of his mouth. She had no idea what his name was, or even whether her assumption that he was Isabella's ex was correct. She didn't know how to take the conversation forward.

'You don't remember who I am, do you?' he said.

'Sorry.'

'Geoff,' he said, and in an instant she remembered. He had been a housemate of Isabella's at university. He had been funny and kind, and had played the guitar. She knew Isabella had liked him, in a non-romantic way. Esther recalled vaguely that he had gone to America after he had graduated. He hadn't crossed her mind in more than twenty years.

'It's funny to look at you,' he said conversationally. 'You look so like her, still. You always did. Like sisters. You must be really devastated.' There seemed no possible answer to this, so Esther said nothing. He laughed suddenly. 'You really were the two musketeers, weren't you? I remember you coming up to uni for parties... There was one in particular, when we all went clubbing together. The two of you were dancing, hanging onto one another. You were wearing a black dress, and Isabella was wearing white... I often imagined what it would be like to—'

'Excuse me,' said Esther. 'Must go to the loo.' She saw Stephen approaching with a plate full of food and she gestured to let him know where she was going.

She locked herself in a cubicle, put the lid down and sat on it, her head on her knees. Geoff's behaviour was so hilariously inappropriate, she hadn't been sure whether to slap him or laugh. Neither would have been fitting at Isabella's wake. It was a first, though. She had never before been retrospectively presented with someone's fantasy of a threesome at the funeral of the prospective third party. At some point in the future, it would make a grand anecdote – and naturally, the one person who would most have enjoyed hearing it would never be able to.

She should go back out to the gathering. She would, as soon as she could persuade herself to stand up. Someone else came into the bathroom, and so she sat still and silent. She wasn't going out now and risking small talk by the basins. She listened to the person pee, flush and wash their hands, and she waited to hear the door open and close, but whoever it was remained in the room. Were they redoing their make-up? Praying? Crying?

Then she heard a voice say hesitantly, 'Are you all right? Hello?' And someone tapped on the door of her cubicle.

She swore inwardly. 'Fine,' she said, as cheerfully as she could manage. She stood up and flushed, and made some pretence of straightening her clothes before she emerged.

Sally stood by the basins.

'Oh, it's you,' she said, and hugged Esther warmly.

'How are you doing?' Esther asked.

Sally smiled. 'Oh, fine. Glad it's over. Hoping we don't run out of Scotch eggs. You know.'

'How's your mum?'

'Well, she's as you'd imagine. Bearing up most of the time. It comes in waves. The last few weeks, we had a lot of time to sit and talk quietly, so it's not a terrible shock, you know, like a sudden death would be. Not like my dad.'

Isabella and Sally's father had died of a heart attack on the train on his way to work one day, when Isabella was at university and Sally was still at school. It had devastated Sally, who had been very close to him, and left Joan frail and wobbly for years. Isabella always said it felt unreal. She had learned of her father's death in a crackly call on a street-corner payphone in Edinburgh, where she was living in digs. She hadn't managed to get back to London until the morning of the funeral. Joan had discouraged the girls from viewing the body, so for Isabella, the bereavement was oddly theoretical. She had gone from having a father to having none, merely because she had been told that that was what had happened. Sally, left at home, had had to bear the brunt of it – the practicalities of settling the estate, her mother's grief.

And here she was, bearing the brunt again. Esther squeezed her hand. Sally smiled and turned to the mirror to tidy her hair and put on some lipstick. She was a pretty woman, but she didn't look anything like Isabella. Where Isabella had had straight dark hair, Sally had a halo of blonde curls. She had wide blue eyes and a sweet, curved, pink mouth. She had been an adorable toddler, but the cuteness of her features did not sit quite as well on the face of an adult woman. She was much shorter than Isabella had been, and tended towards the curvy, a similar shape to their mother.

'My mum sends her love and condolences,' said Esther. 'She told me she sent flowers...'

'Yes, thank you,' said Sally. 'We got them. They're beautiful, of course. I wouldn't expect anything different. Your mum always had such amazing taste. I'll write and thank her.'

'Please don't worry about it,' Esther said quickly. 'She lives on the Isle of Wight now, and she just wanted you to know she was thinking of you. She was very fond of Isabella.'

'I know Isabella loved her too,' said Sally. 'They were both artistic...' Her voice trailed off, as if the effort of sustaining conversation had suddenly become too much.

'What are your plans now?' Esther asked, then inwardly cursed herself. 'Now that your sister's dead,' seemed to be the implied end of that question. 'I mean... what are your plans for the future?'

'Oh, there's still a lot to do,' said Sally, carefully combing her fluffy hair. 'I'll have to wind up the estate, sell Isabella's house and so on. There's a lot of medical equipment which needs to go back to the NHS. Then I hope to take a little holiday maybe. Bit of a break. After that it's back to work. I'm very lucky they've kept my job open.'

'Where are you working?'

'Same place. I'm an office manager for an estate agent's, not far from here. I've been there ten years. I kept meaning to move on, maybe study something new. Isabella was always on at me to do it. But it never seemed the right time.'

'Well, maybe now's the right time,' said Esther, smiling at Sally's reflection. 'New horizons. Use some of Isabella's bravery and go for it.'

'You might be right.' Sally smiled back. 'Just need to get my courage up, eh?'

'Let me come and say hi to your mum,' said Esther. 'Stephen needs to get back to work, so we really must be going soon.'

'Of course,' said Sally, popping her lipstick and comb back into her bag. 'Just understand, she's, well, she's not at her best right now.'

'Of course she isn't.' Esther followed Sally out of the toilet. What an odd comment to make. Of course Joan wasn't doing very well. She had just cremated her beloved elder daughter.

Joan was sitting at a table, a plate of snacks in front of her and a cup of tea at her elbow, staring into the distance. Two of her friends sat at the table with her, but they weren't speaking. Joan had been a young mother, just twenty-one when Isabella was born, so Esther calculated that she couldn't be more than sixty now. She looked a decade older than that, her face grey and pouchy, an inch of frizzy grey showing at her roots. None of this was a surprise. Not after what she had just endured. Esther hadn't allowed herself – couldn't allow herself – to think about burying a child. No parent could. The horror was too extreme.

Sally took her over and they sat down in two vacant chairs at the table. 'Mum, Esther's here,' she said, touching Joan's arm.

'Hello there,' said Joan, mustering a smile. 'How nice to see you. You look well. How are you?'

'I'm fine, thank you,' said Esther. 'I... I'm so sorry for your loss.'

'Beautiful day,' said Joan.

'Yes. And the service was lovely. The music especially.'

'I always preferred David Cassidy myself,' said Joan. 'Or Donny Osmond. Lovely teeth.'

Esther laughed gently. It was good she could make jokes on a day like this. That she still had a little spirit. She caught Sally's eye across the table and was surprised to see that Sally looked strained, embarrassed even. The two other women at the table were looking away, not joining in the conversation.

'I've got one question though,' said Joan.

'Mum...' said Sally warningly, but Joan would not be hushed.

'Where's Isabella? I'm sure she said she'd be here by now. She said she was going to take me to the theatre.'

CHAPTER TWO

eight years later

The same church. The same brilliant blue sky. But not the same crowd. Not even a crowd at all, just a handful of mourners – some elderly, frail ladies, Esther and Sally.

Esther wouldn't have been there, wouldn't even have known that Joan had died, had she not got a letter from Sally. It was odd to get a handwritten, physical letter – she couldn't remember the last time she'd received one. But that was what Sally had chosen; she clearly felt one shouldn't announce the death of one's mother in an email or on social media. Perhaps if it had been an email or a text, Esther might have made her excuses. But there was something about Sally's careful, round handwriting on the old-fashioned notepaper (which was peach coloured, with an illustration of a bunny in a basket of flowers in the bottom right-hand corner). She felt she should go, if Sally had made the effort to write to her, so she took the afternoon off, found a simple black dress in her wardrobe (noting that it was considerably looser round the waist than it had been the last time she wore it), and went to Joan's funeral.

It wasn't the same vicar who had done Isabella's service. This one was young and had a posh, drawling accent that suggested Cambridge. He had clearly never met Joan, which was a little surprising, as Esther remembered her as a regular churchgoer. Even if she had been too ill to attend, surely he would have visited? It seemed not.

Sally was sitting alone in the front pew. The vicar finished his remarks and said, 'Joan's daughter Sally will now say a few words.'

Sally stood and went to the lectern. Esther was sitting towards the back of the church, quite far away, but even at that distance she was shocked at Sally's appearance. Since she had last seen her, Sally had gained weight — a lot of weight. Possibly three or four stone. Her bright blonde curls had faded to an unkempt mess of mouse and grey. She looked like an overweight, middle-aged woman defeated by life. There was no trace of the attractive blonde of eight years before.

Esther assumed Sally would give some kind of eulogy, but instead she read from Revelations, the reading that began 'And I saw a new heaven and a new earth'. Her voice sounded softer and more hesitant than Esther remembered. When she finished reading, she paused for a moment and glanced at the small coffin, her expression unreadable, then stepped down.

The service was concluded. This time there were no hymns, which was a mercy. There really weren't enough people to sing them. The organist played a rather mangled and soulless version of Elgar's 'Nimrod' and the mourners straggled out behind the coffin.

There was no private cremation, no escape to the pub for Esther. Joan was to be buried, and they followed the hearse in convoy to a large, featureless, modern cemetery about a mile away. Most of the old ladies were obviously not up to the trip to the graveside, so it was an even smaller crowd of just five or six people and the vicar that watched Joan get lowered into her grave. Sally stepped forward when invited to scatter some earth on the coffin. She turned and gestured to Esther, inviting her to do the same. It seemed rude, almost sacrilegious, to do so – she hadn't seen Joan for nearly a decade, had seen her only very infrequently in the years before that. But there genuinely was no one else, and it would have been even ruder, and hurtful to Sally, to refuse. She bent and gathered a clod of earth and dropped it on the polished lid. She found a tissue in her pocket to clean off her hand and stood awkwardly by as the old ladies did the same. The gravedigger was waiting impatiently nearby, leaning on his small earth-moving machine. Clearly they didn't do this job with a shovel anymore. Esther didn't think Sally would want to stand by and watch the man fill in the grave like a trench in some roadworks, so she looped her arm through hers and prepared to lead her away.

'You will come back to the house, won't you?' Sally looked up at her, her blue eyes pale and watery. 'There didn't seem much point in organizing a wake, so I just did some sandwiches and cake at home.'

'Of course,' said Esther.

She had not been to Joan's house for nigh on twenty-five years. Once Isabella had graduated and moved into her own place, Esther had had no reason to visit her friend's childhood home. From the outside, the house looked as one might have expected – shabbier and smaller, but much as she remembered it. But as soon as she came through the door, she was assailed by the oppressive sadness of the place. The furniture seemed to be the same as it had been when they were children – she remembered the brown velour sofa, the seascape prints and the glass coffee table. Sally had obviously made an effort to clean and tidy the place, but it had the deeply ingrained dullness of a home that had not been redecorated for decades. Despite an almost oppressive miasma of sweet air-freshener, the underlying scent of urine and unwashed old person was unmistakeable.

Sally settled two old ladies into armchairs and then bustled into the kitchen to make tea. Esther, unsure what to do, followed her. The Formica kitchen table was the same one she remembered from teatimes when she was nine. The chairs were the same too, although the seat covers were now faded and stained and the arched chrome backs and legs were spotted with rust. Sally clicked on the kettle and started taking cling-film off plates of sandwiches. She seemed to have made enough for twenty or thirty people, and there was also a large, bought chocolate cake and several platefuls of biscuits.

'I don't think we'll need all these', said Esther. 'Maybe pop some in the fridge for later.'

'Of course.' Sally smiled faintly. 'I always worry there won't be enough, so I tend to over-cater.'

She bent to get the milk out of the fridge, and Esther noted how broad she looked from behind. She was even heavier than Esther had first thought. She knew that carers often put on weight – it was a sedentary occupation, and often boring and disheartening. One couldn't judge someone for self-medicating with the odd packet of ginger nuts, but it was a worry.

She helped Sally to carry the plates and cups through, then sat on the edge of the sofa, trying to make small talk with the two old ladies. They were much more interested in the sandwiches and cakes, piling their plates high and calling Sally to bring more tea. Esther couldn't help feeling they didn't seem very grief-stricken, and it turned out they were in fact two of Sally and Joan's neighbours. They both freely admitted they hadn't seen Joan for some years.

'Since she went doolally,' one of them said, 'I didn't see much point in coming to see her. She never knew who I was. And I'm sure five minutes after I left she'd forgotten I'd been here.'

'Memory like a goldfish,' said the other, helping herself to another slice of cake.

Esther wondered if they were there out of neither grief nor duty but simply because it gave them a day out, a free meal and possibly a chance to snoop inside the house. Sure enough, once they'd both had their fill of tea, they took turns to go to the toilet, obviously having a good look into all the rooms on their way to and from the bathroom. Then they said their goodbyes and left, walking up the road together, their heads almost touching as they exchanged gossip. To their credit, they didn't promise to come back and visit Sally again.

Sally smiled rather weakly, then heaved herself out of her armchair and began clearing the plates. Esther leapt up to help her, but there was very little to do. She would have loved to have gone too, but it seemed brutal to leave Sally alone after the sad insufficiency of this goodbye to her mother. Esther glanced at her watch.

'I think this might call for something stronger than tea,' she said. 'Have you got any wine, or shall I nip out and get some?'

'Oh...' Sally dithered, clutching a dishtowel in both hands. 'I don't usually... I've got nothing in the house...'

'You don't usually, but do you drink at all?'

'Well, I used to... The odd glass...'

'Red or white?'

'Oh, white. Never could see the point of red.'

'I'll be back in two minutes,' said Esther, heading for the door as she spoke. 'Dust off some glasses.'

She had walked the few hundred yards from that front door to the corner shop more times than she could remember. She and

Isabella had gone there for sweets and crisps when they were little, then for magazines and fizzy drinks. From the age of about fifteen, they had lurked outside, yearning for bottles of Lambrini. Occasionally they'd been able to persuade someone's big brother to go in and buy some, and then they would take it to the park and pretend to be tipsier than they really were.

Now she could walk right in and peruse the wine shelf. She wasn't even going to be asked for ID. The old Indian couple who had run the shop for decades had obviously sold up and left, and it was now a chain mini-supermarket. There were a number of two-for-one special offers on well-known wines, but, rather incongruously, there was a bottle of Veuve Clicquot in the chiller, and Esther grabbed it. It was expensive, but somehow she knew it was the right thing to buy. She also picked up a couple of bottles of Californian Sauvignon Blanc and went to pay.

Back at the house, Sally gasped and giggled when she saw the champagne.

'Let's give your mum a proper send-off,' said Esther, peeling the foil off the cork.

Sally fussed around and found a dingy ice bucket and they took the bottle and their glasses into the living room and sat down. They toasted Joan, and Sally took a small sip and then a bigger one. Her cheeks instantly flushed pink, and she appeared to relax a little.

'So,' Esther said, 'how are you bearing up?'

'Gosh,' said Sally. 'Oh, I'm all right. It's lovely to see you. Have a catch-up. It seems we only get to chat when someone in my family dies.'

'I'm sorry,' said Esther uncomfortably. 'I should have called. Been around more...'

'Nonsense, why should you? You were Isabella's friend.'

'It looks like...' Esther said carefully. 'It looks like the last few years might have been pretty hard for you. And lonely.'

'Well, yes, and yes,' said Sally. 'Dementia is very ugly. Or at least the kind Mother had was. She was very distrustful. And rude. It wasn't nice for people to come round here, because she'd insult them. Or do something awful... Break things, or hide her face and refuse to talk. And I couldn't risk taking her out, because she'd wander off, or sit down on the pavement and refuse to move. I couldn't get her up and shift her if she did.'

'That sounds awful. I'm so sorry.'

'Oh, it wasn't so bad.' Sally managed a smile. 'As long as I kept the routine absolutely rigid – meals at the same time every day, the same food, the same TV programmes – she was mostly all right.'

'And did you not have any help?'

'We had carers in every day, or most days – I couldn't manage to bathe her alone. And they'd sometimes come and sit with her for an hour or so, so I could get a bit of shopping in.'

Esther was stunned into silence. It seemed Sally had barely left the house for eight years. No wonder she had aged. It sounded like prison. There was no point in asking her about friends, boyfriends, her job. It was clear that she had been denied all of these. She refilled Sally's glass, and her own, which mysteriously seemed to be empty.

'So what have you been up to?' asked Sally.

'Oh, you know. I joined the university as a junior lecturer in English literature, and I'm still there. Still teaching Dickens and Austen.'

'Not a junior lecturer anymore though.'

'No,' said Esther. 'I'm, er... a professor now. And currently also head of the English Department.'

'Oh my.'

'Sounds more impressive than it is. Everyone in the department gets a go at being head for a few years, then they get tired of the administration and the meetings and want to go back to teaching and research. Then someone else has a pop at it.'

Sally nodded. Esther had a feeling she might as well have been speaking Chinese. Her world and her life would make no sense at all to a woman who hadn't been able to work for more than a decade.

'And your husband? Stephen, is it?' said Sally. As she spoke, she glanced at Esther's left hand and Esther saw her regret the question.

'We split up.'

'I'm so sorry.'

'Don't be. It's all very amicable. He's remarried and lives in Manchester now.'

'And Lucie?'

'She's twelve. She's amazing. Very together. Very confident and articulate. Much more so than I was at her age.'

'Isabella was her godmother.'

'Yes.'

'Lucky,' said Sally, and Esther wasn't sure if she meant Lucie was lucky, or Isabella, or Esther herself.

Much later, woozy from too much wine, Esther wandered back out to her car. It felt like midnight, although it was only late afternoon. She was in no state to drive, so she made sure the car was locked and wasn't going to get a fine, and then walked on towards the Tube station. What a depressing day. She'd come back the next day to pick up the car, and she'd never ever have to come to this miserable corner of town again.

CHAPTER THREE

'That's the saddest story I ever heard,' said Lucie later, sitting at the dining room table, leaning forward and fixing Esther with her clear gaze. 'It's like she never really lived.'

'I suppose so.'

'Is she very sad?'

'Well, she's sad her mum died,' said Esther, but as she spoke, she wondered if Sally really was sad. She would have lost Joan, the Joan she knew, years ago. This final break might have been a relief. 'She's doing her best to be cheerful.'

'That's terrible.'

'What is?'

'People should be able to be sad. Especially when someone's died. They should have friends to care for them so they can be as sad as they like. It's awful to have to be cheerful for other people.'

Esther marvelled, not for the first time, at her daughter's emotional intelligence. She was compassionate to a fault, forever giving her pocket money to charitable causes and making friends with the least appealing children at school. If Esther hadn't been allergic, she had no doubt Lucie would be out rescuing stray animals too.

'Well, we need to invite her over,' said Lucie firmly.

'What? Oh, darling, that's lovely of you, but it's not as if she was ever really my friend. Isabella was.'

'Isabella was, and she was Isabella's sister.'

'Yes.'

'Isabella was my godmother, which means if you died, she was supposed to look after me.'

Esther's heart sank. She could see where this was going. She had no doubt that Lucie was destined for a career in law. She had the argument all worked out.

Sure enough, Lucie said, 'And so, in return, you should look after Isabella's nearest and dearest... Now she's dead.'

'You're right. I know you're right. It's just...'

'Just what?' Lucie fixed her with her steady, dark gaze, so like Esther's own. So like Isabella's.

'Well, we don't really have anything in common. She... Well, she never went to university, she hasn't worked in years... What would we talk about?'

'Mother!' said Lucie, shocked. 'Are you being a snob? And judgemental? All the things you nag me not to be?'

Esther dropped her head on her folded arms. 'I am, I am. You're right. How hard can it be to make a little space in our lives for someone who's lonely? I'll ring her this evening and ask her over for tea.'

'Dinner.'

'All right. For dinner.'

Lucie nodded, satisfied. Her sense of right and justice had been appeased. And Esther knew she would not be allowed conveniently to 'forget' to call. Lucie would ask insistently until she did it. So she might as well get it out of the way.

She didn't have a mobile or landline number for Sally. She could try Directory Enquiries (when had she last rung them? Ten years ago?), but it might just be worth ringing the old house number, the one she had indelibly committed to memory from years of ringing Isabella when they were children.

She dialled it and it rang for a long time. She was beginning to think it had probably been changed or disconnected, when Sally's voice, fuzzy and blurred with sleep, or sleep and wine, answered. Esther checked her watch. It was not quite nine o'clock. Not an unconscionably late hour to ring.

'Sally, it's Esther,' she said briskly.

'Esther. Oh, hello! What a lovely surprise!'

Lucie had been right. Sally's forced cheeriness was heart-breaking.

'I just wanted to… say thanks for today, and check you were all right,' she said carefully.

'Oh, I'm okay,' Sally replied, and Esther could hear the wide smile in her voice. 'Right as rain. Just dozed off in front of the telly. Not used to the wine, you know. But thank you so much for that. So lovely of you.'

'Well, I was just chatting to my daughter,' Esther said, 'and we wondered if you might be free for dinner sometime soon? Maybe Friday evening?'

'Dinner? Oh my,' said Sally, as if it was not a meal she was familiar with. 'Well, that's very kind of you, but…'

'Nothing fancy,' said Esther, trying to keep her voice gentle, listening to Sally flutter anxiously on the other end of the line. 'Just you, me and Lucie, here at home. I'll make us some pasta or something. Now the evenings are nicer, we might even be able to sit outside.'

'Where are you? I mean, where do you live?' Sally sounded genuinely anxious now.

'Not far from you.' Esther gave the address. 'I pass near you on my way home from work. I could stop by and pick you up in the car.'

'Well, that would be nice...'

'I'll drop you back too,' said Esther, and that seemed to reassure Sally. How very small her world must be. She probably hadn't left the borough she lived in for years. She didn't drive, and navigating the complexities of London public transport would be very scary if you weren't used to it, especially at night.

Lucie was satisfied with the arrangements and announced that she would bake a cake for dessert. On the Thursday evening Esther prepared a lasagne and put it in the fridge, ready to be cooked on their return the following evening. She checked they had salad ingredients and a bottle of chilled white wine as well as the usual selection of soft drinks.

Esther wasn't quite sure why she was dreading the dinner so much. She wasn't unkind by nature, or ungenerous. It was just... Sally was from a different part of her life. A long-ago time. Her split from Stephen had made her wary of looking back. She had reinvented herself, and she wasn't at all sure she wanted to be reminded of the Esther that had been. She had worked so hard to look forward, to build a new life for herself and Lucie. She had taken her half of the proceeds from the sale of the family home and bought a neat, new-build, two-bedroomed townhouse. She had furnished it with new things, except for Lucie's room, which still contained her old white-painted bed and her collection of soft toys.

As much as Esther tried to shed her past, Lucie seemed determined to hang onto hers. Many of her friends had chucked out their Barbie duvet covers and Sylvanian Families collections, replacing them with posters of boy bands and rejecting outright all that was pink and princessy. But Lucie's room was still determinedly the bedroom of a little girl. Esther knew better than to argue; Lucie had lost enough in the divorce. If she wanted to hang onto her My Little Ponies for a few more years, that was fine by her.

For herself, however, she loved the clean, blank newness of their home – the pale sofa and carpets she could never have had when Lucie was a toddler, the framed prints which held no memories of other walls. She had bought them all together, in a single morning, from a faceless, upmarket poster shop. She found the townhouse calming and peaceful, an expression of the person she had worked so hard to become. She wasn't sure how she felt about sad, dowdy Sally, with all her associations with Isabella, coming into the space.

Esther had her open-door office hours on Friday afternoons, between two and five. However, if she had finished seeing students and no one new arrived by 4.45, she often shut up shop in order to get home a little early. Today was such a day, and at twenty to she turned off her computer, tidied her desk and switched off the light. Traffic was unusually light for a Friday and she was outside Sally's house by just after five. It was a little earlier than they had arranged. She spent a few minutes checking her email on her phone and then squared her shoulders and went to ring the doorbell.

Sally answered almost immediately. She had her bag in her hand and her coat on and buttoned up. She still spent ten minutes fussing, going back to check the kitchen windows were locked and the correct lights had been switched off or left on. She dithered by the front door for a few minutes, wondering if she should take her umbrella until Esther, with barely concealed impatience, pointed out that the sky was clear and she would be going directly from house to car to house and was unlikely to be caught in an unseasonable and unexpected downpour.

It was like managing a frail and elderly lady who was leaving the house for the first time in years. Esther had to remind herself that Sally was in fact six years her junior. Her uncertain behaviour, frumpy clothes and bulky physique added decades to her age. Eventually, she got Sally out of the house, but only after she'd locked, unlocked, double-locked and double-checked the front door. She would have gone back in one more time to check the windows were all closed if Esther hadn't practically shoved her into the car.

Esther took a moment to text Lucie, who would already be home from school, and ask her to turn the oven on. Meanwhile, Sally fussed and settled herself in the passenger seat, taking an age to find a place for her handbag at her feet, then pulling the seatbelt across. She couldn't seem to find the clasp to fasten it, so after feeling about for it, she simply held the seatbelt across herself. Esther couldn't help smiling – she remembered her grandma doing the same thing, as if presenting the appearance of wearing a seatbelt was what counted, rather than actually being safe. She reached over gently and took the belt from Sally's hand, pulling it down and clipping it into the buckle. It was odd to touch her, and Esther couldn't help thinking that Sally probably didn't get touched a lot. That said, she could hardly talk. She hadn't had any physical intimacy since her divorce, and her experience of touch was limited to cheek kisses from friends and hugs from Lucie.

She pulled out into the traffic and headed for home. Sally seemed fascinated by everything around her, looking avidly out of the window. Once they'd got more than a mile or so from her house, she began reading the names of shops aloud. 'Magic Kebab!' she said happily, as if she had never seen a kebab shop before. 'Paddy Power. My, there are a lot of betting shops, aren't there?'

Esther nodded and concentrated on getting through the Friday evening traffic. Sally was content to witter on. She didn't seem to expect a reply to her remarks. Esther supposed she had spent years talking to, or rather at Joan, once Joan's faculties had deserted her. She had probably got out of the habit of reciprocal conversation.

When they got to Esther's street, dusk was beginning to fall.

'Oh, this is lovely!' Sally breathed, totally agog, as if she'd been brought to the Palace of Versailles.

'It is nice, isn't it?' said Esther, parking the car. Seeing it through Sally's eyes, she was struck anew at how pretty it was, with its grassy verges and evenly spaced trees laden with blossom. She could see the lights were on in the house, and she glimpsed Lucie's sleek dark head moving around in the living room on the first floor. This would be all right. Of course it would be.

Sally stumped up the stairs and just from that brief exertion became a little out of breath. Esther steeled herself for ten minutes of gushing, and out it came – about how pretty the house was, how nicely appointed, what a lovely view. What a beauty Lucie was, and the image of Esther, how tasty the bowl of crisps was, how delicious her glass of sparkling water. Esther quickly realized that Sally's constant stream of chatter came from nervousness and shyness; she was determined to try and put her at her ease. She eventually persuaded Sally to sit down and asked Lucie to keep her company while she checked on dinner. 'Maybe you could put some music on, Lucie,' she suggested as she went into the kitchen.

She enjoyed her few minutes alone in there, getting salad ingredients out of the fridge and pouring herself a glass of wine. She'd only be able to have one as she was driving Sally home, so she might as well enjoy it now. The lasagne was bubbling away in the oven. She popped in a loaf of frozen garlic bread and went out to see how Lucie and Sally were getting on.

They were standing close together, going through the CD rack, chatting animatedly.

'I saw the Pet Shop Boys at Wembley in 1989,' Sally was saying, taking a copy of *Elysium* off the shelf and turning it over to look at the track list. 'It was a gradual slide downhill from there for them, till this album. This was their last with Parlophone. I'm interested to see how they do with their new label.'

Lucie turned to look at Esther, her eyes wide and her mouth in a round little O. Esther returned the open-mouthed gaze.

Sally looked up and saw both of them staring. 'What? You're surprised I know about the Pet Shop Boys? I've always loved music.'

And as she said it, Esther remembered. Sally had always had music playing in her room when she was young – cassette tapes piled up on her bedside table beside her clunky top-loading old tape player. She had generally been more knowledgeable about the pop acts of the day than either Isabella or Esther, and had often recommended things for them to listen to. There was no reason why that interest should have faded, and even if she perhaps wasn't internet-savvy, music magazines and radio could have kept her connected to the world of music. It gave them a conversational opening, and she encouraged Sally to choose things for them to listen to and talk about. That got them through until dinner, and they sat down to eat with Prince's 'Raspberry Beret' playing in the background and Sally flushed and happy.

Over dinner, talk turned to computers and the internet. To Esther and Lucie's surprise, Sally didn't own a computer, had never owned one, hadn't used one for more than ten years and didn't even have an email address.

'I didn't see the point,' she said, helping herself to a second portion of lasagne. 'When I was working, it was all still Windows

95 and dial-up, even in the office. It was slow and clunky and I didn't enjoy using it at work. Why would I have wanted a computer at home?'

Esther imagined for a moment what a difference it might have made – an opportunity for her to connect with people or maybe join an online forum for carers. Friends. Support. Information. What a difference indeed.

After dinner, Lucie went to her room and returned with her laptop. She got Sally to sit beside her on the sofa and showed her YouTube, asking her to name bands then calling up their videos. Then she showed her Spotify and set up a playlist of obscure recordings as Sally named them, excitedly. There was a moment of confusion when Sally noticed that there were no cables attached to Lucie's laptop, and they had to explain wireless broadband to her.

'Could I have that at home?' she asked.

'Well, you have a landline telephone, so I can't imagine why not,' said Esther. 'I'll look into it.' She went to fetch her iPad to research setting up broadband connections. That was briefly delayed because Sally had never seen an iPad, or indeed any kind of tablet computer. She was excited by it, clearly preferring the touch-screen technology to a keyboard and mouse. Once she had reluctantly given it back, Esther ran a search and found a useful page on the BT website. 'You'd need to get a computer,' she said, 'but there's no reason why we couldn't set up your broadband package and get it connected within a few days. It depends which service you want.'

'I want the best one. All the bells and whistles. Everything.'

Esther was a little surprised. 'Okay, well, you can get a package with extra TV channels—'

'I don't need more TV. I've watched enough TV to last me a lifetime,' said Sally. 'And I'll go out tomorrow to buy a computer.

I've seen those PC World shops. There's one near me. Would they be able to help me with a computer?'

'I'm sure they would,' she said. 'Well, as soon as you've got your computer, I'd be happy to help you order your broadband.'

'Can we do it now? So it's all set up sooner?'

Esther was astonished at this forcefulness. It was as if a light had gone on in meek little Sally. She had glimpsed something new and she clearly wanted it.

Sally rummaged in her bag. 'I've got my bank card,' she said, 'if we need to pay for it now.'

Later, after Esther had driven an excited, chattering Sally home, she returned to find Lucie curled up in the corner of the sofa, her feet tucked under her, looking at something on her laptop. It wasn't late, and it was Friday night, so she didn't mind that Lucie hadn't gone to bed.

'Thanks, sweetheart,' she said, flopping down on the sofa beside Lucie and patting her ankle. 'You were very nice to Sally. And kind.'

'I liked her,' said Lucie. 'I've never met anyone like her before.'

'Like her how?'

'She's like the man in the story, the one who goes to sleep for a hundred years.'

'Rip Van Winkle.'

'Yes. It's like the world has moved on, into the future, but she's been left behind.'

'I think it's at least partially deliberate,' said Esther. 'I mean, she must have seen stuff on television. It's not like she's been living in a bunker.'

'It must have felt a bit like that. So cut off... Even if she saw something she was interested in but didn't understand it, who could she ask about it?'

'I suppose,' said Esther, but she still felt a little unconvinced by Sally's total innocence. Or maybe she was just annoyed by it.

Imparting and gaining knowledge were the cornerstones of her life. She couldn't understand wilful ignorance. It made no sense to her. She found it perverse.

'I'm a bit worried about her though,' said Lucie, looking up from her screen. 'I mean, how is she going to pay for all of this?'

'Pay for what?'

'The computer, broadband… She doesn't work, does she?'

'No. Well, I imagine she has some kind of carer's allowance. Although possibly not anymore. I have no idea what her financial situation is. She's a grown woman, I'm sure she knows what she's doing.'

And even though Esther wasn't convinced this was the case, she wasn't about to quiz Sally on her income and outgoings.

CHAPTER FOUR

Some people talked to their mothers every day. Other people lived with theirs. Esther rang her mother once a week on a Saturday morning. It was an arrangement which suited them both, and other than birthday cards and a pre-Christmas annual visit, this was their sole contact. It wasn't that they didn't love each other, it was just the way they had always conducted their relationship.

Esther's mother Laura was a fit, strong woman in her mid-seventies. She had been born on the Isle of Wight and, with Esther grown up and her husband gone, had opted to return there fifteen years before. Her life was full, busy and active – she gardened and was involved in the local church, she was a member of a local walking group and she read widely and critically. She loved Esther and Lucie, of that there was no doubt, but she was fiercely independent and not grandmotherly at all. Not even especially motherly, Esther had to admit.

Laura had always worked; she was a teacher and it had been her transfer to a north London school that had caused the family to move from Richmond. She had cared for Esther, been kind, fair and reliable, but somehow separate. As an only child, Esther had quickly learned to be self-sufficient, particularly emotionally. She didn't resent this at all – she hadn't been a clingy, needy child. She hadn't missed having a stay-at-home mum like Isabella had, to fuss her; she had liked the fact that her mother didn't need her. Joan had always seemed to be waiting for Isabella and Sally to come home and had always wanted to know the details of their lives. When she was younger, she had rather liked going round to their house and hearing Sally and Isabella sharing accounts of their days as their mum bustled about preparing an after-school snack. But as they got older, they found ways to avoid Joan's incessant questioning. Isabella began spending much more time at Esther's house, where Laura, even if she were there, would leave them to their own devices and other than asking if they wanted anything to eat, never questioned them about anything.

When Esther rang her mum, she would share the week's news, and usually Lucie would take the phone and have a chat with her grandmother too. Laura would fill them in on the goings-on on the island, and would tell them about the season's growth in her garden. She was very even-tempered – always positive, always full of energy and plans for the weeks and months ahead.

After Joan's funeral and the evening with Sally, Esther felt unaccountably low, and she was looking forward to hearing Laura's cheerful voice. 'Hi, Mum,' she said, and she inserted a little fake merriness into her tone.

'Hello, Esther,' said her mum. 'I haven't a long time to talk. I'm off to the garden centre with some friends. They've started doing lunch there, and we thought we might do some shopping and then sample their menu. I've got to get back by mid-afternoon though – we're going to a play tonight, and I have to sort out my hair. It looks like a bird's nest.'

Esther had to smile. She lived in London, the cultural capital of the world. Her mum lived on a tiny island and yet she seemed to find more to do.

'I shan't keep you, just wanted to let you know Joan died – you remember Isabella's mum? I went to her funeral the other day.'

'I'm sorry to hear that,' said Laura. 'What did she die of? She was a bit younger than me, I think.'

'Dementia, as far as I know. That's what she'd been suffering from. Sally had been looking after her, ever since Isabella died.'

'Sally? Oh, the funny little sister, the one with the blonde curls. Such a little cherub she was.'

'I think the past few years have been hard on her,' said Esther carefully.

'Still… dementia. The worst possible way to go. You die long before you die. I should hate it.'

'Well, you're showing no signs of it yet.' Esther smiled.

'Still seem to be in possession of most of the marbles. Now, before I go, how's my wonderful granddaughter?'

'Lovely. A delight as always. Doing well at school, being sweet to her mother.'

'She needs to rebel a bit, that girl. Tell her I said so. She needs to get a tattoo or start smoking.'

'I shall not tell her that!' Esther laughed. 'She's twelve! Plenty of time for rebellion yet.'

'Must dash. Love to you both,' said Laura, and blew a noisy kiss down the phone. Esther rang off, feeling somehow better.

Late one evening about a week later, Esther was curled up in the corner of the sofa, absent-mindedly flicking through some news articles on her iPad while the television droned on in the background. Lucie had gone to bed, and she was trying to work up the energy to go up herself. When the phone rang, she jumped. She glanced at the clock reflexively – it was after ten o'clock. Her mum had always told her not to ring anyone later than nine, otherwise they would assume it was bad news. Was this bad news? Or just an annoying cold call? Either way, she didn't want the ringing phone to wake Lucie, or alarm her, so she leapt up from the sofa and answered it.

'I'm so sorry.' Sally's breathy voice cut in immediately, almost before Esther had finished saying hello. 'As the phone started ringing, I looked at the clock and realized it really was too late to be calling. But then I didn't want to hang up and make you worry.'

'It's no problem,' said Esther, taking the cordless phone and sitting back down on the sofa. 'No problem at all. I wasn't in bed or anything. Just watching a bit of TV.'

'Ah,' said Sally. 'Did you see the sewing thing earlier?'

'The sewing thing?'

'A very interesting programme, all about the history of patterned textiles. They had to be imported, you see. English manufacturers couldn't make them.'

'Sounds interesting,' said Esther neutrally. 'Sorry I missed it.'

'The fabrics were printed, you know, not woven. I mean, they were woven, but the patterns were printed on, not woven in.'

'I didn't know that.'

'Beautiful, some of them.'

'I'm sure.'

There was a longish pause.

'How are you keeping, Sally? Everything all right?'

'Oh, fine, fine, right as rain. All a bit quiet, that's all.'

'I'm sure. After all that time looking after your mum, it must be strange having time to yourself.'

'It's lovely,' said Sally, but she didn't sound convinced. 'I mean, I can go anywhere, don't have to worry about when to be back, or whether someone's here for Mum...'

'That must be a big change.'

'I went for a walk today. I haven't been able to go out just for a stroll for so long. I happened by your old house, actually.'

That was a bit odd. Esther's parents had lived down a narrow, crooked cul-de-sac, off a small side street. The road didn't lead anywhere, nor was it near any major roads or shops. One wouldn't 'happen by' there – either you'd be going directly there, or you wouldn't be there at all.

'I haven't been there for years,' said Esther. 'After my dad died, and my mum retired, she moved to the Isle of Wight. She sold that house and I've never had cause to go back. It's only a few miles from here and I haven't thought about it in years. How funny.'

'I remember it so clearly,' said Sally. 'I went there a few times with Isabella, to visit you. It was so lovely, hidden away among the trees, all white and serene... And you, like a fairy princess, living there alone.'

'Gosh, is that how you saw it?'

'When I was little, yes. We had our little house, and Isabella and I shared a room. She was always nagging me about staying on my side. And if any of my stuff ended up on her side, she'd take it, or break it, or throw it in the bin. And you had that big house all to yourself, with your mum and dad. And your own lovely room with a four-poster bed.'

'It wasn't a four-poster!' Esther laughed. 'It was just one of those funny cheap canopy things you hang from a hook on the ceiling above a single bed. So eighties. The drapes were nasty nylon things. They were very scratchy, and they used to make me all hot and claustrophobic. In the end, I just tied them in a big knot above the bed and left them to gather dust.'

Sally laughed too. 'Now you've spoiled a lifelong illusion for me. I always used to think of you as a princess in your beautiful white house, sleeping in your golden four-poster bed.'

'How funny! How differently we all see things. I was an only child, all alone in our boring house and I envied you and Isabella, together in your cosy room, sharing things, having each other to talk to before you fell asleep.'

'Well, you had nothing to envy! We weren't cosy and close like some sisters are. I think the age gap was just that little bit too big. Just as you said when you spoke at Isabella's funeral, she thought I was just an annoying little sister. A pain. Never a friend. She told me a thousand times when we were children that she wished she could swap me for you.' Sally sounded as if this still genuinely upset her.

'That's just sibling talk,' Esther said. 'Not that I'd know, not having any of my own. And when the chips were down, when she really needed someone, who did she need? You. Her sister. Her real sister.' Sally didn't respond, and Esther found herself pushing on insistently. 'And you were there for her.'

'Right till the end,' said Sally.

Sally rang again two days later, also late in the evening. This time she wanted to talk about a birthday party Esther had had when she was ten. 'Your mum made you one of those Barbie cakes, where you use a real doll and she has a crinoline skirt made of cake. I always wanted one of those.'

'I remember it!' said Esther, delighted. 'Oh, I haven't thought about that in years. My mum always did such beautiful cakes. I got a whole castle one year, I remember. She's still a wonderful baker, and she's always producing lovely cakes for her church on the island.'

'I remember that castle cake too,' said Sally, and then added quickly, 'I mean, I didn't see that one. I didn't come to your birthday party that year. Isabella told me about it. I thought it sounded amazing.'

'I might have photos of it,' mused Esther. 'Although my parents weren't great photographers. No one was, in those days. Lucie probably has more pictures of her school dinners than I do of my entire childhood.'

'You do have some, though,' said Sally.

'Some what?'

'Pictures from when we... From when you and Isabella were children. It would be lovely to see them sometime, if you do. Our parents didn't have a camera at all.'

'Really?'

'There's one studio portrait of Isabella and me together – I was about eighteen months old, she must have been seven or so. Then nothing, until Isabella was given a Polaroid camera when she was a teenager. I've got a few from then. But nothing from when we were little.'

'I'll have a dig,' Esther promised. 'See what I can find.'

Sally rang a few times after that, although never more than twice a week. She wanted to talk about the old days, about their childhoods, and about Isabella. She didn't seem to want to chat about how she was now, and if Esther asked what she'd been up to, she'd say, 'Oh, this and that,' and bring the conversation back to their reminiscences. She invariably rang when Esther was relaxing alone in the evenings, after Lucie had gone to bed, and Esther didn't begrudge her the time. It was wonderful to talk about Isabella. No one in her day-to-day life had known Isabella, and it was hard to keep her memory alive. But Isabella the child, the teenager and the student lived so vividly in Sally's memories that Esther was often surprised at the accuracy and sharpness of her recollections.

Then one week Sally didn't ring. Esther had started anticipating the calls, almost looking forward to them, every second or third day. When the call didn't come, she felt a mixture of relief and sadness. Relief that Sally's need to reach out seemed to have passed and sadness for exactly the same reasons. She thought of ringing Sally herself. She would do it the following evening. But for the next few nights she was snowed under with work until it was too late to call, and then it just never seemed the right time. She decided to leave it for now and see if Sally would ring again. She didn't.

CHAPTER FIVE

Just one more minute. Esther glanced at her GPS watch and saw she was close to a personal best for five kilometres. She gritted her teeth, put her head down and picked up the pace as she ran up the slight incline towards her house. She could feel a low ache in her calves, and her lungs were burning, but she kept going. She heard her watch give a faint bleep, signalling the end of the kilometre, and she slowed to a walk, still panting. She had equalled but not bettered her best time.

It was definitely warmer, and as soon as she stopped outside her house, the sweat began to bloom along her hairline and she could feel drops running down her rib cage. She glanced at her watch again. She had twenty minutes before she had to be out of the house if she was to have enough time to prepare for the faculty meeting. A quick shower, wet hair in a sleek bun, and she could be away.

The house was quiet – Lucie was at school. She went up to her bedroom, set the shower running in her en-suite bathroom and began to strip off her running gear. As she turned to put the things in the laundry basket, she caught a glimpse of her reflection in the mirror. The regular running was paying off – her legs looked slimmer and more toned, and she could see two distinct dents below her rib cage where her abs had got firmer and flatter. She had never been fat, and had always been relatively fit, but she had recently decided to embark on a more ambitious exercise programme. She had always liked running, but it had generally been a small part of her exercise regime, and usually done on the treadmill in the gym as a warm-up for a weights session or class. A few months before, she had started running outside on some of the crisp, clear, winter mornings and had found she liked it very much. She did some research and learned that long-distance running was a sport dominated by older people and that the majority of marathon runners were over forty. She was gradually building up to longer distances and kept trying to improve her speed, and she had a vague idea that she might aim for a marathon at some point. In the meantime, she loved the solitude of her morning runs, the opportunity for contemplation, and the undeniable effect they were having on her figure and general fitness.

She stood up straight and looked at herself, naked, in the mirror. Not bad for forty-seven, nearly forty-eight. Not bad at all. Slim legs and a flat belly, with the narrow line of her caesarean scar barely visible. Firm, small breasts and a long, slender neck. She thought of her own mother at the same age. She had seemed middle-aged, almost old. Esther didn't feel old at all. She felt stronger and fitter than she had in years. She dressed to suit her figure, not a perception of her age. Her mother, for example, would be horrified to be seen in jeans, but Esther, when she wasn't at work, lived in them. Her mother had always worn her hair short and either had it 'done' by the hairdresser or set it herself with curlers. Esther had kept her straight dark hair long, as she always had. There were threads of silver in it, but not many, and every three months or so she got her hairdresser to do a few highlights to keep the colour fresh. She was happy with the way she looked, and more importantly with the way she felt.

She padded through to the bathroom and got into the shower. The question, however, was this. Would anyone else ever get to be happy with the way she looked and felt? It had been four years since her divorce. At first, she had been utterly focused on getting through the process – finding a new home, making sure Lucie was as settled and happy as she could be, concentrating on her career. But now, things were on a pretty even keel. She wouldn't be averse to meeting someone. She didn't know if she would ever marry again, or even if she wanted to live with someone, but she missed male companionship. She missed touch, and intimacy. And by God, she missed sex. Even though she and Stephen hadn't been particularly compatible, they'd had great sex, and she missed it very much indeed. It had been a very long time. Too long.

So what was she to do, she wondered, as she shampooed her hair. Ask a friend to set her up? She was pretty sure that if any of her friends knew any eligible single men, she would know about it. Start hanging out in cocktail bars? Pounce on a colleague? Try internet dating? None of the options seemed very appealing. Maybe she would just leave it in the lap of the gods and hope that now she had acknowledged the desire, the universe would deliver. She snorted with laughter as she got out of the shower and dried herself. Chance would be a fine thing. She might be in good shape, but she was a woman in her late forties. According to friends of a similar age who were also on the market, the men on offer were either damaged goods or were looking for a woman half their age.

Anyway, it was all theoretical. It wasn't as if she was in a position to go on nights out. Lucie was old enough to come home from school alone, let herself in and be there alone for the hour or so until Esther got in, but she had never left her daughter alone for any length of time at night, and nor was she ready to. With Stephen living in Manchester, her mother living on the Isle of Wight, and no siblings, it wasn't as if she had a convenient babysitter to hand (how Lucie would hate the idea of being babysat anyway!). Ah well, she thought philosophically, gathering glasses, papers and purse and scooping them into her briefcase. Perhaps she might reconsider the whole thing in a few years' time, when Lucie was a teenager and more independent.

But it seemed the subject had been on Lucie's mind too. On the Friday of that week, they went to the local shopping centre for an early bite to eat at a sushi restaurant. After dinner they were strolling around, looking in shop windows.

'What do you fancy doing this weekend?' Esther said.

'Don't know,' Lucie replied guardedly.

Esther glanced at her. 'I thought we might go to the garden centre tomorrow morning and get some bits to liven up the front flower beds. Maybe a film?'

'Hmm,' said Lucie, a little noncommittally.

'Why? What do you fancy?'

'I mean, it sounds nice, but...'

'You'd prefer to do something exciting with your friends rather than hanging with your old mum?' She nudged Lucie gently. 'That's fine, sweetie, do whatever you like. I've got plenty of work to keep me busy this weekend.'

'But that just makes me feel bad,' said Lucie, looking up at her. 'Why?'

'Well, because if you don't do things with me, all you do is work, or run. And then I feel like I'm letting you down by leaving you alone.'

Esther was a little stung by this assessment. 'Gracious, Lucie. I'm not your responsibility. I'm perfectly capable of looking after myself.'

'I know. But you need to have fun too. See some friends. Go on some dates.'

'Dates?' She laughed nervously.

'You are allowed to go on dates, Mum. I don't expect you to be a nun, you know. In fact, I wish you would find a boyfriend.'

'What? Don't be silly.'

'Why is it silly? You're really good-looking. All my friends say so. You could find a boyfriend easily, if you ever went anywhere without me.'

'I like being with you.' Esther knew her words sounded plaintive and manipulative. It wasn't fair to guilt-trip Lucie into being her lifelong companion. One only had to look at Sally's life to see how damaging that could be. 'Okay, okay,' she conceded. 'I will do my best to get out and about more and meet people and have "fun", as you young people say. Now what plans do you have for this weekend?'

'Well, Rebecca invited me for a sleepover tomorrow night,' said Lucie hesitantly. 'And we thought we might go swimming on Sunday morning, and then meet up with Clara and Zoe. I'd be back by four or so on Sunday afternoon?'

Esther felt a little pang, both in anticipation of a weekend which would be spent largely without Lucie's company, and at the fact that Lucie had been so tentative about sharing her plans. She didn't want to be a brake on her daughter's social life. Lucie had always been quite shy, and if she had friends and wanted to go out with them, she should be going without a backward glance. She shouldn't be worrying about what her mum would be doing.

'Go,' she said, giving Lucie's shoulders a squeeze. 'It sounds like fun.'

She rang her mother, as was customary, on Saturday morning. Esther generally enjoyed her call with Laura, but on this particular morning she felt a little fragile. When Laura asked about what she was planning to do, how could she admit that Lucie was heading off for a weekend of fun but that she had no arrangements of her own? Laura, with her own busy, sociable existence, would find Esther's wasteland of a social life bemusing. Esther didn't like to fib, but she would keep the call as brief as she could and if in doubt would possibly tell a little white lie about some possible plans. She dialled Laura's number and when it went to answerphone she breathed a small sigh of relief. She left a cheerful message and said she would be out for the rest of the day. It wasn't true, and it was a bit of a cheat, but better than the alternative.

She dropped Lucie at Rebecca's that afternoon, with fervent promises that she was going to have a fun-filled sociable weekend herself. But by the time she had been for an eight-mile run and showered, it was, of course, too late to make arrangements with anyone. She texted a few friends to see if they fancied seeing a film, but they all had plans for the evening already. She considered going by herself but couldn't face wedging herself in at the end of a row of happy couples out on date night. Equally, a solo restaurant dinner seemed out of the question. There was nothing on TV that she wanted to watch, so she marked some first-year essays. So in the end, her weekend would consist entirely of running and working – exactly what she'd promised Lucie wouldn't happen.

Sunday was not much better. She did manage to take herself off to the local farmers' market and get some cheese and bread, but she went alone and didn't meet anyone she knew. She rang up her friends Paul and Tim, who lived locally, to see if they wanted to meet for coffee or a drink, but they weren't answering their phones. She had a vague feeling they were away on holiday. They were a dual-income couple with no children and they always seemed to be away on exotic trips.

Another friend turned out to be away in Berkshire on a spa retreat. Why wasn't Esther at a girlie spa weekend? Did no one invite her to things anymore? With a sigh, she realized that the invitations had probably halved upon her divorce, then dwindled to almost nothing when she kept saying no because she was with Lucie all the time. She couldn't blame her friends. Well, Lucie was right, it was time to take charge and claim her social life back.

On Monday morning she had her regular catch-up with Regina, the English Department administrator. Regina had been at the university for as long as Esther and knew everything there was to know about the department. She was warm, funny and kind to all the students, if a little fierce with disorganized junior lecturers who failed to submit the correct paperwork. Esther considered her a dear friend as well as a respected colleague.

They went to the senior common room and got coffee. Regina ran through the details on a couple of upcoming open lectures and reminded Esther about her quarterly meeting with the principal. Business concluded, she sat back in her chair and dunked a rich tea biscuit in her coffee. 'So how was the weekend?'

'Oh, you know,' said Esther ruefully. 'Lucie had a fabulously busy one, sleeping over at a friend's, gadding about.'

'And you?'

'I realized I really am Billy No-Mates. My twelve-year-old daughter all but shoved me out of the door and told me to go and get a boyfriend. And I realized that not only do I not know any eligible single men, I barely have any friends left.'

'Nonsense. You have loads of friends. People just get very busy with their own lives, that's all. Everyone would be thrilled to spend time with you if they knew you were available. Go on, make some dates with people. Pedro and I are always happy to get together and do something. Anytime.'

'Thanks, sweetie. Does Pedro happen to have a handsome Hugh Jackman lookalike single colleague who's been begging him to set up a double-date?'

'Funnily enough, no. And if he did, the line of women applying for the position would stretch around the block.'

Esther sighed. 'I know. I can't begin to imagine how I would go about meeting anyone.'

'There are always groups to join, you know.'

'Oh Lord, like what? The Women's Institute? Or sad singles groups?'

'Come on, Esther, this is London! There are hundreds of groups for people interested in all sorts of things – drama, art, sports… Why don't you join a running club?'

'I could…' said Esther doubtfully. She'd never run with other people. Would it be odd? Competitive? Would she hate it?

'Seriously. Do a search online. I bet you find something that appeals to you. And start emailing and ringing everyone you know. Lucie's right. You need to get out there.'

Later, Esther got an email from Regina with a list of running clubs in her area, and details of the local parkrun, a free five-kilometre race that took place in local parks around London every Saturday morning. Maybe she could give that a go. Regina had also found a few social groups that met in London on a weekly basis to go for a meal or perhaps to the theatre or an art gallery. They seemed aimed at people who were new to the city, but Esther reasoned that in a sense she was new to socializing in the city as a single woman. She pinged off a quick thank you to Regina and invited her and Pedro for dinner the following week.

CHAPTER SIX

Esther had barely given Sally a thought since the brief flurry of late-night calls – Lucie had asked after her a few times and she had replied in vague terms, promising that she would ring soon and see how Sally was. But one evening as she worked at the dining room table, she was surprised to see an email arrive from Sally Millais. It was so unexpected, it took her a moment to recognize the name.

Dear Esther and Lucie,

I wanted to drop you a line and say thank you so much for encouraging me to get a computer and get connected. It has changed my life! I got a laptop, and an iPad mini for when I am out and about, and I now have a high-speed internet connection at home. I have been attending classes at the local library, which has opened my eyes to the wonders of the internet. I can't believe I missed out on it for so many years! I have made some good friends in my computer class, and I have a new set of online friends on the help forum our teacher has introduced us to.

I was excited to discover that the fingers don't forget, and I can still type as fast as I used to. I may even think about looking for a job!

I am also thinking about taking some driving lessons and getting a car. Perhaps once I have done that I would be able to drive over and visit you! That is going to take a bit of time though. I have learned I need to get a provisional licence and that the whole thing is quite a palaver.

I would love to see you in the meantime. Can we meet for lunch this Sunday? I did some research and found a nice-looking Italian restaurant near my house, and I have seen that I can book a table online.

Love,
Sally

Esther found herself smiling at the email. What a transformation. Access to the internet, something most people took for granted, had wrought such change in Sally's life. Driving lessons, groups, forums – it looked as if Sally's social life was more active than her own. She called Lucie, who was sitting curled up on the sofa with her laptop.

'I just got the most amazing email from Sally. Come and read it.'

'I got it too,' said Lucie. 'I'm reading it now.'

'You got it too? I didn't know she had your email address.'

'Neither did I,' said Lucie, but she didn't seem very concerned about it.

'I wonder how she got it. Mine is easy to find – it's on my page on the university website – but yours shouldn't be accessible to anyone you don't know.'

'Maybe she made a note of it when we were looking at things on my laptop together.'

'Still, it's a bit of an odd thing to do,' said Esther.

'I don't mind,' said Lucie. 'I like Sally and I'm glad she's happy. Are we going to meet her for lunch?'

'Don't you have things to do this weekend?'

'Not on Sunday. How about you?'

'I'm also free.' Esther wasn't sure why she felt a little reluctant to agree to this. Still, it meant a day out with Lucie. Maybe they could go earlier and have a walk in the local park before lunch, or visit a gallery afterwards.

They met Sally in the restaurant she had chosen, a pizza place with a view of the park. She was sitting at a window table and beamed widely when they came in. She looked as though she had had her hair done; it was still mousy, but the grey was largely gone. It had been set in a rather stiff style – great bobbly curls, frozen with hairspray – as if she had gone to the sort of hairdresser her mother would have used, one of those narrow salons that populate suburban high streets with their rows of hood dryers and the eternal stench of perm lotion and who do the same hairstyle for every one of their customers no matter what their age. Sally looked happier though, bright-eyed and animated, and she jumped up to greet them and kiss them both on the cheek.

She started chattering as soon as they sat down, a non-stop stream of questions for which she had no time to wait for an answer, what with all the anecdotes about her computer class, her journey to the restaurant, the weather, how pretty Lucie looked. It was as if she had been storing up a flood of conversation ready for this moment and hadn't been able to wait beyond their sitting down to open the gates in the dam wall.

Esther managed to stem the flow for long enough to order a bottle of sparkling water and get menus for them all. Eventually Sally slowed down and put on her glasses to look at the menu. 'This is my treat, by the way,' she said quickly, 'so please order anything you'd like. Shall we get some champagne? Or whatsisname... Is it Cinzano? Whatever the Italian version of champagne is?'

'Prosecco,' said Esther. 'Oh no, Sally, please don't feel you have to.'

'I want to. You made me such a lovely dinner in your lovely home.'

'It was just a lasagne,' said Esther. She felt slightly panicked. She couldn't accept a meal from Sally. The woman hadn't worked in a decade. She was probably eking out her carer's allowance, or living on savings.

'Please,' said Sally, and she looked hard at Esther. 'I don't want to feel I'm always taking advantage of your charity.'

'Oh, I—' Esther was stung by Sally's use of the word charity. But before she could find the words to say anything more, Lucie had flung her arms around Sally's neck.

'How can it be charity when you're our friend?'

Tears brimmed in Sally's eyes and Esther thanked the heavens, not for the first or last time, for Lucie's sweet, unaffected nature.

She ordered carefully, choosing an inexpensive salad. Lucie took the hint and chose a plain pasta dish. But Sally was undeterred, calling the waiter over and ordering the best Prosecco they had and asking for a platter of antipasto for the table. She beamed at them both. 'This is such a treat!' she said. 'Now, tell me, Lucie, what have you been up to?'

Lucie sipped her Appletiser and chatted about her schoolwork and her involvement with the debating society. The waiter brought the Prosecco and opened it. Sally raised her glass and interrupted Lucie.

'A toast!' she said excitedly. 'To new beginnings and to good friends.'

'A lovely toast,' said Esther.

Sally took a big gulp from her glass and turned back to Lucie. 'So sorry, dear, what were you saying?'

There seemed to be a slightly manic edge to her. She seemed very animated, but not entirely engaged. She was drinking fast, and her hands never seemed to stop moving – going up to touch her hair, fiddling with her glass, folding and unfolding her napkin.

When Lucie had finished telling the story of a recent debating competition, Esther turned to Sally and said gently, 'And how have you been, Sally?'

'Oh fine, fine.'

'From your email, it seems you've been busy.'

'Busier than you know!' said Sally. 'The computer has opened up a whole world to me. There's so much to discover.'

She told them about the computer forum she had joined, where beginner users could ask questions and share tips. She had made a few connections – people she was chatting to regularly – and she talked about them as if they were real, close friends. Esther could see it made Lucie a little sad; it somehow made Sally look even more isolated that these distant connections should mean so much to her.

'You need to get on Facebook,' said Lucie sagely. 'That's the best way to connect with all the people you know.'

'Not that Lucie would know,' said Esther. 'She's still too young to have a Facebook account.'

Lucie made a face. 'Mum's very strict about it. She says there's plenty of time for me to get into social media.'

'Well, maybe I should give it a go,' said Sally uncertainly. 'I'm not sure who I could ask to be my "friends". That is the right term, isn't it? Friends?'

'Mum will be your friend,' said Lucie.

'Of course I will,' said Esther. 'And there's a Facebook group from our old school, so you could connect with people from your year, I'm sure.'

'Golly,' said Sally. 'Well, it would be interesting to see what everyone is up to.'

The antipasto arrived and Sally, who wasn't familiar with some items on the platter, had a lot of questions. She had never eaten an artichoke heart and wasn't sure what she thought about olives. She really did seem to be having the time of her life. Eventually, she made herself a little plateful of things she thought she might like to try and energetically encouraged Lucie and Esther to eat everything else.

'It's taken me a little bit of time,' Sally said, draining her glass and reaching for the bottle for a refill, 'to realize that I have got my life back. And I intend to have some fun!'

'You should!' said Lucie. 'You looked after your mum, and before that you looked after Isabella. It's time you looked after yourself.'

'I felt so guilty after Mum went.' Sally's cheeks were decidedly pinker from the Prosecco. 'But it wasn't easy, especially not the last few months.'

'I'm sure,' Esther said soothingly.

'She was like a small baby – she used to wake up nine or ten times a night. She kept trying to get up and go outside, but she could barely walk, so she'd keep falling over. I had to sleep on a mattress in her room to try and stop her. I was exhausted of course, but if I tried to go and have a little nap in the daytime, she'd sit in her chair and scream over and over, "Isabella! Isabella? Where are you?"' She gave an uncanny imitation of Joan's querulous tone. 'In the morning, she'd start asking what time it was and worrying about her meals. Then she'd forget she'd eaten and she'd ask me over and over to make her breakfast. Sometimes I'd give her seven or eight meals a day, just to shut her up. She started weeing everywhere too, like an old dog. I was always finding her in corners. No amount of bleach will get that smell out. I've had to have all the carpets ripped out. I used to try to take her for a walk every day, but she'd just cry the whole time and beg to go home, and one time she tried to take her clothes off in Sainsbury's. I stopped after that. And when the carers came to help, especially towards the end of the day, her behaviour just got worse. She'd spit at them, or swear, or call them terrible names – "Darkie" or "Chinkie". She was never like that – racist – before the dementia. Makes you wonder what ugly thoughts people are hiding.'

The whole monologue was delivered in flat and unemotional tone, except for this last observation, which Sally made with a cheerful smile.

Esther glanced at Lucie, who looked horrified. She was sure her own expression was much the same. It wasn't so much the litany of sadness and misery that Sally had spilled out, but the coolness of her delivery. She hadn't expressed any sorrow or self-pity. She had just calmly told the story. It was impossible to know what response she hoped for.

'I'm so sorry,' Esther said carefully. 'That must have been very hard.'

Sally shrugged and picked up an artichoke heart with her fingers. 'It was all right, until she started hitting me. Every time

I took her to the toilet or helped her into a chair, she'd hit me on the head and face. And pull my hair. I had bald spots. I'm still waiting for it to grow back properly.' She popped the artichoke heart into her mouth and touched her temple. For the first time Esther noticed there was fuzzy new growth there. 'Anyway, I haven't really been out in the world or been able to do anything, so lunch – just a lunch like this, which must be something you two do every week – is the most exciting thing I've done in years! Lots more excitement to come though.'

The main courses arrived and the mood seemed to lighten a little as they occupied themselves with tasting each other's food. They shared three desserts between them and Sally insisted she and Esther should have a little liqueur too.

When the bill came, she opened her handbag. She took out a great wedge of twenties and counted out some notes. Esther noted she hadn't left a tip. Perhaps she had forgotten the niceties of eating out. Sally excused herself to go to the toilet, and Esther took out a ten-pound note and slipped it under the edge of her plate for the waiter.

On the Monday, when Regina asked her what she had been up to at the weekend, Esther found herself telling her all about Sally – her years of isolation and her slow emergence.

'It's very odd,' she said. 'She appears to be both very much younger than me, in terms of her innocence and lack of worldly experience, but also very much older. She dresses like an old lady, she has old lady hair, she even has an old lady turn of phrase. She says "golly".'

'I'd love to meet her,' said Regina. 'She sounds fascinating.'

'She really isn't,' said Esther. 'She's sadly a little bit dull, but I feel… responsible somehow, because she's Isabella's younger sister and Isabella was my best friend.'

'I presume Isabella wasn't dull.'

'Isabella was beautiful and brilliant and mercurial. She was a very talented architect, she drew wonderful pictures, she was charismatic and popular...'

'And she died?'

'Eight... nearly nine years ago. Cervical cancer.'

'Was she married? Kids?'

'No... she hadn't got round to settling down – I think she always imagined she'd have time at some point in the future. She was too busy having a brilliant career and travelling all over the world.'

'The opposite of her sister.'

'Polar opposite.'

'Although it sounds like Sally is trying to give it a go now she doesn't have her mum to look after. She's getting online, wanting to learn to drive... It's a start.'

'I suppose so.'

'We could all take a leaf out of her book,' Regina said. 'Get out there a bit more.' Esther looked quizzically at her. 'When I say "we", I mean "you", you know,' said Regina. 'You can make big innocent eyes at me, but you know I'm right. At least Sally's trying, in her own modest way. When are you going to take the plunge?'

'Into what?'

'A more adventurous life.'

'I've invited some friends round for dinner...' Esther said defensively.

'By "friends" you mean me and Pedro and, let me guess, other friends who are all couples. All old, safe friends you've known for years.'

'Maybe, but... Anyway. I've been to the parkrun thing you

suggested a couple of times too.'

'Did you actually talk to anyone?'

'I will, soon. Next time. And I keep meaning to go to one of the Meetup groups you suggested. I just really haven't had a chance.'

'But, let me get this right… the Easter holidays start next week, don't they?'

'Yes.'

'And Lucie will be going to Manchester to stay with her dad?'

'Yes.'

'So no excuses. You need to get out there. If you don't do it, I'll take charge of your diary – I have access, you know – and I'll just start booking things in. Salsa classes, taxidermy, life drawing…'

'Okay, okay.' Esther laughed. 'I'll do some things while Lucie's away.'

CHAPTER SEVEN

Esther had never been brave. She'd been a cautious, shy child and a quiet, bookish teenager. She'd had a very modest view of her own skills and accomplishments, so it was Isabella, with her firm, no-nonsense attitude, who shoved her out of her comfort zone and got her to aim a little higher. Without her, Esther would probably have ended up as a primary-school teacher. She certainly would never have had the courage to seek and pursue a career in academia. It was always Isabella who encouraged her, Isabella who persuaded her to break the rules, pushed her into the limelight or dragged her on adventures. She could have done with a little of Isabella's cajoling now. As she clicked through a list of social clubs on the Time Out website, she remembered a poetry competition, when they were in the third year.

It was a stupid poem. Esther didn't know why she'd spent so long on it. And even though she'd been working on it – changing a word here, altering a rhyme there – for almost three weeks, it was still stupid. She had no idea why she still cared. Anyway, there was no point. She was only in the third year, and no one from the third year ever got anywhere in the poetry competition; the prizes always went to girls doing their O levels, or girls in the lower sixth. It was a stupid competition anyway.

She didn't show the poem to anyone. Well, no one except Isabella. They were doing their homework at Esther's kitchen table one afternoon, or at least Esther was doing homework and Isabella was sketching an elaborate art nouveau pattern of swirls and elegant female forms around the margins of her maths worksheet.

'I hate algebra,' Isabella said absently. 'I can't imagine a world where I will ever, ever care what the value of x is.'

'You can copy mine,' Esther said, and pushed her completed sheet across the table. 'If you do something for me.'

'What?' said Isabella suspiciously as she began copying the answers into the empty spaces on her sheet.

'I want you to read something, and then not say a word.'

'Not say a word about what?'

'I wrote something. And I want you to read it, but then don't say, "That's nice", or "Well done" or "That's rubbish". Just don't say anything, okay?'

She'd thought about this for a long time. She knew the poem was terrible and would never be entered into the competition, and she knew she couldn't bear to give it to just anyone to read – not her mum or dad, or Miss Holford, the English teacher. But Isabella was different. She'd be okay about it. She wouldn't say something patronizing or insincere. And now she'd been warned, she wouldn't say anything at all. Esther knew she shouldn't care. After all, she hated the poem. But it had occupied so much time in her head, and there were bits of it she thought were, well, if not good, at least not totally horrific. It deserved to be read by at least one person before she tore it up and chucked it away.

She pulled a sheet of paper from her homework diary; it was the latest iteration of the poem, which she had neatly copied out that morning. She flipped it round and pushed it across the table to Isabella.

Isabella finished writing the answers onto the algebra worksheet, handed Esther back her page, then picked up the poem and headed for the door.

'Where are you going?'

'I'm not going to read it with you staring at my face like a hungry puppy. I'm going to take it to the bathroom where you can't see me.'

She was gone forever. For hours, it seemed. Esther sat staring at her algebra homework. She spotted a mistake and painstakingly crossed it out and corrected it. She didn't correct it in Isabella's work – that would be too obvious. At least this way they wouldn't get the exact same mark. Esther thought the maths teacher was already a little suspicious. Isabella still wasn't back. What was she doing? Tearing the poem into tiny shreds and flushing it? Was it that bad?

Isabella came back from the bathroom. She was holding the piece of paper in her hand. Instead of sitting back down across from Esther, she stayed standing in the doorway, gripping the page tightly. 'I'm not going to say anything,' she said calmly. 'I'm also not giving it back.'

'Why?'

'You know why you gave this to me.'

'To read. And not say anything.'

'Bollocks,' said Isabella crisply. It was her new favourite word. 'You gave it to me because you know how good it is and because you want me to bully you to give it in for the competition.'

'No I didn't!' said Esther, her face flaring hotly.

'Whatever. Anyway, I'm not going to argue with you, or say nice things or beg. I'm just going to keep this very nicely written copy and hand it in to Miss Holford tomorrow, all right?' Isabella edged her way around the room, keeping the page behind her back, as if Esther might lunge and grab it. She swept her book and notes together with one hand, then slipped the page between the leaves of a notebook and tipped everything into her open school bag. 'See you tomorrow.' She turned to go.

'Stop!' Esther yelled, suddenly furious. 'Give it back!'

'No,' said Isabella firmly. 'I'm not going to let you torture yourself and me about how maybe you should give it in for the competition or maybe you shouldn't, until it's too late, and then you'll go on for weeks about how maybe you should have after all. It's boring. The poem is good. You should enter it. If I didn't push you into things, you'd spend your life dithering. This is my job in your life. Your job is to save me from my maths homework and stop me doing something stupid and dying by accident.'

She didn't win the competition, but she was the first third year in the school's history to get a 'Highly Commended' certificate. There seemed no way to thank Isabella adequately except to take over her maths homework when asked and to catch her hand whenever she was about to dash headlong across a road without looking.

CHAPTER EIGHT

Imagining Isabella's slim hand between her shoulder blades. That was what had got her to Tate Britain at eight o'clock on a Friday night, to wander around with a glass of chilled wine while a performance poet with a megaphone shouted incomprehensibly in the echoing main vestibule. She immediately regretted coming. She'd imagined some kind of civilized soiree, with people standing around chatting and looking at the paintings. Instead, it seemed there were events in every room, starting every half an hour – performances, lectures, classes and debates. She didn't know enough about art for this. She was considering ducking out and going home, or at least going to a pub where no one with a megaphone would shout at her, when a gallery assistant walking through the rooms announced loudly that the talk on Francis Bacon would be starting in five minutes. Bacon had been Isabella's favourite artist. She had written her major sixth-form essay on his work and prints of his disturbing paintings had hung on the walls of her room at university. Esther saw it as a sign – a message from Isabella – and followed the assistant into a room where rows of chairs faced a screen.

She took a seat on the edge and towards the back. More people drifted in, and eventually the seats were around two-thirds full. She looked to see who would be giving the lecture but couldn't identify anyone in the room who might be an art expert. Once everyone was seated, however, a slim young woman with a sheet of raven-black hair stood up and went to the podium. She had something of the young Isabella about her. She spoke eloquently for forty-five minutes on Bacon's intense relationship with George Dyer. Dyer was an East End gangster who broke into Bacon's home to burgle it, and this was the start of a tumultuous relationship which ended with Dyer's suicide. The woman spoke well, the subject matter was fascinating, and the photographs and paintings were compelling.

When the lecture was finished, Esther took the time to walk around all the Bacon paintings on display. She felt a little woozy from the wine. She hadn't spoken to anyone directly, but she'd had a fascinating evening and she'd learned something new. It was almost time for the gallery to close, and as she prepared to leave, she realized she was ravenous. She knew of a reasonably nice pub around the corner in Pimlico. Hopefully they would still be serving and she could get a plate of something – fish and chips, she decided; definitely fish and chips – before heading to the Tube and going home.

The pub was much busier than she would have expected, but she managed to find a space at the bar and stood patiently waiting to place her order. Someone jogged her elbow slightly, and she turned to see who it was. A tall man with a pleasant, boyish face and sandy hair was standing beside her.

'Sorry,' he said, and smiled.

She smiled back and turned away to try and catch the eye of the barman who was currently serving down the far end of the bar. When she glanced back the other way, the man was still looking at her. She smiled again, a little uncertainly.

'So sorry, I don't mean to stare,' he said, 'but were you just at the Bacon talk at the Tate?'

'Yes.'

'So were we,' he said. 'What did you think?'

'Fascinating. I didn't know much about him before. I mean, I'd seen his work – an old friend of mine was a big fan – but I had no idea about his...'

'... rather chaotic life?'

Esther laughed. 'A fair description.' She looked back down the bar at the barman, who seemed to have skipped her and moved on to another customer.

The man, who was considerably taller than her, gestured and managed to catch the eye of another barman, who came over. 'You were here first,' he said politely. 'Go ahead.'

'Thanks,' said Esther, and ordered a glass of white wine and her dinner.

The man hesitated for a moment, then turned to her and said, 'Look, I don't mean to be forward, but as you've just ordered for one, I assume you're here alone?'

Esther looked up at him, a little surprised.

Before she could say anything, he cut in hastily. 'I'm here with a few friends – we've all ordered food too. Might you like to join our table? We could all talk Bacon while we eat.'

Carpe diem, thought Esther. At least this way she could tell Regina on Monday that she had met some new people. And she wasn't going off with a lone strange man – he was there with friends, so it was a potentially less stressful situation. A friendly meet-up rather than a pick-up.

'Thanks, that's very kind of you,' she said, picking up her glass and following him.

On the way over to the table, he introduced himself, rather formally – his name was Philip Osborne. Esther stole another quick glance at him. He was probably around her age, in good shape, with the slender physique of a lifelong sportsman. She'd have put her money on tennis or cycling. He had an open face and closely cut sandy hair, which on inspection showed a sprinkling of grey but didn't appear to be thinning. His eyes were a light, clear blue, and he was well, if casually, dressed in a blue open-necked shirt and chinos.

His friends were both work colleagues. There was a woman called Gillian, who was sturdy and wore her brown hair short, and Benjamin, a man with a long, narrow face and a slow, deliberate way of speaking. They all worked together at an environmental charity, something to do with rare British wildlife. Gillian was the campaigns manager, Benjamin did something in IT and Philip was the financial manager. They all seemed nice and were perfectly happy to shuffle round their smallish circular table to make space for Esther and her glass of wine.

The conversation began a little haltingly, but Philip encouraged everyone to talk about the Bacon lecture and then to discuss some of the other events. Benjamin painstakingly explained the intention behind the performance art piece with the man and the megaphone. It was something to do with alienation. 'Well, in my limited experience, stomping around shouting at people through a megaphone will lead to alienation,' Esther said, and was surprised when Philip chuckled at her not-very-funny joke. She glanced at him and he was watching her closely. Good grief, she thought. He fancies me. It's been so long, I'm not sure what to do. Self-consciously, she tucked her hair behind her ear. She was sure she was blushing. Luckily, at that moment the food arrived and there was the usual fussing with cutlery and asking for ketchup.

Esther ate her fish and chips enthusiastically. Gillian, across the table, picked at a rather limp and unappetizing Caesar salad. 'Should have gone with the fish and chips,' she said, eyeing Esther's plate. 'I was trying to make a healthy choice, but as this is four leaves soaked in a bucket of cheesy dressing with two baby tomatoes and oily croutons – loads of calories, rubbish taste, and maybe only one of my five a day – I needn't have bothered.'

Esther smiled. 'Have some chips,' she said, pushing her plate closer to Gillian. 'Life is always better when you have chips.'

Gillian grabbed a few. 'I agree, but sadly, as much as I love chips, they seem to love me more.'

'A moment on the lips...' Benjamin drawled slowly.

'Honestly, Benjie, I'll smack you with this chip if you finish that sentence,' said Gillian, dipping her golden fry in a pool of ketchup.

Esther laughed. Gillian looked her up and down. 'To be fair, you don't look like a woman who's eaten too many chips,' she observed. 'You're skinny as anything.'

Esther was used to this – a touch of friendly accusation from women of her age; as if by being slim she had betrayed some unwritten rule of the sisterhood. 'I was a bit rounder until recently. Now I run,' she said, shoving a chip in her mouth. 'It burns off a multitude of sins.'

'How much do you run? I mean, how far do you have to run to offset dessert? Is ten kilometres equal to one chocolate brownie?'

'I don't really think of it like that,' said Esther. 'I run four times a week because I like it and it keeps me sane and, amazingly, I've found that then I can eat pretty much what I like.'

'I run,' said Philip suddenly.

'Oh, Phil is the ultimate running bore,' said Gillian. 'Five London marathons.'

'Marathons?' Esther noticed for the first time that Philip's plate held a plain-grilled chicken breast and a heap of salad.

'Yes. Are you aiming for one?'

'I'm not really a competitive runner, and I'm nowhere near that kind of distance.'

'It doesn't take a lot of preparation,' Philip commented, efficiently assembling a forkful of pure protein and raw vegetables.

'I'm sure it does, if you do it properly.'

Benjamin and Gillian lost interest in the conversation and started talking to one another about a big blockbuster film that was opening that weekend and whether or not they wanted to see it. Philip seemed happy to chat about running and diet and training programmes. She could see that even though he had been brave enough to invite her to the table, he was quite shy; being able to discuss something he was knowledgeable about obviously made things easier for him. He seemed a nice man. There, you see, she thought, I've gone out, I've done something new, and I've met a nice man.

She wasn't surprised when, after they had all finished their food and were preparing to go, he hesitantly asked for her telephone number. She was happy to give it to him. What had started out as rather an unpromising evening had turned into something quite pleasant.

He rang the next afternoon. Clearly he had no plans to play hard to get. With almost comical formality, he introduced himself with his full name and said how lovely it had been to meet her the previous evening. He wondered if she might like to join him for a walk on Hampstead Heath tomorrow, Sunday, as the weather forecast suggested it would be a lovely day. Might she like to have tea? She might indeed. They arranged to meet at Kenwood House at two o'clock, and said their goodbyes.

Esther sat looking at her phone for some time. This was a

date. Definitely a date. She hadn't been on a date in more than twenty years, and even then she'd known Stephen since university and they had been friends first, so they hadn't dated in the conventional sense. It was more that they just started sleeping together. Oh dear heavens, she thought. That was where this was leading, wasn't it? Not this Sunday, but if that date was a success, and Philip asked her on another one, and another, at some point in the nearish future, they would…

She jumped up from the kitchen table, where she'd been sitting doing some lecture preparation, and headed upstairs to pull on her running things. She needed to think about this.

Within a few minutes, she was running at a slow warm-up pace towards the park. If sex was the ultimate aim, she would have to get naked with Philip. How did she feel about that? Her first response was a flurry of almost teenaged self-consciousness. No man but Stephen had seen her naked in years. No man but Stephen had seen her naked since she'd had a baby. What if Philip was horrified at her ageing body? She checked herself immediately. That was ridiculous, and she was being juvenile. Her body was fine, and he was middle-aged himself – he was fit, but not some buff young Adonis.

More importantly, did she want to get naked with Philip? It was too early to know for sure, but could she foresee wanting to at some point? He wasn't unattractive, she thought, as she laboured up a steep hill. He was pleasant-looking rather than sexy and she hadn't felt an instant buzz of electricity when she met him. But then, would she recognize a buzz if she experienced it? It had been so long since she had gone looking for someone to be attracted to, she wasn't sure she'd know the signs anymore. The fact was, he had chosen her and not vice versa. How she felt about him, and whether there was the possibility of something real happening between them, was yet to be seen.

She woke the next morning cross with herself for over-analysing the whole thing. She deliberately didn't take too much time choosing what to wear, selecting a new pair of jeans and a crisp white shirt. She added a light, raspberry-coloured cardigan in case it was cold or windy on the Heath and opted for comfortable flat shoes which would handle any but the most rugged walking terrain. She left her hair loose and applied minimal make-up and the faintest spritz of a light floral perfume.

She was punctual by nature and allowed extra time to drive to the Heath and park the car. This being one of the first properly sunny weekends of the year, she knew it was likely to be very busy, and so it was. She found parking in a side road some distance away and walked briskly up the hill and down the driveway to Kenwood House. It was a beautiful stately home, recently restored, which commanded a sweeping view of lawns and a lake. It had featured as a location in many films, and the lawns were the scene of an annual series of concerts in the summer. She had always liked it and often visited with Lucie or with friends, either trailing through the house to look at the paintings, or going to the tea garden for cake after a walk.

Despite the parking and walking delays, she still got there early enough that she could take a stroll around the outside of the house before it was time to meet Philip. She saw immediately that they would be lucky to get near the tea garden today. Every table was taken and she could see a line of people stretching out of the door, queuing to be served, even though there would be nowhere to sit once they had their scones and pot of Earl Grey. She had been too nervous to eat any lunch, and she realized that she was now quite hungry. She knew that The Spaniard's Inn, another famous historic spot, was a short walk away, but she imagined it too would be busy at the height of Sunday lunchtime. Perhaps they could find a kiosk that sold sandwiches or something.

She glanced at her watch. She had ten minutes until she was due to meet Philip. She nipped into the ladies' toilet. Luckily she didn't need to go, as there was a queue of ten women waiting for a cubicle. She took a moment to check her reflection and tidy her hair, then squared her shoulders and set forth.

Although it was only five to two, Philip was already standing outside the entrance of the house as she rounded the corner. He hadn't seen her yet, so she had a moment to observe him. He was as she remembered: tall, slim and in possession of all his hair. He was dressed pretty much exactly as he had been on Friday night – in an open-necked shirt and chinos. A conservative man in his dress, then, who would be considered by most to be reasonably attractive. But how did she feel about him? Attracted? She still didn't know. Then she spotted the wicker basket at his feet. Clearly, he had anticipated that the place might be crowded and had brought a picnic. Foresight, consideration and sandwiches. She instantly found him more fanciable.

She walked over and touched his elbow, and he turned quickly. His face lit up at the sight of her, and there was an awkward moment when she could see him trying to decide whether he should kiss her. She made it simple for him by leaning in to kiss his cheek, inhaling as she did so. He wore no aftershave, but his skin smelled clean and faintly of shaving foam. Not unpleasant. Not unpleasant at all.

They walked side by side around the house and surveyed the lawns, which were already fairly crowded with picnicking families and groups playing with Frisbees or balls.

'Shall we go round towards Parliament Hill?' he suggested, and she nodded.

It was less crowded that way, although without any manicured lawns to sit on, but Philip found a bench with a splendid view and they made themselves comfortable on it.

'I thought it might be very busy,' he said, opening his basket, 'so I decided to make us self-sufficient.'

He had done an excellent job, or at least Marks & Spencer had – there was a good selection of tapas-style snacks, bread and cheese, and a chilled bottle of wine ('I remembered you ordered a Sauvignon Blanc in the pub, so I got that,' he said). He'd brought picnic plates and cutlery, and wine glasses, which, although plastic, were still nicer than paper cups. He even had cloth napkins. Esther was impressed and said so.

'I've been looking after myself for quite a few years now,' he said. 'I've got fairly capable.'

It seemed a good time to exchange biographical information. Philip ('Call me Phil' he said hastily, when she used the full version of his name) was also forty-seven, about six months younger than Esther. When she tentatively asked about his marital status, he said, 'Widowed.'

She nodded, not sure if she should enquire further. Before she could, he asked the same of her. 'Divorced,' she replied. 'With one daughter. Lucie. She's twelve, going on forty-five, but in a good way. Do you have kids?'

'No, no, none,' he said, but didn't elaborate.

He filled her wine glass and his own, and they began to eat, chatting more generally about the weather, the Heath, and a little about their respective careers.

When they had finished eating, Phil packed the leftovers and dishes neatly back into his basket, and stood. 'Shall we walk? Or would you rather just relax?'

'Let's walk,' said Esther, jumping up. It seemed natural to loop her arm through his free one as they strolled down the hill.

They walked in silence for a while and then chatted sporadically. But then, abruptly, Phil brought the conversation back to his marriage. He seemed to need to tell her his story.

He had married his university sweetheart, a woman called Sue. They had agreed early on that they didn't want children, but in her mid-thirties Sue had changed her mind and persuaded Phil that they should try. When she didn't fall pregnant after a few months, she went to the doctor. A check-up revealed that she had stage four cervical cancer. She died just before her fortieth birthday.

'I'm so sorry,' said Esther. 'I lost my best friend to cervical cancer. It's brutal.'

'I was heartbroken, as you can imagine,' Phil said. 'And even though I wasn't sure I wanted children, I've spent a long time being even more heartbroken that we never had any. At the time, it seemed as if she just disappeared from the world and there was nothing left of her. I started running after she died, because I couldn't sleep. It was very therapeutic to be able to pull on my running shoes and go out at two or three in the morning and run myself into exhaustion.'

It seemed a revealing and personal thing to tell an almost stranger, and Esther was a little taken aback. 'I'm sorry,' she said again. 'It must have been very hard.'

He nodded his thanks and kept walking in silence.

Esther understood now. This story was Phil. It was the essence of him, and he clearly felt that if she was to know him, she would need to understand how this marriage, Sue's death and his regrets underpinned everything. Did it mean he was broken? Unable to commit? She didn't think so – he had been eager to ask her out, seemed keen to extend their interaction. He just needed her to know. And that was all right. She gave his arm a squeeze. 'I'm sure the tea garden has quietened down now. Can I buy you a coffee and a cupcake?'

'Tea and a scone and you have a deal,' he said, and smiled down at her gratefully.

Over tea, she found herself telling him about the demise of her marriage to Stephen – the irritable exchanges that gradually morphed into constant sniping and point-scoring, the weekends spent deliberately apart, and finally, the New Year's party where, on going into the kitchen, she had come upon Stephen kissing an acquaintance of theirs. It wasn't his putative infidelity that was the last straw, but her own response to it – she felt no anger or jealousy, just a quick rush of relief that this was a big enough reason for them to end the whole tiresome, brittle charade. As soon as they agreed to part, they found they got on much better. It had been the most civilized and amicable divorce.

Stephen had always loved Lucie and been a good father, but once he left, he became increasingly distant. He kept his weekly visitation dates but often didn't bother to ring her in between. He started dating pretty much as soon as he moved out of the family home and had a few short-lived relationships before meeting Melissa. They had married within a year, and when her work had offered her a transfer to Manchester, Stephen seemed content to relocate. By necessity, he became a part-time father.

Esther surprised herself with her frankness – in twenty minutes, she had told Phil more than she had shared with many of her friends. Was this middle-aged dating? Was it usual to embark on a first date by laying your baggage down on the table and inviting the other person to paw through it? It seemed odd and rather un-English, but it was practical, she conceded. Everyone of their age had damage. At least this way, you knew up front what dents and scratches you were buying.

The sun was starting to sink and the shadows were getting longer. Esther shivered a little in her thin cardigan. Phil looked concerned. 'You're cold,' he said. 'Shall we move on somewhere indoors? A pub? Would you like some dinner?'

Esther could so easily have said yes, but she felt vulnerable, almost peeled. She had revealed more than she had intended to. She could imagine the two of them at a small table in a dimly lit Hampstead pub, sharing a bottle of wine and more confidences, maybe some kisses. It was tempting, but she didn't feel ready for it. She needed to go back to her safe house and regroup.

'Thanks, but I need to get home,' she said, and then cursed inwardly when Phil looked crestfallen. She had told him Lucie was away with her dad, so what could she possibly need to get home for? She considered inventing a dog, but in the end settled for, 'Work, you know, never ends.'

She had been uncharacteristically open and honest already, but she wasn't going to say, 'This is my first date in two and a half decades and if we drink and you keep being nice and sensitive, I might end up naked with you and I'm not ready for that.'

Phil nodded, as if he understood, but he still looked a little sad. Walking back towards their cars, Esther found herself overcompensating. She kept finding excuses to touch him, and she kept her tone light and flirtatious, so he would know she was still interested.

He insisted on walking her all the way to her car, although his was parked much nearer to the entrance to the Heath. At the car, he became awkward and clumsy again, shifting from foot to foot and making inane small talk, as if he didn't want her to go but was too scared to do anything compelling enough to make her stay. Eventually, Esther found herself leaning in to kiss him. It hadn't been her plan to do so, but it seemed the correct way to end the date, and he was clearly too scared to initiate anything. He kissed her back – sweetly and dryly. It was a mouth kiss, definitely more than a friendly peck, but far from a passionate snog.

She was furious at herself as she drove away. She should have left it – either let him kiss her or said goodbye without any kiss at all. Now she was worried that he might feel she had stolen the initiative or think she was more eager than she really was. Curse this strange and unfamiliar dance, an unfathomable process of advances, retreats and failed attempts to anticipate the movements and intentions of one's partner. It was all too difficult, this middle-class, middle-aged dating.

CHAPTER NINE

Phil emailed her on the Monday morning.

Dear Esther,

Thank you so much for yesterday. I enjoyed it very much.
If I am not being too forward, I was wondering if you were
free on Wednesday evening? I got an email inviting me
to a wine-tasting event, and I thought it would be more
fun not to go alone, and much more fun to go with you. I
am not a wine bore, promise, and not a big drinker. I just
thought it might be interesting to do something new.

Anyway. Let me know.

Phil x

It made Esther smile. He was clearly trying to play it cool, but the fact was that he had emailed by ten o'clock on the morning after they'd been out, and she could imagine him agonizing over the kiss at the end. She decided to wait a couple of hours before replying. Not to play games – in fact, just the opposite. She wanted to temper her rather gushy behaviour at the end of their date the day before. She liked him, of course she did. But she wasn't sure how much. He was perfectly fine, on paper, but she needed to think about how she really felt. Was it genuine attraction or the novelty of having someone attracted to her? She was so out of practice, she just didn't know. She was keen to go to the wine tasting, to have another evening out, to get to know him a little better. But she wasn't feeling any great swoops of emotion or electric currents of attraction. It was probably just too early to know.

Regina came into her office with a handful of post.

'Good weekend? How was the Tate?'

'Good. Good. Interesting.' Esther turned back to her computer. She wasn't ready to talk about Phil. She couldn't discuss him with someone else if she didn't know what she thought herself yet, and she was certain that Regina would be terribly excited by the whole story and would make all sorts of assumptions. After Wednesday perhaps. There might be more to tell then.

The wine tasting was held in a cellar bar in Mayfair, around the corner from Claridge's and down a narrow flight of stairs. Esther approached the venue and once more saw Phil standing outside waiting for her. He smiled carefully when he saw her. He had obviously given himself a talking-to and decided not to look too eager. Esther had, rather uncharacteristically, gone shopping for a dress. She had decided it was worth splashing out on something new, as much to celebrate going on a date as to impress Phil. It was a silky jersey wrap dress in a deep burgundy (appropriate for the event, she thought), and it accentuated her shape. As she passed him to go down the stairs into the bar, she noticed him noticing and smiled quietly to herself.

The wine tasting was not, as she had expected, a thinly veiled excuse for a piss-up, but a formal teaching event, with bottles wrapped in paper sleeves and questionnaires to fill in. The activity kept them busy but rather ruled out any in-depth conversation. Esther put on her glasses, took it seriously and got stuck in, tasting, thinking and writing detailed notes. She was so engrossed that it took some time for her to notice that Phil had gone quiet. When she glanced over, she noticed a sheen of perspiration at his hairline. He saw her watching and looked up – guiltily, she thought. His eyes were watery and unfocused. He was drunk. Of course, she thought. He's a marathon runner, supremely fit, and the small amount of alcohol we've drunk has gone straight to his head. She gave him a gentle smile.

'Can I order you something to eat?'

'Hmm? Me? No! I'm fine. Unless you're hungry.' He was definitely slurring a little.

'I could eat something,' she said. She called over a waiter and ordered a cheese platter with some extra bread. That should do the trick.

Eating something did seem to slow Phil down a little and he lost his slightly glassy look. Esther was relieved. She was too old to be nursing a man who was vomiting or passing out. They tasted the last round of wine, and she suggested they take a stroll around Grosvenor Square before they went their separate ways. The bar was dark, intimate and a little claustrophobic, and she thought a breath of fresh air, or the London equivalent, would do them both good.

Phil had been very quiet all evening, and he remained so as they strolled up South Audley Street towards the square. Esther made small talk about the wines they had tasted and mentioned some of the interesting facts she had gleaned from the notes. He made a few brief replies to her comments but didn't seem particularly interested. Then he said, abruptly, 'Tell me about your friend.'

'Pardon?'

'Your friend. You said you had a friend who died of cervical cancer.'

'Isabella, yes.'

'When did she die?'

'Eight years ago.' She felt odd. She didn't really want to talk about Isabella, although she wasn't sure if it was more that she didn't want to talk about her, or she didn't want to talk about her to Phil.

'Were you close?'

'Very. We met at primary school and stayed friends through university and beyond.'

'What was she like?'

'An architect – brilliant, creative, braver than me.'

'An architect? Was she well known? Would I have heard of her?'

'If you were a real architecture buff, possibly, otherwise not. She won some competitions, had a few good commissions, but then she got sick. She didn't live long enough to reach her true potential. That's the thing about cancer...' She stopped. Phil knew all too well the cost of cancer. 'Her name was Isabella Millais,' she finished.

'Millais?'

'Like John Everett Millais, the painter.'

He nodded. 'Was she married? Are you in touch with her husband?'

'No husband. No children either – just a mum and a sister. Her mum died recently.'

'Are you still friendly with the sister?'

Esther wasn't sure how to answer this. Was she Sally's friend? It seemed an extravagant word to use for their tentative connection. 'We're still in touch, yes,' she said.

They reached the corner of the square nearest the American Embassy. Two heavily armed policemen stood in a pool of light in front of the imposing building. Phil stopped and Esther turned to ask if he was all right. He grasped her upper arms and abruptly pulled her in towards him, then kissed her hard on the mouth. She was surprised, and a little embarrassed that this was happening in the line of sight of two men wearing Kevlar and carrying semi-automatic weapons. But Phil's ardour was unmistakeable. His mouth was firm on hers, and she could feel his arousal against her stomach. He wound his arms around her tightly, so the softness of her body pressed against him, and she heard him groan – actually groan – against her mouth. Then, just as abruptly, he let her go.

'I'm so sorry,' he said.

'Why are you sorry?'

'I… I haven't done that for so long… I don't know… I'm out of practice… But you… in that dress… Oh God… what an idiot.'

'Don't be silly,' she said gently. 'I'm out of practice too. And for the record, it was very nice.'

As they walked up towards the Tube, the silence between them felt awkward, so she tentatively took his hand. After the quiet of Grosvenor Square, Oxford Street was busy and buzzing. They got to Bond Street station and people were thronging in and out. Phil drew her to him again and began to kiss her. It seemed so odd to be snogging outside a Tube station like a couple of teenagers. She stiffened for a second, self-conscious, and then decided just to go with it. After all, she was supposed to be embracing new opportunities. She relaxed into Phil's arms and ran her hands up and down his back. He was strong and fit, and after months –

years – of sensory deprivation, it was novel and exciting to feel male muscles and smell his warm, musky skin. He clasped her even closer and she could feel he was very turned on. Then he drew back for a second, and his gaze was unfocused with desire and drink.

'I know this is going to come out wrong,' he said, his breathing uneven, 'but I know a hotel...'

'Yes,' said Esther, before she had time to think. 'Let's do it.'

The hotel he had in mind was a few blocks away. Phil walked quickly, holding her hand tightly, almost dragging her along, so she had to half-trot to keep up. In the five minutes it took to walk there, Esther began to wonder if she was making a terrible mistake. Was she about to have a... well, it wasn't a one-night stand, they had been on a couple of dates after all, but... an unplanned sexual encounter? It seemed crazy. She had imagined that if they were going to sleep together it would be more sedate and would involve dinner out or at home, music and soft lighting, not a mad rush to an inner-city hotel. And what kind of hotel did he have in mind? Was he about to drop hundreds of pounds on some five-star establishment? Or would it be a shabby, squalid place with grubby sheets and neon lights flashing in the windows? She was about to bring their speedy march to a halt and call the whole thing off when Phil stopped outside a boxy business hotel – not seedy, but impersonal.

He seemed in an enormous hurry, striding in and banging his hand on the counter, his credit card firmly held between two fingers. The night clerk looked up, unsurprised. He was obviously used to people checking in at short notice and without luggage, and within minutes, Phil had a room card key and they were in the lift.

They started kissing again in the lift, and Phil barely drew breath as they spilled out into the corridor, found their room and got the door open. Rather than being transported with desire, she felt uncomfortable, aware of Phil's slightly sour wine breath and the pressure points his grip had left on her shoulders. But perhaps she was expecting too much. She pushed her misgivings to the back of her mind. A blip, that was all. She'd try to fancy him more. There was certainly no way to back out of the encounter now.

Half an hour later, she sat propped up on the pillows in the hotel room, looking down on Phil lying beside her. It had been… well, all right, she supposed. She hadn't had an orgasm, but then, why would she? It took time to establish rhythms, find what the other person liked, surely? It had been years, decades since she had slept with someone for the first time, so she had very little to compare it to. Sex with Stephen, refined during years of familiarity and mutual knowledge, had been an entirely different experience. Still, this encounter seemed to have been over very quickly, and Phil had certainly… gone straight for the prize, as it were. No leisurely foreplay or time taken to explore her body or his. And as soon as it was over, he had drawn away and lain quite still, staring at the ceiling and not speaking or touching her. Then he had fallen asleep.

She glanced at her watch; it was only just midnight. Suddenly, there was nothing she wanted more than to have a bath in her own bathroom and then fall asleep, alone, in her own bed. If she hurried, she would make the last Tube home. She slipped out of the bed and began to gather her clothes and dress as quietly as she could. She wasn't sure what to do about Phil. Should she wake him to say goodbye? Leave a note? Send a text? She wasn't familiar with the etiquette in these situations. But when she looked up, he was lying, eyes open, watching her.

'You're going,' he said.

'Yes. Work tomorrow. Early start.' She didn't have a lecture till eleven, but the urge to leave was becoming stronger.

'Of course.' He propped himself up on one elbow. 'Well, be careful how you go. Can't imagine what the bloke on the front desk will think. I didn't even get the whole hour.'

Esther finished dressing, grabbed her handbag and hesitated before leaning over the bed and giving him a quick peck on the lips. He seemed to have no intention of dressing or leaving with her. As she rode down in the lift, she mulled over his last comment. Maybe he had intended it as a joke, but it had a hint of real nastiness... suggesting she was a prostitute, and not even a very good one at that. She held her head high and didn't make eye contact or greet the clerk as she left the hotel.

The next morning, she woke up feeling slightly ill. What had she done? Her behaviour had been very out of character. Having sex with Phil had been a mistake, a precipitous, drunken error. Well, chalk it up to experience. She never had to see him again. But when she got to the office, an email from him popped up in her inbox. The subject line said 'Sorry'.

Dearest Esther,

What a pig I am. I let you go out into the night alone. I wanted to say I am so, so sorry. The whole experience last night was so overwhelming for me, as I am sure you can imagine, and I kind of... lost myself. I hope you can forgive me. Please let me see you again. As soon as possible. Please. Let's go back a step and get to know each other properly.

Phil

PS. I'll ring you later and try to set something up for Friday, if you're free.

The email was so reasonable and thoughtful that she softened. Of course, he had not slept with anyone other than his wife for years. It must have been huge for him, and very emotionally fraught. She would do her best to be more understanding.

When he rang at around lunchtime, she was on her way to a tutorial and didn't have time to chat, but she agreed to see him on the following evening.

On the Friday evening they went to a comedy club. This time Phil didn't drink, sticking to lime and soda the whole evening. He told Esther it was because he was running the next day, but she suspected he wanted to maintain his self-control. He seemed to avoid touching her at all costs – indeed, when they met and she went to kiss him hello, he almost recoiled. Like the wine tasting, watching comedy meant that they had little opportunity to talk to one another. She found the evening frustrating and confusing. This adolescent dancing around one another was not at all what she had imagined when she started dating. Surely adults didn't behave like this? She was angry with herself. She seemed to be taking all her leads from Phil, and she felt she needed to be back in the driving seat a little. She wanted to see him on her own terms, on her own turf, where she could set the pace and tone of the encounter. Thus it was that she found herself boldly suggesting he come to her house for dinner early the next week. It was the last week before Lucie would be back, and if things were going to move on, she would have to move them on herself. Only then would she know if there was anything real there.

CHAPTER TEN

In the end, the dinner with Phil was not to be. They scheduled it for the Wednesday, but then Esther received an urgent request to attend a meeting with the university principal, for all department heads, early on Wednesday evening. She rang Phil, full of apologies, to see if they could change the date for their dinner. Could they possibly make it Friday instead? Phil said that was fine and Esther made the change in her diary, but then Lucie rang.

She had been due to come back from Manchester at lunchtime on Saturday, but she wanted to come home earlier. Could she get a train on Thursday morning instead? Esther could hear from her tone of voice that all was far from well, but she could also hear that Stephen was in the room with Lucie so there was no point in quizzing her because she wouldn't be able to answer honestly. 'Of course, darling,' she said. I'll take Thursday afternoon off and meet you at Euston.' She would ring Stephen later and find out what had happened. She hung up and rang Philip immediately, cancelling their dinner.

'Lucie's upset about something,' she explained. 'I'm so sorry about our plans, and I'm doubly sorry that this is the second time I'm doing this. I'm not normally unreliable, honestly. Let me get her home and work out what's wrong, and we can reschedule for the weekend.'

He said it was fine and that he understood, but there was an unmistakeable hint of impatient confusion in his voice. He didn't have kids of his own, she recalled, and couldn't begin to understand that no matter what age they were, their needs trumped everyone else's in their parents' lives. She foresaw arguments whenever she put Lucie's needs ahead of his, and it gave her pause. She didn't have time to think about it immediately though. She had to find out why Lucie had cut her visit short.

She tried to ring Stephen later that day, but his phone went straight to message. He then left her a message while she was lecturing, just saying he was returning her call. He didn't sound unduly concerned. She dropped him a quick email asking why Lucie was coming back early. She got his reply when she woke up on Thursday morning. Like all of Stephen's communications, it was terse and to the point. Lucie had been fine and seemed to be having a nice time but then suddenly said she wanted to get back early to see her friends. He thought it was a standard pre-teen whim. He didn't seem put out that he was missing out on a few days of his daughter's company. Esther thought there was probably more to Lucie's decision than a whim, but she wasn't going to get anything out of Stephen. He was surly and taciturn, the original man of few words. In the last few years of their marriage, he had become a man of almost no words at all. It never ceased to amaze her that he had gone on to marry Melissa, a lively, curvaceous, strawberry-blonde woman who never seemed to stop chattering. She was the first person Esther had ever met who could legitimately be called 'bubbly'. Presumably she drowned Stephen's grumpy silences in a babbling brook of happy words.

Esther was waiting outside the barriers when the train pulled in. It was the middle of the day, so the station wasn't too busy. She had a good view along the length of the platform, and she could see Lucie clearly as she stepped out of a carriage about halfway down the train. Esther noticed, for the first time, a slight roundness to Lucie's hips and thighs. Her slender little daughter was growing up. She had her head down, her long dark hair obscuring her face, and although she was too far away for Esther to be sure, it looked as if, uncharacteristically, her shoulders were drooping. Lucie was normally a confident walker – she had good posture and tended to stride forth quickly and with purpose, but to Esther observing her unseen, she looked as if a little of the stuffing had been knocked out of her.

However, as soon as she saw Esther, she straightened up and plastered on a bright smile. It made Esther's heart ache, and she wondered how often Lucie faked that smile, which she had to admit was worryingly believable if you hadn't seen it being put in place.

'Hello, lovely girl,' she said, and kissed her daughter warmly. She slipped Lucie's bag off her arm and shouldered it herself. 'I'm so happy to see you. I've taken the afternoon off, as promised. Shall we do a naughty trip to Patisserie Valerie?'

'Oh, Mum,' said Lucie, trying to keep the smile going, 'that'd be lovely, but I'm so tired. Can we just go home?'

'Of course,' Esther said, and together they started to walk towards the Tube. She had never known Lucie turn down a visit to Patisserie Valerie. It had always been their favourite mother-and-daughter indulgence, choosing two beautiful pastries to share and sipping on hot chocolate. She also couldn't really see why Lucie would be tired – it wasn't an especially long train journey and it was only two o'clock. Still, now didn't seem to be the time to interrogate her about it, so she merely got them onto the Northern Line going north, to be home as soon as possible.

As soon as they got back to the house, Lucie took her bag and went up to her room, and Esther heard the door close. She assumed Lucie was unpacking (she had always been very neat) and would come back down shortly, but she stayed in her room. After half an hour or so, Esther made a cup of hot chocolate and carried it up. She tapped softly on the door but received no answer. When she pushed it open, she saw Lucie sprawled asleep on her bed. She had opened her bag and the contents were strewn across the floor. She'd clearly just been digging for her phone and laptop, which were beside the bed. It looked like any typical teenage bedroom, expect Lucie was neither typical nor a teenager. Nor was she behaving like the sweet girl Esther had packed off to her dad's a week or so before.

Esther gently closed the door and went back downstairs. As she reached the living room, a chilling thought struck her. She hadn't said anything to Lucie about Phil, but what if Lucie had found out? She couldn't think how – she had eventually told Regina that she'd met a man but had refused to give any details, and she knew Regina would never say something to Lucie. She hadn't mentioned it to anyone else. Could Lucie have gone into her emails? It seemed unlikely. But what else could it be? Or was it nothing? Was she merely witnessing the beginning of teenage sulks and hormones? She decided to try and talk to Stephen one more time. She rang his office number and, to her surprise, he answered.

'Hi there,' she said. 'Glad I caught you.'

'Oh, hello,' he replied, and from those three syllables, she knew he knew something. He sounded guarded and uncomfortable.

'Lucie's back.'

'Good. Good. So she made it back all right? Train not too bad?'

'Seems to have been fine. She's tired. She's gone straight to her room and now she's asleep.'

'Ah.' He didn't have anything to add to that. There was a long pause.

'Steve, did something happen when she was with you? She seems... not right. Did you have a row?'

'Us? No, no.'

'Did she fight with someone else? Melissa, maybe?'

'Fight with Melissa? Of course not!' His faux outrage gave Esther another hint. Whatever the problem was, it had something to do with Melissa.

'Do you have any idea what might have upset her? Anything at all?'

'Well, there's one thing... Just a possibility...'

'What?'

'Melissa thinks... Well...'

'Melissa thinks what?'

'That Lucie might have... seen something. Found something she shouldn't have.'

'Found something? Found what?' What the hell did he mean? Drugs? A gun? He made it sound so sinister.

'We... Well, we haven't told anyone yet. We weren't ready, not till we'd had all the tests and scans...'

'Scans?' Dear God, did Stephen have cancer? Did Melissa?

'But... well, Melissa was so excited, she went and bought a pair of little booties, and she accidentally left them on our bed, still in the bag...'

Booties? In a bag? It took her just a nanosecond to change gear, but Esther cursed herself for her slowness.

'Melissa's pregnant,' she said flatly.

'Just eight weeks along.' Stephen couldn't keep the pride out of his voice. 'But it's all going really well so far.'

'So, let me get this straight,' Esther said, and almost surprised herself with the venom in her voice. 'Your wife is pregnant. I assume this was planned. You hadn't told Lucie you were planning to have a baby. You hadn't told me either, to give me a chance to prepare her, and your... *idiot* wife left cute booties lying around for Lucie to find?'

'Don't be vile, Esther.'

'Don't make this about me, or about manners, Stephen. This is our daughter. Her feelings. She shouldn't have found out like that. She shouldn't have. You know that.'

'I know,' said Stephen testily. 'But you must understand that this is a big deal for us. And maybe we weren't as thoughtful as we should have been. This baby means a lot to us.'

Esther could have sworn, could have screamed, could have told Stephen in no uncertain terms that Lucie should mean a lot to him, Lucie should mean everything to him, and he should have put her feelings first. But she didn't do any of these things. Instead, she gently replaced the phone on its base and walked away. It rang again immediately, so she picked it up, pressed reject and then removed the batteries, so the incessant ringing wouldn't wake Lucie. She scribbled a quick note in case Lucie woke up, went and changed into her running things and left the house. As she closed the door, she heard her mobile, which was set to vibrate, begin to buzz on the kitchen counter.

She ran hard and fast, choosing a route that included a number of long, exhausting hills. She came back an hour later, her legs shaking, red in the face and dripping sweat. Lucie was sitting at the kitchen counter. She looked up when Esther came in. 'You've got about a million missed calls on your phone from Dad,' she said.

'Really?' Esther went to the sink and filled a glass with water.

'And why did you take the batteries out of the landline phone?'

'Hmm? Oh. To replace them.'

'Dad eventually just rang my phone,' said Lucie coolly. 'He said you hung up on him and that you've gone mad.'

The woman's gone mad – the defence used by many a man perplexed by the reaction his behaviour has caused. Esther didn't respond. She just drank her water and pulled off a square of kitchen paper to mop her sweaty neck and forehead.

'Why did you fight with Dad?'

'I didn't.'

'Mum...'

'I didn't fight with him. He said something stupid; I put the phone down and went out for a run. I didn't fight.'

'Was it about me?'

'Not directly.'

Lucie stood up abruptly and headed for the stairs.

'Where are you going?'

'Upstairs.'

'Can't we talk?'

'About what?' said Lucie warily.

'About what happened at Dad's.'

'Nothing happened at Dad's.'

'Really?'

'I wanted to come home, that's all.'

'That's not what Dad says.'

'What did Dad say?'

'He said you found the booties that Melissa bought and left on their bed, and—'

'Booties? What booties?' The shock on Lucie's face was real. She wasn't faking it. 'Do you mean baby booties?'

Never before had Esther wished so earnestly that she could snatch words out of the air and make them unsaid.

'Baby booties?' Lucie said again. 'Is Melissa having a baby? Am I getting a brother or sister?'

'Half-brother or sister,' Esther said, before she could stop herself. For the second time in as many minutes, she wished she could unsay the words. Now was not the time for point-scoring.

'Why didn't they just tell me?' Lucie looked bewildered and suddenly very young.

'Lots of people prefer not to say anything until the pregnancy has got past the twelve-week mark,' Esther said, gently.

'To other people, maybe.' Lucie's voice was shaking. 'To work people, or friends, or something, But he's my dad. Why didn't he tell me?'

'I'm sorry, love. I didn't even know they were trying, or that Melissa was pregnant, or anything, until I spoke to Dad an hour ago. I would have done my best to get him to tell you. Honestly I would.'

Lucie didn't say anything. She just stood, wavering in the doorway, her laptop under one arm, turning her phone over and over in her other hand. Hesitantly, Esther went over and laid a hand on her arm. Lucie stood stock-still for a second and then abruptly shrugged Esther's fingers off her arm, jerking her elbow so hard that her phone flew out of her hand and skittered across the floor. She rushed over and scooped it up, the turned to face Esther, her face a tense mask.

'I bet you love this.'

'What?' said Esther, shocked.

'You love this. Me hating Dad, Dad not wanting me, replacing me with a cute little baby. You win. Well, I hope you're happy now.'

She pushed past Esther and rushed upstairs, slamming her room door so hard it boomed through the house like thunder.

Esther stood where she was for a minute, then, legs shaking, went through to the living room and sat carefully on the edge of a chair. She was trembling all over, and her eyes were blurred with tears. Lucie had not yelled at her since she was a toddler. Her daughter was usually the sunniest, most even-tempered of girls. She had no idea how to respond to Lucie's anger. But more than anything, she was utterly furious with herself for the awful, clumsy way she had handled the situation. She'd blundered in, assuming Stephen's theory about the booties had been correct and that Lucie had known about Melissa's pregnancy. In doing so, she had given Lucie the news in the worst, most tactless way, causing untold pain and damage, and alienating her. No wonder Lucie had turned on her.

She genuinely didn't know what to do. Lucie had never slammed a door on her before, never shouted at her in anger. How best to approach this?

Esther calmed her breathing and went into the downstairs bathroom, where she washed her face and tidied her hair. She went upstairs and knocked softly at Lucie's door.

'Go away.' Lucie's voice was muffled, as if she had her face buried in her pillow.

'Lucie...'

'Go away!' This time her voice was clearer, as if she had raised her head. Her tone was vehement.

'I'm very, very sorry I made such a mess of telling you,' said Esther, leaning her forehead against the door. 'I know you're angry with me, and you have every right to be. I'm going to check back with you every half an hour, until you're ready to talk to me.'

'Go away.'

Esther wasn't sure, but she thought Lucie's voice sounded a little less angry that time. Not much, but a little. She took herself off to shower and change out of her running things. In exactly half an hour she would be back outside Lucie's door. And if Lucie wouldn't let her in, she'd come back half an hour after that. Whatever happened, her daughter would know she had one parent she could rely on, 100 per cent.

She went into the bathroom, started the shower running and began to strip off. As she put her things in the laundry basket, she noticed that the door of the bathroom cabinet beneath the sink was slightly ajar. She went to push it closed, but something was obstructing it. A box of sanitary towels had been clumsily ripped open and left half-hanging off the shelf. It was this that had jammed the door open. She realized immediately that these were the sanitary towels she had bought for Lucie when they had talked about the fact that her first period might come at any time. Esther had explained how to use the towels and had put them in the cupboard so they would be there when Lucie needed them. They had sat there, unopened, for more than a year. Suddenly, Lucie's desire to come home made awful, simple sense.

She showered quickly and dressed, and went and tapped on Lucie's door again.

'Go away.'

'I'm going to make a risotto,' Esther said. 'Dinner's at 6.30.'

She was standing at the cooker, listening to the radio and stirring, when Lucie came downstairs wearing an oversized jumper, one that Stephen had left behind. She poured herself a glass of orange juice and sat on one of the kitchen stools. Esther kept stirring and didn't say anything for a while. Rodrigo's *Concierto de Aranjuez* poured into the warm, quiet kitchen, the music swelling and rising. After a few minutes, she asked Lucie to grate some Parmesan. Without answering, Lucie fetched the cheese and the grater and soon brought a bowl of fluffy white cheese to Esther at the cooker. She took it and lightly touched

Lucie on the arm in thanks. Lucie didn't pull her arm away or complain, but she didn't lean in for a hug, or kiss Esther's cheek, as she would usually have done. Small steps.

When the meal was ready, they sat across the kitchen counter from one another with their steaming bowls. Lucie ate slowly, picking out tiny spoonfuls. Esther let the silence grow, and then said quietly, 'So did your period start when you were up at Dad's?'

Lucie threw down her spoon. 'What? How did you know?' Her face was dark with sullen suspicion.

'You left the bathroom cabinet open. I saw you'd opened the box of pads. I wasn't prying, Lucie, honestly.'

She could see Lucie wrestling with anger and embarrassment, and considering fleeing to her room. She kept her eyes down and continued eating.

Eventually Lucie said, 'Yes.'

'What did you do?'

'Melissa had some pads in the bathroom. I took a few.'

'But you didn't tell her.'

'No.'

'I'm sorry you had to go through that alone. I wish I'd been there.'

'Yeah,' said Lucie. 'Well, you weren't.' And this time she did push her plate away, hop off the stool and go back up to her bedroom, shutting her door with finality.

Esther sighed, finished her food and cleared away the bowls. She had some business she needed to sort out. She had been unsure what to do, but it was now clear that there was only one possible choice.

Subject: So sorry

Dear Phil,

For someone who teaches English for a living, I'm finding this email surprisingly difficult to write. You can't tell, but this first line has been deleted and rewritten countless times. I've hit undo and redo so often, I'm surprised they're not worn out. Anyway, here goes.

I am so glad I met you. I'd decided to try going out and doing something new that evening at the Tate, and you made my first evening out such fun. I also so enjoyed our time on the Heath last weekend, and our two subsequent evenings too. It has been wonderful to meet someone new and begin to get to know you.

I'm sorry our plans for dinner this week haven't worked out, and I wish I was writing this email to reschedule, but I've had something of a minor family crisis. As you know, my daughter came back unexpectedly from visiting her father in Manchester today. There have been a few rather unfortunate events, and she's really terribly upset. I'm going to need to make her my sole priority for a little while, and I'm afraid that rather precludes inviting you for dinner, or indeed going out in the evenings. I'm so sorry.

This won't be forever, but I'm afraid I can't say how long I'll need to cry off having a social life. I don't expect you to wait around while I resolve my family issues. I do hope you understand.

She typed the words 'Perhaps someday', deleted them, typed 'Maybe at some future date' and backspaced the words away. It really wasn't fair to keep him hanging on, especially when she wasn't at all sure she liked him. In the end, she typed:

Again, I'm so sorry.

Warmest wishes,

Esther

She hovered the mouse over the send button for a full minute. Then she saved the email to Drafts, half got out of her chair, sat down again, called the email up and hit send rapidly. Now it was done.

What a mess she had made of everything. What did Woody Allen say? 'If you want to make God laugh, tell him about your plans.' She'd imagined that her life was on an even keel, but it had taken only a week to show how precarious everything was. Lucie, whose happiness was more important to her than anything, felt hurt and betrayed and saw Esther as the author of her misfortunes. On top of that, she had treated Phil badly – not deliberately, of course, but through circumstance. There was just no way, however, she could start something with him at this point. The last thing Lucie needed was more uncertainty. She might feel she was low on Stephen's list of priorities, but she would never be made to feel that about Esther.

CHAPTER ELEVEN

Subject: Re: So sorry

Dear Esther,

Thank you for your email. I have to say, I'm not surprised.
I found your behaviour a little unbalanced and your
mood swings disconcerting. It was very clear to me from
our meetings that you were not stable enough for any
kind of long-term relationship. You blew hot and cold,
sharing inappropriate confidences, then being sexually
aggressive, then pushing me away. My colleague Gillian,
who met you that night after the Tate, said to me that she
thought you were a hysterical female.

I thought you were very attractive, but I am afraid I cannot involve myself in the chaotic goings-on of your family.

Best wishes,

Phil

The email came in at around ten the following morning. Esther was in her office alone. She read it once, twice, then sat staring at individual phrases for some time. 'Unbalanced'; 'sexually aggressive'; 'hysterical female'. She closed the email, left her office and went to get a glass of water in the kitchen, then came back and read it again. She had absolutely no idea how to respond. It was a piece of sheer ugliness. It was malicious and unpleasant. It exposed Phil as a mean, narrow-minded misogynist and Gillian as a conniving cow, who probably wanted Phil for herself. He had managed to turn the whole thing around, to make it look as if he was rejecting her. He was a nasty man, Esther realized. A nasty, cruel, unpleasant man that she was well shot of. She had only just met him, and it was a lucky escape. She was fortunate not to have him in her life. And yet the injustice stung so fiercely, it took great willpower not to pick up the phone and ring him. She wanted very much to set him right on so many points. But she knew how he would interpret such a call, and the names he would call her. There was no way to win this one. Dignified silence was the only option. Well, dignified silence and a good bitching session. She gathered up her laptop and went to find Regina.

'Coffee. Out,' she said. 'And we won't be talking work.'

Esther filled Regina in on the happenings of the last few weeks, from the Friday night at the Tate to Lucie's return, her email and Phil's reply. She opened the email and handed over the laptop for Regina to read it herself. Regina's response was satisfyingly dramatic. She gasped, hissed and even swore. She read it twice, then pushed the laptop back across the table.

'Well, my darling girl, you dodged a bullet there,' she said.

'I know! But you would never have known. He seemed so nice. So normal. Never in a million years would I have guessed... would I ever have imagined...'

'He hates and distrusts women. And he's a freak.'

'It looks that way. But how are you supposed to spot them? If they walk around wearing nicely ironed chinos and talking normally, packing picnics and taking you to comedy clubs? Are all the men out there scary misogynist freaks?'

'Of course they aren't. You just landed a bad one on your very first fishing trip. There are loads of lovely, sane, sensible men.'

'Where? I thought the Tate was a pretty safe place to go looking for one. It's not a dodgy bar or a nightclub. I was supposed to meet some pleasant, polite, *Guardian*-reading fellow who plays the oboe and has an allotment. Not Jack the Self-Esteem-Ripper.'

'At least you can laugh about it.'

'The alternative isn't really available. Costa frowns upon people sobbing into their flat whites. And to be fair, Psycho Phil is the least of my problems. Lucie is much more of a worry.' She told Regina briefly about what had happened following Lucie's return from Manchester.

'Oh dear.'

'Oh dear indeed. Maybe Phil's right. Maybe my life is in chaos and I am a hysterical female.'

'Nonsense. You're the most level-headed, reliable, loving mum I know. Just keep doing what you're doing. Love Lucie. Be there for her. She'll be fine. You know she will.'

Esther wasn't so sure. Lucie remained sullen and closed. She appeared certain that everything that had gone wrong in Manchester was in some way Esther's fault. Esther understood that it was easier for Lucie to be angry with her, and awful to her, secure in the knowledge that Esther's love was total and unconditional, than for her to be angry with her father, whose affections must have seemed very conditional and fickle indeed. Knowing this didn't stop it hurting, though, and it hurt a great deal.

At first it looked as if Lucie had undergone some kind of radical personality change, but as the weeks stretched on, Esther had to admit that the signs had been there for a while. Lucie had gradually been shedding her good-girl persona – wanting to spend more time away from home, wanting to be with her friends, resisting Esther on small issues. She was growing up, on the verge of becoming a teenager. Esther also realized, with an ache, that Lucie had spent the last few years trying to be very, very good, as if, through her parents' divorce, she was concerned she might be too much trouble. If she was now being sullen and sulky but at least expressing her true self and her own opinions, that had to be a good thing. Didn't it?

Still, a lot of the time it felt like war, and Lucie would answer even the most banal questions in a sarcastic monotone. It took all Esther's willpower not to snap at her. She maintained a cheerful tone no matter what and kept doing the same things she had always done. She cooked the dishes Lucie had always liked, even though Lucie rolled her eyes and refused to eat them. She offered to take her shopping, to the cinema, out to dinner, even though she knew Lucie would say no to all of them. Through it all, Esther did not lose her temper, even though, deep down, she was boiling at the injustice of it.

Her life felt suddenly joyless. Until comparatively recently, she had thought herself happy – working, running, being with Lucie. But the awful, abortive interaction with Phil, and the family crisis brought about by Stephen's new baby seemed to have sucked all the pleasure out of her existence. She felt lonely and hollow. Even though she hadn't felt deprived by her lack of a social life before, she found herself resenting the endless evenings at home. Even when Lucie went out to visit friends, she avoided going out herself. It seemed best to stay at home, to be on call. She knew she was being perverse and that she was only doing it so that, in contrast to Stephen, she would appear reliable and steady.

Now she kept thinking of all the things she might have been doing – the events she might have attended, the groups she might have joined. The nice men, the anti-Phils, might well be out there, waiting to meet her. But where was she? Sitting at her kitchen table for the umpteenth Saturday night in a row, marking essays or filling in endless forms as part of her head-of-department duties.

But then the conference came along. It was a gathering of academic leaders from universities around the country to discuss new techniques for recruiting students. 'It's a vital networking opportunity,' said the principal. He had called Esther into his office for a special meeting. 'Student numbers are down with the new fee structures, and your department is especially hard hit. We need to get out there, press the flesh. Build some new relationships. See if there aren't some other universities we can get into bed with, maybe create some new joint courses, unique offerings for the marketplace.'

The principal had been attending some marketing conferences himself. He had learned a lot of new buzzwords and liked to use them. Esther wished he wouldn't. She had preferred it when he was a slightly woolly ex-professor of geography who never knew what was going on. To her the conference sounded like hell on earth – four days stuck in some stately home in the middle of Buckinghamshire with a load of crusty academics. Nothing came of these events, she was certain. It was just an excuse for four days of eating and drinking at the university's expense. Hang on a minute – four days of eating and drinking at someone else's expense? Away from home and Lucie's huffy sulks? Meeting new people? Going to a part of the country that she didn't know especially well? Perhaps it wasn't such a bad idea after all.

The conference fell on the Monday, Tuesday, Wednesday and Thursday of a week in May. It was term-time, so Lucie couldn't go up to stay with Stephen, which was probably a mercy. However, when Esther tentatively mentioned that she might have to go away for work, Lucie showed uncharacteristic animation and said she was sure she could stay at Rebecca's for a few days. A call to Rebecca's mum proved this to be true, and the arrangement was quickly made. Lucie seemed thrilled at the prospect. Esther examined her own feelings – a complex cocktail of a sneaky, desperate desire to escape her day-to-day life, albeit temporarily, resentment at Lucie apparently being happier without her than with her, and crushing parental guilt. Eventually she reasoned that the first two balanced each other out and removed the need for the last, so she resolved to go to the conference and make the best of it, confident that Lucie would have fun and might well be in a better frame of mind when she returned.

She looked at the website of the place where they would be staying and discovered that it had both a spa and a gym, as well as acres of grounds in which she could run. The formal events took place between ten and five, and even if she did 'flesh-pressing' and 'networking' over dinner, it would still give her hours to herself to relax, regroup and breathe.

CHAPTER TWELVE

She opted to take the train up on the Sunday evening rather than drive – it was easier to get the university to pay for a train ticket than for mileage, and it also meant she could get a bit of work done on the journey. It also, oddly, made it feel more like a holiday. She went through her conference pack on the train – she hadn't had time to give it more than a cursory glance before. There were a couple of interesting sessions that she was looking forward to attending, as well as a talk by the head of the English Department of a big American university, whom she had always wanted to meet. At the back of the pack there was a full list of attendees. She glanced down it. Unsurprisingly, she knew quite a few of them – academics she had collaborated with on various projects, a smattering of people she had got to know during her undergraduate and postgraduate studies, and Michael Wolfson. Michael had taught Medieval English at her university for some years. He was a sound academic and a good colleague. For a long time she'd considered him one of her better friends at the university. Five or so years earlier, he'd been offered a professorship in the Midlands and had left London. They had stayed in sporadic email contact, but, inevitably, that had waned to nothing. He was warm and funny and was married to a mathematician called Lisette, with whom he had two teenaged sons. She was delighted to know he would be there. He would make a good dinner companion and gossip partner.

The event organizers sent a minibus to collect her at the station, and she arrived in plenty of time to get ready for the drinks reception on the first evening. She showered and changed into the red jersey dress she had bought for her wine-tasting date with Phil. She was determined to wear the dress again to erase the negative associations it had inevitably acquired.

As usual, she was ready too early, so she decided to stroll down to the gym and spa complex and see what was on offer. It was a warm, golden evening and the rolling lawns of the stately home looked velvety and well tended. The gym was small, with a reasonable selection of treadmills, cross-trainers and weights, more or less what you would expect from a five-star hotel. The spa was closed for the evening. She could hear splashing from the far side of the complex, however, so she crossed the gym floor to have a look at the swimming pool.

It wasn't quite full size – maybe eighteen metres or so, rather than twenty-five – but certainly long enough to swim decent lengths. And indeed a man was swimming, a fast, economical freestyle, slicing his way up the length of the pool, performing a professional tumble-turn at the end, and continuing. It was rather mesmerizing to watch. Esther became conscious that she was staring and was about to turn and go when the man finished his last length and stood up in the shallow end, shaking the water from his eyes and hair. He had his back to her and her first thought was that he was beautiful – his skin was an even golden olive and his back smoothly muscled. In an instant, however, she realized that she recognized the shape of his head. It was Michael Wolfson. He put his hands on the edge of the pool and vaulted out smoothly. He was wearing black shorts which sat low on his hips, and as he bent to retrieve his towel, she found herself looking at his muscular calves and thighs. He hadn't spotted her, and somehow it didn't seem an appropriate moment to step out of the shadows and renew their acquaintance. He wasn't wearing much, and she didn't want him to think she was some kind of voyeur. She walked back quietly through the door into the gym and left the complex. She'd see him at the drinks reception.

She was handed a name badge and a glass of Prosecco as she arrived and was ushered into a windowless conference suite, where there was a low buzz of chatter from a smallish group of people. There had been quite a lot of name badges still on the table – she suspected many of the delegates had not yet arrived. People were clustered around the food table and were mainly chatting in pairs. She didn't see anyone she recognized and hung back a little. A veteran of many conferences, she knew the dangers of rushing in and chatting to the first stranger you saw. Inevitably, you picked the biggest bore in the room and were then stuck with them for the rest of the evening or, worse, the rest of the conference.

A few moments later, someone she knew entered – a professor from a university in Scotland called Biddy Bates. She had worked with Biddy on a research project on teaching methods and had liked her very much. She had a dry sense of humour and a wicked twinkle in her eye and could be counted on to not take events like this too seriously. She waved, and Biddy's face lit up when she spotted her. She hurried over, scooping up a glass as she came.

'Ah, a sane and familiar face,' she said, smiling and kissing Esther on the cheek. 'Good to see you.'

They exchanged news, and Biddy, who was a notorious gossip, shared a few scurrilous details about various delegates and speakers. Esther enjoyed talking to Biddy and began to relax, but she couldn't quite resist keeping half an eye on the door. Even though she was focused on Biddy's face and what she was saying, she had a heightened awareness of the rest of the room and who was in it.

Biddy broke off for a second and turned to grab a canapé, and Esther glanced towards the door just as Michael walked in. He stopped and surveyed the room, and his eyes locked with hers. She saw something, an emotion that was more than happy recognition, cross his face. Then he collected himself and smiled and walked over to greet her and Biddy. He was a few inches taller than her, broad-shouldered and strong, with a dark complexion (she recalled that his mother was Italian or Spanish). His black hair was greying attractively at the temples and, as it was receding slightly, he wore it very short. His eyes were a deep chocolate brown and they danced with amusement.

He kissed Biddy first, warmly, and said something softly to her that made her giggle. Then he turned to Esther. 'Professor Hart,' he said, holding out his hand.

'Professor Wolfson,' she replied, equally seriously.

Then he grinned and pulled her into his arms for a firm bear-hug. She could feel the smooth skin of his back, warm through his thin shirt, and she had a flashback of him standing by the side of the pool.

'May I say, you look very foxy in that red dress, Professor,' he said, looking her up and down.

'Why thank you, Professor. You don't look too shabby yourself,' she replied. It was the sort of light banter they had always shared, except now it seemed to carry a charge of real electricity. She knew it was all in her own head. She had to stop it. He was married. This was a work conference, and he was a valued colleague. Behaving like a flirtatious, desperate divorcée who had been let out for the weekend just wouldn't do. She exchanged the necessary pleasantries, then forced herself to spot someone else she knew across the room, make her excuses and move on, leaving Michael and Biddy to chat to one another. A few minutes later, one of the conference organizers came in and announced that dinner was served, and they all moved into the dining room.

A colleague who held the same post in another London university introduced herself, and Esther, mindful of her professional responsibilities, opted to sit with her at dinner. She was a dry, rather humourless woman, an expert on *Beowulf*, who had taken to her administrative duties as head of department with zealous seriousness. She talked statistics with dull relish, and Esther couldn't help glancing over at the table where Biddy, Michael and a few other colleagues seemed to be having an uproarious time, laughing and drinking wine. She had definitely cut off her nose to spite her face. The *Beowulf* woman was drinking still water (not even sparkling, Esther noted gloomily). She defiantly refilled her own wine glass. If she was going to be bored to death by grade quotas, she may as well be tipsy and bored.

After dessert was served, there seemed to be a general shift as people took their coffees and began to mingle, moving from table to table. Madame Beowulf seemed to be going nowhere, however. Esther was about to make her excuses and move on when she sensed someone slipping into the empty chair on her other side.

'So, Professor Hart, it's been a while.'

'It has indeed, Professor Wolfson. Some years. A lot has changed.'

'That's true. For one thing, I'm no longer a professor.'

'You're not?'

'Didn't really work out in the Midlands. I hated the department, and the teaching load was too heavy to allow time for any meaningful research. So I've taken a step down the ladder and I'm now at a college in Surrey where I supervise a few PhD and master's students and by and large they leave me to my own devices. I'm not even a head of department, just a deputy, but my boss is on maternity leave, so here I am.'

'Surrey?'

'About half an hour from London by train.'

'How has that worked out for Lisette? Is she at the same university as you?'

'Lisette is still in the Midlands. We split up about three years ago.'

'I'm sorry,' said Esther, but she felt a small thrill deep in her belly, as if she had just gone over the top on a rollercoaster. 'Well, I'm in the same boat. Stephen and I split up about four years ago.'

'I'm sorry too,' said Michael, although he didn't look even slightly sorry. 'How's Lucie?'

'On the verge of being a teenager and struggling a bit because Stephen has remarried and she's about to get a new half-brother or sister. How are your kids?'

'Both at university now – Oliver's at Durham, Luke's at Cardiff. They split their holidays between their mum and me, when they're not off gallivanting with friends.'

'Gosh, so a lot has changed for both of us,' she said, taking a sip of her wine.

'A lot has changed,' he said quietly. 'Some things are the same.'

She looked up and caught his eye. He was watching her intently, searching her face.

The conference organizer tapped her glass with a fork and

stood up to make a series of housekeeping announcements. She concluded by suggesting, none too subtly, that an early night might be in order, as there was rather a full programme the next day. Most people took the hint, finishing their coffees and saying their goodbyes.

Michael had turned back towards the table and was drawing circles in the sugar with the spoon, lost in thought.

'Are you all right?' said Esther.

He looked up at her. 'I have a really nice room, with a balcony that overlooks the lawns. Number 23, in case you were wondering. I was trying to think of a way to suggest we get a bottle of wine from the bar and go and sit out there. But every sentence I frame sounds like a proposition.' He gave her a crooked smile.

'A proposition?'

He nodded. 'I suppose mainly because it is. A proposition.'

It was her turn to be pensive for a moment.

'I think I might be amenable to that,' she said finally.

'Should we be having a grown-up conversation about whether this is a good idea, and whether we're both in the right place emotionally, and whether this will ruin our friendship?'

'It's an excellent idea, I'm fine, hope you are too, and meh, we weren't that good friends anyway – I didn't even know you'd got divorced.'

He chewed his lip for a second. 'I... kind of knew you had.'

'You did?'

'Grapevine. You know how it is. So when I heard you were attending this conference... that bit of news may have been a deciding factor in my choosing to come.'

'Interesting,' she said coolly. 'Well, since we're laying our cards on the table, I took a walk down to the pool earlier, and I may have, unobserved, watched you swimming for a while. You have very fine form, sir. And your freestyle is excellent.'

He broke into a broad grin. 'Just wait…' he began, but she laid a finger over his lips.

'You're doing so well, Michael, this had better not be a breaststroke joke.'

He laughed, a deep chuckle. She remembered that laugh, and the way his eyes crinkled when he smiled. It gave her a warm, sweet glow.

'Let me go to my room to freshen up, and I'll meet you in yours in fifteen minutes,' she said, standing up.

'Are you leaving first so I can watch your bottom as you walk out of the room?'

'What you do is entirely up to you.' She smiled over her shoulder and put a little extra sway into her hips as she left.

She couldn't help grinning broadly and even skipping a little as she made her way down the long carpeted corridors back to her room. As she walked, she offered up fervent thanks to Phil and released any bitterness she might have harboured towards him for their brief and ill-fated encounter – because Phil had served his purpose. In being so utterly wrong for her, he had helped her to know when someone utterly right was there in front of her. Her worries about Phil, her soul-searching about whether or not she was attracted to him, her doubts about her own behaviour and her trying to understand his – all were swept away instantly in this reconnection with someone who was, in the simplest way, perfect.

Michael Wolfson. Sexy, warm, delightful Michael, whom she knew so well and yet didn't know at all. Of all the scenarios she had imagined in which she might meet a man, getting together with someone she'd known for years was not something she had considered. And yet it made so much sense. She knew he was a good, kind and honourable person. She knew his life story, knew they shared knowledge and interests, even many mutual friends.

And as for attraction, just looking at him made something melt and fizz in her. She had been acutely conscious of the heat of his arm as he sat next to her at the table, and she had found herself staring at his hands and mouth and thinking profoundly unacademic thoughts.

Although she was absolutely set on her course of action for the evening, she was still nervous, so she hurried into her room, stripped off and had a lightning-quick shower, before putting on fresh underwear, retouching her make-up and applying a little perfume. She hesitated for a second about what to wear and then put the red dress back on. It seemed to be doing the trick. No point in messing with something that was working. She gave her teeth a quick brush, tidied her hair, and she was ready to go.

Michael's room was on the other side of the hotel, and she felt a little as if she were doing a premature walk of shame as she crossed the reception area and went down the corridor into the other wing. A few people who were sitting having coffee glanced up as she passed, though no one spoke to her. But as she turned into the corridor where Michael's room was, Biddy stepped out of a room a few doors along.

'Hello there,' she said cheerfully. 'Is your room down this side as well? Michael's along here too!'

'Um… no,' said Esther carefully, looking at the room numbers. 'I seem to have got turned about. I'm on completely the wrong side. Night!' She gave Biddy a wave, turned on her heel and re-crossed reception. Once she was back in her room, she sat on the edge of the bed for a moment. Her hands were shaking. Then she looked in the room service directory and worked out how to dial another room in the hotel.

'Cold feet?' Michael answered.

'Not exactly. I bumped into Biddy, a few doors from your room.'

'Oh dear.'

'It was a proper bedroom-farce moment – I did consider hiding in a broom cupboard and then chasing a curate up and down the stairs with a feather duster.'

He laughed. 'And so…?'

'Well, maybe it's a sign.'

'It's definitely not a sign. I taught a course on signs and signifiers. I'm practically a world expert. That wasn't a sign. Come on over.'

'How do I get past Biddy? She's gone to sit in the reception area and drink coffee and gossip. I'd have to crawl through a flower bed, or wear a false moustache or something.'

'Shall I keep an eye out and let you know when she's gone to bed?'

'She might stay up for hours.'

'So… where does that leave us?' He sounded uncertain and suddenly serious.

'Not… shagging?' she said, trying to lighten the mood. 'At least, not tonight.'

He was quiet for so long, she wondered if the connection had been cut, but then he said, 'I had a speech all prepared, you know, for when you got here.'

'A speech?'

'I could do the telephonic version if you like.'

'I'd like,' she said.

'Okay.' She heard him take a deep breath. 'This isn't just about sex, you know. I didn't imagine this as a saucy conference one-night stand. I'm really not that bloke.'

'I'm relieved. I'm really not that woman either.'

'Don't get me wrong,' he said, 'I fancy you immensely. I've spent an unconscionable amount of time over the years imagining what you might look like without your clothes on. But it's more than that.'

She smiled at what he'd said but didn't interrupt. She just let him talk.

'I've never been a Lothario. I was faithful to Lisette for all of our marriage and since we split up, I've gone on a few dates, but there's been nothing, or no one, significant. I know that you aren't in a position to take things lightly. You've got Lucie to think of, and even though my boys are older, I worry about them too. I don't want to embarrass them by parading a succession of women in front of them that don't stick around. I like you... a lot. I'm not the most thrilling of fellows. I think I'm what they call a serial monogamist. So when I invited you to my room, what I was saying was... I would very much like to have a go at... embarking on a relationship with you.'

'That's wonderful to hear,' Esther said, 'but we're adults, and we have to accept that there are no guarantees. I mean, I recently met someone—'

'Oh God, I didn't even consider that. That you might have a boyfriend. What an idiot. I'm so sorry.'

'I definitely, definitely don't have boyfriend,' she said, and briefly she told him about Phil.

'Well, firstly, he sounds like a bell-end,' said Michael. 'And secondly, I'm not him. I have kids too, and I understand that Lucie always has to take priority, especially now when things are a bit tricky for her. We can take things as slowly as you like. I really do understand.' He suddenly caught himself. 'If you... you know... want to take things at all.'

'I want to take things,' she said softly. 'Or at least I want to try.'

'I would very much like to smell your hair right now,' he said. 'I hope that doesn't sound weird. It's just that when I came to sit next to you at dinner, I caught the scent of your hair as I sat down. It smelled wonderful.'

'Thank you – I think. I don't think anyone has ever complimented me on the smell of my hair before.'

'I should warn you, I'm quite rubbish at this. I've never had any good chat-up lines. My main methods are bumbling honesty and desperation.'

'So far, they're working a treat.' She smiled.

There was a loud burst of laughter from the foyer, which was audible in both of their rooms.

'It doesn't sound like Biddy and her cronies are going to be winding up the party anytime soon,' he said regretfully. 'Can we try again tomorrow night?'

'If I have to abseil down the building to your window.'

'Will this abseiling involve any kind of close-fitting black Lycra outfit?'

'Possibly. Now we should both get some sleep. Tomorrow, you know… Big day and all that. Lots of plenary sessions and breakouts.'

'Hmmm… I'm trying to…'

'… think of a double entendre involving plenary sessions? I know you are.'

'Ah, Esther, we've been dating for fifteen minutes and you already find me predictable.'

'It's okay,' she said, quietly. 'I rather like predictability.'

'Well, predictably, I shall be staring at you through breakfast, finding an excuse to stand near you during the coffee breaks, and fantasizing about you during the afternoon discussion on research grants.'

'Sounds delightful.' She smiled. 'Good night, lovely Michael.'

'Good night, delectable Esther,' he said softly.

She passed a fitful, broken night and got up at dawn to go for a run around the quiet, misty grounds. She may as well not have attended the conference at all, for all the attention she paid to the sessions that day. Michael came to sit beside her at breakfast, but, regrettably, so did a number of other colleagues, and there was no opportunity for them to talk privately. He kept his leg pressed up against hers under the table, and at one point managed to take her hand and stroke it briefly.

They were both well aware of how swiftly gossip spreads in academic circles, so they were careful not to spend too much time together. They chose different breakout sessions in the morning and sat separately at lunch. But Michael risked sitting beside her in the afternoon talk on funding and distracted her throughout by drawing saucy cartoons in the margins of his notepad and then angling the page so she could see them.

At the end of the afternoon session, the conference organizer explained that there would be a couple of free hours before dinner and that they were all welcome to make use of the hotel facilities. Biddy, who was sitting two rows in front of Esther and Michael, stood up, stretched and turned to face them.

'Right, I'm off for a swim in the pool. Either of you fancy joining me?'

'No thanks,' said Esther, as casually as she could manage. 'I need to catch up on some emails.'

'I swam this morning,' said Michael. 'I think I might just go for a lie-down.'

'Righto, see you at dinner,' Biddy said cheerfully, and set off.

They walked nonchalantly out into the foyer and stood chatting until they saw Biddy leave her room and head for the leisure complex. The reception area cleared, and as the last stragglers left, Michael caught Esther's hand and hurried her down the corridor, pulling his key card from his pocket as they walked. Within seconds they were inside his room, with the door closed.

He drew her into his arms and held her, very lightly and carefully, as if she was precious, and then he kissed her for the first time. It was the polar opposite of Phil's clumsy lunge in Grosvenor Square – a sweet and sensual kiss – and Esther felt desire leap in her like a flame.

They didn't make it to dinner. Around nine o'clock, Michael rang room service and ordered bacon, eggs and toast, which they devoured sitting cross-legged on the bed. Then they showered together and fell back into bed.

Esther's thighs were aching, she felt deliciously bruised inside. Her lips were puffy and swollen and her hair was a bird's nest. Michael flopped down on the pillows beside her, and entwined their fingers.

'Well, my dear, I think we can safely say our friendship is over.'

She glanced over at him. They hadn't drawn the curtains or turned any lights on, and in the pale light coming in from outside, she could see he was smiling.

'Yup,' she said, 'I think it's clear we're no longer mates and work colleagues.'

'There might be a few things we haven't done – we might need a few more goes, just to make sure that period of our lives is over.'

'We have plenty of time,' she said, rolling over and putting her head on his shoulder and stroking his chest.

He wrapped his arms around her, pulling her close to him. 'We do. But despite all my brave talk, I'm not as young or as virile as I used to be.'

'I found you pretty virile, Dr Wolfson.' She smiled, hugging him back.

'Feel free to spread that information around. Maybe tweet it. Or submit a paper on it to a reputable journal.'

'I'll get onto it.'

'Do you know what I'd like to do now, very much indeed? I'd like to sleep with you.'

'Again?'

'I mean sleep. I want you to turn on your side so I can wrap my arm around the curve of your waist, and I want to bury my face in your hair and sleep.'

'It sounds divine, but maybe I should get back to my room...'

'By all means,' he said. 'But I can still hear people laughing and talking in reception. We skipped dinner, and if you emerge from my room, still wearing what you were wearing this afternoon, I think that people – and by people I mean Biddy, world-champion gossip – might notice. I might also point out that your hair isn't quite as smooth and tidy as it was when you arrived.'

'You make a good point,' she said. 'But I haven't even got my toothbrush.'

'To be fair, I think we've been intimate enough in the last few hours that you could use mine. In fact, it's an electric one and I have a few spare heads with me, so you don't even have to do that. You can have your own brand-new one.'

'Practical and virile. I like that in a man.'

'Why thank you, ma'am.'

'One last thing,' she said. 'Do you snore?'

'Like a foghorn, apparently.'

'Seriously?'

'No. I don't think I do, but to be fair, the only living thing to have slept in the same room as me for some time is my cat, Geoffrey.'

'Your cat is called Geoffrey?'

'Chaucer, obviously.'

'Obviously. Well, thank you. I accept your invitation to sleep over,' she said. 'I'll set an alarm and sneak back to my room at about six.'

They got out of bed and went into the bathroom, where they took turns to brush their teeth. It was oddly domestic and companionable. As they got back into bed, he turned to her as he snuggled down in the pillows. 'I forgot to ask you. Do you snore?'

'Like a St Bernard with sinus problems,' she said, lying down beside him. 'Too late, though, I'm staying now.'

They woke before Esther's alarm went off, and in the grey light of dawn, made love again, slowly and deliciously. She reluctantly dragged herself out of bed and found her clothes, which were strewn across the floor. He lay in bed and watched her dress.

'There's a small possibility I might not make it to breakfast,' he said. 'I might need a little lie-in. Just to get my strength up.'

'Lazy,' said Esther briskly. 'I'm going back to my room to get changed and go for a run now.'

'Oh Lord. Are you one of those perky morning people?'

'The perkiest.'

'Well, that might need some negotiation.' He smiled up at her as she came over to kiss him goodbye. 'I need very gentle handling when I wake up.'

She did her best to tidy her hair with her fingers – she had neither a comb nor a brush and Michael's hair was cropped so short, he required neither. Then she scooped up her handbag, blew him a kiss and slipped out into the deserted corridor. She hurried across the foyer – mercifully whoever was supposed to be at the desk was in a back office somewhere – and made it back to her own room without encountering anyone.

She plugged in her phone, stripped off her crumpled clothes and crawled into her neatly made bed. She'd get up and go for a run in a minute. What a delicious, glorious and unforgettable night. She relived a few choice moments and smiled. Then she thought about what Michael had said about mornings, and her euphoria faded slightly. It had been an incredible night, but this was not real life. Big hotel beds, room service, no commitments – it was a million miles from her tightly scheduled day-to-day existence. How many long nights would she and Michael get to spend together? How many lazy mornings in bed would they have? There was no way she could have a man sleep over when Lucie was in the house. And with the changes in Stephen's home life, Lucie might be more reluctant to go and see her dad. Michael had swept her along with his certainty, but how long would it take for his patience to become exhausted? These were uncharted waters, and she was far from sure that they could make it work.

They had fallen asleep late the previous night, and she had slept relatively fitfully – it had been a very long time since she had shared a bed with anyone. Her bed was so comfortable, she found herself dozing off. She should get up. Even if she didn't run, she needed to shower, wash her hair, make herself look respectable. She would get up, any minute now. She would just close her eyes for a minute… Just a minute…

It was the chambermaid's knock that woke her, and as soon as she heard it and opened her eyes, she saw the bright mid-morning sunlight streaming in through the curtains. She looked at the clock on the TV. Ten o'clock. She'd slept through breakfast and the first session. 'Still here!' she yelled, and mercifully the chambermaid apologized and withdrew. She jumped out of bed, gathered up her hastily discarded clothes and headed for the bathroom.

Fifteen minutes later, she emerged from her room, freshly showered and with her wet hair neatly pulled back in a twist. The first talk had just ended, and everyone was having coffee before the breakout sessions. She slipped in quietly and made for the coffee table. She was starving, but breakfast was long finished. She'd have to fill up on biscuits and fruit and hang on for lunch.

She had a cup of coffee and was stacking ginger nuts and rich tea biscuits on her saucer when Biddy came over.

'Morning,' she said. 'You all right? We missed you at dinner last night, and I didn't see you this morning either.'

'Hmm? Oh, I was feeling a bit under the weather,' said Esther. 'I slept in this morning. I feel a bit better now.'

'Not food poisoning or anything?' asked Biddy. 'Only Michael says he thinks he had something dodgy at lunch yesterday. He wasn't around last night either.'

'Oh no, nothing like that. Just... hay fever.' She couldn't resist looking over Biddy's shoulder and, sure enough, Michael was standing just behind her, smiling cheekily.

'Hay fever?' he said, with mock concern. 'That must have stopped you running this morning.'

'It did. I was so tired from all the... sneezing, I ended up having a little lie-down instead.'

'Well, that's best. It's the best remedy. For sneezing.'

'I've always sworn by Piriton,' said Biddy. 'And locally sourced honey.'

'Locally sourced honey?' Esther focused intently on Biddy and refused to catch Michael's eye. 'I must try that.'

'Me too,' said Michael. 'I do like my honey.'

This time she did look at him; his smile, while cheeky, was so tender and affectionate, it made her a little wobbly.

They had two more nights at the conference – two long, delicious nights, plus one wicked, knee-trembling quickie just inside Esther's room door in the coffee break on the last afternoon. But then it was time to go home to their real lives. Many of the delegates left on the final night, but Esther was booked on a morning train. She left Michael's room at six and went back to her own to pack. They had breakfast together in the almost empty restaurant and then went to check out.

'Are you sure I can't drive you home?' Michael said, for the umpteenth time.

'Really, don't worry. It's miles out of your way, and I'm going straight from the station to work and then on to collect Lucie from school.'

'It would mean I'd get another couple of hours with you though.'

'You're going to see me at the weekend. Besides, I like the idea of you missing me a little bit.'

'I shall miss you more than a little bit.'

'And I you,' she said. She wanted so much to slip into his arms and hold him, but there were still a few delegates around. She contented herself with taking his hand briefly and stroking the skin inside his wrist. 'I miss you already.'

The person in front of them finished checking out, and Esther stepped up to the desk to hand in her key card. As she was doing so, Biddy came out of her room dragging her case. 'Either of you headed to the station?' she asked.

'I am,' said Esther.

'Well, I'll be your minibus buddy then,' said Biddy.

Esther took her case and stepped off to one side, while Michael and Biddy checked out. They all left the reception area together, and Michael waited with them outside the front door until the hotel minibus pulled up to take them to the station. He kissed Biddy on the cheek and wished her well on her journey. She climbed into the bus. Esther took his hand briefly. Looking into his eyes, she felt her own fill with tears. She wasn't ready to say goodbye, and the urge to hold him was very strong indeed.

'Bye,' she whispered. 'I'll ring you as soon as I can, when I'm home.'

'Bye, my lovely,' he said, and kissed her cheek very softly, very sweetly.

Esther turned to get into the minibus, desperately blinking back tears, but Biddy was leaning forward, blocking the doorway. 'For the love of God,' she said brusquely, her Scottish accent particularly strong, 'kiss the man properly. He's going to expire if you don't.'

Michael caught Esther's hand, pulled her back to him and kissed her soundly. Biddy and the minibus driver applauded, and Esther, blushing and still crying a little, climbed into the bus.

As they drove off up the long, sweeping driveway, Esther stared out of the window. She could see Michael walking to his car, but they soon rounded a bend and he was out of sight.

'It took you two long enough to find each other,' Biddy said behind her. 'That's a very good man there. Don't let him go.'

'I don't intend to,' said Esther.

CHAPTER THIRTEEN

She got back to London and went straight to work. She barely had the chance to go through her emails before it was time to leave and go and collect Lucie. It felt as if she had been away for weeks – so much had changed in those few days. She was heading for the stairs, Oyster card in hand, when the principal emerged from his office. 'Esther!' he called cheerfully. 'Good conference?'

'Very good,' she said, smiling.

'Did you do some good networking?'

'I believe so. I think I made some useful connections.'

'Well, I look forward to reading your report on it.' The principal smiled broadly and set off towards the common room.

She grinned at his retreating back. She hoped that in her distracted state she had managed to make some halfway coherent notes and collect some business cards. She may not have given the conference her full attention, but one thing she had learned about was social media. There had been an excellent seminar on the value of university social media accounts and especially personal accounts for academics.

Esther had a Facebook account, which she had set up to keep in touch with friends who were scattered across the world. She used it cautiously and infrequently. She knew nothing about Twitter, Instagram or any of the other platforms, however. The bright young fellow who had given the session had taken them all through the process of setting up a Twitter account. 'It's an excellent way to connect with others in your field,' he'd said. 'And it's also an easy way for students and prospective students to connect with you in real time.'

Esther had wondered why an abbreviated 140-character message was more 'real-time' than a phone call, but she knew better than to raise her hand and ask. She duly set up her account, followed, on the instructor's suggestion, everyone else in the room, and set a reminder in her electronic diary to log on at least once a week. Well, at least she could put that in her report to the principal, she thought. She had to have something to show for the four days away, and she was fairly sure that 'I have a new boyfriend' wasn't going to win the principal over.

I have a new boyfriend, she thought. How very odd. It seemed an enormous shift, but at the same time it made such perfect sense. Michael was gentle and sexy and she fancied him rotten, and being with him felt as comfortable as if they had been together for years. Now, if she could just find a way to ease him into her day-to-day life, and into Lucie's life too.

When she emerged from the Tube station near home, her phone pinged with a text.

'I haven't seen you for six whole hours,' it said. 'I'll have you know, you've turned me into a drippy, moping, teenage boy.

Please can I take you and Lucie out for an ice cream tomorrow? I think I can just about hang on until then to see you.'

She grinned from ear to ear as she walked up the hill from the station towards Lucie's school. She had a couple of minutes in hand, and she stopped outside the school gates to reply to the text.

'I miss you too. I'll run it past Lucie. I can't make you any promises, but I would say frozen yoghurt rather than ice cream might just swing the deal.'

She had thought long and hard on the train journey home about how best to handle telling Lucie about Michael, and she had decided that (close to) total honesty was the best policy. Lucie came bounding out of school with Rebecca and seemed genuinely happy to see her. She gave Esther a warm hug and looped her arm through hers as they walked home.

'How was your conference?'

'Good. The hotel was very posh. I've brought home all the miniature soaps and shampoos for you.'

'Fab,' said Lucie. 'I love tiny soaps.'

'I know. I even kept some little pots of jam and honey for you from the breakfast buffet.'

'Honestly, Mum, you're a proper hotel kleptomaniac. You didn't steal any towels, did you?'

'No... although I was very tempted by the lovely robes.'

'What are you like? I can't let you out on your own.'

'Probably not,' said Esther cheerfully.

'So, did you manage to have any fun?'

'I... did.' They were just passing the café on the corner of their road. 'Why don't we go in and have a hot chocolate and I'll tell you all about it?'

She chose her words carefully, but she told Lucie that she had met up with an old friend at the conference. She spent some time explaining who Michael was, and Lucie said she thought she remembered meeting him, although she would only have been around six or seven when he had last been around.

'We've found that we... really like each other, and we would like to start dating,' Esther said.

'Is he married?'

'No!' said Esther, shocked. 'He was, but he's divorced. I would never date someone who's married.'

'Just checking,' said Lucie. 'I know lots of adults aren't that fussy.'

'I'm fussy. Anyway, he's asked if he could take us out tomorrow. So he can meet you again, and you can meet him.'

'Wow, that's moving a bit fast, isn't it? You only just met each other.'

'Well, I think if you've been friends before, things can move a bit faster. Because you already know the person.'

'Has he got children?'

'Two boys, Oliver and Luke. They're away at university.'

'So we wouldn't all be going out together, having an awkward stepchildren date.' Lucie was smiling and didn't seem upset, so Esther smiled back.

'I think we're some way from people being stepchildren, my lovely.'

'We could end up like the Brady Bunch though.'

'But with better hair.'

'That's true.'

'So... will you? Meet him tomorrow?'

'Sure,' said Lucie, looking remarkably unconcerned. 'He's not going to be all smarmy and condescending and treat me like I'm six years old, though, is he? And you're not going to get all kissy-face?'

'I promise not to get kissy-face, and Michael's not a condescending person at all. Also, he knows you're not six, and I'm sure he'll behave properly. If he doesn't, I'll kick him.'

'Where are we going?'

'I suggested frozen yoghurt. He's paying.'

'Well, that changes everything. I like him already.'

And, remarkably, she did. He was wonderful with her. He listened to her, took her opinions seriously and never talked down to her. He teased Esther gently, and was funny, easy and kind. They went to Lucie's favourite frozen yoghurt shop, and he encouraged her to have a bowl with two scoops and all the toppings. Afterwards, they all went for a walk in the park, and Lucie chatted so easily and warmly, Esther dared to hope it might all work out. Michael, ever sensitive, stayed with them for exactly an hour and a half, then regretfully looked at his watch.

'I'd better get back home, before the M25 turns into a car park.'

'Why don't you come to our house for dinner?' Lucie said impulsively.

Surprised, Esther and Michael looked at one another.

'That would be lovely,' he said. 'Really lovely. But I'm going to say no, for today. If your mum would like to invite me for another evening, I'd be very happy to say yes.'

'Mum?' said Lucie pleadingly. 'Tell him to come tonight.'

Esther looked into Michael's warm, chocolate-brown eyes. She knew he was doing the right thing – this first meeting had been a great success, and he wanted to quit while he was ahead. But she would so love to have him sitting in her kitchen, maybe staying till after Lucie had gone to bed, when they could be alone and could touch each other...

It took all her strength to say, 'Michael's right. You've got homework to do tonight, and we're going out with Sally tomorrow. Maybe Michael could come up one night in the week? If he had a day when he wasn't too busy...'

'Tuesday,' said Michael eagerly. 'Tuesday would be ideal.'

'It's a date,' said Esther. And when Lucie spontaneously kissed Michael on the cheek when they parted, she felt almost impossibly optimistic.

CHAPTER FOURTEEN

Sally had called a week or so before and asked Esther and Lucie to accompany her to an event. 'I've gone along to the local amateur dramatic group a few times,' she told Esther. 'Not to be in a play or anything.' She gave a self-conscious giggle. 'I just thought I could... you know... help backstage, or work in the box office or something. But the people are ever such a giggle, and they're having a quiz night to raise some funds. Might you come along and be on my table? I'm happy to pay, but it should be a jolly occasion.'

Esther said she wouldn't hear of Sally paying and they would love to come. She was fairly sure it would be anything but a jolly occasion, but she felt guilty that she hadn't made more of an effort to see Sally. When she tentatively suggested the arrangement to Lucie, her daughter rolled her eyes. 'It sounds awful, Mum,' she said. 'Just awful. A quiz night? In a church hall?'

'There's a fish-and-chip supper.' Esther gave a small smile. The withering look Lucie returned made her burst out laughing. 'Come on,' she said. 'It's Sally. She's trying to build new friendships. Let's go and support her. It's one night out of our lives.'

Lucie was forced to agree. It was she, after all, who had pushed Esther to maintain the friendship in the first place.

On the Sunday afternoon they went round to Sally's place to pick her up and drove to the church where the amateur dramatic group met, which was some distance away. Sally kept up an excited chatter, explaining how she took two buses to get there on the evenings she went along to the meetings, and how, once or twice, she had been given a lift home by one of the nice ladies.

When they got there, Esther understood why members might offer one another lifts – it wasn't in a very nice part of town. The church sat a little way down the street from a small parade of down-at-heel shops and was surrounded by unkempt blocks of flats and cramped-looking semi-detached houses. Several of the streetlights were out, and the pavement was obstructed by an abandoned mattress. It wouldn't be ideal to leave a place like this late at night and walk to the ill-lit bus stop.

There was a small parking lot in front of the church, and Esther managed to find a spot under a feeble streetlamp, close to the door. They all got out of the car and went into the hall, which was brightly lit and full of people bustling around, setting up trestle tables and chairs. Sally greeted a number of people excitedly, telling anyone who would listen that this was her old friend Esther and Esther's lovely daughter. She looked around her eagerly and stood, oblivious, in the middle of the room. This caused them all to be in the way of the busy set-up team, so Esther took it upon herself to start unfolding the chairs which were stacked against the wall. She began to set them up around a nearby table. She had done two or three when a thickset woman with iron-grey hair came over.

'Those don't go there,' she said sharply. 'The green chairs go with the round tables.' She gestured to the other side of the hall.

Esther glanced across the room. She was tempted to ask why, since surely any chairs could go with any tables, but she knew that the answer would be 'because we have always done it this way', so she nodded, refolded the chairs and carried them across the room. Soon enough, Mrs Iron-Grey came over again and told her off for putting six chairs around a table instead of eight. At that point, she gave up and went back to stand with Sally and Lucie.

Despite the large number of people scurrying about and bossing one another around, it took quite some time for all the chairs and tables to be set out and for everyone then to be allocated a place. Esther found herself at a round table (with the green chairs) alongside Sally, Lucie and two older ladies who seemed determined only to speak to one another. There was also a man in his mid-fifties whose sideburns were only slightly more impressive than the brocade waistcoat stretched across his belly, and a painfully shy, awkward boy of about fifteen with bad skin and nails bitten to the quick.

Mrs Iron-Grey circulated among the tables and dropped quiz sheets on each of them. The man in the waistcoat officiously drew the pages towards him and took a gold pen from his top pocket. 'I'll write, shall I?' he said, smiling benignly at the table.

Esther had met his sort before. Unbendingly convinced of his own superior knowledge, whatever the topic, he would clearly steamroller any opposition and write what he believed to be the correct answer, no matter what. She could fight him for possession of the quiz pages and at least try to make it a collaborative effort, but as this was Sally's evening, and she had no wish to cause a scene, she opted to leave it.

The evening unfolded with dreary predictability. There was a picture-round page separate from the main quiz that Waistcoat Man considered beneath him, so he allowed the others to work through it. Given Lucie's familiarity with popular culture (and a few hesitant interjections from the spotty young man), the old ladies' eclectic general knowledge, Esther's knowledge of literature and Sally's of music of all types, they managed to identify all of the images.

Sure enough, when the quiz itself started, Waistcoat Man bulldozed his answers through for almost all of the questions. A few times Esther tried, mildly, to disagree, particularly on the ones about literature, but he kindly explained that she must be mistaken and that he was sure he was right. She was tempted to pull rank and tell him what her job was, but decided it would be more fun to watch his face when the correct answers were read out at the end. Sally took his rejection of her answers to musical questions less happily. She went a little pink when he told her categorically that 'Return to Sender' had been written by Elvis Presley himself.

'I'm pretty sure it was Winfield Scott and Otis Blackwell,' said Sally, her voice wavering a little.

'Never heard of them,' he said, as he wrote 'Elvis Presley' in firm black letters on the page.

Their table came second from last, and Mr Waistcoat perfected a regretful tilt of the head every time an answer was read out that differed from his own. However, they won the picture round outright and were each given a small box of chocolates. Sally and Lucie seemed happy with that, and Esther felt, in a petty way, vindicated.

By the time the chairs and tables had been restored to their rightful places, stacked along the walls of the hall ('Not over there, over here!' barked Mrs Iron-Grey, more than once), it was gone

11 p.m. 'Let's get you two home,' said Esther, and ushered Sally and Lucie towards the door.

Now that it was properly dark, the area around the church looked even seedier. A group of youngsters hung around outside the kebab shop, drinking from cans and laughing loudly, and the pavement was liberally scattered with litter. Esther instinctively pressed the button that locked all the car doors, as they waited at the traffic lights. She was looking forward to getting out of this grotty part of town and putting the interminable evening firmly behind her. Sally was clearly nursing a grudge against their bombastic table companion, and she kept repeating that she'd known all along who wrote 'Return to Sender', which would have given them one extra point at least. Lucie, who had looked more and more sulky and bored as the night had progressed, had lain down on the back seat and seemed to be asleep.

The traffic light change seemed to take forever, and Esther tapped her fingers impatiently on the steering wheel. She planned to run in the morning and at this rate wouldn't be in bed before midnight. She glanced casually to her right, just as a man rounded the corner, walking swiftly, clearly heading for the corner shop to make a late-night purchase. With a shock, she realized it was Phil. On one of their dates, he had vaguely mentioned that he too lived in north London, but she hadn't registered that this was his neighbourhood. He wasn't looking at the cars on the road, so she knew he hadn't seen her, and she had a moment to observe him. His expression was grim and set, his mouth pursed in a thin, humourless line. How could she ever have thought him even vaguely attractive? With the wisdom of hindsight, his face looked pinched, nasty and unpleasant. She watched him turn into the corner shop, and at that moment the traffic lights changed and she could pull away. Horrid man, she thought. She didn't say anything to Sally.

CHAPTER FIFTEEN

Tuesday morning dawned, and as Esther awoke, her first thought was that Michael was coming for dinner. She got up, padded through to the kitchen to make coffee, and looked around her home with new eyes. It would be so strange to have him in her space. Strange and lovely. She imagined him sitting on a bar stool at the kitchen counter as she cooked, imagined him relaxing on the sofa in her living room, imagined him in her bed. They were all very pleasing images, especially the last one, although she thought it very unlikely that he would be in her bed that evening. Not with Lucie in the house.

Mercifully, her cleaner came on a Monday, so the house was clean and tidy. She had shopped for ingredients for dinner and would be home early enough to cook, shower and change in relative calm before Michael arrived at around seven. She put her coffee cup in the dishwasher and popped some bread in the toaster just as Lucie came yawning into the kitchen.

'Morning, beautiful,' she said cheerfully.

'Morning, Mamma. I'm not feeling beautiful.' Lucie came to rest her head on Esther's shoulder.

'Are you not well?'

'No, just tired.'

'Really? What time did you go to bed?'

'I dunno,' said Lucie guardedly. 'Normal time.'

'And what time did you go to sleep?'

'Er...'

'Were you watching stuff on your computer by any chance?'

'A bit, maybe...'

'You know I'm not one of those heavy-handed mums, but if you're not getting enough sleep, I might have to have to start turning off the router at night.'

'And then how would I do my homework?' said Lucie, horrified.

'I know it's almost incomprehensible, but I did all my schoolwork and three degrees without access to Wikipedia.'

'Yes, back in the Dark Ages. We don't get our information from medieval illuminated manuscripts these days, you know. All our coursework is online.' Lucie had a face like thunder, and Esther regretted starting this discussion first thing in the morning.

'I know, sweetie,' she said soothingly. 'I don't want to cut you off from the lifeblood of the internet, so I need you to police yourself. Okay? No more *Gossip Girl* marathons till midnight on a school night.'

'*Gossip Girl*?' said Lucie disdainfully, as if Esther had suggested something so absurd as to be beneath contempt.

Once again, Esther realized that she could not keep pace with the speed at which her daughter was growing up. Lucie had seemed better at the weekend, happier and more even-tempered. She hoped this was just a morning blip. She couldn't face Lucie being sulky and foul when Michael was there.

'You haven't forgotten Michael is coming for dinner tonight?' she said tentatively.

Lucie, who was getting a yoghurt out of the fridge, gave a very teenage, non-specific grunt, which may have been assent, or may not have been.

'I thought I'd do the chicken casserole with chorizo.'

Grunt.

'And maybe a fruit salad for after.'

Silence.

'Does that sound okay?'

Shrug.

Esther took a deep breath and bit down hard on her toast. It was very difficult not to come out with a schoolmistressy admonition to be nice when Michael came, but she knew that would engender more eye-rolling and would almost certainly have the opposite effect. She also knew reminding Lucie that the invitation had in fact come from her and not Esther would be unhelpful. Rock. Hard place. She'd just have to hope that Lucie would have cheered up by the evening. She might stop off at the newsagent and buy a few magazines as bribes. Bribery, enforced silence and occasional yelling – her parenting techniques weren't quite as noble as she'd envisaged.

She went into work with the best intentions, but what should have been a normal, calm day turned into something of a nightmare. She started the morning with a quick chat with Regina – neglecting to mention who was coming for dinner or that her social life had moved into a new phase. Then she went to her own office, believing she had three free hours for admin and lecture planning before her afternoon tutorials. But two minutes after she'd sat down, Regina followed her there in a flat panic – she had just had a phone call from on high. The principal had moved his deadline for a key report, and needed it that day. It should all still have been manageable, but when Esther turned on her PC, she got an ominous blue screen, and the computer refused to boot up. She rang IT support, but there was no technician available. Naturally, the materials she needed for the report were saved on her PC alone, as were her incomplete lecture notes. Regina called in one of the PhD students, who fancied himself as something of an IT expert, and he sat at Esther's desk, clicking on things and staring at the screen. She couldn't see anything much happening, and the clock was ticking. Her three free hours were trickling away. She gave up then and went to the library, thinking that at least she could do some sort of planning; she would email the principal and beg him for twenty-four hours' grace on the report. She found a free computer on the quiet floor, which was earmarked for silent study. Unfortunately these rules were hard to enforce, and there was a group of rowdy students sitting around a machine two desks along, chatting and laughing. She frowned at them a few times, but they seemed oblivious to her displeasure.

She couldn't access her online diary, so she had to make a guess at the order of her tutorials that afternoon. She managed to sketch out a plan for the classes she thought she had and fired off an email to the principal. When she glanced at her watch, it was already midday. She had achieved less than half what she had hoped to. There was no time to get something to eat. She dashed back to her office to find, to her great relief, that her computer was working again. The phone rang, but she ignored it. She just didn't have time. She spent a feverish half-hour finishing her preparations for the afternoon classes and then discovered she was unable to print anything out. She raced round to Regina's office with a memory stick and found Regina sitting there looking miserable.

'I need to print out these lesson plans. Can I use your machine?' she said breathlessly. 'I've got about seven minutes before my first class.'

'I've just got off the phone with the principal,' said Regina. 'He's been trying to get hold of you. He's not best pleased we can't deliver the report.'

'Did you tell him we had an IT disaster?'

'I did, but he doesn't seem interested. He has to meet with council this evening – it's been moved up, for some reason – and he needs to know about our student recruitment. It's urgent, apparently. He really tore a strip off me.'

'The principal? But he's a lamb.'

'Not today.'

Esther glanced at her watch as the pages spooled, too slowly, out of Regina's printer. 'Well, I have three tutorials back-to-back. I can get back here around four. If you can pull the figures, I'll write something up as soon as I get back. I was hoping to leave early, but clearly that's not going to happen.'

She didn't manage to get away from work until well after six o'clock – much later than she'd planned and much later than she usually left. She hadn't factored in the traffic either, and she sat in a long line of stationary cars, seething with frustration, watching the minutes tick away. She rang both Lucie and Michael to say she was running late and eventually pulled up in front of the house at five past seven, just as Michael arrived. He came to meet her by her car and kissed her. Then he drew her into his arms and held her.

She was desperate to get inside. She'd had no opportunity to cook dinner, and she had no idea whether Lucie had made a mess in the house in her absence. She had wanted to shower and change before he arrived – as it was, her make-up had worn off and her hair was tangled and messy after the stress of the day.

Michael paused and looked at her, still holding her around the waist. 'You're vibrating like a plucked string, my lovely. Was it such a bad day?'

'Awful day. And now I have nothing to give you for dinner and I look a mess...'

'You look beautiful, and we can get fish and chips if needs be. Please relax. I'm just happy to be with you. I've brought a nice bottle of wine, and I'm looking forward to an evening with you and Lucie.'

'You're a nice man, Michael Wolfson,' she said, and kissed him.

'I was never any good at being one of those mean, chiselled bastards,' he said. 'So I've decided to embrace my inner niceness.'

'Works for me,' she said, looping an arm around his waist and walking him up to the front door. 'Well, welcome to my house.'

They opened the door, and immediately Esther could smell the aroma of cooking. As they entered, Lucie came into the hallway, clutching a dishtowel.

'I didn't know how to do your chicken and chorizo thing,' she began anxiously, 'but I did manage to roast the chicken. Hope that's okay. And I made salad.'

'Darling, darling girl.' Esther kissed her warmly. 'You're an absolute star.'

Lucie and Michael kept each other company while she dashed upstairs to wash, change and repair her face and tidy her hair. In all the craziness, she had failed to notice that it had been a beautiful day and was now a warm and balmy evening. When she came downstairs, she saw that they had set the table out on the deck behind the house. Michael handed her a glass of wine as she walked outside.

'Well, you two have managed to transform a disaster of a day into rather a delight,' she said, sitting down gratefully and sipping her wine.

'You haven't tasted my chicken yet,' said Lucie.

'It smells wonderful. And best of all, I didn't cook it. I may just take you out of school and keep you at home as a permanent chef and housekeeper. You can take care of me.'

'No thanks. I'm not Sally. If you go gaga, I'm putting you in a home.'

'Who's Sally?' asked Michael.

'Sally is Mum's friend Isabella's sister. She gave up like her whole life to look after Isabella, who got cancer and died, and then she looked after her mum when she got dementia. She's like this princess who's spent her whole life locked away, and she's never had any contact with the real world. She's all innocent and wide-eyed. She didn't even know about Wi-Fi until we told her.'

Esther marvelled at Lucie's romanticized interpretation of Sally's life.

'And now?' Michael asked.

'Now she's starting to do things,' said Lucie. 'She's got a computer and she's learning to drive. And she's selling all her mum's stuff on eBay.'

'Well, well, well,' said Michael. 'You two know some interesting people. I look forward to meeting this Sally.'

'Oooh, chicken!' Lucie jumped up.

Esther followed her into the kitchen to help her. 'Thank you so much for doing dinner,' she said quietly.

'You might not thank me once you've tried it.'

'I'm sure it'll be delicious. And on top of that, it really was a lifesaver.'

'Well, I know you hate it when you have to work late, and today of all days, with your boyfriend coming...'

'He's not my boyfriend,' said Esther, like a sulky teenager, but she was smiling.

'He is so your boyfriend.' Lucie grinned. 'And I knew you'd be all like "Oooh, there's no dill for the salad dressing, what about the balsamic vinegar, does my hair look all right, where's my Cath Kidston apron…"'

'I do not talk like that!'

'Of course you don't.' Lucie raised a cynical eyebrow. 'Anyway, now dinner's all done, you can go and be all soppy with your boyfriend on the deck.'

'Not my boyfriend.'

'So your boyfriend. He looks at you like he's a puppy and you're a choccy treat.'

Esther beamed, then swiftly hugged Lucie and kissed her temple. 'I love you, cheeky girl.' Lucie permitted the hug for a second, then wriggled free and went to get the salad out of the fridge. Esther picked up her wine glass and walked to the door. 'Mind you hurry up serving our dinner. I'm expecting five-star service now.'

Lucie had indeed done a good, if workmanlike, job with dinner. They all tucked in, and Lucie was ebullient and proud of her achievement. Michael, with his usual charm and ease, kept the conversation flowing and the mood light. After the awfulness of the day, the evening could cautiously be pronounced a success. Esther, sipping wine and looking at her spring garden, allowed herself a moment to imagine a future where golden evenings like this might be commonplace.

CHAPTER SIXTEEN

Within just a few weeks, Esther, Michael and Lucie were established in a tentative routine. Michael would come round for dinner twice during the week – on a Tuesday and Thursday evening. Then they would generally meet on one or both days of the weekend and go on an outing. Indeed, he quickly became such a big part of their lives that Esther felt it best to mention him to her mother in their usual weekly call – before Lucie did.

'So, Mum,' she said carefully one Saturday, after she had heard all the gossip from Laura's church and the latest on her allotment. 'I have a new... friend.'

'Friend?'

'Male friend. Partner.'

'That all sounds a bit formal and sterile. Are we not saying "lover"?'

'Not to our mothers we're not. Good grief.'

'Please take all the concerned questions as read. You're not a fool. I'm assuming he's a decent man, kind and reliable, and that Lucie approves.'

'Yes to all.'

'And he makes you happy?'

'Very.'

'Well, I'm thrilled. I hope he encourages you to be a bit silly and you have lots of lovely sex.'

'Mum!'

'Got to go. Have to hack back my rhubarb, don't you know. Love to all. Kiss, kiss.'

On the weekends when Lucie was away with friends, Esther and Michael abandoned all pretence of worthy activity and spent the days in bed. But if they made love on nights when Lucie was in the house, he didn't stay over but would doze for a while and then manfully get up and dress to go home in the early hours. Esther was grateful for his sensitivity, but she also yearned for nights when she could sleep in his arms and wake up with him.

One night, he had stayed until about three in the morning. He groaned as he got out of bed. 'This is not fun,' he said, but she knew he wasn't guilt-tripping her, just having a little whinge.

'Sorry, my love. At some point it'll be different, I promise. And I so appreciate your patience.'

Michael gathered up his things and pulled on his trousers. 'Just popping to the loo before I start the long drive,' he said, leaving his shirt on the bed.

Esther heard Lucie get out of bed and open her door when Michael was in the bathroom. She heard her pad down the passage – she obviously needed the loo herself. Oh Lord. There was nothing to be done. Esther herself was naked in bed; there wasn't enough time to leap up and fling on her dressing gown, and anyway, what would she say – 'Don't go into the bathroom,

Michael's in there'? That would raise more questions than she had answers for. Perhaps Lucie would see the toilet door was closed, assume it was Esther in there and go back to bed.

Of course, that wasn't what happened. As Lucie stood outside the toilet door, Michael flushed and emerged. Esther heard a note of surprise in Lucie's voice, although she couldn't make out what she said, and then she heard Michael saying a few words, low and reassuring. Then Lucie went into the loo and shut the door and Michael came back into the bedroom.

'Well, that was a bit awkward,' he said.

'I'm so sorry.' Esther sat up. 'What did she say?'

'Just "Hello". And I said something idiotic about being on my way home. But my natural gravitas was somewhat dampened by my being shirtless.'

'Well, there's nothing to be done about it,' said Esther resignedly. 'I expect we'll have a fantastically embarrassing conversation about it in the morning.'

'I'll be heartbroken to miss it,' said Michael, pulling on his shirt. 'Let me know how it goes. I may be away some time – it's going to take weeks for my blushes to subside.'

In the end, Esther overslept and the morning was a mad rush. In the chaos of breakfast and teeth-brushing, Lucie showed no inclination to discuss the issue. Esther spent the day feeling mortified and trying to work out how to raise it when she got home. When she did get back, Lucie was in her customary corner of the sofa, laptop on her knees, typing away.

'Hi, lovely!' said Esther, and even she could hear the false note of cheerfulness in her voice. 'Good day?'

'Fine,' said Lucie, seemingly calm and unconcerned.

'Plans for the weekend?'

'Sleepover at Rebecca's tomorrow night, if that's okay.' Lucie continued typing.

'Fine, fine!' Esther took a deep breath. 'Listen, Lucie, about last night...'

'Mum, it's perfectly fine by me if Michael stays the night here. I know adults do sex and stuff. Just ask him to put a shirt on when he goes to the bathroom, okay? His hairy chest is icky.'

And so they moved into warmer days as a comfortable, if carefully balanced unit. Michael stayed over three or four nights a week, and on a couple of occasions Esther and Lucie went down to his house in Surrey, where they met Oliver and Luke, his sons. They were a pair of tall, blonde, muscular boys, who looked more like their mother than Michael. They were both nice, and Luke in particular made an effort to be kind to Lucie. Esther liked them immensely, and she was very grateful for their calm acceptance of her place in their dad's life.

As the school summer holidays approached, they began to talk about what they might do in those six long weeks. Esther had always found the summer holidays a stressful time – even though there were no students on campus, her work continued and she had to find ways to look after Lucie. There was only so much time she could spend working from home and only so many times she could take Lucie into work with her. Lucie, rather reluctantly, had agreed to go and see her dad in Manchester. She would be with him for the first fortnight, which would include going to Malta for a week with him and the now visibly pregnant Melissa.

'Can we steal a few days away while Lucie's in Malta, just for us?' asked Michael one Friday evening.

'I don't know,' said Esther. 'I've had to save all my leave for later in the summer, when Lucie gets back.'

'Were you planning to go away in that time?'

'I was hoping she and I could take a short break somewhere in the UK. I've not booked anything yet though.'

'Well, here's my proposal,' said Michael. 'If you can squeeze even one day's leave at the beginning, you and I could take a city break over a long weekend – I thought Venice, or maybe Paris would be nice.'

'Nice? That'd be glorious. It sounds too wonderful for words.'

Esther's wider social life had brightened up too. The work colleagues and friends who knew Michael were universally thrilled that he and Esther were an item, and the friends who had not come across him before warmed to him instantly. She met some of his friends too, and many weekends now incorporated picnics or drinks with their growing social circle. He got on especially well with Esther's friends Paul and Tim, who lived close by. Both Michael and Paul considered themselves barbecue experts, so they liked to get together at weekends to test new recipes, and Esther, Lucie and Tim were all very happy to be guinea pigs.

When Esther's birthday came round in mid-July, it therefore seemed natural to plan some sort of a party. She had a lot of invitations to repay and a great many friends she would like to share her day with.

'There are a couple of possible options,' she said to Lucie and Michael over dinner one evening. 'We could have a party here, but that would restrict the numbers a bit. Or we could go for a pub garden, where we get in some food and wine, and people could come and go.'

'The pub garden might be a bit impersonal,' said Michael, 'but if we do it here, you'll end up running yourself ragged, cooking and entertaining. It's your birthday and you should be able to relax and enjoy yourself.'

'Michael and I could do all the cooking,' said Lucie.

Michael laughed. 'Did you see the look your mum gave us? I'm not sure we're up to her high standards.'

'Of course you are,' said Esther. 'You're the barbecue king, after all. But...'

'Oh,' said Lucie, rolling her eyes and looking at Michael. 'There's a "but"...'

'I was just going to say I quite like the idea of absolving us all of responsibility. If we're in a pub, someone else cooks, clears away and washes up. We just get to have fun. All of us.'

'Good point,' said Michael. 'I hadn't thought about the clearing up. I'd only got as far as standing at the barbecue in a "Kiss the Cook" apron, getting compliments for my burgers.'

'Washing up after a barbecue for loads of people would be no fun at all,' admitted Lucie. 'I vote for the pub.'

Esther researched a number of local venues, checking out their canapé menus, negotiating exclusive space and wrangling about drinks prices. In the end she chose a pleasant gastro-pub about a mile from her house that offered her exclusive use of their small, walled garden. She had to guarantee a small minimum spend on the bar, but she didn't foresee this as a problem. She compiled a guest list and was gratified to see that there were upwards of thirty people she wanted to invite.

It being a summer weekend, a few people couldn't make it, so the final tally would probably be closer to twenty than thirty. She was going over the guest list one evening when Lucie came to lean over her shoulder and have a look.

'Can I invite a friend?' she asked.

'Sure. Do you want to ask Rebecca? I don't think her mum will mind her being in a pub garden if she's going to be with us.'

'Yeah,' said Lucie, a little reluctantly. 'Maybe not. Maybe Clara. Or Zoe.'

'Why not Rebecca?'

'She's just...' Lucie didn't seem to want to go on.

'Just what?'

'Being a bit weird. You know... She's all obsessed with this TV show about vampires, and she spends all her time on the fan forums, and stalking the main actor on Twitter...'

'Ah,' said Esther. 'Well, people's tastes change as they get older. And sometimes our friends like stuff we don't like. I'm sure you and she will find something you're both interested in soon.'

'Not if she keeps calling me lame and babyish.' Esther looked round, and Lucie was frowning. She didn't seem hurt, just angry. 'I can just imagine what she'd say about being asked to my mum's birthday party.'

'Well, ask Clara or Zoe instead then.' Her heart ached for the fraught teenage path Lucie had yet to navigate. At least she'd had Isabella by her side. She hadn't had to negotiate it alone.

'What about Sally?' Lucie asked suddenly.

'What about her?'

'Are you inviting her?'

'I haven't,' said Esther. 'I could, I suppose.'

'You should,' said Lucie emphatically. 'We haven't seen her since that awful quiz night.'

Indeed they had not, nor had they heard from her. Esther felt a little guilty that she hadn't made contact, but truth be told, Sally had barely crossed her mind. She felt a pang of guilt. She should have.

'I'm not sure,' she said hesitantly. 'I mean, she won't know anyone.'

'She'll know you, she'll know me,' said Lucie. 'Clara or Zoe wouldn't know anyone either.'

'And I don't know that she would fit in,' finished Esther lamely. She imagined Sally in a group of her friends. They would all be warm and polite and kind, of that she had no doubt. But she had a vision of Sally sitting on the edge of her chair on the edge of a group, handbag in her lap, trying to keep up with the conversation.

However, even before Lucie began berating her for being a snob, she knew she had lost the battle. She didn't understand why Lucie had taken such a liking to Sally, but she had. The whole thing made Esther anxious, and she just hoped that Sally would be otherwise occupied and would refuse the invitation.

CHAPTER SEVENTEEN

The day of Esther's birthday party dawned, unsettled and a little blustery. Clouds scudded cross the sky and the wind gusted and abated. In the course of the morning there were a few brief flurries of rain, but by midday the sky had cleared, the wind had died down, and it was warm and bright. Esther dressed carefully in an emerald-green dress which went well with her light honey tan. She'd had her hair trimmed and blow-dried, and she applied simple make-up. Lucie looked lovely in jeans and a bright-orange T-shirt, although Esther had a small moment of shock noticing how her breasts had grown and her shape had become more womanly. Because she saw her daughter every day, she didn't always notice the changes, but every now and then she was surprised.

Michael arrived at around four, looking smart in a crisp white shirt. He kissed her and looked at her appreciatively.

The venue had done a great job – there was a long table down one side of the garden area laden with plates, cutlery, napkins and glasses. 'We'll bring out jugs of Pimm's once people start to arrive,' the manager said.

'Perhaps you could bring one out now,' suggested Michael.

'No problem. And the canapés are set to come out at around six.'

'It all sounds fine,' said Esther. She was beginning to feel a little anxious. What if people didn't turn up? Or the party was dull? Or it rained? She glanced up at the bright blue sky. Well, that was one worry she could scratch off her list. Lucie and Michael followed the manager inside and she smiled. She suspected there were dastardly birthday cake plans afoot. She was fine with that, but she hoped they hadn't put the correct number of candles on the cake. She didn't think she would have enough puff to blow them all out.

Regina and her husband were the first to arrive. As Esther might have predicted, Regina had been utterly thrilled when Esther had confessed sheepishly that she was seeing Michael.

'The lovely Dr Wolfson!' she had said excitedly. 'I always liked him. And, to be fair, I always thought he was a total fox. Good work!'

Esther kissed Regina and Pedro, grateful to see their friendly faces, and handed them each a Pimm's. Somewhere inside the pub, music began to play, and then someone turned the outside speakers on so that it was playing in the courtyard too. Lucie and Michael came back outside and helped themselves to drinks. Within a few minutes three more couples had arrived, and the party began to feel like it might just be a success. Paul and Tim came, bearing a beautiful bouquet of flowers, which took pride of place in the middle of the food table. Esther relaxed a fraction and found a seat at the head of a long table, where she could hold court and chat to friends as they arrived. Michael was the perfect host, circulating among groups, making sure everyone had a drink and putting people at their ease. Clara arrived and she and Lucie found a corner to huddle and giggle in. People kept refilling Esther's Pimm's glass, and she felt bathed in a warm glow – she was a little tipsy, surrounded by all her favourite people, celebrating her birthday on a sunny summer afternoon. What more could she ask for?

The canapés arrived and were surprisingly good. The sun dipped a little so the courtyard was in shadow, and the manager came out to light the tall gas heaters. Lights twinkled in the flower borders and the courtyard had a magical, almost continental feel. Someone turned the music up a little louder and Paul and Tim started the dancing in a cleared area in front of the food table. Michael came to sit beside Esther and she rested her head, which was swimming a little, on his shoulder.

Through the haze of Pimm's, warm feelings and fairy lights, she saw someone – a blonde woman – standing talking to Lucie and Clara. The woman had her back to Esther, and she didn't recognize her. She was wearing a cherry-red summer dress. Maybe she was a punter from inside the pub who had ignored the 'Private Party' sign and had come into the courtyard hoping to score some food or a free drink. Esther was about to ask Michael to go and play bouncer when the woman turned and surveyed the garden. To her shock, Esther saw it was Sally. Or at least it was a version of Sally, a woman so transformed it was hard to imagine she was the same person Esther had last seen six weeks or so before.

It wasn't that she had lost an enormous amount of weight – she had lost some, but was still decidedly curvy. She was wearing a dress that accentuated the best aspects of her shape, not least her voluptuous bosom, and was nipped in to show her waist. She had lost the old-lady, mousy hairdo; instead, her hair was back to the bright blonde Esther remembered from childhood, and it had been blow-dried in soft waves rather than frozen in harsh curls. She had caught a little sun and had a slight tan and a healthy rosy glow to her cheeks. She still looked a little awkward and nervous, but the change in her clothes and hair had taken years off her.

'Sally!' Esther called, half-standing. She was conscious her voice was a little loud, but it was hard to know how to be heard above the music and hum of conversation.

Sally turned towards the voice, and when she saw Esther, her face lit up like a star. She seemed so genuinely happy, Esther felt embarrassed at how churlish she'd been about inviting her. Sally made her way across the courtyard and kissed Esther warmly.

'You look absolutely fantastic!' said Esther.

'So do you!' said Sally. 'Summer must suit us.'

Michael stood up and Esther turned to introduce them. 'This is…' and for the first time, she heard herself say, '… my boyfriend, Michael. Michael, Sally.'

She sensed Michael glancing at her, surprised. They hadn't had a conversation about the state of their relationship, nor had they agreed appropriate terms of address. For a minute she thought she might have upset him, but then she felt his hand warm on her back, and he held her waist firmly and drew her closer to him.

'Nice to meet you, Sally,' he said, extending his free hand to shake hers.

Sally stared at him, a little wide-eyed, and didn't say anything for a second. There was a strange hiatus in the conversation, as if Sally had dropped an obvious cue to say something, and then she spoke.

'This is a lovely venue,' she said, looking around her. 'Gosh, and they do lay on a good spread!' Although she looked different, she had the same awkward manner and old-fashioned turn of phrase.

'They certainly do!'

'Have you had something to eat, Sally?' asked Michael. 'Let me take you on a tour of the finest canapés in north London. I could do with a plateful myself.'

While Michael and Sally were getting food, Lucie came over and slipped into the chair next to Esther.

'Did you see Sally, Mum?' she whispered. 'She looks amazing!'

'I did. What a transformation.'

'She told me and Clara she'd had a whatchamacallit. A makeover.'

'Really?'

'Yes. She went to some posh department store and got a personal shopper to help her choose new clothes and then someone to tell her what to do with her hair and redo her make-up and everything.'

'They did a very good job.' Esther looked over at Sally, who was smiling up at Michael. 'She looks...'

'Looks what?'

'Like I imagined she would look when I knew her as a teenager, if that makes sense. She went through a lot, and it made her old before her time. Now she looks the way she should look. She looks her age.'

'She looks better than her age,' said Lucie. 'She's quite a babe.'

Later in the evening, Esther saw Sally on the dance floor, bouncing up and down, laughing and being swung around by Paul, who loved to dance. Tim came to sit beside her.

'Your friend Sally's a hoot,' he said. 'Where's she been hiding?'

'She's the princess in the tower,' Esther mumbled, by now definitely on the downward slope from tipsy to maudlin. 'And now she's letting down her hair.'

CHAPTER EIGHTEEN

The summer holidays finally came around and, predictably, the weather immediately changed for the worse. It seemed to rain night and day, and in the moments when it stopped, the sky was leaden and low. Lucie had a few days at home before she was to go up to Stephen's, and her misery was palpable. Esther was working from home, and she seemed to spend all her time either creeping around to avoid Lucie's sulks and wrath or cuddling her and soothing her sudden and unpredictable fits of crying and clinginess. She wanted so badly to tell her she didn't have to go to her dad's, but it wouldn't be fair to do that. She had a responsibility to encourage a healthy relationship between Lucie and her father. And, on a purely selfish and practical note, she couldn't afford to spend any more work days away from the university, especially as she and Michael were due to fly to Venice in a week's time.

She knew Lucie had to go, but going to the station and putting her red-eyed, silent daughter onto the train was one of the hardest things she had ever done. She got back on the Tube to go to work and wedged herself into a seat by the door, beside the glass partition. Then she covered her face with her hands and allowed herself a few discreet tears. She felt hollow and awful.

That evening, Lucie rang and sounded a little more cheerful. It seemed Melissa had redecorated her bedroom, and she now had her own TV and DVD player. Esther was none too happy with this set-up, nor did she feel bribery was the best way for Stephen and Melissa to win Lucie over, but she held her tongue. She said a lot of warm and encouraging things, and promised to pack up some of Lucie's favourite DVDs and post them up to Manchester that evening. Now that she knew Lucie was settled and happier, she found she didn't like the quiet of the house, so, on impulse, she rang Michael. He was thrilled to hear from her, and within half an hour she was driving round the M25 to spend the evening – and the night – with him.

She took two days' worth of clothing and went back to stay with Michael again the following evening. So, in all, it was forty-eight hours before she returned to her own house. It took her a good few hours before she noticed the blinking red light on the telephone handset. People seldom rang her on her landline, so she wasn't in the habit of checking her messages. She picked up the phone, expecting a message from some cold-calling company, and was surprised to hear a clipped female voice saying, 'If this is the home of Esther Hart, could you please call us with some urgency. This is the fourth message I've left. This is Sister Marilyn Brent. I'm calling from the Intensive Care Unit at Saint Mary's Hospital on the Isle of Wight.'

Laura. Esther felt sick. She played the message again and jotted down the number and then dialled, her fingers shaking. She asked to be put through to the ICU, and the sister who answered the phone had the same clipped tones she had heard on the message.

'Sister Brent? This is Esther Hart; I assume you're calling about my mother, Laura Hart?'

'We have been trying to reach you for two days. We only had a landline number for you on your mother's medical records.'

'I'm so sorry. I've been staying… away from home. What's happened? Is she…?'

'Your mother was brought in two days ago. When would you be able to get here?'

'What happened?'

'I'm afraid I'm unable to give detailed medical information over the phone.' It was a stock response, but Esther could tell from the firmness of the tone that arguing would get her nowhere. She thought fast. She considered the time it would take her to get to Southampton and the frequency of the ferries. It was already 7 p.m. If she drove like the wind, she might catch a late-night one. The ferry journey was an hour, then a lightning-quick drive to the hospital… but would they let her in at midnight or 1 a.m.?

'I can leave immediately,' she said breathlessly. 'Catch the last ferry…'

'Er… I would…' The sister paused on the other end of the phone. 'I would get here as quickly as you can, but we don't anticipate any change in her condition in the next twelve hours. Tomorrow morning would be fine.'

'Would you let me in if I could get there tonight?'

'Of course.'

'I'm on my way.'

Esther ran upstairs, emptied the bag she'd brought back from Michael's house and began to shove in a few things. She had no idea what to pack – no idea how long she would be away, or indeed what she would face when she got there. She packed a few pairs of jeans, boots and tops, as well as handfuls of underwear. As she raced back downstairs, she grabbed the hands-free kit for her mobile. She would let people know as she travelled, to save time.

She rang Stephen first. He was surprisingly kind and understanding. 'I'm so sorry,' he said. 'I always liked Laura. She's a tough old bird. Give her my best when you see her.'

'I don't know...' said Esther, and for the first time she felt tears threaten. 'I don't know that I'll be able to tell her anything. She's in intensive care.'

'What was it? A stroke?'

'They didn't say. They won't, as you know, tell you anything over the phone.'

'Well, let us know what's going on as soon as you know.'

'I will. And Stephen—'

'I won't tell Lucie any details. Just that she's ill. Don't worry.'

'Thanks.'

She rang Michael, who immediately offered to get in his car and come and meet her.

'Thanks, my lovely,' she said, grateful for his immediate and unconditional support. 'But I need to just get there and find out what's going on. If it's... appropriate for you to come, I'll let you know.'

'I'll be waiting for your call. Ring anytime. Esther...'

'Yes?'

He hesitated, and then seemed to think better of what he was going to say. 'Lots of love, okay? Look after yourself.'

Her last call was to Regina, explaining where she was going and asking Regina to clear her diary for the next few days at least. 'Will you be back before you go on holiday?' Regina asked. Oh heavens. Holiday. She and Michael were due to fly to Venice in less than a week. It had gone right out of her head and, she realized, he had had the sensitivity not to mention it. Well, there was no point in worrying about it until she got to the hospital and found out what had happened.

'I don't know,' she said shortly. 'As soon as I know more, I'll let you know. Right now, I just have to get there.'

'Of course,' Regina said, and then added uncharacteristically, 'I'll pray for her.'

The traffic was merciful and she got to Southampton in under two hours. She drove straight to the ferry terminal and was able to get a place on the next crossing. The forward movement of her journey had sustained her and kept the panic at bay, but once she was aboard the ferry, there was nothing to do. She could only sit for an hour. She went to the upstairs lounge and got a cup of coffee and a dry pastry. She sat staring at a television screen, seeing nothing. What had happened? She had spoken to Laura just that weekend. Or, wait... had she? She had been so busy getting Lucie ready for the trip, and Michael had stayed over on Friday night... Had she forgotten to ring her mum? She genuinely couldn't remember. What if she hadn't rung and that was the last time she could have spoken to her?

She jumped up and began to walk around the ship. She felt as if she were trying to will the ferry to go faster through her own motion, but it would not be hurried.

The moment the announcement came through that passengers could return to their vehicles, she headed down to her car and sat in it, seatbelt fastened, ready to go as soon as she could.

By the time she disembarked, it was after eleven and the roads were very quiet. She drove straight to the hospital. It was largely in darkness, but she managed to find her way to the Intensive Care Unit. She hesitated for a second, then reasoned that they would be used to late-night arrivals and rang the intercom beside the door. A quiet voice answered, and a nursing sister came to meet her.

'I'm Laura Hart's daughter,' she said softly. 'I've just heard and come down from London.'

'There's no one here who can give you much information,' said the nurse gently. 'If you come back in the morning, the doctors do their ward rounds at eight.'

Esther looked at her, stricken. 'Please...' she said, and was mortified to find her eyes filling with tears.

The nurse touched her arm lightly. 'It must have been a big shock to you, and I know you've come a long way. You can come in and see her for a minute.'

Now she was there, walking through the door, Esther wanted to turn and run. The unit was dimly lit, and there was a symphony of bleeps and hums from machines and monitors. The nurse led her to a private room and stepped aside to let her enter.

It wasn't Laura. Whoever the shrunken, wizened woman in the bed was, hooked up to wires and with her mouth open around the unfeasibly large tube of the ventilator, it wasn't Laura. There was none of her fierce, crackling energy in the room.

She turned to look at the nurse. 'She's dead, isn't she?'

The nurse hesitated and then said quietly, 'It really is best if you come back to talk to the doctors in the morning. Do you have somewhere to stay?'

She hadn't even thought about that. Somehow she had imagined she would be sitting beside Laura's bed all night, but that didn't seem practical, and it didn't look as if the nurse would allow it. A hotel? She'd never stayed in a hotel on the island – she wouldn't even know where to find one, let alone one that would give her a room at midnight. Then she remembered. 'I have my mum's spare key on my key ring. I can go back to her house.'

She took one last look at the still figure in the bed. She wanted to touch her or kiss her, but she didn't think she could bear to feel how unyielding and unresponsive Laura's skin might be. 'I'll be back first thing,' she said, and the nurse nodded. As she passed her, the nurse very gently touched her arm again. Esther wished she hadn't. It made the tears spill over, and she could barely see as she left the hospital and made her way back to her car.

Her mother's house, in nearby Wootton Bridge, was down a quiet side street. The house was in darkness when she pulled up outside. She had never been there when Laura wasn't there.

As she walked up the path to the front door, she stumbled over a small object. It was so dark, she couldn't see what it was, so she stepped around it and kept walking. Once she was a little closer, the motion sensor kicked in and the light above the door came on. She glanced back to see what she'd tripped on and saw that the path was strewn with leaves and clods of earth, and that the garden was choked with weeds. Her mother's garden? It was almost unbelievable. She fumbled with the key and let herself into the house. It smelled dusty and undisturbed, with a faint undertone of real, sour-smelling dirt, as if it had not been cleaned for some time. She wandered from room to room, turning lights on, and indeed, the house did look neglected. Newspapers were piled high on the coffee table, there were dirty dishes in the kitchen and dust was thick on the shelves. She went up to her mother's bedroom and saw that the bed was unmade. In all her life, she had never known Laura to leave her bed unmade. Was this where she had been found?

She felt so tired and overwhelmed with sadness, she didn't know what to do. She went to the linen cupboard, found some bedclothes and made up a single bed in one of the spare rooms. She felt grubby from travelling so had a quick shower and got into bed. She was desperately tired, but sleep would not come. There were so many unanswered questions. She could see no connection between the Laura she had spoken to on the phone, who had been cheerful and positive as always, and the wretchedness she found in this house. What had been going on? And why had Laura not said anything to her?

After half an hour or so, she realized that she wasn't going to doze off, so she got up and went back into her mother's bedroom, looking for clues. The first thing she noticed was the absence of books. Laura's bedside table had always groaned under a teetering pile of volumes – an eclectic mix of fiction and non-fiction. She usually had three or more books on the go and would mark her place with scraps of paper. Reference books, about gardening or cookery, would have a bristling fringe of the torn scraps. But now the bedside table was empty. There was a dusty glass, which Esther assumed had contained water, and that was all. Next, she went into the bathroom. The bathroom cabinet stood ajar; again, she assumed whoever had taken Laura to hospital had come in to get her toiletries and any medication. The cabinet was all but empty except for a tube of antiseptic cream and some plasters, and an empty pill bottle lying on its side. It had a prescription label. Esther picked it up. It was labelled 'Madopar', not a drug she was familiar with. She would have to google it.

It took a moment to type the name in, and the answer came back from the NHS site, listed under 'Parkinson's Disease Medicines and Drugs'. Good grief. Had Laura been diagnosed with Parkinson's? Why hadn't she said anything? And how had that led to her current condition? Esther didn't know much about Parkinson's, but she did know it was a degenerative disease characterized by tremors and a gradual restriction of movement. Laura couldn't have been showing symptoms for long; it was just seven months since Esther had seen her, and she had been fine in December – if anything, more energetic and hearty than usual. Esther glanced at her watch. It was 2 a.m. She knew for certain that she wouldn't be able to sleep; all she could do was wait until morning.

CHAPTER NINETEEN

She wandered the house restlessly until, unable to bear the mess and neglect, she resolved to clean. She dusted, scrubbed and hoovered until the sun came up, but it was still only 5 a.m., far too early to go the hospital. Maybe she'd go for a run. But despite her nervous energy, she was shaky with exhaustion and misery, so that probably wasn't a good idea. She made a cup of tea and sat down in a chair in the living room, planning just to rest for a couple of minutes. Some three hours later, she woke up to bright sunlight slanting through a gap in the curtains. She jumped up, looking around wildly, trying to make sense of the numbers on her watch. It took her a full thirty seconds to put together the time, the place and what she had to do. She tidied her hair and brushed her teeth and then set off for the hospital.

When she got to the ICU, the doctor was in with Laura, and she was asked to wait outside. They showed her into the little family room. It was, as these rooms always are, awful – featureless, with waiting room chairs, a waiting room chipboard coffee table and, most awfully, a box of tissues, as if tears were inevitable. She hadn't been in there long when the doctor came in to see her. She was a slim, tall woman in her mid-fifties, her greying blonde hair drawn back in a messy bun. She looked tired already, even though she had just begun her shift.

'I'm Dr Willis,' she said and briefly shook hands before sitting down in the chair opposite Esther. 'I believe you came down from London last night.'

'Yes, I'd been... away from home...' Esther couldn't bring herself to say 'staying with my boyfriend'. 'And you only had my landline number.'

'That seems to have been the case,' said the doctor. 'Your mother had filed some "in case of emergency" details with her GP, and that was the only number we had. I'm sorry.'

'No, I'm sorry. I should have picked up the messages sooner.'

'In most cases, that could have been a problem, but I'm afraid in this instance, twenty-four hours has not... made much difference.'

'Is she...?'

'We have run the full battery of tests, and we have concluded that she is brain-dead. I'm so sorry. The ventilator is keeping her body going, but there is no brain activity at all.'

'So you need me...' Esther couldn't finish.

'We wanted to give you a chance to say goodbye and, if you would be willing to consider it, to talk to you about organ donation.'

'Yes, yes of course,' said Esther quickly. 'I know Mum wanted to donate her organs. I think she had a card and everything.'

'Would you like to call someone? Get someone to come here to be with you?'

'There's really no one I could call. Most of all, I want to understand what happened. I spoke to her just a few days ago. She was fine. What changed? I found some medication in her house... Madopar? Did she have Parkinson's?'

Dr Willis looked uncomfortable. 'I know there were some neurological issues and she had recently had a diagnosis... I think it might be best for you to speak to her GP about the details.'

'But that wasn't what killed her?'

'No.'

'Was it a stroke? A heart attack?'

'We think... Well, it appears that she had carbon monoxide poisoning. When her neighbour found her, she was unconscious and barely breathing. When we got her to the hospital, she suffered a bleed on the brain. We did what we could, but...'

'Carbon monoxide poisoning?' Esther was horrified. 'How? Was it a defective appliance? The cooker? Is the house safe?'

The doctor hesitated. 'It wasn't in the house. It was in the garage. It appears... she got into her car and turned on the engine. There was a pipe from the exhaust to the—'

'No!' said Esther aggressively, as if saying it would make the doctor's words go away.

'It was an old car,' the doctor said, somewhat unnecessarily. Esther knew what car her mother drove – a fifteen-year-old Ford Escort.

'But... why?' The tears were flowing freely down her cheeks. She understood now why there were tissues in the room – it was a room where people received bad news like hammer blows. Dr Willis touched her hand kindly, in sympathy, but didn't reply. She wasn't going to speculate. But Esther knew why. If there had been some kind of diagnosis, if Laura had begun to have tremors, to fall, to anticipate a gradual loss of independence and control, she could not have borne it. Knowing that didn't make it any easier to hear.

'Was your mother religious at all? Would you like us to call a priest?'

'She was. She was a very active member of her church, and I'm sure her own priest would be the best person.' Esther gulped. 'Can I call him?'

'Of course.'

Esther suddenly felt overwhelmed by the oppressive little room. 'I think... I think I might go and see him, if that's all right. If we come back... later today... would that be all right?'

Dr Willis hesitated. 'Of course. Take as much time as you need.'

But as she said it, Esther could see she didn't really mean it. She didn't mean 'Take as much time as you need to process this cataclysmic turn of events.' There wasn't enough time in the world for that. She meant, 'Take the time required to manage the immediate practicalities, because we need to turn the machines off, let your mother die and free up the bed for another desperately ill patient.' Intellectually, Esther could understand this and knew that this was what had to happen, but emotionally she felt at sea – bereft, alone, unable to begin to do what needed to be done. 'I'll... I'll be back,' she said, standing abruptly.

She walked blindly through the corridors of the hospital. As if by reflex, she checked her phone. Of course, she'd turned it off when she'd got there, as ordered to by signs on the doors of the ICU. She switched it back on, and immediately it began to bleep. Ten missed calls and multiple voicemails – from Michael, from a wobbly-sounding Lucie, from Stephen and from a couple of work colleagues. She flicked from one message to the next without listening to any of them in their entirety – they all expressed concern and asked for news. How could she begin to reply? Especially to Lucie. Oh God. Lucie. She was going to have to put this all into words... explain it all. And there was still so much she didn't know. She wasn't sure she could bear any more revelations.

A wave of nausea overwhelmed her. She hadn't eaten anything since the desiccated pastry on the ferry, and she'd had three hours' sleep. Nevertheless, she was going to be sick. She looked around the reception area of the hospital but couldn't see a toilet. The car park it would have to be. She ran outside, into the blessed fresh air, found a nearby bush, bent over and retched dryly. Unsurprisingly, nothing came up. She stayed bent over, hands on her knees. Straightening up, walking to her car – that felt like just too much effort. She wanted to crawl under the bush and hide like an injured animal. Then, unexpectedly, she felt a warm hand on her back. She started a little. It must be a passer-by, a good Samaritan.

'Are you all right?' The voice was concerned, and very familiar.

'Michael,' she said, turning into his arms.

'You didn't ring or answer your phone. I thought it had to be bad. I came down as early as I could,' he said, holding her close.

In another life, or if they had been different people, Michael would have taken charge. He would have made all the decisions and arrangements and phone calls, and Esther could have collapsed in a grieving heap. But she wasn't that woman, and he was sensitive enough not to try and be that man. He took her back into the hospital and up to the café, where he ordered food – bacon, eggs and toast – and made her eat. Once she was on her second cup of tea, she was sufficiently revived to tell him. She had to spell it out and actually say the words aloud – carbon monoxide poisoning, attempted suicide, brain-dead. It was horrific, but she managed to say it all without crying or vomiting.

He listened quietly and asked a few questions. Then he said, 'What needs to be done?'

'I need to find her priest. He needs to come and give her the last rites. She would want that. Then... they turn the machines off, and she dies, I suppose, or stops breathing, as technically she's already dead. I don't know what that will be like. I've never seen someone die.'

'Me neither,' said Michael. 'Do you want me to be there?'

'Is it all right if I say no? She didn't know you, and she was very private.'

'Of course. What else can I do to help?'

'I have no idea. Just stay with me, for every moment except for that part. And could you find us a hotel? I don't think I can bear to stay in her house.'

'Consider it done. I'll reserve a few rooms. I imagine Lucie will need to come down. Will her dad bring her?'

'Oh dear God, I suppose she will. Stephen will come, I imagine. He was fond of my mum. And we'll have to organize the funeral.'

'Should it be here or in London?'

'Here. Definitely here. This was her community, and where she was born. She wanted to end up here.'

Michael took out a notebook and in his sloping, tidy handwriting made a list of what needed to be done, in chronological order, checking each step with Esther. He used his phone to look up the number of the church and then handed her the phone to ring it.

Esther had met Father Daniel a few times on her visits to the island. He was a cheery, ruddy-faced man with a bristle of white beard. She explained who she was and what had happened. He asked where she was and told her he could be there in ten minutes. She hung up, and he duly arrived. She had forgotten that death and bereavement were part of a priest's day-to-day work and that good priests were good at handling it. He was a very good priest – warm, practical and compassionate – and clearly deeply shaken by Laura's death. In an odd way, Esther found this even more comforting. It meant that Laura had genuinely meant something to him and also that she was not alone in not having foreseen the awful events.

He kept shaking his head and saying, 'I can't believe it.'

'Did you know she was ill?'

'I knew she had been a little unwell, and she looked frailer. She started walking with a stick, but that's not unusual for those of us in our seventies. It's often just a sensible precaution.'

'So she hadn't told you about the Parkinson's, or whatever it was?'

'She hadn't spoken to me about it, no. But you should probably talk to some of her friends. And to Dr Preston. He was her GP.'

'I will,' said Esther. 'And now we had better go back to the ward. I get the feeling they're waiting for us.'

'Let them wait,' said Father Daniel. 'What matters is that you feel Laura has the final journey that is best for her, and that you have said your goodbyes as best you can. There's no hurry. If they give you a hard time, they can deal with me.'

Impulsively Esther reached across the table and took his hand. 'Thank you.'

'Not at all. I loved her too. And this is a horrible blow, make no mistake. The Lord and I will be having words over this one.'

Esther explained that she had some other calls to make and that they needed to check into a hotel. She and Father Daniel arranged to meet in a few hours' time. She rang Stephen first. He and Lucie were in Southampton, waiting for the ferry. She told him the facts, baldly and briefly. He was shocked but kept his responses brief. She sensed that Lucie was nearby, and he didn't want to alarm her.

'What should I tell Lucie?'

'I don't know. I think it's important for her to know that Nanny Laura is dead. Maybe she doesn't need to know we'll have to turn off the life support. As to what she died of... well... I suppose we can address that later. Say you don't know, or that she got ill suddenly, for now.'

She and Michael drove in his car to Laura's house and she went in and packed her things as quickly as she could. He had done a web search and had found a hotel for them. He gave her the address, then dropped her back at the hospital before going on to the hotel to check in and unload their luggage.

She met Father Daniel outside the hospital, and together they went to the unit. The nurses there were kind and respectful and showed them into Laura's room. Esther was surprised to find a short, elderly man with a bald head and a fringe of white hair standing beside Laura's bed. He turned when she came in.

'You must be Esther,' he said, offering a broad, strong hand for her to shake. 'Dr Preston.'

She shook his hand, and he and Father Daniel exchanged nods of greeting. 'I'm so very sorry,' he said to Esther. 'This must be very difficult for you.'

She wasn't sure how to respond to that. She had no frame of reference for the situation she found herself in. She looked over at Laura lying on the bed, then went to sit in the chair beside her and took her hand. To her surprise, Laura's skin was warm. When she'd been there the previous night, she had been in no doubt that Laura was dead, but now she was not so sure. She looked frail and small and still, but there was life and colour in her skin and her chest rose and fell. Esther knew she wasn't breathing on her own, that it was the ventilator inflating her lungs which was keeping her alive, but it was very hard to see all the usual outward signs of life and yet intellectually accept that she was dead. What if Laura wasn't brain-dead? What if they switched off the ventilator and killed her? How could she live with herself? She looked up at Dr Preston, who seemed to understand.

'They do a series of tests to determine brain-death,' he said quietly. 'They're performed by two highly experienced doctors who have no involvement in organ transplantation. They are very careful and very thorough about these things, I assure you. I know it's hard, because she appears still to be with us, but I promise she isn't.'

'What do we do now?' she asked the room at large.

Father Daniel answered. 'You should have as much time with her as you want. I can stay with you or leave you on your own. When you're ready, I will pray for her and anoint her with oil. If you want to stay after that, do so. For as long as you need. If you want anyone else to come and say goodbye, that's also all right. If I have to beat the medical staff off with a drip stand, I will. When, and only when you are ready, you say your goodbyes, and we leave.'

Dr Preston took over. 'As you know, she wanted to donate her organs, and the transplant team is on standby. She'll be taken into surgery, where the ventilator tube will be removed, and within a few minutes her heart will stop. I know it's hard to say goodbye when she still seems to be alive, so if, after the transplant surgery, you'd like to see her again…'

'No,' said Esther. 'No.'

'Do you want us to leave you alone for a while?' Dr Preston asked gently.

Esther knew she was supposed to say yes, but she didn't know what she would say if she was alone with Laura. Whatever she said, she would be saying to herself alone. She was an atheist, she didn't believe in an immortal spirit. Laura had checked out and gone. And even if Laura could hear, what would she say? 'How could you? How could you do this to me, to Lucie?' She felt cold and bleak, and she felt the deep stirrings of anger. She wanted this to be over.

'No,' she said firmly, not caring what the two men thought. 'Father Daniel should do the prayers now.'

She stood beside the bed through the prayers, dry-eyed and still, and watched Father Daniel make the cross on Laura's forehead in oil. He touched her with great tenderness, and she could hear a catch in his voice. He was affected by this loss. But all Esther could feel was a growing coldness, as if something inside her had turned to ice. She had no idea who this woman was. This breathing corpse was a stranger. All she wanted to do was get away.

For form as much as anything else, she stroked Laura's hair and kissed her forehead. And then she heard a voice that didn't sound like her own saying, 'Goodbye, Mamma.' It was as if the voice of a child had risen unbidden from deep inside her, and it startled her so much she began to cry. She stepped back from the bed, shocked, and Father Daniel caught her with an arm around her shoulders.

'Do you want to go now?' he said softly.

She nodded.

'Are you sure?'

'Yes.'

He led her from the room, and she didn't look back. She could see the nurses and a few people in surgical scrubs standing by the nurses station. In her peripheral vision she saw Dr Preston stepping into the doorway of the room, obviously alerting them that the process could begin. The process.

The rest of the day passed in a blur. She got into her car and, using the satnav, found her way to the hotel, which was close to her mother's house, on the banks of the Old Mill Pond. She would have liked to have lain down on the bed, alone or with Michael, and rested, but while she was at the hospital, Lucie and Stephen had arrived. They were sitting with Michael at a table in the reception area of the hotel, having tea. She didn't have time to consider the deeply awkward nature of this meeting. Lucie rushed into her arms in a storm of sobs. She held her and comforted her, stroking her hair.

'Is she dead?' Lucie asked, looking up into Esther's face, her expression pleading.

'I'm sorry, my darling. Yes she is. She was in no pain at all though.'

'I can't believe it,' said Lucie.

Stephen stood up and gave Esther a self-conscious pat on the shoulder. She managed a weak smile for him.

'Thanks for bringing her,' she said.

He nodded, without saying anything, and she found herself grateful for his taciturn and unemotional nature. Stephen didn't make a fuss. He wouldn't make a fuss about Laura's death, nor about having to have tea with his ex-wife's new boyfriend. She had found his coldness alienating when they were married. Now she was thankful for it. She would have to carry the burden of so many people's emotions over the coming days; at least his would not be among them.

She sat down at the table and Lucie poured her a cup of tea. It was lukewarm and a bit stewed, but she drank it anyway. They were all looking at her expectantly.

'They took her body into surgery, for the organ donation,' she said carefully. 'I imagine we can start organizing the funeral within the next day or so.'

'Do we need to let anyone else know?' asked Michael. 'Other family? Friends?'

Esther thought. 'I'll make a list of cousins and so on, but they're all quite distant relations. We weren't a close family. I was an only child. She was an only child.'

'What about your friends?'

'I'll let people know. But I can't imagine many of them can drop everything to come to a funeral on the Isle of Wight. This was her place. Her friends were all here, especially at the church. Letting them know should be our priority.'

'I'm sure the priest could help us with that,' said Michael.

'Father Daniel. Yes, he's a lovely old fellow, and was obviously very close to her.'

They talked through a variety of practical concerns – timings, logistics, what was to happen with Laura's will and her house in the short and longer term. After fifteen minutes or so, Esther glanced over at Lucie, who was slumped in her chair, clearly poleaxed by misery. How could she help her daughter? This was the first time Lucie had experienced the death of someone close to her. And what an awful death. There was no way she wouldn't find out how Laura had died – someone was bound to let something slip, and Esther knew from what Laura had told her that the island was rife with gossip. It would of course be better if Lucie heard it from her and not via a cruel chance comment made by a stranger. But how should she tell her? Not for the first time, she was struck by how different real parenting was from the fantasy version she'd imagined in her youth. Deep down, she felt no cleverer or wiser than she had when she was a teenager herself, and yet she was expected to have the answers, to know what to do in a crisis, to know how to manage this massive, significant event in her daughter's life. She didn't know how to do it. All she knew was that she had to do it alone.

'Do you mind if Lucie and I go for a walk?' she said, conscious that this would leave her ex-husband and her boyfriend to make small talk with one another. But they were perfectly capable of looking after themselves.

'Go ahead,' said Stephen. 'I need to go up to the room and make some calls for work.'

'Me too,' said Michael.

'I don't want to go for a walk,' said Lucie miserably.

'Come on,' said Esther. 'You've been stuck in cars and ferries and now the hotel. Let's go down to the lake and get some fresh air.'

The hotel had elegant, groomed lawns which rolled down to the lakeside. The wind whipped around their legs and tangled their hair. Esther took Lucie's arm and they found a bench, overlooking an expanse of velvety turf.

She sat down and drew Lucie into the circle of her arm.

'Lucie…' she began hesitantly.

'Are you going to tell me how Nanny died?'

'Yes.'

'I don't want to know.'

'All right…' said Esther gently. 'My one worry is that if you don't hear it from me, you might hear it by accident from someone else, and I think that might be worse.'

'I still don't want to know.'

'Okay.' She wasn't going to fight. She let herself relax just a little. It was so lovely, sitting there with Lucie's sweet, narrow shoulders in the curve of her arm. With her girl close to her, everything would be all right. But then Lucie spoke again.

'This is our fault.'

'What do you mean?'

'We should have been looking after her. Lots of people have their grandparents living with them. We hardly ever saw Nanny Laura. You neglected her, and now she's dead.'

Esther had to get up and move away. She walked fast down the lawn towards the lake, pulling her cardigan tightly around her. The alternatives – slapping Lucie's face hard, or weeping uncontrollably, because what she said was true – weren't open to her. She stood, breathing raggedly, looking out at the water. Eventually, she turned back. Lucie was still sitting on the bench, hunched over, not looking at her.

CHAPTER TWENTY

The following morning, Esther wrote an enormous to-do list of things she needed to deal with over the next few days, but every time she tried to do something, someone else seemed to step in and do it more competently. Even though she would happily never have gone back to her mum's house again, she had to go there to find all the necessary paperwork. Unsurprisingly, it was all in order, neatly filed and easily accessible in shelves above her desk. There were folders marked 'Will', 'Funeral Policy' (Laura had paid for it in full, including a plot in a woodland cemetery on the island), 'House' (this contained all the information relating to the ownership of the house, which was fully paid off), and 'Finances' (all her accounts, insurance policies and pension). Esther merely had to hand these over to the named solicitor, who was also the executor of the will. She and Lucie were the main beneficiaries, but there was also a substantial bequest to the church and some smaller ones to local organizations. The solicitors asked her if she wanted to sell the house and said that they would take care of everything.

She set about trying to organize the funeral. She had no idea what to do about choosing readings and hymns, so Father Daniel came up with a list of suggestions. She started looking for a venue to host the wake, but the church ladies made it clear they wanted to cater it in the church hall. And on the day she decided she would begin the mammoth job of sorting and clearing out Laura's effects, a group of six women from the church turned up with bags, boxes and labels, ready to help. All Esther had to do was choose the mementoes she wanted to keep – a task made so much harder by the fact that everything seemed tainted by Laura's illness and death. She didn't want any of it, but she knew that that was a choice she would come to regret, and besides, it wasn't fair on Lucie. She forced herself to pick some paintings and jewellery, as well as photo albums and a few other articles, like her mother's handmade quilts, which were unique and irreplaceable. Beyond that, she was glad to let the ladies get on with it and parcel up everything else to be dispersed to various charities.

During the packing-up, she checked every nook and cranny in the house – the desk drawers, Laura's bedside table, the kitchen counters – but there was no note, no letter for her or anyone else to explain why Laura had done what she did.

It took all her courage to lift the key off the wall and make her way across the little courtyard to the garage. Perhaps Laura had left something in the car. The hardest thing was walking through the door and seeing Laura's dusty red Ford. The driver's door still stood ajar, and the pipe she had run from the exhaust was lying on the garage floor. The dust on the floor was scuffed with the marks of many feet, and there were a few discarded packets from medical paraphernalia, which must have been left there by the ambulance crew.

Esther could see that the locking bar that ran across the up-and-over garage door was twisted and bent. The door had been pulled closed but was unfastened and could no longer be locked. The emergency services must have forced it open to get inside. She walked slowly around the car, looking in each of the windows, and could see nothing on any of the seats. After a long while, she tried the passenger door and it opened. She checked the glove compartment and under all of the seats. No note. Nothing.

Perhaps the police had taken something away; but if they had, surely they would have told her? She decided to go and see the next-door neighbour – the one who had found Laura in the garage – to ask if she had seen anything in the car.

She had met the neighbour, a Mrs Hardy, a few times before. Laura hadn't particularly liked her, finding her to be a fussy busybody who had an opinion on everything in the street. She always had something to say about the way people parked their cars, put their bins out or kept their front gardens. She had a detailed knowledge of everyone's comings and goings and seemed to disapprove of most of them.

She was a short, thickset, grey-haired woman with heavy-lidded eyes that made her look like a squat bird of prey. She answered the door and when she saw Esther, nodded for her to follow, then walked back into her living room. In layout, her house was the mirror image of Laura's, but it could not have been more different. Though Laura's house had usually been clean and neat, it was also brightly decorated with all of her craft items – tapestries, quilts and rugs; the shelves bulged with books and the walls were full of artwork. Mrs Hardy's surgically spotless house was decorated in shades of beige and magnolia. There were no paintings on the walls and no books to be seen, just a single pristine-looking copy of the *Radio Times* on the coffee table.

She sat down squarely in a chair and indicated that Esther should sit on the sofa opposite.

'Thought you'd have come by before,' she said, a little sourly.

'I'm so sorry,' Esther found herself saying. 'I should have. This has all been a terrible shock.'

Mrs Hardy gave a curt nod, as if the apology was merited and, if not accepted, at least acknowledged.

'Thank you so much for... finding her,' said Esther. 'And calling the ambulance.'

'I heard the car. Bloody noisy thing. I was out in the front garden, doing some weeding, and the engine just kept rumbling on and on. I couldn't understand why she hadn't opened the garage door if she was going out. So I went to have a look – there's that little window in the side wall – and I could see her in the car, leaning back against the headrest. I thought maybe she'd been taken ill, so I called out, but she didn't answer. The garage door was locked and so was the side gate. So I came back here and dialled 999. You know the rest.'

Somehow, Esther had imagined Mrs Hardy going into the garage herself, maybe trying to pull Laura out of the car. She hadn't even been inside. Nevertheless, she had to ask. 'Was there anything found, do you know? A note? A letter?'

'I don't know,' said Mrs Hardy. 'I don't think so. I watched them pull her out of the car and put her on the floor to see if she was breathing, and then they got her in the ambulance and off they went. The police came later, but I didn't see them take anything away.'

Esther was fairly sure that she would have watched the police like a hawk. She would have noticed them taking something out of the car, or an evidence bag. Mrs Hardy didn't miss anything.

'Well, thank you,' she said. 'And thank you again for what you did. I wish... things had turned out differently.'

Mrs Hardy showed her to the door, and as Esther was about to step outside, she said abruptly, 'She fell, you know. Twice.'

Esther stared at her. Mrs Hardy continued. 'Once outside her front door, once in the road. The first time, she got up by herself and went inside. Didn't speak to anyone. The second time, she couldn't get up. Had to call out to some young feller who was passing by.'

She didn't say anything further, but in her bald recounting of these facts, Esther heard an accusation. 'You should have known. How could you not know?' Perhaps the accusation was not in Mrs Hardy's tone but in her own head. She had spent every waking moment since Laura had died thinking about their last few telephone conversations. Was there a clue she had missed? It was impossible to remember if Laura's speech had been slurred, or different in any way – she hadn't noticed it or commented on it, that was for sure. And she was sure Laura had sounded cheerful, normal, busy – herself. She might have believed Laura's death was an accident, or even foul play, if it wasn't for the 'neurological issues' mentioned at the hospital, the Parkinson's drugs, and the anecdotal evidence of falls and the use of a stick. What had been wrong with Laura? How bad was it and how long had she known? She had no idea if patient confidentiality applied after death, but she had to try. She had to go and speak to the police and Dr Preston.

She rang the local police station and was passed from person to person until eventually she was given the name of the officer who had been first on the scene. She left a message, asking him to ring her, and half an hour later a man whose voice sounded reedy and young called her on her mobile.

'There was no note in the car,' he said, slightly defensively. 'I got there at the same time as the paramedics, and while they were helping the lady, trying to get her to breathe, we checked the car over. If we'd found any evidence, we would have got forensics in.'

She sensed he was terrified that he had done something wrong and might be in trouble. She was sure he had checked for a note, and she had to conclude that there simply had not been one.

She made an appointment with Dr Preston's surgery, explaining who she was. When she went into his consulting room, he didn't seem at all surprised to see her. 'Esther,' he said gently. 'I'm glad you came.'

'I don't know if you're allowed to...' she began, but her voice wobbled and she couldn't finish the sentence.

'Talk about Laura's medical history? To be honest, I wasn't sure, so I've consulted a few colleagues and the General Medical Council guidelines. She didn't ask me not to talk to you, which would have made things tricky. And the general view is that if the facts can help you make sense of her death, I am at liberty, or even encouraged, to share them with you.'

'And the facts are?'

'When she came into the surgery that first time, I didn't know who she was. She had never been to see me before, although she'd been registered with us for upwards of fifteen years. She had begun to experience some worrying symptoms in November last year. The first time she came to see me, it was because she had fallen in the street and bruised a knee very badly. When I questioned her further, it transpired she'd had some dizziness, bumping into things, falling over, that sort of thing. I suggested we run some tests, and she laughed and said no. But a week later, she was back. She'd had another fall.'

'November?' said Esther.

'Yes, why?'

'So she already knew she was ill at Christmas? When we came to see her?'

'She'd had some tests, but we didn't get anything like a firm diagnosis till the January. I'm sure she didn't want to worry you.'

Esther nodded. Dr Preston continued. 'At first I was pretty sure it was Parkinson's, but then she started to show some very specific symptoms – she was losing the ability to move her eyes, and she was having trouble swallowing. We did some further investigations and it transpired she had a Parkinson's-plus syndrome.'

'Parkinson's-plus?'

'Similar to Parkinson's but often more rapidly progressive, and with additional symptoms. She had a thing we call progressive supranuclear palsy. PSP.'

'Rapidly progressive?'

'With PSP, we can usually expect a patient to live around seven years, with progressive degeneration over that time. But Laura's case was severe and moving very fast.'

'And so she just decided to opt out. Without telling me. Without telling anybody who could have helped her.' Esther was surprised at the venom in her own voice.

'I'm so sorry,' said Dr Preston gently. 'All I can say is I had absolutely no inkling that she was planning to do what she did. She asked a great many questions about the disease, and I know she read up on it. We did speak recently about the fact that she would need care as it progressed, and she said that she had a plan in place. That was all. I had an appointment to meet with her this week to discuss it further. I was going to contact social services on her behalf and so on. But...' He shrugged helplessly.

A more cynical doctor might have been afraid that Esther would complain to the NHS trust or report him for negligence, but Dr Preston was remarkably open and frank and seemed genuinely distressed by what had happened. Esther had no plans to report him. How could she accuse a doctor of failing to spot her mother's plan to commit suicide when she had been utterly clueless herself? She hadn't even known Laura was ill. She thanked Dr Preston for his time and made her way out into the unfeasibly bright sunshine. The funeral was the next day, and she still had so much to organize.

CHAPTER TWENTY-ONE

The church was full by the time Esther arrived from the funeral home. Standing in the doorway, she could see a sea of bent, grey heads, all leaning together and talking in urgent undertones. She knew they were gossiping. Well, let them gossip. They couldn't make her feel worse than she already did. She held her head high and, taking Lucie's elbow, walked to the front pew and sat down. They were all behind her now. Michael and Stephen took their seats separately a little way back – they had been unable to come up with a seating arrangement where they could all sit together without sparking more gossip or unnecessary questions. Esther was hot in her scratchy black wool dress. She hadn't had anything but jeans in her hastily packed bag, so she had had to go shopping for something to wear. It was an unappealing, plain, black, sack-like dress, but it didn't matter. She would never wear it again after today.

Father Daniel conducted the service with warmth and kindness. Lucie did a short Bible reading (she had wanted to do something), and Father Daniel himself gave a lovely, personal eulogy. The service seemed to go on and on, and Esther felt desperate for it to end. Laura's wicker coffin, woven with flowers, hovered in her peripheral vision. When finally the service was over, she steeled herself for greeting and thanking people. Once they had said hello to everyone, they would accompany the funeral directors out to the cemetery then return to the wake an hour or so later.

She and Lucie followed the pallbearers to the door of the church and watched them load the coffin into the hearse. Lucie was trembling. She had never been to a funeral before. Esther took her hand and Lucie clutched her fingers tightly. Then they took their places by the door to shake hands with people as they came out. It was slow going – everyone wanted to stop and give their condolences and share a story about Laura. Esther lost count of the number of wrinkled cheeks she kissed and the number of times she said, 'Thank you so much.' Michael and Stephen were among the last to leave the church. Stephen gave her a firm hug, and she realized with surprise that it was the first time he had held her in his arms in years – they had stopped touching long before their split and divorce. Then he moved along, curled his arm around Lucie and led her away. Michael came and stood beside her, putting his hand on her back. His warm touch gave her strength to greet the last few people.

To her astonishment, Paul and Tim were the next people to come out of the church. She hadn't seen them when she came in. She hugged Paul and felt tears prick her eyes.

'Thank you. Thank you so much for coming,' she said fervently. 'I had no idea you were here. It means so much.'

'Of course we'd be here,' said Tim, hugging her too. 'We all wanted to give you support, precious friend.'

'All...?' asked Esther. Looking up, she saw Sally standing beside Tim.

'I'm so sorry for your loss,' said Sally, hugging her and kissing her cheek.

'How... er...?' Esther was confused. Sally had not been one of the people she'd rung to inform of Laura's death. She had called only her closest friends and a few key work colleagues, reasoning that most people would find out when she got back to London.

'Paul and Tim rang me and told me what had happened. I wanted to be here to support you too,' Sally said. 'I remember your mum so well. She was always so beautiful and elegant, always making things, or out in the garden.'

Esther swallowed hard and fought back yet another terrible wave of guilt. Of course. Of all the people she might have invited, Sally was one of very few who had actually known Laura. She should have been one of the first people Esther had thought of. But she hadn't been.

'I'm so, so glad you came,' she said, rather more fervently than she intended, and she hugged Sally. 'We're going to the cemetery – well, it's a bit of managed woodland, really – and we'll be coming back to the hall in about an hour.'

'Are you going in a funeral car or driving yourselves?' Sally asked.

'We're driving ourselves. We didn't go for funeral cars in the end, it seemed a bit... old-fashioned. Not really Mum's style.'

'I'm happy to squeeze in with you, if there's room,' said Sally, and Esther realized she was asking to come to the burial, or expecting she should come. She couldn't say, 'It's family only,' because of course Michael was coming with her and he wasn't family and had never even met Laura. She'd already made a faux pas by not ringing Sally herself. She couldn't snub her again.

'There's room in our car, of course,' she said. 'Lucie will be travelling with her dad.'

Sally moved away to chat to Lucie, and Esther looked across at Michael.

'Did I hear that right? She's coming to the burial?' he asked.

'I didn't know how to say no,' Esther said, realizing as she did so how pathetic that sounded.

'That's kind of you,' he said, coming to stand beside her and putting his hand on her back.

'I feel – confused. I'm not quite sure how it happened,' Esther looked over at Sally, who was talking earnestly to Lucie. 'I don't know even why she's here.'

'She knew your mum, didn't she?' Michael said.

'Well, yes. She seems to have admired my mum a lot. She went through a phase, after her mum died, of ringing me to talk about our childhoods. She remembered things I didn't even know she knew, about my bedroom, and birthday parties, cakes my mum baked...'

'Wow. You must have been close. I thought Isabella was your friend, not Sally.'

'She was, but Sally was her little sister, so she was around a lot.'

'How little? I mean... how much younger?'

'Six years younger, I think. Something like that.'

'That's a big gap to be trailing around after your sister's friends. Didn't she have friends of her own?'

Esther thought. 'Not that I can remember, but then, why would I? We barely paid any attention to one annoying little girl, so I doubt we'd have noticed if there were two.'

Michael looked over at Sally, thoughtfully. There was something tender in his expression – was it sympathy? Pity?

'It seems likely to me that you and your mum were important to her, so coming to the burial would probably mean a lot.' He looked back to Esther. 'As long as you're sure you don't mind.'

Esther did mind. She minded a lot. Now her memories of

Laura's internment would always include Sally. But without causing an awkward scene, she could see no way out of it.

'Will Lucie object?' said Michael.

Esther saw Sally standing with an arm around Lucie's shoulders. They had their heads close together and were talking. She could read Lucie's body language pretty well, and she seemed to be leaning into Sally, as if she were happy to be close to her.

'Lucie really likes her,' she said grudgingly. 'I don't think she'll mind. I'll ask her, as soon as I can get her alone.'

She didn't get the chance, because Lucie came over a minute or so later and said, 'Sally says she's coming to the burial with us. I'm so pleased. I wanted everyone to come to say goodbye to Nanny Laura.'

Esther glanced at Michael and he gave a small nod. 'I'll go and get the car,' he said.

Later, in the church hall, Esther looked across the room and saw Sally chatting animatedly to a group of Laura's friends from church. She was well dressed and well groomed, and she seemed to have found new confidence. The Sally of old would have hung around on the periphery, blurting platitudes at anyone who talked to her. Now, Esther saw a bright, outgoing, pretty woman who seemed happy to talk to anyone. She had certainly won over Paul and Tim – Esther hadn't known that a friendship had developed since they'd met at her birthday party. She noticed they'd all gathered by the food table now and were sharing a joke. She would have loved to have gone over to Paul and Tim, and she could have done with one of Tim's warm bear hugs, but she couldn't face Sally right now. Sally had sniffled and sobbed quietly at Laura's graveside. This had elicited a warm hug from Lucie, but had left Esther wanting to slap her. She herself had been dried eyed, stiff and quiet.

She should be mingling more herself. These kind people had

made such an effort in Laura's memory; she needed to thank them all. She went over to a knot of ladies, whom she knew had been responsible for the food.

'I just wanted to thank you all,' she said. 'The food is magnificent. You did my mum proud.'

'We did our best, but none of us could come close to Laura on the baking front,' said one wiry old lady. 'No church spread would be complete without her lemon drizzle cake.' Her bright blue eyes reminded Esther of Laura's own, and as she registered this, she had a powerful memory of her mother's lemon cake – a deliciously moist and delicate creation with a sharp, crystalline crust of sugar and lemon. Her breath caught in her throat and tears started in her eyes. She took a tiny step back and forced a smile, but the women had all seen. They crowded around and patted her, murmuring kind words. This of course made the tears flow faster.

It was mortifying to be crying in front of complete strangers, but, worse than that, she felt like such a fraud. She had so neglected her mother that Laura had committed suicide rather than ask for help. How they must all be judging her. How they must despise her. She certainly despised herself. She pulled herself together, thanked them all for their kindness and withdrew. All she could do was count the minutes until she could leave this wake, and the days and hours until she could leave the island.

Stephen and Lucie and the friends who had come to the funeral left the same day. It took another interminable two days to wind up the details for the lawyers handling the estate and the sale of the house. Esther and Michael drove onto the ferry in convoy and then went to sit in the lounge, ready to sail. As the ship moved towards the mainland, Esther looked back and watched the coastline of the island recede. She had left Laura there, beneath the chilly ground in the woodland cemetery. Her grave would be unmarked, as she had wished it to be. And Esther was returning home with no mother and no answers.

CHAPTER TWENTY-TWO

Esther got home in the afternoon, after a hot, grubby, frustrating three hours spent crawling up the M3 and around the M25. Michael had gone back to his own house, having promised to come by later. Esther pushed open her front door, feeling the resistance of the pile of letters behind it. No one had been in the house in ten days. The air smelled of dust and the unemptied rubbish bin. She had left in a hurry, and the shoes she had been wearing that day were discarded beside the sofa. A pile of student papers sat on the dusty coffee table where she had dropped them, and there were still cups and plates on the draining board. It was as if the house were frozen in the moment before everything had come crashing down. When she had kicked off those shoes, she had been happy and her life had seemed to be coming together very nicely. She had been looking forward to her time in Venice. Oh God. Venice. She had completely lost track of the days. She went into the kitchen to look at the calendar. They should have flown three days ago. She picked up her phone and rang Michael.

'Hi there,' he said. 'Just on my way.'

'Venice.'

'What about it?'

'We were supposed to leave for Venice three days ago.'

'As soon as I got to the Isle of Wight, it was obvious we weren't going. I cancelled the trip and put in a claim with the travel insurance. It's covered, don't worry.'

'You didn't say anything.'

'I would have if you'd asked, but I figured, in the greater scheme of things, I should just make it one less thing for you to worry about.'

'You're a good man, Michael Wolfson.'

'Just an ordinary man,' he said quietly, 'who loves you.'

Her breath caught in her throat. It was the first time he had said it.

'Thank you,' she said, her voice barely a whisper. 'Thank you. I don't deserve you.'

'I'll see you in a bit,' he said. She could hear he was disappointed she hadn't said she loved him in return, but she had been caught off guard. She would say it, when the moment was right.

She wandered through the house, taking note of what needed doing. She'd have to get some shopping in and throw away all the spoiled food. But first she'd get the first lot of laundry on – she had completely run out of clean clothes and had had to buy underwear and a few bits and pieces on the island. She put a load of darks on, straight from her open suitcase, then went to collect the stack of post from the hallway. She sat at her desk and began leafing through the letters while she listened to her landline phone messages. She had missed an appointment for a boiler safety check, and the optometrist had rung to remind them that Lucie was due for an eye test. Was that all? She knew her landline was seldom used, but there were usually more messages than that. She clicked replay, and the automated voice told her she had one saved message. She usually deleted everything – perhaps this was an important call she had forgotten to return. The automated voice gave the date of the message; a Saturday two weeks before. And before Esther had time to think what it might be, Laura's voice filled the room.

'Morning, busy daughter,' she said, and her voice sounded as it always had, cheerful and strong. 'I expect you've gone out for a run. Give me a tinkle when you get back. Love you. Bye.'

And now Esther remembered. She had heard the message when she got back from her run but had been on her way out of the door to go grocery shopping. She had deliberately not deleted it, as a reminder to ring Laura when she got back. But she hadn't. And now...

It wasn't possible to feel worse. How could she feel worse than she had for these last ten awful, nightmarish days? She sat down on the sofa, then lay down, her head on a cushion that smelled musty and sad. She wanted to play the message again, to hear Laura's voice one more time. But simultaneously she never wanted to hear it again. Laura's voice, calling out to her forever, the call unreturned.

Eventually, curiosity drove her back to the phone and she replayed the message. Was there a clue in Laura's voice? Any sadness? Or, for that matter, any sign of her illness? A slurring or fuzziness to her speech? Was there any hint of a goodbye? She had left the message just two days before she went into the garage. Surely she must have known by then that she was going to do it? Esther played the message again and again, until the words lost meaning.

When Michael rang the doorbell, she was still sitting at her desk in the dark. It took all her strength to go to the door and let him in. He looked at her, and drew her into his arms. She couldn't relax into him. Her body felt stiff and brittle, as if she might snap. In as few words as she could, she told him about the message. Then she made him come and sit at her desk and listen to it.

'What can you hear?' she asked desperately. 'Can you hear anger? Or resignation? Does she sound ill to you? Can you hear any slurring in her voice?'

'Esther, I never spoke to her when she was alive,' he said gently. 'It's impossible for me to tell. To me, she comes across as perfectly normal, and it sounds like an ordinary message from a mother to her daughter. But as I say, I didn't know her. You can't torture yourself like this.'

She looked at him as if he was mad. 'What else can I possibly do?'

He gently bullied her into tidying the place up a little and got her to unpack the rest of her things. He cleaned up the kitchen and emptied the bins and then urged her out of the door. He drove her to a local Italian restaurant and ordered them both starter portions of pasta. She stared at her plate when it arrived, as if food were an alien substance she had once heard about but had no experience of or interest in.

'You have to eat,' said Michael, and for the first time ever, she heard a note of impatience in his voice. 'You're getting so thin.'

'I can't.'

'Starving yourself won't bring her back.'

She looked up sharply. His tone was harsh.

'What?' she said blankly.

'I know this has been horrible for you,' he said. 'But you cannot fall apart. You just can't. Laura may be gone, but Lucie isn't. Your job hasn't disappeared. I'm not going anywhere. You're needed.'

'Hang on,' she said coldly. 'I got back from my mother's funeral two hours ago. I found a message from her on the phone an hour ago, and you're telling me to get over it?'

'I'm not saying get over it...'

'You're saying my grief is inconvenient for you.'

'Esther...'

'I know this is a comparatively new relationship. I know it's not ideal that my mother committed suicide when we'd only been dating a few months. I'm sorry. I didn't schedule it that way.'

'Please don't be sarcastic.'

'Why not?' she said, caught off guard by the uncharacteristic coldness and anger in his voice.

'Because it's how you shut people out. You speak very clearly in your Jane Austen voice and you get very cutting and there's no way to break through that. I'm trying to tell you that I love you. We love you. We need you. This is a terrible thing that has happened, but I'm asking you, please, don't give up on yourself. Don't give up on Lucie or me.'

'Can you say that again?' she said, so softly she wasn't sure he'd heard.

'Which part?'

'The first part.'

'I love you.'

'I love you too, Michael. This is the worst thing that has ever happened in my life. I will do my best, and I won't give up. But please, don't give up on me either.'

'I give you my word. Now will you eat something? Please? There's nothing of you. I'm scared you'll blow away in a strong gust of wind.'

Michael had an early start, so he dropped Esther at home after dinner and went back to his own place. She wandered aimlessly around the house; her body ached with tiredness, but her mind would not let her sleep yet. She poured herself a glass of wine and went up to the bedroom to put fresh linen on her bed and clean the bathroom. She hadn't slept in her own bed for a fortnight, and her room looked entirely unfamiliar. There was a novel on her bedside table, with a bookmark between the pages. She had no recollection of having started to read the book, nor any idea what it was about. And even worse, when she glanced at the stack of notes on the dresser in her bedroom, it reminded her that she had just four days before she was due back at work. The university felt like some kind of foreign planet. After years of keeping up with her emails day and night, and worrying about work even when she was supposed to be on holiday, she hadn't given it a moment's thought for the past ten days. When she forced herself to think about it, she recalled that she was probably a week overdue in returning a collection of second-year essays, that she had promised to submit a chapter for a new Austen publication, which was also overdue, and that she had had no contact with Regina for days. The department could have burned to the ground for all she knew – and she wouldn't much care if it had.

Michael was right. She was going to have to pull herself together. She just had no idea how to do so. She sat down on the edge of her half-made bed, a pillow on her lap. One day at a time, she told herself, and if that was too much, one hour at a time. Or one minute. Or breath by breath.

When the phone rang, it sounded so loud in the quiet room, she jumped. She snatched it up.

'Hello?'

'Esther?' It was Sally.

'Oh, hello, Sally,' she said, trying to sound warm and friendly.

'I thought you might be coming back from the Isle of Wight

today. I called an hour or so ago but didn't get an answer. Have you just got back?'

'I got back this afternoon, but Michael took me out for dinner.'

'That's a nice man you've got there.'

'Well, I think so.' This time Esther managed a smile.

'I wasn't ringing for anything special. I just thought I'd see how you were doing.'

'Awful,' said Esther, surprising herself with her own honesty. 'Absolutely awful. I've come back to my house, to my life, to work… and I have no idea how to pick up where I left off. How can I?'

'It seems impossible, doesn't it? When something so dreadful has happened, worrying about ordinary everyday things like whether or not you've got milk, well, it feels almost disloyal, doesn't it?'

'Yes. That's exactly how I feel,' said Esther. 'I know there are things I have to do, but if I do, if life goes on… if I'm not thinking about her…'

'Then she's still dead,' said Sally gently. 'If you believe in God, then you'll believe she's watching you from heaven and knows what's in your heart. If you don't, then you'll believe she's gone completely, so how can your actions hurt her?'

'It's easy for you to think like that,' said Esther bitterly. 'You cared for your mum – and for Isabella. My mother killed herself rather than let me care for her. That's how little she thought of me.'

'Is that what you think? Really?'

'What else can I possibly think?'

'That maybe it wasn't about you? When people are ill, they turn inwards. Often, they think only of themselves. It's not surprising. And sometimes they do and say things… that they wouldn't if they were entirely in their right minds.'

'But…'

'There are a lot of things I don't know about,' said Sally softly, 'but I do know about sick and dying people. And I know about grief.'

'That's true,' said Esther. 'Thank you.'

'I'm going to call you every day,' said Sally. 'At around this time. If you don't want to talk, or you're busy, don't pick up. I'll understand. But I'm going to keep calling, in case you do need to talk. And of course you can ring me anytime you want to. Anytime. Day or night. I'm a very light sleeper.'

'Thank you. I don't deserve your kindness.'

'Of course you do. Sleep tight.'

Lucie came back from Stephen's, Esther went back to work and, at least on the surface, life regained some semblance of normality. She lectured, she administrated, she cooked meals and started running again. She spent nights and weekends with Michael and took Lucie out to do things whenever she could get a slot in her daughter's busy social calendar. And every night, give or take the odd one when she was out, she sat on the edge of her bed and talked to Sally.

Sometimes the calls were short. Sally would just say, 'How are you?' and Esther would reply, 'A little better today,' and they'd make small talk for a couple of minutes and then ring off. Sometimes the phone rang and she didn't want to answer it because she felt almost happy that day, and she didn't want to have to think about Laura. But guilt would make her pick up the phone and, somehow, talking to Sally would make her feel a little less like she was betraying her mother's memory by carrying on with her life.

And some days she was barely able to drag herself through the hours of work and beyond, so heavy was her heart. She'd count the minutes until half past nine, the magical hour when Sally would ring. And on those days, when she could barely croak 'Hello', Sally would understand and would keep up a quiet, murmuring monologue, as if she was speaking to an invalid or someone who was unconscious.

'I had my driving lesson today', she said on one such evening. 'Harry, my driving teacher, says I'm making very good progress. I'm planning to take my test next month. I got him to drop me on the high street, and I went to that posh new coffee shop, do you know the one I mean? They have macarons. Fancy that! I'd never had a macaron before. I didn't even know what they were. They came in all sorts of pretty colours – pinks and peaches and yellows – and they're so light.'

'My mum...' Esther began, but then couldn't continue.

'Your mum?' prompted Sally gently.

'My mum... made the most beautiful macarons. Light as a feather and so delicious. Lucie loved them.'

'Do you bake?'

'A bit. But I don't have a tenth of Mum's skill, or her artistic flair.'

'She was very artistic. She worked, didn't she?'

'Yes, she was a junior school teacher. Never at our school – she never wanted me to be the teacher's child – but at another school in the area.'

'I bet she was a wonderful teacher.'

'I think she was firm but fair, as they say. She certainly didn't stand for any nonsense from me, so I can't imagine she'd have put up with it from children in her class. I know she used to come up with wonderful art projects for the children. She always had the most brilliant classroom displays. She'd transform the whole room into an undersea wonderland, or put castle battlements around all the walls and get the children to design flags and shields.'

As she spoke, it became clear to her that just talking about Laura had lifted the weight from her chest a little. It was so good to remember her – remember what she had been like before the terrible end she had chosen. Sally was right. She did know about grief. Her simple acts of kindness, the daily phone calls, were saving Esther's life. And yet Esther couldn't help thinking the kindness, the intimacy was – disproportionate. What kind of person made an effort like that for an acquaintance? What kind indeed?

CHAPTER TWENTY-THREE

One Monday morning, Esther was sitting at her desk, working through her emails when her office phone rang.

'Professor Hart?' Esther recognized the breathy voice. Abigail from the press office, an enthusiastic young woman with a tendency to flap in a crisis. This was not an ideal quality in someone who sometimes had to firefight bad-news stories about the university or deal with insistent journalists.

'Yes,' said Esther cautiously.

'Have you seen the news?' said Abigail. 'It's all over the BBC and the broadsheets.'

'Er... what news?' Esther opened her internet browser and called up the BBC site. She couldn't immediately see anything on the front page that might overexcite someone in the press office of a university. But then she spotted it in the 'Most Read' stories in the bottom right-hand corner: 'Possible new Dickens manuscript discovered'.

'Is it the Dickens thing?' she asked, opening the story and scanning it.

'Yes!' said Abigail. 'Isn't it wonderful?'

Academics at a small university in the South East had been approached by an anonymous person who had found a boxful of papers that he said had been in his family for some generations. Among them was a handwritten story, full of corrections and crossings-out. He could see it was very old but had no idea how old exactly or who might have written it. The academics at the university had suspected from the handwriting and the style that it might be an early story by Charles Dickens himself, although none of them had ever seen it before. They had approached a few experts confidentially and asked their opinions. They were now so cautiously optimistic that they had made a public announcement, little thinking, Esther assumed, that it would break as a national news story.

Abigail had been waiting impatiently on the other end of the phone for Esther to finish reading the article.

'What do you think?' she asked.

'I can't really offer an opinion,' said Esther. 'I haven't seen the manuscript, and besides, I'm not an expert in Dickens' handwriting. I just wouldn't have a clue one way or the other.'

'Do you think you could arrange to have a clue by lunchtime? You see, we have a news crew coming to the university, and they want to ask whether you, as a Dickens expert, think it's genuine.'

'What?' said Esther, horrified.

'I've got a transcript of the story, which I'm emailing over now.' Abigail was persistent, Esther had to give her that. 'You just need to say a few words on camera. Say you don't have very much information, but you think it might be genuine. Or probably isn't genuine. Just say something. Please.'

'Abigail, I really can't—'

'This is the first approach we've had from a national television station in years. It would do wonders for the profile of the university. And to have a woman professor—'

'What about my professional credibility? I can't just pop up on TV, offering opinions on something I've skimmed over in an email.'

'Just a few words. A sound bite,' pleaded Abigail. And then she played her trump card. 'The principal himself has asked that you do it.'

Esther sighed. There was no way she could say no now. Not if the order had come from the boss himself. 'All right. But I'm going to need some time to read the story.'

'It's in your inbox already!' Abigail was almost squealing with delight. 'Thank you, Professor Hart. Thank you so much. I'll come over to your office at eleven and we'll decide where to do the interview.'

Esther didn't open the email with the transcript. Not yet. She left her office and went to the bathroom to look at her reflection in the mirror. She looked dreadful – washed out, and too thin. Michael had been right. Her hair was long overdue a trim, and she didn't have any make-up on. At least she was wearing a vaguely presentable blouse and dark blue pencil skirt. She'd put her hair up and slap on some make-up. That would have to do.

She went back to her desk and, taking a deep breath, opened the email. She spent the next hour and a half going through the transcript (in which, fortunately, all the changes and corrections from the original had been indicated in the typed text) and reading the theories about when the story might have been written. She checked various Dickens biographies, comparing dates and other writings from the time. It was by no means exhaustive, but at least she could fudge a few answers.

She was massively over-prepared. The interviewer arrived with a cameraman, who couldn't have looked more bored if he tried. The interviewer was a glossy and ambitious young man and didn't bother hiding the fact that he thought this assignment beneath him. He clearly imagined himself standing outside Number Ten, opining on the political news of the day, not interviewing some stuffy old-lady academic about a long-dead writer who may or may not have written something.

They set up in a corner of the library so that there was a background of leather-bound spines over Esther's shoulder. The cameraman arranged a light or two to illuminate the scene. Then he got behind the camera and began to shoot.

'So do you think this manuscript is a real Dickens story?' asked the interviewer, in a way that suggested he didn't much care.

'I'm not an expert in the forensics of handwriting, and I also haven't seen the original, however—'

'Cut, Peter,' the interviewer said to the cameraman. He turned to Esther. 'Listen, can you just answer the question without loads of qualifications?'

'Not really. I can't just throw out a random view.'

'Why not?'

'Well, the information I'm basing my opinion on is scanty at best. I have to explain the limitations of what I'm saying.'

'No one's going to hold you to it,' he said insistently. 'It's for five seconds on the five o'clock news. We'll have dropped this story by tomorrow.'

'Except my academic colleagues,' said Esther firmly. 'Anyway, why didn't you interview the academics who were given the manuscript?'

'They're all the way down in Surrey,' said the interviewer. He didn't even bother to look ashamed.

'Seriously? This is the way the BBC does things?'

'Oh, we're not from the BBC. We're Channel 5.'

She relaxed a fraction then. The Channel 5 news at five? She had thought it a little odd when he'd said the five o'clock, not the six o'clock. She couldn't imagine anyone she knew would be watching a five o'clock news bulletin on Channel 5 on a weekday. She'd still be very careful what she said, but it was unlikely to cause a stir.

She and the presenter wrangled over it for a while, but in the end she got away with saying that the manuscript looked very interesting and promising, and that it contained a few references which might relate to where Dickens was purported to have been at the time. He pressed her quite hard and eventually she said, hesitantly, that she thought there was a possibility it might be genuine. It wasn't too overt a confirmation, she hoped. On balance, she thought she had escaped with her academic credentials intact, even if her hair wasn't up to much. Hopefully press-office Abigail and the principal would be satisfied. She dashed off a text message to Lucie and sent Michael an email, in case he was anywhere near a TV at five o'clock. Then she promptly forgot about it and got on with the real business of the day.

She was just pulling up outside her house at about 5.30 that evening when her phone bleeped with a text message, and before she could reach for it, it started to ring. It was a very excited Abigail. Esther had the sense that this was the biggest coup of her publicity career. Abigail was thrilled and said they had given Esther more screen time than she had expected.

'I've just got in the door,' Esther said, trying to stem Abigail's flood of enthusiastic chatter. 'I haven't actually seen it yet.' Nor would she see it, she realized. There wasn't a catch-up website for Channel 5 like there was for the BBC, was there? She had no idea.

Lucie came to meet her at the door and took the stack of books and papers out of her arms. She was clearly trying to get her attention too. Esther nodded and kept trying to get a word in edgewise so she could get off the call with Abigail. Eventually, she spoke a little sharply. 'Abigail. Abigail!' she barked, in the split second when Abigail drew breath. 'I've just got home. I need to see to my daughter. Can I call you back later?'

'Of course, of course! Ring me back whenever you can. I'm just going to email the principal.'

Esther ended the call and then deliberately switched her phone off before it could ring or beep again.

'See to me?' said Lucie. 'That makes me sound like an infant, or a dog.'

'I had to say something. I was trying to get rid of the press-office lady.'

'You have a press-office lady now? My mum's a celeb.'

'Hardly. Did you see it?'

'Saw it, recorded it, posted pictures on the internet.'

'What?'

'I'm kidding about the last one. I haven't posted any. Yet. I got some with my phone – look.' Lucie held up her phone and Esther saw a pixelated image of her own face, clearly snapped from the TV screen.

'Oh Lord, I look like some kind of mad old-lady academic,' she said, horrified.

'You looked fine. And hardly mad at all,' said Lucie. 'Come and watch it.'

Esther went through to the living room, pausing long enough in the kitchen to grab a glass of wine.

Lucie found the clip with the remote, and Esther watched as a blank-faced news anchor she didn't recognize introduced the story. The young presenter who had come to interview her gave a short introduction over a montage of images from Dickens book covers and TV adaptations. And then suddenly Esther saw herself on screen. She knew many of her lectures were filmed or recorded for students to use as reference, but she had never watched more than a few moments of any of them. This was completely different. There she was in high definition, on her own TV screen at home. She had heard from colleagues who did a lot of television and radio that it was always a shock the first time you saw yourself on screen or heard your voice. They weren't lying. To her own eyes, she looked old. Very old, and haggard; her hair was scraped back from her too-thin face, and her voice sounded high and reedy. She had thought she was relaxed and confident, but she looked ill at ease and amateurish. Worst of all, they had cut what she said to ribbons. They showed her making a few introductory remarks about the context and the time in which the story was written. Then they had shots of her hands (veined and thin, she noted), moving over the copy of the manuscript they had brought with them. But when they cut to her face, they had edited her words significantly. 'Yes,' she said, and then they cut away to her sitting looking at her PC screen, and she heard her own voice saying, 'Every possibility it's genuine'. She knew she hadn't said that in those exact words – it was clearly a clever splicing job, to make her sound more definite than she had been.

'Oh, this is awful!' she said, covering her mouth with her hand. 'I look terrible, and I sound worse... and they've made me say things I didn't say!'

'No, it isn't awful,' said Lucie. 'You look fine. And you sound very professional.'

'If you say I look fine, that means I always look like that. And that makes it worse. That means I've been walking around looking like a haggard old mad cat-lady for years, and no one has told me!'

'Not a haggard old mad cat-lady. Not one of the ones with fur-covered clothes that smell of cat pee. More like a slightly eccentric academic lady who might have a cat or two.'

'Thanks.'

'I'm teasing. You looked fine. And you still have a boyfriend, so you can't be a total hag.'

'That's true. Although I clearly need feeding up. Shall we order pizza?'

'Well, now you're a celebrity, we obviously can't go out to a restaurant. What with the paparazzi and the autograph hunters.'

'And I've given the bodyguards the night off.'

'Pizza it is then. Is Michael coming over?'

'Not tonight. He's got some thrilling faculty meeting that's due to go on till eight or so. He will have missed my star appearance.'

'Poor guy. Can we get pepperoni? And dough balls too?'

Esther ordered pizza and pottered around putting laundry on and tidying the house. The pizza arrived and she and Lucie ate it in front of the TV. She heard the landline phone ring, at the time that Sally usually called, but she left it to go to message. She was grateful for the thought, but she was cautiously content this evening and wanted to enjoy this small bubble of peace with Lucie. Sally would understand.

Lucie found a film she wanted to watch and by the time it had ended and Esther had persuaded her to go to bed it was nearly ten o'clock. She glanced at her watch and idly thought that it was a bit odd that Michael hadn't rung her. Then she remembered clicking off her mobile as she came through the door. She switched it back on and it bleeped several times with texts and voice messages. She was astonished. There were five or six texts and a couple of messages from friends who had seen her on TV, as well as two voice messages from Michael. 'I didn't want to ring the landline,' he said in the second one, 'in case Lucie's already in bed. I'll be up late. Call me.'

That was the third of six messages on her phone. The last three seemed just to be silent, although she thought she could hear someone breathing. Maybe Michael had called again – but why would he have waited for the message tone? Or perhaps it was just a wrong number. She rang Michael. He sounded tired; the meeting had gone on late. He hadn't seen her TV appearance but said he looked forward to seeing the recorded version when he was round at her house the following evening.

'I've just put some toast in and the bath is running,' he said.

'Go,' she said. 'Have a good sleep. I'll see you tomorrow. Love you.'

'Thanks, ditto, ditto and ditto,' he said, and rang off.

She walked through the house, put the last few dishes away in the kitchen and turned off the lights. She was about to head upstairs when her mobile rang again. It could only be Michael at this hour, surely? But the caller display said 'Withheld', and when she answered it, there was silence and breathing on the other end of the line. She said 'Hello?' a few times, but the person didn't reply. She rang off, but the phone rang again immediately.

'Hello?' she answered, then listened to the quiet breathing for a moment. 'I don't know who this is, but stop it, all right? I'm turning my phone off now,' she said. She ended the call and switched her mobile off immediately. Her hands were shaking. It was almost certainly nothing – probably one of those automated cold calls where a machine rang hundreds of numbers and operators answered whoever picked up first. She must have imagined the breathing. Still, it was disconcerting.

She went to her room and plugged her phone into its charger, then went to the bathroom to shower and get ready for bed. When she got into bed ten minutes later, she hesitated, then switched her phone on again. There were three voice messages from the 'Withheld' number. The first two were silent, and in the quiet of her bedroom she could hear the breathing distinctly. She hadn't imagined it. She was about to delete the third message when she heard something, so quick and indistinct she thought she might have imagined it. She played the message again and turned the volume up on her phone. It was quite clear this time. Breath. Breath. And then a whisper. 'Esther.' Click.

CHAPTER TWENTY-FOUR

She didn't mention the whispered message to anyone, although she did leave her mobile phone switched off for the majority of the following day, only turning it on briefly once every few hours to check for messages. There were none, and nor did there appear to be any missed calls.

The principal seemed thrilled by her TV appearance and, just as Michael had predicted, Abigail put a link to the clip on the home-page of the university's website. Esther put up with a little good-natured teasing from her colleagues and from every student she met or taught that day. They had all seen it, but only, she suspected, because Channel 5 showed the Aussie soap operas that all students seemed to adore. If only they would give what happened in *Northanger Abbey* the same attention they gave events on Ramsay Street. Her email pinged constantly with notifications from her Twitter account, people following her or sending congratulations.

She was just getting out of her car that evening when Michael pulled into the road behind her. She waited as he got out of his. He took her in his arms and kissed her, then held her close.

'I've missed you,' he said and, taking her hand, led her into the house.

She made a quick pasta sauce with tomatoes and chilli, and Lucie and Michael set the table. They were all about to sit down to dinner when her mobile, which she'd turned on when she got home, bleeped with a text message. She didn't recognize the number – it wasn't one in her contacts list. Perhaps an advertising message? She clicked to open it. It contained a single word.

'Slut.'

She dropped the phone on the kitchen counter. Michael and Lucie were laughing about something as they carried bowls of pasta to the table. Now wasn't the time. She'd tell Michael about this and the voice mails after dinner. She turned the phone off again, poured herself an enormous glass of wine and joined them at the table.

She drank too much wine with her dinner and kept refilling her glass when they went to sit in the living room. Lucie was pleased to see Michael after a few days' absence and kept chattering excitedly at him. Esther knew she should tell her to go to bed, but she couldn't find the energy. Michael came to sit beside her on the sofa and took her hand. He gently massaged her palm and fingers, all the while listening to Lucie talk about a swimming gala at school. She knew he was being patient and sweet, as he always was, and that she should make a move, take control, send Lucie to bed. But she felt overwhelmed with a horrible lethargy. The little flurry of excitement around her TV appearance had given her a brief respite from her misery about Laura, but somehow the horrible text and the voice message from the night before had thrust her back into a dark place. She didn't want to have to talk about it, to theorize about who it might be, or to deal with it in any way. Maybe she could pretend to lose her phone and have to change her number.

The landline phone rang and she jumped to her feet, adrenaline coursing through her. She could hear her own breath quickening and knew Lucie and Michael were looking at her curiously. Her first thought, irrationally, was that the secret message-leaver had got hold of her home number. But then she glanced at the clock and realized that it was more likely to be Sally. She let out a sigh of relief. 'That'll be Sally,' she said. 'I'll take it upstairs. Lucie, it's time for bed, my lovely.'

She heard Lucie's wail of protest behind her as she grabbed the cordless phone and made for the stairs. But her issuing the order gave Michael tacit authority. She could hear him talking soothingly to Lucie, no doubt offering some breakfast treat as a bribe for an argument-free going to bed.

In the split second before she answered the call, fear almost overcame her. Maybe it wasn't Sally. Maybe it was the anonymous message-leaver after all. 'Hello?' she said cautiously into the phone.

'You're talking very quietly,' said Sally. 'Is this a bad time?'

'No, no… It's a perfect time. I was sinking into the sofa, and I really needed to get moving. You gave me the nudge.'

'How've you been?'

'Busy couple of days. Sorry we didn't get to talk yesterday. I did this television thing…'

'Television thing?' Sally said excitedly.

Esther gave a brief explanation. Sally was disproportionately thrilled. 'Well, that's quite something. I don't think I've ever met anyone who's been on television before. Oh, no, wait… except for Isabella, that time she won the competition.'

Esther smiled. 'I remember that now.' There'd been a competition to find a young architect to design a new canal-side arts centre in Birmingham. It had to incorporate a listed building that took up half the proposed site. Isabella's audacious idea, which incorporated walls covered in plants, solar panels and a water mill, had won. It had led to a brief appearance on the news, Esther recalled. Isabella had been diagnosed with cancer some six months later and hadn't lived to see the centre completed. 'Did they finish the building? After she died?'

'I think so,' said Sally. 'Although I think the design changed quite a bit in the building of it. Budget constraints, you know how it goes.'

Esther did know how it went. She also knew that, had Isabella been fit and well, she would have fought fiercely for the integrity of her design. She wouldn't have stood for contractor kickbacks, or time-wasting, or whatever profligacy had frittered the money away. 'We should go up and see it sometime,' she said vaguely.

'I would love that!' Sally enthused, and Esther instantly regretted her off-hand comment. She couldn't imagine when she might have time to go to Birmingham. And she wasn't sure she would want to spend a weekend away with Sally, no matter how grateful she was for her patient friendship.

'It's one of the things I'm going to do when my car gets delivered,' Sally said. 'Drive around and look at all Isabella's buildings.'

'Wait… Your car?'

'Yes! I passed my test yesterday.'

Esther cursed herself. She had known that Sally was doing her driving test the day before. A good friend would have rung or texted to wish her luck. And a good friend would definitely have remembered to ask her how it went. 'I'm so sorry. I should have asked…'

'Oh, don't worry!' said Sally cheerfully. 'You have such a lot on your plate.'

'How did it go?'

'All right. I had a few minors, but I passed. So now I've ordered the car I always wanted, a Mini convertible. I'll have to wait a few months for them to make it. In the meantime, I've hired a car. Just a little hatchback.'

'Well, huge congratulations! Great to hear you're already on the road.'

'I'll let you know when I'm out and about and which routes to avoid.' Sally giggled.

'I'm sure you'll be fine.' Esther imagined for a moment the freedom that a car would give Sally. She thought of the timid woman she had brought to her house for dinner all those months ago – a woman who had barely left her neighbourhood in years.

'I'd better go,' she said, a little regretfully. Talking to Sally was simpler than the conversation she would have to have with Michael when she went back downstairs. 'Have a lovely evening.'

'I will. I'm going to pick up Paul and Tim and we're off to a pub quiz. They want me to win the music round for them.'

Esther laughed. 'You're a formidable secret weapon. I remember how well you did, the night of the quiz with the amateur dramatics lot.'

'Oh, don't get me started on that evening. That Gavin with the waistcoat? Thought he knew everything? We was robbed!'

Esther felt a tiny pang that she hadn't got an invitation to the pub quiz with Tim and Paul – in the days before she and Stephen had split, she'd been a fixture on the team. But once she became a single parent, she'd had to drop out. At least Sally was getting out more, she told herself.

She popped her head round Lucie's door and delivered the standard admonishments about turning her laptop and phone off and being asleep by ten. Lucie nodded in the standard way, which Esther knew meant she had no intention of doing so. She'd have to come back up and nag in half an hour's time, she knew.

She walked slowly down the stairs, pausing in the kitchen to refill her wine glass and pick up her mobile phone. When she came into the living room, she smiled to see that Michael had dozed off. His head was resting on a cushion and he was snoring very softly. She liked to look at him when he was unaware of her gaze – his face, usually so lively with humour and intelligence, was simply handsome in repose. Absent-mindedly, she clicked her phone on. Immediately it beeped, a sign that she had a message. She was scared to look at it, but she had to.

'Screwing your gigolo with your child in the house? Whore.'

Now she was afraid. Properly, chillingly afraid. The first text might have been a random insult, but this was someone who knew her, someone who had been watching her house and had seen Michael go in with her.

She walked to the window. She wished she was brave enough to whisk the curtains open and stand, defiantly backlit, looking out. But she wasn't. She knew whoever it was might be watching for movement in the middle of the window, so she stepped to one side, pushed back the edge of the curtain and peered out. The street was quiet – she couldn't see any cars she didn't recognize, and there were no pedestrians in sight. Could the stranger be concealed in one of the other houses? Or had he gone?

'What's up?' Michael's voice made her jump. She hadn't realized he was awake. She turned around. 'Just having a look outside,' she said, not sure why she sounded guilty.

'Is everything all right?'

'Yes. No.' She went to sit beside him on the sofa, then opened the text messages and handed him her phone. 'There's a voice message too. Just my name, whispered, so you can't identify the voice. I can't even tell if it's male or female.'

Michael read the texts and then without a word took out his own phone and dialled the sender's number. He listened for a second, then passed the phone to Esther. A recorded voice said, 'The number you have dialled is unavailable. Please try again later.'

'I can google the number, but my guess is that whoever it is has got an unregistered pay-as-you-go SIM card,' he said. 'Do you have any idea who this might be?'

'Not a clue.'

'When did the first one come through?'

'I had a few missed calls on my phone yesterday, after the TV appearance. Then the texts today. Who would have the need to be so nasty? I just don't get it.'

'I don't know what to say. In my experience, some people are just awful – cruel, selfish, desperately trying to make up for inadequacies in their own lives by being cruel to others. Do you want me to ring the police?'

'And tell them what? There are no threats in the messages. I think they'd probably tell us they couldn't do anything.'

'So do we wait for real threats? Or for someone to hurt you?' Michael looked genuinely distressed. 'You think it's some crank who saw you on TV?'

'A crank who has my mobile number and knows where I live?'

'So it has to be someone you know. A disgruntled colleague?'

'In the cut-and-thrust world of Victorian literature? I think that's unlikely.'

'So what do you want to do?' he asked, taking her hand.

'For the moment? Nothing, I think. As I say, there are no actual threats. It's just the sort of nastiness that happens when someone, particularly a woman, is in the public eye, however fleetingly. You read about it happening all the time in the press.'

'Fair point. Still, for the next while, just be careful, okay? Try and come home in daylight. And as much as I can, or as much as you'll let me, I'll be here.'

CHAPTER TWENTY-FIVE

Grief, Esther realized, was a guerrilla fighter. It didn't engage in honest warfare. It didn't plan a sustained attack or agree to a ceasefire. It hid in the jungle and ambushed you when you were least expecting it, when complacency had made you vulnerable, or when your mind was occupied elsewhere. It came for her at 4 a.m. Michael was sleeping peacefully beside her, and she was suddenly awake. As her eyes snapped open in the dim room, she recalled that, moments before, she'd been dreaming about Laura. She was in Laura's kitchen on the Isle of Wight, and they were chatting easily. Laura was pottering around, cooking, baking, tidying, moving constantly, as she always seemed to. Then, without warning, she turned, smiled at Esther and walked out of the kitchen door. In the dream, Esther saw her cross the courtyard to the garage, open the door and close it behind her. She knew Laura was going to gas herself, but, with dreamlike logic, she couldn't be bothered to go and stop her. She'd get round to it, eventually. She had to be on TV first.

Grief and guilt. Twins. How quickly life had crowded in. Here she was, working, living, making love with Michael, worrying about some scumbag who was trying to frighten her with text messages, getting on with things. And Laura was dead, decomposing in her unmarked forest grave. Dead by choice, because she knew Esther would have been too busy to look after her. What would she have done if Laura had asked? She didn't know. She couldn't have dropped everything and gone to the Isle of Wight, or could she? How would she have supported herself? And what about Lucie? Could she have uprooted her daughter? Or could she have brought Laura back to London? How long might Laura have lived? What kind of care would she have needed? She didn't have answers to any of these questions, because she hadn't been given the chance to try and look for them.

She began to imagine scenarios where she might have made it work. The university would undoubtedly have granted her a sabbatical, and she had an income-protection plan, so she might well have been able to make ends meet for a year or so. As for Lucie, she had adored Laura and might have been happy to go to the Isle of Wight, or to have her here in the house in London. Yes, that would have been the more logical choice. London. And Laura would have contributed financially towards her own care; Esther knew from the breakdown of the estate that she had had money. It could have worked. She could have done it, in theory at least.

But then she began to imagine what it might really have been like. She had read up on the condition, and the inevitable outcome was horrible. Slurring, visual impairment, incontinence, dementia. How Laura would have hated the loss of dignity, the increased reliance on help for basic physical needs. As a family, they had never been all that comfortable with physical intimacy; she had no memory of having seen Laura naked, for example. How would they both have felt had she needed to bathe her? Or help her on the toilet? But how minor these things seemed in the face of the alternative – the alternative that Laura had chosen. And how crushing an indictment, that Laura had deemed her incapable of doing these normal, kind, human things. Things that daughters and sons had done for their parents for generations.

She knew then that sleep wouldn't come again that night. Slipping out of bed, she grabbed a dressing gown and went downstairs. She might as well get some work done. Since getting back from the Isle of Wight, she still hadn't fully taken up the reins again at the university. She was fighting fires, lurching from task to task, with no long-term sense of what she was supposed to be doing. Her current research project, a chapter for a new book on Jane Austen, was still just a Word file of sketchy notes. She opened the folder on her computer and looked at the date when it was last saved – well over six weeks ago. She was sure she was supposed to have submitted something by now. She must have a note in her diary somewhere. There were also dozens of emails in her 'Action' folder. She'd skimmed them when they'd come in and then flagged them as needing replies. She did a quick count – there were fifty-two. Well, that was as good a thing as any to do at 4.30 a.m. It wasn't as if there would be any interruptions.

As she worked through the emails, she began to get a disquieting sense that hers was a department in chaos. Maybe chaos was a bit of a strong term, but disarray at least. There seemed to be timetabling issues, budgetary concerns and definitely no real sense of how they would be moving into the new academic year. She knew she should have led all sorts of steering committees and insisted that they had a range of new, exciting and irresistibly relevant modules to offer students for the next year. But she hadn't, and now it was probably too late. In previous years, she would have been able to recite the timetable for submitting module outlines by heart. She'd have known when course guides were being designed, proofed and printed. But this year she had let it slip. Perhaps, during the summer, she could claw it back – beg the communications office to print her some new course guides, maybe set up a series of public lectures or events to improve the profile of English at the university. Perhaps she could call in some favours and get some top-flight guest lecturers, maybe a famous author or two for the twentieth-century modules. She would do her best.

The other rather disquieting thing was a series of emails from the principal's office, the admissions department and the finance office, all asking for statistics on the English Department. Individually, none of these emails was a worry, and they asked for fairly standard information. But opening one after the other, it seemed to Esther that they amounted to a concerted attempt by Central Services to gather data on all aspects of the running of her department. Was this happening across the board? She would have to ask other department heads. And whether it was all departments or just hers, why did they suddenly need to know all these details? She knew from past experience that when senior management started asking for figures, it was because something was wrong and they were looking for something or someone to blame. Was the university in trouble? The humanities faculty? Or just her department?

She spent an hour or so replying to the emails she was able to answer immediately and sent polite holding-off notes to the others, saying she was gathering data and naming a firm date by which she would respond more fully. By the time she had finished, the sun was fully up. She had the heady dizziness and empty feeling that comes from a night without sleep. But she wasn't tired, and the desperate misery of the night had passed, to a certain extent. She wanted to get to work early, try to get things back under control. But Lucie wouldn't be up for another hour, and she'd have to get Michael out of the house too. She'd run. That would use up some time. Luckily she had a full set of running gear in a gym bag downstairs, so she didn't have to risk waking Michael. She got dressed in the downstairs loo, laced up her trainers and slipped out of the front door, pulling it silently closed behind her. She'd do a speedy three-mile loop around the neighbourhood and be back home in half an hour.

It was quiet. The air had the clean, silent expectancy of dawn. A brief rainfall the previous night had freshened the sky and the trees, and the pavement glistened underfoot. She began to jog, slowly, and then, as her muscles warmed up, she picked up the pace. For the first time since she had woken in the night, she felt less frightened and desperate. Running somehow made everything simpler. It was just her body, doing what it was designed to do, being pushed, getting stronger. There were no nuances, no hidden agendas. Just pounding feet and burning lungs.

She ran up a steep incline to the top of a ridge. That climb was a little easier than it had been the week before, although not as easy as it had been at her peak. Maybe she'd put in an extra run a week, try to get back to her optimum levels of fitness. She checked her watch – it was still well before 7 a.m. Maybe she'd make this a slightly longer run; she could go the full length of the ridge before she doubled back to head home. She got her breath back and began to set an easy, loping pace along the road. She had come out without a phone or iPod, so she was running without any music. She liked hearing the muffled thud of her feet on the pavement and the even sound of her breathing. There was no one else about.

It was because it was so quiet that she heard the car well before it reached her. It was moving slowly, in a low gear, coming along the road behind her. She half-glanced back as it drew abreast. It was a silver Vauxhall Corsa or something similarly nondescript. The person who was driving saw her, slowed down, then came to a halt some ten feet in front of her. She stopped dead. What a fool. Here she was, out in the deserted street, alone. The houses in this road were set well back from the road – even if she called out, she wasn't sure anyone would hear her, assuming they were awake. And she had no phone to alert the police. If this was the stalker message person, or indeed anyone who wished her harm, she had made herself as vulnerable as she possibly could be. Well, unless they were going to mount the pavement and run her down, they would have to get out of the car to catch her. She wasn't going to make it easy for them. She started to run again, staying close to the hedges of the houses – out of grabbing range, should someone from the passenger side try and lunge at her. She passed the car and began to run faster, heading up a slight rise. There was a side road up ahead, which would take her back down to the main road. She was just about to cross the road and run down it when she heard a voice calling her name.

'Esther!'

A female voice. She broke stride for a second and glanced back at the car. The driver had opened the door and stepped out beside the vehicle. It was a woman, not very tall, but the sun was behind her and Esther couldn't see her face.

'Esther!' the voice said again. 'Sorry, did I scare you?'

Sally. It was Sally. Esther stopped running and, rather shamefacedly, walked back towards the car.

'Sorry,' she said lamely. 'Running alone, this early, it's not usually a good idea to stop for cars you don't know.'

'Of course not. I'm so sorry. I couldn't sleep, so I thought I'd go out for a drive, and there you were. It was lovely to see you, so I stopped. I didn't mean to give you a fright.'

'Don't worry,' said Esther. 'It's just me being a bit paranoid. I'm not usually like this.'

'Bad night?'

'You could say that. I also couldn't sleep, so I've been up for hours, working.'

'Is it your mum?'

'Partly. Lots of other stuff too, but mainly Mum.'

'I don't want to keep you, if you're running. But... just to say, if you want to talk, you know, get a cup of coffee...'

Esther was suddenly tired of her own company, of struggling with the demons inside her own head. 'That'd be nice,' she said gratefully. 'I've run far enough, I think.'

'There's a nice little café at the roundabout down the hill,' said Sally. 'I think they cater for the building trade, so they're open early. It's a bit basic, but the coffee is very good.'

'It sounds lovely, but I'm worried Lucie and Michael will wake up and not know where I am. I don't even have my phone with me. We could go back to mine, if you like.'

'Are you sure? I mean, I don't want to be in the way...'

'Of course you won't be in the way.' Esther smiled. 'Lucie would love to see you, you know that.'

'Well, only if you're sure.' Sally hesitantly got back into the car.

Esther went round to the passenger side and got in. She watched Sally in the driving seat and was reminded of the time she had collected her for dinner. This version of Sally looked very different – slimmer, brighter, more confident – but deep down, that fussy, old-lady uncertainty was still apparent if you knew her well. Sally took long moments to fasten her seatbelt and settle it comfortably across her lap and over her shoulder. Then she started the car, checked all her mirrors, put on the indicator even though there was no other car or person visible anywhere nearby, and pulled slowly back out on to the road. She drove tentatively and carefully, checking her mirrors with textbook regularity and slowing down to a crawl for every corner. She seemed uncertain of the route, and Esther had to tell her where to turn.

'I haven't quite got the hang of this navigation thing yet.' She smiled. 'The bus just takes you where you want to go. Now I have to work out where to turn and whether there's parking – it's a whole new world.'

They pulled up outside Esther's house, and Esther looked up at the windows. The living room curtains were still closed – a sign that the inhabitants were still asleep. 'Come on,' she said. 'We may have to be a bit quiet if Lucie and Michael aren't up yet.'

They came through the front door and into the warm, still air of the slumbering house. Esther kicked off her running shoes. 'Let's go into the kitchen,' she said softly. She put on a pot of coffee and drank down a big glass of water. When the coffee had finished brewing, she heated some milk and frothed it to make them each a latte.

'Oooh, posh coffee!' said Sally appreciatively, sniffing it as Esther put it down in front of her.

'Any more in the pot?' A sleepy-eyed Michael came into the kitchen. To Esther's relief, he was wearing pyjama bottoms and a T-shirt. Nevertheless, he looked rumpled and sexy and very much just tumbled out of bed. He came over and kissed her. 'Been running, you two?'

Sally giggled. 'She has, not me. I was just out for an early-morning drive.'

Michael glanced at the clock. 'A very early-morning drive,' he said.

'Sally's just got her licence,' said Esther. 'It's still a novelty, I think.'

'I wish I had the courage to drive a bit further,' said Sally. 'I'd be in Wales by now.'

'You'll get more confident,' said Esther. 'The world is yours now.'

She poured Michael a coffee and then ran upstairs to rouse Lucie for school. Lucie, who had been a chirpy, morning person as a small child, had gradually become more sullen and difficult in the mornings. She always stayed up too late and then found it almost impossible to get up on time. She hated rushing but ended up doing so every morning and then taking out her frustrations on Esther. Mornings had become something of a battleground, and Esther rather dreaded them. When Michael was there, Lucie made a small effort to be civil at least, but Esther was by no means sure how she would react to hearing that Sally was in the kitchen too.

'Hi, lovely,' she said softly, speaking to the top of Lucie's head, which was all she could see above the duvet. 'It's 7.30.'

Silence.

'Lucie,' she said a little bit louder.

Still nothing.

'Lucie.' She allowed a little annoyance to creep into her voice. Time was moving on, and she also had to shower and dress.

At that moment, Sally and Michael both laughed loudly in the kitchen below. Lucie rolled over and one baleful eye stared out over the top of the duvet. 'Who the hell is that?'

Esther sighed. 'Sally.'

'Sally? What's she doing here?'

'I bumped into her when I was out running. She came back for coffee.'

Michael said something quite loudly, downstairs. The words weren't clear, but it was obviously the punchline of a joke, because he and Sally laughed again.

'It's like a bloody bus station down there. Bloody hell, Mum.' Lucie turned over onto her stomach and pressed her face into the pillow.

'Firstly, language. I know you've just woken up, but there's no need to swear. And secondly, I thought you liked Sally.'

'I do. But not at dawn. I don't like anyone at dawn. Especially not cheerful people.'

'I know that. You make that abundantly clear. But Sally's here, and Michael's here, and the clock is ticking.'

'Is there going to be a queue for the bloody... For the shower?'

'I don't think Sally came round here planning to shower, and you have to be out of the house first, so if I were you, I'd dive into the bathroom now, while Michael finishes his stand-up routine downstairs. I'll hop in when you're done. And in the meantime I'll make you some toast.'

'How about pancakes?'

'In your dreams, sunshine. Toast or porridge, that's my final offer.'

'Porridge and brown sugar,' said Lucie, throwing back the duvet. On her way out of the room, she kissed Esther quickly on the cheek. It might require bribery to keep her daughter sweet, but she'd take it.

She went into her room and put clothes out ready to get dressed in after her shower. She was about to head back down to make Lucie's breakfast when a wave of tiredness overcame her. She had been up for hours already, and the day had hardly begun. She lay down on the bed for a second, resting her head on the cool of the pillow. She could so easily doze off, but there was so much to do. She needed to get into work to begin to sort out the mess and neglect she had uncovered in the early hours. But it wasn't her sense of duty that got her up and moving – it was the sound of Sally's laughter, drifting up the stairs again.

Esther padded down the stairs silently, in her socks. She could have stepped directly from the hallway into the kitchen, but instead she went through the living room. Michael was leaning against the kitchen counter, his back to her, his ankles crossed and his arms folded. He looked relaxed and happy and was telling a story about a work colleague who had fallen off his bicycle as he arrived on campus the previous week. Michael told a good story. He had a vivid turn of phrase and good comic timing. And there was no doubt that Sally was an appreciative audience. She stood by the sink, the sun glinting off her blonde curls. Her eyes were bright with laughter, and she watched Michael eagerly, waiting for his next punchline.

'…arse over tit in front of the statue of Queen Victoria, in the middle of the quadrangle!' He finished, and Sally let out a delighted peal of laughter. Her breasts rose and fell under her sheer, white blouse.

As Esther stepped into the room, she watched Sally's face. She was visibly surprised to see Esther entering from another direction, and was Esther imagining it or did she look a little guilty? Simultaneously, she saw her own reflection in the kitchen window, over Sally's shoulder – her sweaty hair still scraped back in a ponytail, the lines that ran from her nose to her mouth like two deep, dark grooves, and her own small breasts, flattened and shrunken under her sports bra and Lycra running top.

'I'm making porridge,' she said shortly. 'Anyone want some?'

'Oh, er, not for me,' said Sally. 'I should probably be getting back…'

'I'd better run through a shower,' said Michael.

'Lucie's gazumped you, so you'll have to wait.' Esther began measuring out oats and milk. Her entrance seemed to have caused an odd tension in the room, and the laughter and jollity had ebbed away instantly. She should have felt guilty, but she didn't.

CHAPTER TWENTY-SIX

It had been two days since the last message, and Esther allowed herself to relax slightly. It had probably been some crank from her past, offended somehow by seeing her on TV. She got into work early each day and powered through as much as she could, trying to make up for the weeks of inattention that had followed Laura's death. The deeper she dug, the more disquieting the information she discovered. Student numbers were down, and a few of the more lucrative research grants were coming to an end without any new investments to replace them. Was it just a bad time for humanities? With the rise in tuition fees, were students investing in degrees that would be more likely to get them a high-paying job? Certainly the principal seemed to think so, with his marketing buzzwords and his relentless drive for every piece of literature to contain information on 'employability'. It didn't sit comfortably with Esther. She believed in old-fashioned scholarship – in learning for the sake of learning, in the beauty of discovery for young people. She didn't want to create modules that pushed them into narrow career paths before they'd even begun to open their minds.

After a frustrating morning spent editing a brochure for an upcoming recruitment fair, she set off to get coffee in the staff common room. The head of the Drama Department was ahead of her in the queue. Craig Shaw was a compact, bouncy man of forty. He came from a professional theatre background, not as an actor but as an agent. He'd worked in the industry for a number of years before opting to return to university to do a PhD. He'd stayed on as a lecturer and with his uncommon energy and drive had risen swiftly through the ranks to become head of department. He was short and chunky with blonde hair cut in a bristly cap. He always appeared to exude great passion when he spoke (he had worked in LA and seemed to have absorbed some American positivity), and the more excited he got, the pinker his cheeks glowed. Esther had always found him congenial enough, although he had a tendency to get camp and bitchy after a few drinks, which made her a little wary.

'Craig,' she said, by way of greeting.

'Lovely Esther,' he replied, swooping in to kiss her cheek. 'It's been ages.'

She took a step back, surprised by both the kiss and the miasma of aftershave that surrounded him. He was usually effusive, but this was super-friendly, even for Craig.

'All good?' he asked.

'All… okay.'

'I heard about your mother.' He affected a sympathetic frown. 'Condolences.'

'Thank you.'

'Well, these things take time. Make sure you look after yourself. You're looking strained.'

'I will,' she said, not sure how to respond to his blunt assessment of her appearance. 'Listen, Craig, are you in a hurry? Do you have five minutes to chat?'

He pulled out his phone and scrolled quickly through his calendar. 'I've got five minutes, yes. Not much more than that. Let's grab a seat.'

Esther got her coffee and joined him at the table he'd chosen, right in the middle of the room. She'd have preferred to be in one of the window seats, or a corner, but she didn't want to cause a fuss by asking to move.

'So, what's up?' Craig took a container of sweeteners out of his pocket and dropped a tablet into his coffee.

'It's not so much that something's up,' said Esther carefully. 'I just wanted to get a sense of what you thought about the… climate.'

'Climate?'

'In higher education. In humanities. In the university.'

'It's cooking!' Craig said with uncommon enthusiasm. 'We've had a bit of a shift in application and enrolment…' By 'shift', Esther assumed he meant 'reduction'. '… but I feel really bullish. If we create an irresistible offering, and we prove to students that if they graduate with us, they'll have enhanced—'

'If you say employability, I may have to scream,' said Esther drily.

'Well, that's what it's all about.'

'Is it?'

'In the current climate, if we want to keep our jobs, it is,' he said flatly, and she saw he wasn't being quite as affable and twinkly as before.

'Really? Do you think it's that bad?'

'The days of the dusty ivory tower, where we all sit around day-dreaming and having deep thoughts about art and literature, are over. We have to move with the times.'

'Like sharks,' said Esther.

'Sharks?'

'Move or die.'

She got home that evening feeling weary, sticky and grimy in the oppressive summer heat. It was a Friday, and Lucie had gone to a friend's house for a sleepover and movie evening. Michael had drinks after work and would be coming round later. Esther was too hot and uncomfortable to eat anything, so she had a quick, cool shower and put on a loose cotton shift dress. She poured herself a glass of cold white wine and went out to water the garden, which was wilting.

It was mercifully quiet, and she could hear the birds singing and the distant hum of traffic. The garden was ragged and neglected. She would have to do some work on it over the weekend. How Laura would have frowned to see the weeds and unkempt lawn. It was in quiet moments like this that Esther allowed herself to fantasize about what might have been – how Laura might have sat on the back veranda telling her what to do, pointing out which plants needed cutting back and which needed moving to a sunnier spot. How she might have told Laura about her concerns about work, and what her mother would have said. It was Laura who had given Esther her love for teaching and her faith in the value of education. Laura had had a clear-eyed and definite view about the vistas that were opened up to young people through reading and discussion. Esther could just imagine Laura's sardonic expression on hearing about the principal's PowerPoint presentations full of visions and mission statements and marketing objectives. 'Good grief,' she'd have said, 'just teach them. Get them to read everything, get them to question everything. They'll be fine.'

Esther attached the sprinkler head to the hosepipe and put it into a flower bed, turning it on and watching rainbows forming in the droplets. A moment of peace. The pain didn't go away, and her anger at Laura came and went, but for the moment she just missed her, and wished things had turned out differently.

Her phone, which she had left on the patio table, beeped with a message. Maybe Michael had got bored at the drinks event and was coming over early. She scooped it up and opened the message without looking at who it had come from.

'Scrawny female,' it said. 'No one would want to fuck you.'

Later that evening, she logged on to her computer. Her email inbox instantly filled with Twitter notifications. She had been mentioned in twenty or so tweets. Each one came from a different account and each account had an anonymous egg as its avatar, a gibberish name, no followers and no previous tweets. The tweets were much the same as the phone messages – invariably insulting and usually obscene. As soon as she blocked and reported a tweet, another few accounts would spring up, hydra-like, spewing more of the same ugly invective.

The messages and tweets trickled in throughout the weekend. Vile as they were, none of them contained threats of violence or rape, so as there was no direct risk to her safety, Esther knew that the police would be unlikely to do anything. The phone messages came from three or four different numbers, but she didn't try to ring any of them to see if someone would answer. As each one arrived, she read it, then closed the messages folder on her phone. She wished she could delete them all, but she knew that she would need them as evidence. She also didn't tell anyone, not even Michael, that they were still coming. She knew if she told him, he would stop her from doing what she knew she had to do.

On Monday morning, she left home very early and went into town. A Google search had given her the location of the offices, and she stationed herself across the road, opposite the entrance, from 8 a.m.

He arrived at work at about ten to nine. She saw his tall, gangly frame hurrying up the pavement towards his office, head bowed, leather satchel over his shoulder. For a moment, she regarded him dispassionately. How had she thought, even for an instant, that he was attractive? There was something pinched and nasty in his face, just as there had been that night she'd glimpsed him in the street after the amateur dramatics quiz.

She crossed the road quickly and stood in front of him, just as he turned to walk into the office building.

'Phil,' she said, trying to make her voice as firm and authoritative as she knew how.

A kaleidoscope of expressions crossed his face. She couldn't hope to read them all, but she thought she saw shock, guilt and triumph. Equally quickly, he wiped his features clean and smiled at her with bland politeness.

'Hello,' he said carefully. 'What a surprise.'

'It's not a coincidence.'

'No?'

'You have five minutes to talk, I trust?'

He made a show of glancing at his watch. 'Not really...'

'I wasn't actually asking,' she said. 'There's a little independent coffee shop a block or so away. As you have a Starbucks opposite your building and a Costa downstairs, I'm guessing your co-workers don't go to that one. Let's go there, shall we?'

She didn't look to see that he was following, just turned and walked towards the coffee shop.

His curiosity must have got the better of him, because he did follow. She went into the coffee shop, snatched a bottle of water out of the cooler and took it to a table to justify their presence there. She sat down, her back to the wall, and regarded him as he settled himself opposite her.

'You've been leaving me messages and sending me tweets,' she said, without preamble.

'I… what? No.' Despite his protestations, she could see she had him on the back foot.

'At first I had no idea who it was. I remembered our encounter and I wondered if it might be you, but there was no way to prove anything. Then in the message you sent on Friday, you referred to me as a "female". There's something dismissive and hateful about calling a woman a female, and I remembered you'd done it in the nasty email you sent when I cancelled our dinner.'

'You're crazy,' he said coldly. 'I always thought you were unbalanced. Menopausal.'

'Now, now, Phil,' she said coolly. 'Don't add insult to injury, as it were. I have a record of all the numbers you used to send messages, and I've reported all your tweets to Twitter, so they'll have a record too. I'm sure the police will enjoy tracing where the messages were sent from. I'm guessing you were sitting all alone in your sad little flat, or at work, when you sent them? They're very good at pinpointing locations these days. Within a few yards, I believe.'

She had absolutely no way of knowing whether or not this was true, but she was banking on the fact that Phil wouldn't know either. 'And I bet you haven't had the chance to get rid of those SIM cards either. They may well still be at your home. Shall I ring the police now?' She put her hand in her bag to take out her phone.

'It wasn't me,' he said cravenly. 'It was Gillian.'

'Who?' She was momentarily stumped, and then she remembered Phil's colleague, whom she'd met that first night after the Tate. The woman had taken a dislike to her there and then and, she recalled, had said some nasty things to Phil after the fact, which he'd then relayed to her in his email. 'Gillian? Why?'

'I was very cut up about you,' he admitted, looking down at his long, bony hands, which were resting on the table. 'You were the first woman I had been with after my wife died, and when it didn't work out, well...'

'Well what?'

'I was quite bitter. Quite... put off women.'

'And Gillian offered you a shoulder to cry on.'

'She was very supportive.'

'Did she have an ulterior motive perhaps?'

'Like what?' Phil looked baffled.

'Wanting you for herself?'

Phil looked at Esther as if she was mad. 'But she's not my type at all. She's much too old, and she's very... hefty.' The way he said it, so dismissively, made Esther realize that he didn't see Gillian as a woman at all. If she knew how he viewed her, it was unsurprising she was bitter and vengeful.

'So...?'

'I was just starting to get over it, and then I saw you on television. Showing off. Making yourself the centre of attention, as usual.'

His take on that was so deranged and irrational, it wasn't even worth questioning. She just sat silently and waited for him to continue.

'I was off work that day, off sick with a cold. I wouldn't usually be sitting on the sofa at five o'clock, watching Channel 5. It was almost like a sign, seeing you. And you looked... I don't know. Like I remembered you. But sad.'

'My mother died,' she heard herself saying. She wasn't sure why she felt the need to tell him that.

'So I tried to ring you, but it kept going to message. And then I started remembering what it was like to touch you, and how I hadn't got to do it again, and I started to drink. I opened a bottle of wine.'

He was bad with alcohol. She remembered that. He was fit, and couldn't hold his drink, and didn't seem to know when to stop.

'I kept trying to get you, and finally, quite late, you answered the phone, and then I couldn't speak. It was too much, hearing you speak. Then you turned the phone off again, and all I could do was listen to your voice in the outgoing message.'

'You whispered my name,' she said.

'Did I? I don't remember.'

'But you didn't stop there. You came and parked outside my house.'

'I'd done it before,' he said, as if in some way this made it better. 'But I always seemed to miss you coming and going. And then I did see you, with that man...'

She nodded. She wasn't going to say Michael's name to him, or give him any more information or ammunition.

'That man... touching you.' She was disturbed to see that his hands were actually shaking. 'I left then, and I went to see Gillian and told her what I'd seen.'

'And she comforted you.'

'She was very nice. And she said you were obviously someone of loose morals, and you probably needed to be taught a lesson. She had a collection of these pay-as-you-go SIM cards at her flat, the kind you get in a bundle when you buy a new phone. "Text her," she said, "Tell her what you think of her."'

'Slut.'

'Yes.'

'That's what you texted. What you thought. That because I'm in a relationship with someone that isn't you, I'm a slut? You need help, Phil, honestly.'

His face twisted into a grimace. She couldn't quite work out what it was. Was he angry? Laughing at her? But then, to her horror, she saw he was crying.

'I didn't want to do it. I didn't. But I was so hurt and lonely and Gillian kept telling me I deserved better than you.'

'You don't know anything about me. We met a few times, that's all,' said Esther. 'We had sex once. This has nothing to do with me and everything to do with your own unhappiness.'

'I know.' He sobbed. 'I'm sorry. I won't do it again.'

'I have a record of every message. And I've recorded this conversation,' she said, holding up her phone so he could see the blinking red light on the screen. 'You've admitted it was you. If you ever contact me again, I'm going to the police. If I see you anywhere near my house, I'll have you arrested so fast, you won't know what hit you.'

She clicked the voice recorder off, pocketed her phone and dropped a pound coin on the table to pay for the unopened bottle of water.

'Goodbye, Phil,' she said. 'I'm sorry your life isn't what you want it to be.'

He nodded, staring down at the table, and let out a long, shuddering sigh. And then, in the moment before she turned and walked away from him, he looked up and stared her full in the face. His mouth was twisted in a grin, a ghastly parody of a cheeky smile.

'You may think you're queen bee and in command, but you're still just a scrawny slut no one would want to fuck,' he said, coldly and clearly.

CHAPTER TWENTY-SEVEN

The Dickens story was a fake. Someone had been kind enough to pop into Esther's office and leave a copy of the Metro newspaper on her desk, open at the appropriate page. It had been an elaborate hoax, by a conman who had spent months creating a counterfeit document. He might have got away with it, but an eagle-eyed Dickens specialist in York had spotted a discrepancy in spelling, which meant it was highly unlikely to be a real Dickens story. The academics had called in a forensics expert, who found that while the paper was of the correct age, the ink was modern and had been painstakingly aged. The article took the time to name-check some of the academics who had been taken in by the story, and Esther saw her own name staring up at her from the page. She sat down at her desk and sighed. Naturally, anyone who had fallen for the deception would look like a gullible fool who didn't know their subject, and the newspaper was quick to see this and rub it in. It didn't matter that she hadn't actually said she believed the story was authentic. There was no point in saying that what she'd said had been taken out of context and cunningly edited. Given the choice, she would never have made a statement at all, but she hadn't been given a choice. The university PR machine had been quick to put her on the front page of the website when the story was glamorous and high-profile, but she was certain that they would be very quiet now. She was highly unlikely to get the support of the principal if anyone started asking questions.

Sighing, she booted up her computer and, sure enough, there were two emails from journalists asking her to comment on the fact that she had declared the document authentic. There was also a 'sympathetic' email from a colleague from Loughborough. 'It was a gamble to say something one way or the other. Sorry you bet on the wrong side,' it said. She deleted the email in a fit of pique. She hadn't 'bet'; she'd been bullied. Well, never again.

She wanted to stay in her office and hide, but she had to lecture to a vast crowd of first-year students and then attend a meeting with the other humanities departmental heads. She detested lecturing the first years – it was always an enormous group, often as many as five or six hundred, and very few of them were genuinely interested in the subject. It was just a module to them. It wasn't so much lecturing as speaking blindly into a cloud of indifference, pouring her words into a room full of slouched bodies, their phones held loosely in one hand, thumbs incessantly scrolling.

She gathered her notes and the memory stick that held her PowerPoint presentation and set off for the lecture theatre. She was usually early for lectures, but the emails had delayed her and she got there at one minute past the allotted start time. The lecture theatre was full, and there was an expectant buzz in the room. The students all went quiet as she came in. This in itself was unusual. Normally she had to use a sharp, teacher's voice to call them to attention. 'Sorry I'm late,' she said. 'We'll begin straight away.'

She walked over to the lectern, preparing to plug the memory stick into the PC. She heard a titter pass through the room and looked round. Someone had uploaded a picture to the computer and projected it onto the screen. It was a portrait of Dickens, one of the famous Herbert Watkins photographs. The picture was reproduced twice, but some wag had Photoshopped a dress onto the right-hand image and coloured Dickens' lips a lurid pink. 'Spot the fake' said the caption. The students couldn't contain themselves, and they all burst into delighted laughter as they watched Esther stare at it.

'Yes, yes, very witty,' she said, plugging in her memory stick and bringing up her own PowerPoint slide as quickly as she could. 'I think I can spot the real Dickens in this case.'

It took an age for the students to settle down, and she knew she would struggle to hold their attention. She was speaking on the character of Doctor Manette in *A Tale of Two Cities*. It was one of her favourite lectures, and she usually valued the input from students. It was a book which captured the imagination of many, and she liked to open the floor to questions and get a sense of their views. Today, however, she would not. She would keep talking, no matter what, allowing no time for queries or interjections. She wasn't fielding a series of wise-cracking comments from a bunch of spotty kids who had left school ten minutes ago. She ploughed through the lecture, barely pausing for breath, expanding on some points to fill the time and staring at the computer screen rather than making eye contact with any of the students. When she reached the last slide and glanced at her watch, she was profoundly relieved to see that it was the end of the period. She immediately gave the students their reading

244

assignment for the next class and exited hurriedly without saying goodbye.

The departmental heads meeting was little better. She sensed the ripple that went through the room as she came in and took her place at the table. No one said anything, but she could feel their eyes on her. Aristotle had been right, of course. We like tragedies because they arouse pity and fear. Pity for the victim and fear for ourselves, because we can envision ourselves in that situation. Well, let them enjoy her tragedy, she thought fiercely. It could have happened to any of them.

'Hi there,' said Craig softly, slipping into the seat next to her. 'How are you doing?' he breathed into her ear, his voice honeyed and soft. 'Bad luck,' he whispered. 'Such bad luck.'

Except Craig, she reminded herself. It would never have happened to Craig. He was far too much of a shark to get caught out.

After the meeting, he made a point of walking out with her. He stopped just outside the door. 'Coffee?' he said, his voice dripping with faux sympathy.

'I'd love to,' she said evenly, 'but I really don't have time.'

'Of course you don't. What with everything that's going on. So, this Dickens thing is a bitch, isn't it?' He had managed to stand in such a way that he was blocking her exit. She would have to push past him or ask him to move in order to escape.

'Well, these things happen.'

'Of course they do. Especially when your stock-in-trade has been research and teaching rather than talking to the media. It's easy to make a blunder.'

'I didn't make a—'

'I saw you've been having rather a hard time on Twitter too.'

'On Twitter?'

'I saw your mentions. Some really nasty trolls.'

'Troll, singular. I've dealt with it.'

'It happens, you know, especially to women in the public eye, and especially if you're not internet savvy. Maybe you could get someone to manage your online profile for you? A graduate student? Take the pressure off.'

'I said I dealt with it. It'll stop now,' she said, sounding less convinced than she wanted to.

'Well, think about it. It's not a sign of weakness to ask for help.' He patted her on the arm and walked away before she could respond.

That evening she was viciously chopping vegetables for a stew when Michael arrived. They had exchanged emails during the day, so he knew what had happened. He let himself in – she had given him a key some weeks before – and came to kiss her. She heard the clink of glass in the shopping bag he held. 'I know it's a school night,' he said, 'but I thought it was a good time for a large glass of wine.'

'It is, it really is,' she said gratefully, and he went to find glasses and a corkscrew.

Esther took the glass that Michael offered and wandered through to the living room. Lucie must have brought in the stack of post when she came in from school, and she had left it on Esther's desk. Esther picked up the letters and leafed through them. There were the usual bills and charity requests, a reminder about her tax return, and a square envelope which contained what felt like a card. It was much too late to be a birthday card. It had to be some kind of invitation. She opened it, and sure enough, the front image showed a pretty thatched cottage with window baskets and an apple tree. The word 'Housewarming' curled in pretty script across the top of the card.

Esther opened it.

Dear Esther, Michael and Lucie,
Please join me in wetting the roof of my new home.

There was a date, a Sunday four months or so hence, and an address in an area not far from Esther's house, a leafy, villagey part of north London – expensive and rather fashionable.

The card was from Sally. Esther raised her eyebrows. Sally? She was moving? How had she managed that? And why had she not said anything?

'You look surprised,' said Michael, coming into the living room, glass in hand.

She held out the card to him. He read it quickly. 'Ah, so she managed to get them to complete,' he said.

'What? You knew she was buying a new place?'

'Yes, she told me the morning she came back here with you. I thought you knew.'

'No, I didn't know. And she's bought in Mill Hill? How did she manage? I imagine she's got a tiny little flat.'

'No, I think it's a house. Two or three bedrooms, I think she said. I forget.'

'A three-bedroomed house in Mill Hill? Now? In the middle of a housing boom?' Esther couldn't keep the incredulity out of her voice.

'What do you know about Sally's financial situation?' asked Michael.

'Nothing. Well, nothing but the fact that she's never really worked. And she's not working now. I assumed she was claiming some form of benefit.'

'She's not.'

'Really?' said Esther, surprised. 'What do you know?'

'To put it crudely, she's absolutely loaded.'

'Loaded? Like—'

'A millionaire. More than. Several times over.'

'How? I mean… How?'

'I don't know all the details, but she was your friend Isabella's sole heir, more or less. And Isabella's house was something special, I'm told...'

'She designed it herself. It was unique, and rather beautiful. Very airy.'

'Sally said she hung onto it for a few years before she sold it. I don't know what she got for it, but it was a lot. And Isabella had a life-insurance policy too, which seems to have paid out significantly. Add to that her mum's house and estate...'

'Good grief.'

'She didn't tell me a lot, but it sounds like she was very cautious in her investments, so she weathered the financial crash very well. She's absolutely minted. She'll certainly never have to work, if she doesn't want to.'

'How did I not know this?'

'Because you didn't ask,' said Michael, and there was something in his voice that made her look up sharply.

'I'm not in the habit of enquiring about people's financial situations,' she said defensively. 'I don't usually check my friends' bank statements.'

'But you would usually know something about a friend's situation. You'd know if they owned their own home, and you would have an inkling if they were struggling, I'm sure.'

'What are you saying?'

'I suppose I'm asking why you have a problem with Sally.'

'What? I don't have a problem with Sally. She's a friend, that's all. Not a close one.'

'She thinks of you as a close friend. As a very precious friend, in fact.'

'Oh God,' said Esther, exasperated. 'I can't really be dealing with guilt about Sally right now, from you of all people. I've had a shitty day...'

'What do you mean, from me of all people?'

'I saw you and her cosying up in the kitchen the other day.'

'Cosying... what?' Michael couldn't help himself. He actually laughed out loud. 'Good grief.'

Esther couldn't stop herself; she kept talking. 'You were smiling and laughing, all warm and intimate, and she was wearing that ridiculous transparent blouse...'

'We were talking about house prices. Not really sexy talk.' He looked at her hard. 'Are you accusing me of something?'

'No... I...'

'Are you asking if I fancy Sally? If I'm thinking of running off with the buxom heiress? Because I'm not. And the suggestion is both rude and slightly insane.'

'So I'm a hysterical female, is that it?' Esther found herself yelling.

Michael's voice was cold. 'I'm not even going to dignify that with a response. I'm not your psycho ex, okay?'

They stared at each other, bristling, for a long moment. Esther had a sudden out-of-body experience, a view of herself – angry, irrational, attacking the one person she needed most as her ally. She had to stop.

'You are supposed to be on my side,' she said, a little weakly.

He looked at her, his eyes so dark they were almost black. 'I am utterly on your side, and I don't believe I've ever given you cause to believe otherwise. What I don't understand is why you've decided Sally isn't.'

CHAPTER TWENTY-EIGHT

'Hi, Sally, this is Esther. Just a quick call to see how you're doing. I'm so excited to hear your good news. We'd love to come to your housewarming. What a great new beginning. Anyway, give me a call when you have a moment.'

She would try. She really would. Michael was right. Somehow, she had become resentful of Sally, suspicious even, and there was no cause for this. Sally was a gentle, harmless woman, with limited life experience, who just wanted to be friends. So she would make an effort to be a better friend, to get to know Sally, to repay the compliment Sally had given her by wanting to be her friend. She could do that. After all, everyone else seemed to adore her – there must be more to her than Esther was currently seeing.

Sally returned her call within the hour.

'So sorry I missed you,' she said breathlessly. 'I was out for a run.'

'A run?'

'Well, a little jog and a walk, you know. I'm trying to shift some more weight, and my Weight Watchers' leader says it's all about exercise. Now, how are you?'

Where to begin? Should she tell Sally about the Dickens fiasco at work? About her uneasy truce with Michael? About Lucie, who was reaching maximum sulk now that Stephen's wife Melissa was getting closer to giving birth? Should she tell Sally how she felt scrawny and unfeminine? About how she'd been stalked and harassed by a horrible man she'd gone on three dates with?

'I'm fine,' she said. 'I really rang because I wanted to hear all about you and your new house.'

'Oh, not much to tell,' said Sally, but Esther could hear she was thrilled to be asked. 'I just decided that at my advanced age, it was time to have a place I could call my own. And now I have the car, I'm not so limited by bus routes and so on. I've always loved Mill Hill...'

'It's a lovely area.'

'So I just started looking, and I found a place right on top of the hill that I just fell in love with.'

'I can't wait to see it.'

'Well, would you...' Sally hesitated. 'Would you like to come and see it this weekend? I've completed and I have the keys... I'm just having a few little bits done before I move in.'

'I'd love to,' said Esther. And she meant it.

Sally picked her up in her smart little car on Saturday morning, and they meandered through the suburbs to Mill Hill. It was a lovely area, set in acres of green fields yet still close to town, with access to the Tube. Esther herself would have loved to live there, but it was well beyond her means. Sally's place was much bigger than she had expected, a detached, two-storey house set back from the road. There was a crescent-shaped gravel driveway in front of the house, and a big oak tree nearby cast dappled shade.

On one side of the driveway was a skip filled with broken kitchen cabinets, which made Sally's comment about having a 'few little bits done' seem like rather an understatement.

'Are you putting in a new kitchen?'

'The old one was a bit shabby.' Sally looked a little embarrassed. 'My estate agent suggested I should do it. Make the house more saleable, he said. Not that I plan to sell it.' She scrabbled in her handbag and brought out a key. 'Shall we?'

It was very quiet when Esther stepped out of the car. She couldn't hear any traffic, just the music of birdsong. Sally crunched over the gravel to the front door and she followed. The house was empty of furniture and clean, although there was a fine film of dust on the floor from the renovations.

It was beautiful. The rooms were elegantly proportioned, with big sash windows which looked over a small garden and then out over the fields, as if the house was in the middle of the countryside rather than a few miles off the North Circular. There was something calming about the emptiness of the rooms, with their pristine, newly painted walls. It was as if the house waited, in a hush of expectation, for the new adventures which would unfold within. Quiet adventures, Esther imagined, but adventures nevertheless. She had a moment of envy – the house was exquisite and full of possibility, and she loved it – wished it were hers. But at the same time, she was full of excitement for Sally, for whom the house held such promise. Her first real home. Esther was not demonstrative, but she found herself taking Sally's hand and squeezing it warmly.

'It's lovely, just lovely. I wish you great happiness here.'

'I shall rattle around in it,' Sally said, smiling and blushing.

'Well, you'll have to fill it with friends and parties. Given the size of your living room, you could probably host musical soirees and play-readings too.'

'You don't think I'm crazy? Buying a big place like this?'

'God knows, you've earned it,' said Esther. 'You gave decades of your life to caring for your family. I think you should have anything you want.'

For a moment, Sally's eyes looked as if they were filling with tears, but she blinked rapidly and then smiled broadly. 'All I need is George Clooney in my spare room and I'll be all set!' She paused for a moment and then said, hesitantly, 'As you can see, the house is empty. I wonder if you might maybe help me... fill it?'

And thus they went on a number of shopping trips. Sally was determined to get rid of all the furniture from her mother's house and start afresh. Now Esther had an inkling of Sally's financial position, she felt a great deal less anxious than she might have done as they swept through curtain warehouses and sofa shops, measuring, matching fabric swatches and taking phone snapshots of lamps and cushions. Unsurprisingly, Sally seemed unsure of her own taste and was forever asking Esther to make decisions on her behalf. Very quickly the house began to take shape. It was softer and more feminine than Esther would have chosen for herself, but she sensed it was right for Sally. The living room was decorated in shades of dusky mauve, with accents in a pale green. It looked like a summer garden. The kitchen was all blonde wood and white china, and Sally's bedroom was a riot of pretty floral prints.

Esther quickly realized that it was easy to be nice to Sally. She was so grateful for the slightest display of friendship and kindness, and she seemed to glow with happiness when Esther offered to do something with her. On the surface, it wasn't the easiest friendship Esther had ever had, not least because she and Sally didn't have that much in common. Sally hadn't travelled, and she had never been married or had children, so many of the usual topics of conversation Esther might have shared with a friend were not open to them. Sally watched a lot of television, which Esther didn't, and enjoyed a wide range of music from all eras, also not a major interest of Esther's. Yet somehow Esther began to take comfort in Sally's company. She was warm and open, she liked to laugh, and she was always keen to hear about what Esther had been up to and happy to ask questions about things she didn't understand. She had an easy, open physicality too – she liked to kiss Esther hello and often offered hugs and squeezes of the hand as punctuations to conversation. Esther had always been rather protective of her personal space and was usually only comfortable being touched or hugged by lovers or Lucie. Friends and acquaintances seemed to sense this and tended to opt for handshakes or cool air kisses by way of greeting. Sally had no such qualms, however, and surprisingly Esther didn't mind that.

One Sunday morning Sally rang and asked her if they could go to the garden centre to choose some plants. 'I got some local lads in to weed the beds and mow the lawn, and it's all looking a bit bare. I don't know the first thing about gardening,' she said. 'I just want it to look pretty for the housewarming party, with some flowers in the beds.'

'Well, I'm no expert,' said Esther. 'Not like my mum was.' She said it lightly and unthinkingly, but at the words 'my mum', the weight of missing Laura struck her with a blinding force.

Sally must have heard her hesitate and draw breath. 'Are you all right?'

'Oh, you know...' said Esther weakly. She couldn't get the words out to explain. Fortunately, she didn't need to.

'I do know,' said Sally. 'Look, we really don't have to do this today – or at all.'

'We do. We should,' said Esther firmly. 'Let's let the spirit of Laura guide us through the garden centre.'

'Lobelias are easy to grow,' she said, as they walked down the long rows of plants. 'And geraniums.'

'I need things that are very tough and strong,' said Sally. 'Things that are almost impossible to kill.'

Esther laughed. 'I'll choose super-plants. Some plants really like a bit of ill treatment. You know, some people swear by beating apple trees with a baseball bat to get them to bear more fruit.'

'Good grief! I wasn't planning on abusing my plants. Just neglecting them a little.'

'There is a lovely apple tree in your garden though,' said Esther.

'There is? Well, that's news to me. I have so much to learn.'

When they had loaded their trolley with bedding plants, fertilizer and gardening tools ('I don't have so much as a trowel,' said Sally, 'I don't even really know what a trowel is'), they took themselves to the garden centre coffee shop for tea and cake. Or at least, Esther had tea and cake and Sally had sparkling water and a fruit platter.

'You're being very disciplined,' Esther observed.

'I bought a dress for the housewarming party,' Sally said, picking up a sliver of melon with her fork. 'It's a size ten, and I'm determined the zip will go all the way up.'

'How close are you?'

'Just an inch or so to go. I shan't be able to breathe, but hey, breathing's overrated anyway.'

'You've lost a lot already.'

'Three stone,' said Sally proudly. And my cholesterol is down to safe levels. And my blood pressure.' She gave a broad, sunny grin, and Esther thought, not for the first time, how grateful she was that Michael had pushed her to fix this relationship.

CHAPTER TWENTY-NINE

It was the postcode. She had got the postcode wrong, and the handwriting on the envelope was so shaky, the name of the road was difficult to read. The envelope had been scribbled on and redirected, and was scuffed and marked. But it was there, lying on Esther's desk. She stood back, staring at it.

Lucie came into the living room and stood beside her. 'It's from Nanny Laura, isn't it? I found it on the mat when I came home.'

'Yes,' said Esther quietly. 'Yes, it is. It must have been lost in the post all this time.'

'Months.'

'Yes, months.'

'Are you going to open it?'

'I will. I just...'

'Do you want me to go away?'

'Yes, I think so, darling, if that's all right. I need to read it quietly, by myself.'

'Will you tell me what it says?'

Her mother's suicide note? Would she tell Lucie what it said? The letter was addressed just to Esther, she saw with relief. Had it been addressed to them both, Lucie might well have opened it. She hadn't told Lucie how Laura had died. When they'd been beside the river on the Isle of Wight, Lucie had said she didn't want to know, and she had never brought it up again. The close friends who had attended the funeral knew, of course, but most other people merely assumed she'd died as a result of illness or old age. So far, no one had said anything awful in front of Lucie, and it had seemed best just to let things lie. If she'd asked, Esther would have told her, but she hadn't asked. And now here was a letter which would no doubt make the whole thing explicit, in Laura's own words.

'I don't know,' she said frankly. 'I don't know what it says. If it's private information that Nanny wanted only me to know, then I might not tell you. But if there's a message in the letter for you, then I will tell you for sure.'

'Okay,' said Lucie doubtfully. 'But it's not as if she's here to mind if I read the letter.'

'Even though Nanny Laura is dead,' said Esther carefully, 'we should have the same respect for her privacy as we would have if she were alive. That means only the person to whom she wrote the letter should read it, don't you think?'

Lucie clearly didn't think so, but she had no choice but to agree. She missed Laura, Esther knew, and the thought that this communication had come from her, from beyond the grave, must be very tantalizing.

'I promise if she said anything to you, I will show you,' said Esther again.

The letter lay on her desk in its scuffed envelope. She had to pick it up and open it. She had to. And yet she could hardly bear to. It would be like ripping open wounds that had scarcely begun to scab over. It seemed so absurd, so utterly awful that a letter as crucial as this had gone astray. And that it had arrived now, just as she was thinking she might survive the mortal blow of Laura's death. Would it contain answers? Or would it simply leave her feeling worse? She considered ringing Michael, or Sally even, to come over and be with her when she opened it. But she knew that was not the answer. She had to open it alone, and read it.

She poured herself a large glass of wine, gingerly picked up the envelope and went upstairs to her bedroom. She managed to procrastinate for another few minutes by going downstairs to fetch her letter opener. It didn't seem right to rip the envelope open. She slit it open carefully, and took out the letter. It was many pages long, but she saw with a pang that that was because Laura had managed to get just a few words onto each page. The handwriting was unrecognizable, wobbly and big, rather like Lucie's first attempts when she was tiny. It was nothing like Laura's usual firm, forward-sloping script. It was dated, unsurprisingly, the day of Laura's suicide.

My dearest Esther,

By the time you get this letter, I will be gone. I know you don't believe, so for you, I will just be gone into the void, but I have faith I will be with my God.

I am making the most selfish decision of my life, and I beg you to forgive me. I am choosing dignity and self-determination over months or years of deterioration and reliance on others. I want to die as me, as I am, as you know me, not as some shuddering, incontinent caricature of myself. I am doing it now, while I still can, even though I

am still comparatively well. I don't want to find myself at a point where I am physically incapable of taking my own life.
Please forgive me.

From here, the writing became even bigger and more wobbly.

This is, predictably, all about me. It is no reflection on you, nor on your love or loyalty. I know you would have done what needed to be done. I could not and would not ask you.

She did not end the letter with love, nor with a message for Lucie. Laura's name straggled down the last third of the last page, each letter fainter than the one before, the last 'a' so unclear it was almost not there – fading, ephemeral, like Laura herself.

CHAPTER THIRTY

She lay on her bed for a long time after she read the letter. She knew she had to go downstairs, reassure Lucie, make dinner, and pick up the threads of normal life. However, for the moment, she just couldn't. She just needed to lie there, in the twilight, alone for a moment. It wasn't even as if she was thinking about the letter. She was, for some reason, thinking about the castle birthday cake she'd had for her eleventh birthday.

She was really too old for a castle cake. But she'd been reading the stories of King Arthur, and she was immersed in medieval lore and stirring tales of knights and valour, and when Laura asked her what cake she would like that year, she'd said 'A castle' without thinking. She regretted it immediately. Her classmates would think she was babyish. It would look silly, with a dolly princess in an upper window, and everyone would think she was lame. Because she had come to the school so late, there was an almost imperceptible distance between her and the other children, or so it seemed to Esther. They were nice enough, and civil, and no one bullied her, but they had all known each other since nursery, and it was as if they couldn't be bothered to get to know her properly, especially as, when she'd first arrived, they had just two and a bit years to go before they would all disperse to secondary school.

Other than Isabella, she didn't really have close friends, although she knew she had enough social clout that people would come to her birthday party. It helped immensely that Isabella had chosen her as her friend. Isabella was effortlessly cool – not conventionally popular, and certainly not friends with everyone, but charismatic and a little mysterious. She was the person everyone wished they could be friends with, but in truth they were a little intimidated by her.

They were all too old for party games in the garden, and even though hers was a summer birthday, they couldn't count on the weather being decent. So in a break with tradition, she and six friends would be going to the cinema to see *Grease*, which everyone had been talking about, and then coming back to the house for tea and birthday cake. It seemed like it could be a cool birthday party except for the castle cake, Esther thought.

In years gone by, Laura had involved her in the design of her birthday cakes. Esther had chosen the colours for Barbie's dress the previous year, and the rainbow sprinkles for the pony cake on her eighth birthday. But this year, Laura was unusually secretive. Esther didn't really want to ask about the cake anyway, but she did notice that Laura hadn't shown her any drawings or talked about it. She thought maybe Laura had forgotten, but one day, when she walked into the kitchen, she saw her bent over the counter, pencil in hand. When Laura heard her, she flipped over the drawing and turned quickly to face Esther, moving the piece of paper behind her back. It had to be the cake design.

At that point in their friendship, Esther and Isabella were splitting their time pretty equally between their two houses. However, in the week or so leading up to the birthday party, Esther did notice that whenever she said to Isabella, 'Where shall we go today then?' Isabella would always say, 'Let's go to yours.' And then she'd keep disappearing. She'd leave Esther in the bedroom and go off, ostensibly to the loo or to get a drink of water, but then be gone for ages. Esther was clever enough to know whatever it was Isabella was up to was probably birthday-related – she knew people did funny things in the days leading up to your birthday, and if you liked surprises (which she did), it was best to act unconcerned and pretend you hadn't noticed.

Grease was funny, very American, with lots of great songs, although Esther suspected she hadn't understood all of the jokes, because there were some things the adults in the cinema seemed to find hilarious that she didn't get at all. They had gone to an afternoon showing, and it was still light, so they were all allowed to walk back to Esther's house without an adult. She felt quietly thrilled. The film had definitely been a hit with everyone, and she knew for a fact that Louise and Violet weren't usually allowed to walk home by themselves but had been given special leave to do so because they were in a big group and it was Esther's birthday. So this is what it's like to be cool and popular, she thought. Perhaps this was what it was like to be Isabella. Isabella herself seemed a little antsy. She had been restless through the film, and she seemed to be hurrying them all to get back to Esther's house. 'Come on,' she said, a little impatiently. 'Stop dawdling, you lot.'

It was a perfect summer evening as they turned into Esther's gate. Laura's beautiful garden was heavy with the scent of jasmine and roses, and the house, set back from the trees, gleamed in the late sunlight. Other than Isabella, none of the girls had been here, and there was a collective gasp.

'It's beautiful,' breathed Violet, who lived, Esther knew, in one of the new tower blocks.

'Come in,' she said, suddenly proud, and feeling expansive.

There was a crisp white cloth on the dining room table, and plates of delicate finger sandwiches, scones and sausage rolls, everything homemade. Laura had set out the good teapot and china cups. The girls stopped, open-mouthed, in the doorway and stared, except for Isabella, who ducked past them all and went through into the kitchen, shutting the door behind her. Esther urged all the girls to sit down, and Laura, playing the maître-d', filled teacups and formally offered round the comestibles. Esther tried to get everyone to relax by chattering about the film, but she could see they were somewhat intimidated by the beauty and ceremony of the tea. They were, after all, only eleven-year-old girls from the local junior school. She half-wished they had just put out the splash pool in the garden and had ice lollies. She had tried to be too adult, and now no one was having fun. And Isabella wasn't there. She hadn't yet emerged from the kitchen. Esther felt a hot wave of anger. Isabella was ruining her party. If anyone could get everyone to relax and talk, it would be Isabella. Where was she?

Laura went through to the kitchen then and was gone for a few minutes. Then she came back into the dining room and said excitedly, 'I think it's time for the cake, don't you?' The girls chorused enthusiastic assent. Laura rushed over to the windows and drew the curtains, plunging the bright room into sudden gloom, then she stepped back to the kitchen door and opened it slowly, as if raising a stage curtain. She began to sing 'Happy Birthday' in her deep, tuneful voice, and the girls dutifully joined in.

Isabella entered, carrying the cake carefully in front of her, her face illuminated by the blazing birthday candles. She walked slowly and proudly, and placed the cake in front of Esther, who was sitting at the head of the table.

It was a castle all right, but it couldn't have been further from the boxy, babyish castle of her imagination. It was a tall, crumbling tower, balanced on a rock, which had been iced painstakingly in shades of grey and brown, with each stone of the tower individually carved. The tower was surrounded by a tangle of tiny green ivy leaves made from sugar. A pathway wound its way up the rock towards the castle, and the eleven birthday candles formed torches, lighting the path at regular intervals. But most astonishingly, there was a dragon, with glittering bright red scales (Esther never did find out how the scales were made to glitter), coiled around the roof of the tower. No squared-off battlements, no dolly princess. It was a brooding, dark, medieval castle. Years later, she was able to identify it. It was Childe Rowland's Dark Tower.

The girls were silent, open-mouthed, awed. They had never seen anything like it. Laura looked around the astonished faces and clapped her hands in glee. 'Do you like it? Do you all like it?' The girls could scarcely speak, but they nodded. How would they describe this to their families? This was no bland Victoria sponge; it was a work of art.

Belatedly, Esther remembered to blow out the candles. They had begun to drip wax on the icing pathway. She had to turn the cake slowly to get to all of them. Then Laura whisked open the curtains and went to fetch a knife.

'You can't cut it!' said Louise, horrified. 'It's too beautiful!'

'Nonsense!' said Laura. 'It's a cake! Meant to be enjoyed. If we didn't eat it, it would go stale and rot.'

'It's beautiful,' sad Violet, softly. 'So beautiful. You're so clever, Mrs Hart.'

'Oh, it wasn't me,' said Laura. 'I just baked the cake and did a bit of the assembly. This is all Isabella's work. The idea, the design, the icing…. Everything.'

Esther turned to look at Isabella, who was standing off to one side, smiling and hugging herself, her thin arms wrapped tightly around her own waist.

'Sneaky, huh?' she said. 'Been working in secret with your mum for weeks!'

Esther turned back to look at the cake. It was a work of love. Any misgivings she'd had about the day had been wiped out by the cake. No one at school would ever forget this cake, not even people who hadn't seen it. It made her birthday party unforgettable, unique, special. And it was all because of Isabella. She looked back at her best friend, who had done this astonishing thing, and in that split second she caught the glance that Isabella exchanged with Laura. It was conspiratorial, full of shared understanding and satisfaction at a secret plan successfully carried to completion. Two artists well pleased with their work. And they were so alike – slender, dark, bright-eyed. A casual observer might have thought Isabella was Laura's daughter, rather than Esther.

CHAPTER THIRTY-ONE

It was sunset, and Esther sat in Sally's kitchen, watching the clouds streak blood-red and violet through the window. Sally had put a cup of tea in front of her, and she had wrapped her hands around its smooth, warm surface, although she could not bring herself to drink any.

Sally stood by the window, looking out. She had been listening to Esther talk for the past half-hour. But Esther wasn't finished.

'I'm angry,' she said, squeezing the cup tightly. 'I thought I'd finished being angry. That I had obediently gone through all those prescribed stages of grief, but I haven't. I'm angry again. Just so fucking angry.'

Sally nodded, without turning back from the window.

'She's absolutely right, of course,' said Esther. 'She was selfish. Always so damned selfish. Living her life entirely for herself.

Dying her own death. Not giving a damn about what it would do to me, or Lucie.'

Sally spoke at last. 'I think everyone's a bit selfish, really. Especially near the end. I think when you have so little time, you don't want to waste it on—'

'Waste it?' said Esther incredulously. 'You think she would have been wasting her time, spending it with us?'

'You didn't let me finish. I was going to say, you don't want to waste it on arguing about something you're not going to change your mind about. Your mum was elderly, and she lived alone. I bet long before she got ill she'd thought about what she would do if she got some debilitating illness. I know I've thought about it.'

Esther had come seeking – what? Sympathy? Solace? Sally's soft sweetness? She had got none of that. Sally had read Laura's letter and had then looked at her enquiringly. She hadn't said how sorry she was, or given Esther a hug or held her hand. She'd nodded once, when she had ascertained Esther wasn't going to speak, and had said, 'Well, now you know.'

'Do I?'

'As much as she was able to tell you. It wasn't your fault. Not that I ever thought it was. Just her choice.'

And thus the argument had begun. Esther, furious, saying that Laura had robbed her, denied her the right to do her duty as a daughter. Sally, immovable, supporting Laura's choice. This wasn't what Esther had expected. Not at all.

Now, for the first time, Sally seemed to be losing her temper a little. 'So what you wanted was for Laura to suffer, to go through the indignities she feared most of all, so you could feel okay about what you had done for her?'

'That's not fair.'

'Isn't it? Why should you get to choose?'

Esther exploded. 'You got to choose. Isabella pushed everyone away. She pushed me away. But you went in to care for her. You. You saw her die.'

'I helped her die.'

Esther stopped short. 'What?'

Sally spoke calmly now. 'She was in a lot of pain towards the end. She was struggling to breathe, nauseous a lot of the time and if she moved suddenly, she'd haemorrhage. It wasn't going to get better, only worse. If she'd been older, her body would have given in sooner. But the downside to getting cancer when you're young is that the bits of your body that aren't affected are strong. We talked about it, and over a few weeks we decanted a little of each bottle of oral morphine until we had enough. I helped her to sit up and she drank it. Then she went to sleep.'

Esther was silent. What could she say? Sally was admitting to – what? Assisting a suicide? Murder? Was it classified as murder? She had no idea. Was it a criminal offence? Again, she didn't know.

Sally continued. 'If we hadn't done it, she might have lived another week, maybe more. But she'd had enough. And I respected that. I didn't want her to go. But I didn't want her to suffer anymore either. We didn't tell anyone. Not Mum, obviously, and not the doctors. Because she'd been seen recently by medical professionals, there was no post-mortem.'

'And now you've told me.'

'I can see you're angry with me because I don't agree with you about your mum. I wanted you to know why. You're the only person I have ever told.'

Sally looked out over the fields again. The sky was almost dark now, and her profile was sharply delineated against the window. She had lost even more weight, and Esther could see the line of her jaw, which had for so long been hidden beneath soft flesh. She could see cheekbones too, with small hollows below them.

She had often thought that Sally's baby-doll, childish good looks wouldn't age well, but now Sally's bone structure was emerging from the pudge, she could see it was fine-boned, delicate and well made. And she could see that Sally, more than she had ever imagined, was Isabella's sister.

After she left Sally's house, she knew they wouldn't see each other again for a while. The enormity of the revelation was too great a weight for the fragile new closeness they had built. Was it broken? She didn't know. She hoped not. While she recoiled at what Sally had confessed to, she had to admit to a strange, grudging respect. In the face of a desperate plea from one she loved, could she, would she, have done the same?

CHAPTER THIRTY-TWO

Stephen's wife Melissa was thirty weeks pregnant, and they were moving back to London. It was madness. Stephen was the first to admit this when he rang Esther to tell her.

'Melissa stopped work early for her maternity leave. We'd got more than halfway through decorating the nursery, it was nearly good to go, and one day she sat down and just cried and cried. She said she didn't think she wanted to go back to work after the baby was born, that she wants to be near her mum and dad, and she wants the baby to be close to its big sister.'

'So what does that mean for you?'

'The company's always been happy for me to transfer back to the London office, and I still own my place in Islington. We'll have to rent somewhere for a few months until our tenant's lease runs out, but it's doable. Insane, but doable.'

'Gosh,' said Esther. 'Well, I'm sure Lucie will be thrilled.' For her own part, she was slightly less delighted – she had been able to manage her feelings about her ex-husband with his wife and new baby quite easily when they were a few hundred miles away. Dropping Lucie off in Islington to play happy families might be a little more difficult.

'We'll be able to give you more of a break,' said Stephen, doing his best to sound conciliatory. 'More time to yourself and, you know, time to spend with your fella.'

That didn't necessarily make her feel better, but she saw it for what it was, both an acknowledgement of her relationship with Michael and an admission that Stephen himself hadn't really put in the parenting hours he should have over the last couple of years. If he wanted to change that, that was good.

Lucie took the news with a deadpan lack of concern. 'Yeah, I knew that,' she said, and turned to go to her room.

'Were you planning to tell me?' said Esther, and immediately chided herself. It was exactly the type of provocative question that made Lucie roll her eyes and shut down these days.

Lucie duly looked at her with a mixture of pity and boredom. 'Dad said he would,' was all she could be bothered to say.

'It'll mean you can see the baby whenever you want to,' said Esther, trying to appear enthusiastic.

'Mum, you don't have to try and sound like the textbook divorced parent. It'll be fine. We'll work it out, I'll see them whenever.' Then she paused for a good long moment and said, uncertainly, 'It'll be nice when Dad moves back into the Islington place. I liked my room there. Unless… they give it to the baby.'

'Of course they won't!' Shocked, Esther made a note to email Stephen and make sure that was not his plan. 'It's your room! And it always will be. Besides, they'll have the baby in with them for ages anyway. Maybe when it's a bit older you can share,' she teased. 'You could get bunk-beds.'

Lucie looked horrified for a moment, then saw Esther was joking and went stony-faced. 'It's not funny.'

'Of course it isn't. I was just being light-hearted. It's a lovely thing having your dad back in London. And I'm sure we'll all work out the details together and it'll be fine.' She wished she could reassure herself with as much conviction. But there was no point in fretting about it. One day at a time, she told herself. We'll deal with it one day at a time.

She'd been touched by Stephen's thoughtful comment about Michael. Nearly six months into their relationship, she and Michael had reached a comfortable equilibrium. He was, as he had told her the night they got together, a serial monogamist. He had seemed to like the fireworks and non-stop sex at the beginning of their liaison, but he seemed even happier once things had settled into a predictable routine and they were fully integrated into each other's social circles and universally acknowledged as a couple. He wasn't a player, Michael. When he arrived one Friday and rather shamefacedly asked if he might leave a pair of slippers at her place to wear in the evenings, she knew they had reached a new level of comfortable closeness. She liked it, she supposed, and she valued his kind reliability immensely. But, a little selfishly, she sometimes thought that a bit more champagne, sexiness and danger might have been nice. They'd only been dating half a year after all. Where would they be after a year? Or two? Side by side in matching rocking chairs?

It was with these slight misgivings in mind that she pushed for them to take the long-postponed trip to Venice in the autumn half-term. Stephen and Melissa had moved down to London by then and were staying in a pleasant enough two-bedroomed flat not far from Stephen's place in Islington. There was a room for Lucie, and Esther knew Melissa was dying to drag Lucie off shopping for baby things. Lucie would still be just a Tube or bus ride away from all her friends and so was happy to go to her dad's. Michael, after hesitating for a few days, which made Esther very uncomfortable, eventually agreed; he applied for the few days' annual leave he would need and rebooked the trip. She didn't need anyone to approve her leave application – she was, after all, the head of department, so she merely informed Regina and the principal's office and rescheduled her appointments for those days.

It all seemed to be going smoothly, when she got a message to ring the principal's executive assistant. He was a studious, serious young man with thick-rimmed glasses, who spoke extremely slowly. She knew he had a brace of degrees from Russell Group universities and a cluster of qualifications in educational administration. Nevertheless, he had absolutely no people skills.

'Professor Hart...' he said when she identified herself. For a moment she thought the line had gone dead, but then she remembered he was the master of the long pause.

'Yes?' she said as encouragingly as she could. She had to give a seminar in twenty minutes and it was on the other side of campus. She had no idea how long it would take him to say what he needed to.

'It has come to my attention...' he said, and she resisted the urge to nudge him with another 'Yes...?' Instead she waited, drumming her fingers silently on her desk blotter.

'.... that you have put in a request for annual leave.'

'Not a request,' she said. 'As HOD, I'm merely required to inform the principal of my intentions, as long as it's within my yearly allocation, which it is.'

'Yes...' he said, drawing the word out into several syllables. 'But...'

'But what?' She couldn't keep the impatience out of her voice. 'Look, I have a class to get to, is this urgent?'

'No, no, no... Merely a procedural question. You see, the principal is thinking of calling a meeting... Nothing is as yet formally confirmed, but a possibility has been tabled—'

She couldn't bear his turgid corporate speak for another moment. 'I appreciate that the principal might call a meeting, but the point is I've postponed this trip once already. We've rebooked it now, and if I try to move it again, we'll lose most of our deposit for a second time. I will only be away for three working days and a weekend. Surely the principal could take that into account when arranging his meetings?'

This rapid-fire monologue seemed to flummox the slow-moving young man. 'Ah. Well. Yes,' he said. There seemed to be more full-stops in his speech than there had been previously. 'Well,' he said again. Then, finally, 'I will let the principal know what you've said. And we will take it all into account. Under the circumstances.'

Esther said goodbye and hung up, relieved. She dashed off to give her seminar and didn't give the young man's call another thought that day. It wasn't until much later that she reflected that, his taste for jargon notwithstanding, there was something sinister about that last 'under the circumstances'.

Esther knew that summer in Venice could be disappointing – overcrowded, stiflingly hot and smelly – but in autumn the crumbling city had extraordinary beauty. She found herself grateful that their summer trip had never happened; it could never have competed with the entrancing experience of the city in this golden season. The weather was still sunny and warm, but not too hot, and the city was more or less empty of tourists, or at least of big tourist groups.

For the first two days, Esther was still tense. She worried about work and about Lucie, and fretted about whether her house would be okay. On the afternoon of the second day, Michael gently took her phone out of her hand and switched off the data connection. 'You're on holiday,' he said. 'Your out-of-office is on your email. Work can wait.'

'But...' Esther protested. 'It's not just work. Lucie...'

'I've texted my number to Lucie, and she has the number of the hotel, as does Stephen. This is supposed to be a break from normal life. And if it is a break, you need to relax your iron-fisted grip on the tiny details of life at home and live in the moment, in Venice, here, with me.'

She protested a little more, but she could see the sense in what he said, and she resolved to go off-grid. They made few plans and had brought no guide books; they spent each day wandering the streets and alleyways hand in hand, crossing and re-crossing canal bridges, finding themselves in enchanting courtyards and exquisite corners. They ate extravagantly, drank too much and made love every afternoon before tumbling into long, dreamy naps. Then they would get up and meander under the twinkling lights, looking for new bars, hidden cafés and live-music venues. Somehow the few days they had seemed to stretch infinitely, packed with slow delights.

On the second-last day, they went to the Guggenheim museum. She was pleased that Michael also liked to explore galleries alone. She had always disliked either having to wait for someone who moved slower than her, or being rushed through a space when she wanted to linger. He clearly felt the same, and so they split up pretty much as soon as they went in and moved through the rooms at their own pace. When they had both had their fill of culture, they met up and by silent mutual assent found a café overlooking a canal and ordered a bottle of wine. It was a glorious autumn day, warm and still, and the sky was a deep azure. Michael took her hand, and she sat stroking his fingers and looking out over the water. It was a moment of such perfect contentment, she wanted to bottle it. She heard Michael clear his throat, and she glanced over at him. He was looking particularly serious.

'What?' she said, alarmed. 'Are you all right?'

'I'm very much all right,' he said, smiling. 'I'm having an utterly splendid time. I was very much enjoying looking at you. I just wish I was one of those cool, sexy chaps who could pay you a lovely compliment and make it sound sincere.'

'You could try.'

'I could, but I'm English and self-deprecating, so it's sure to come out somewhere between sarcastic and lame. It's just... you look happier and more relaxed than I've ever seen you, and your... really quite extraordinary beauty is revealed when you're like this.'

'So you're saying I'm normally a dog?'

'I knew it would come out all wrong. What I meant was...'

She laughed and squeezed his hand. 'I'm teasing! Thank you. It came out perfectly, and it may well be the nicest compliment anyone has ever paid me. I am happy and relaxed, you're right, and it's all thanks to you. I've had the most magical time.'

'Ditto,' he said, and his beautiful dark eyes were warm and, she thought, slightly wet. 'Ditto.'

They sat in happy silence for a few more minutes, but she could sense that he was thinking. He kept holding her hand and playing with her fingers, as if he couldn't quite sit still.

'We should...' he began, then stopped.

'We should...?'

'Well, not we should... I mean, I would like to think we might...'

'We might what?'

'Bollocks. I'm rubbish at this, aren't I?'

'It's hard for me to give an assessment, as I haven't a clue what you're talking about.'

'We should... talk about where we are,' he said, finally.

'I assume saying "Venice" would be counterproductive and unhelpful.'

'I meant in life.'

'I know.'

'Well?'

'Happy, I would say,' said Esther. 'At least I am. You've enhanced my life extraordinarily. You're kind and lovely and sexy and a delight, and everything is better when you're there than when you're not.'

'Thank you,' he said. 'And I would agree on all fronts. I was thinking more about... well... the future.'

'The future?'

'Well, I love the way things are, but I can't help thinking that if we're going to stay together, we need to think about... you know... uniting our households.'

'Are we talking about...?'

'Not marriage,' he said quickly. 'At least not yet, unless you want to...'

'No,' she said, equally quickly. 'Thank you. I agree, not yet, and maybe not necessarily at all.'

He looked a little surprised at this, but continued. 'I was thinking more about moving in together. Because of Lucie, it makes more sense for us to live at yours than mine, but if you'd rather, we could sell both places and get somewhere new for all of us. When my boys finish uni, they'll need bedrooms to come home to, even if just temporarily, and I suppose that would mean getting a bigger place...'

'Whoa!' she said, laughing nervously. 'Hang on.'

'What?'

'In a handful of sentences, you've gone from our possibly moving in together to our pooling our resources and buying some kind of four- or five-bedroomed mansion for us and all our offspring. I just need a bit of time to catch up.'

'Okay.' He sat back in his chair, looking at her.

She stared out across the canal. Why was she feeling so uncomfortable with this? Michael was a wonderful man. She loved him, and it made sense that if they stayed together, they should move in together. He was right, of course. She tried her best to come up with an honest, clear response.

'You're probably surprised that I'm responding like this,' she said. 'Any normal woman would be leaping at the chance to move in with you, to make a home and a future together.' He looked suddenly stricken. 'And I want to,' she added quickly and as fervently as she could manage. 'I really do. I just need some time to get my head around it.'

He nodded, and then said, very quietly and with a little edge to his voice, 'How much time?'

And she realized that, after all these months of love and support, all the kindness and generosity, there was a possibility that Michael's patience might be finite. This was, in some crucial way, a make-or-break conversation.

She wasn't good at change. She had always known this about herself. While ending her marriage to Stephen had been a relief, it had taken an enormous effort to build the life she had now, to make a home and a routine that worked for Lucie and herself. And with Stephen now back in London, there was another big change on the horizon. But if she put Michael off because of that, how long would he stick around? There would be another change in her circumstances, another upset. He was so relaxed and even-tempered, it was easy, she realized, to take him for granted. Now was the time to put him first.

'Christmas,' she said firmly. 'I propose you move into my place at Christmas. In the short term, you might consider letting your place out. Let's give it a year of living together and make sure we don't want to kill each other, and then we can talk about selling up and getting a bigger place.'

'All of this, naturally, is subject to Lucie's approval,' said Michael.

'Naturally. I also know that I don't have a room for the boys, but we can work something out – sofa beds in the living room?'

'Or if you'd consider it, we could replace your shed with something a bit more substantial. Like a summer house. If we run power to it—'

'We can't make them sleep in the shed. They're not dogs!'

'You haven't smelled them after a rough night out. Besides, they're practically adults. They'd probably prefer the privacy.'

'Well, let's talk to them about it. And Lucie. We'll find a solution that works for everyone.'

Michael reached across the table and squeezed her hand. 'Thank you.'

'For what?'

'Not freaking out. I was pretty sure you'd panic and run screaming. I had visions of you swimming at great speed down the Grand Canal towards the sea.'

She smiled at him. 'Nope, not panicking. Lots of things to plan and work out, that's for sure, but not panicking. All of this is good, my love. We're moving into a wonderful new part of our lives.'

Much later, they lay side by side in the big white bed in their hotel room. Michael had fallen into a light doze, lying on his side, his back to her. Over his shoulder, through the open French windows, she could see the sky, streaked with pink clouds. She reached out a hand and stroked the smooth skin of his ribs and waist. He murmured softly and leaned slightly against her hand, but she knew he wasn't properly awake. This dear, kind man, a gift beyond price. How lucky she was. If she were to think through the minutiae of what they planned to do, she knew it would overwhelm her. But at the same time, she knew it was the right choice. Yes, they had three grown and growing children between them and not enough space for everyone. Yes, she had never lived with a man except Stephen, and she had no idea if they would want to kill each other if they shared a space. Yes, she would have to relinquish control of her precious little home and share it... Really share it. But all of these worries paled in comparison with the undeniable joy of a deeper, closer, more permanent relationship with Michael.

What might her life have been like if she'd fallen in love with him at twenty instead of forty-seven? Might she have grown into a different person, someone warmer and more open? Someone whose mother would have let her... No. Now was not the time to go there. Twenty-year-old Esther would not have been ready for Michael. She wouldn't have recognized his value. He would have been insufficiently glamorous or dangerous.

When she met Stephen at university, he had been brooding and handsome, with sharp cheekbones and enormous dark eyes fringed with black lashes. She had found him unbelievably sexy and smouldering. When he was silent and cold, which was often, she interpreted this as a sign of his hidden depths, of his fathomless, unknowable soul. Over the years of their marriage, she had come to realize that he really was just a grumpy, aloof bastard. There were no depths, or, if they were, it seemed to her they were just deeper reserves of grumpiness and sour pessimism. It took the smallest thing to spoil his mood – a patch of bad traffic, a poor phone signal, a less than perfect meal. In the early years of her marriage, she tiptoed around him, trying to make him happy. When she realized this was an impossible task, she took to ignoring his sulks and diatribes. He wasn't emotionally cruel or violent, just frequently silent or unpleasant. After a while, ignoring his moods meant largely ignoring him, and their lives became more and more separate.

Being with Michael was different in every way. His default setting was cheerfulness. He had a childlike knack for finding enjoyment in almost anything and was always easy-going. If something went wrong, no matter how large, Michael took it in his stride. A broken-down car, a burnt burger, a traffic jam on the M25 – he treated them all as fleeting inconveniences and immediately began translating them into fodder for jokes and a good anecdote. When Laura died, Esther had seen his response to a larger crisis; he had been calm, practical, loving and helpful. Not only was he the polar opposite of Stephen, he was the perfect counterpoint to her own tendency to shut down, push people away and take refuge in being cold and unemotional.

Lying beside him in this magical bed in this magical city, she took a moment to thank whichever power had brought him into her life. She gave herself one tiny moment to consider where their future plans might take them. For the first time, she allowed herself to think about a lifetime commitment; about, just possibly, marrying this good, kind man, if he would have her. She wriggled closer, wrapped an arm around his waist, and warmed herself on him.

CHAPTER THIRTY-THREE

Esther had once met a maths professor who had worked out a formula for the value of a holiday. He theorized that the value was equal to the cost of the holiday divided by the length of time you retained your sense of inner peace upon your return to work and the real world. If she were to apply the formula to her return from Venice, the holiday's value was a big fat zero. She had not even made it into the building when reality came crashing in.

She and Michael had got home very late the night before; their flight was delayed and they got into Heathrow at around 11 p.m. Michael had parked his car at the airport so they could make a speedy getaway. It should have taken them forty minutes or so to get home, but there had been an accident on the motorway, and they were stuck between two junctions for more than an hour and a half, before they could creep onto the off-ramp and then cut through the sleeping suburbs to get back to Esther's place. She had taken a quick shower and fallen into bed, not even bothering to unpack; unsurprisingly, she'd overslept the next morning.

More traffic, nowhere to park, and the realization that she had forgotten to charge her phone the night before, meant her stress levels were up even before she reached her office at the university. When she approached the Humanities building at about five past nine, she was surprised to see Regina standing outside, wringing her hands and looking quite desperate.

'Hello,' she said. 'Not waiting for me, are you?'

'Yes,' said Regina. 'And thank God you're here. Why is your phone off? And why haven't you responded to any emails?'

'We switched data off in Venice.' Esther felt her stomach clench. It wasn't like Regina to be flustered, and she looked well beyond flustered now. She looked almost as if she might burst into tears.

'I left messages on your home phone. I even tried to get hold of Michael's number...'

'What's happened?'

'We don't have time to go through everything. Right now, you're expected in the principal's office for an extraordinary meeting of the heads of department. I've been trying to warn you, make sure you were prepared...'

'By right now, you mean...?'

'Nine o'clock. Ten minutes ago now. I lied and told them you were only flying in this morning and that you've been a little delayed, so they're waiting for you.'

'What's the meeting about?'

'I don't know for sure. But it's not good, I can tell you that. There are mutterings, rumblings in the School of Humanities...'

'What do I need to do to prepare?'

'Nothing. Well, nothing that we have time for.' Regina walked Esther briskly towards the administration building. 'I've done this for you.' She showed her a folder. 'It's all our statistics, research profiles, student numbers, applications data...'

'Will I need this?'

'You'll need all the ammunition you can get.'

By now they were standing outside the principal's office, and the principal's grey executive assistant, the one who had tried to block Esther's leave application, was waiting to show her into the council boardroom. She had no idea what awaited her on the other side of the door, but she knew it wasn't good. Regina impulsively squeezed her hand as she passed over the folder, and Esther went in.

It was all decided. A bloodless coup. She had no ammunition to fight it, no weapons in her arsenal. She had her thin folder of statistics, with which she was barely familiar. Craig had been preparing for weeks, for months, it seemed. How she hadn't seen it coming, she couldn't imagine. The council had voted to amalgamate the English and Drama departments, to 'rationalize' the administrative staff, cut down on some junior lecturing posts and streamline the budget. By unanimous vote, the council had decided that Craig Shaw, head of Drama, would be the head of the new, larger department.

What this meant in real, non-corporate speak, was that when Esther walked out of the principal's office, she was no longer a head of department. Her own research funding had been subsumed into a bigger pot, and many of her colleagues, including people like Regina, were almost certain to lose their jobs. Worst of all, she knew that it was her fault. If she hadn't been so distracted by Laura's death, by her own personal dramas, she might have seen Craig's poisonous rise, might have observed him angling for power and influence. She might have been able to stop him. She stood outside the administration building, looking up at the iron-grey sky through the branches of the great oak tree. She had to walk back to her office now. She wouldn't be able to tell Regina what had happened. For the next while, she couldn't tell anyone anything, at least not until the powers in the administration departments had drawn up all the necessary documentation and set the HR wheels in motion to relocate people and begin the merger. She would have to lie, prevaricate and hide things from her colleagues and friends, until the moment when she would be forced to convene a meeting of all department staff and let them know that things were changing, and pretty universally for the worse.

She felt a sudden flood of adrenaline through her system, and she had to fight the urge to flee towards her car and freedom. She wanted desperately just to run home and hide. How could it all have gone so wrong, so quickly? If only she could have been better prepared. If only she hadn't let Michael turn off her email in Venice.

Venice. She allowed herself a dry smile. This time yesterday she'd been sipping a cappuccino in a café on the Lido, watching some villainous-looking gents in deep conversation over their espressos. If someone had been planning a Mafia film, they could have cast it then and there in the coffee bar. She and Michael had joked about what crimes might be being hatched. Twenty-four hours later, she knew.

CHAPTER THIRTY-FOUR

Now all pretence was out of the way, Craig showed himself to be the ruthless little shit he truly was. Negotiations between him and Esther were bloody and unpleasant. She had had no inkling of the proposed merger of the departments and was caught entirely on the back foot. He had been plotting it for months so had made detailed strategies and suggestions about joint courses, new modules, and the dropping of those which he considered to be obsolete. Unsurprisingly, many of the modules he saw as outdated were English Department ones. He had budget proposals too, which entailed cutting teaching staff to the bone and choosing which admin staff to keep. She had nothing. Just a record of having been away from the university a great deal in the preceding six months, some shoddy statistics and the knowledge that admissions to the English Department had plummeted under her care. She had failed.

But her past failures were nothing in comparison with the failures to come. All of the negotiations were conducted under conditions of utter secrecy. She wasn't able to speak to any of the staff about what was on the cards, as the plans were all still unconfirmed. She simply had to carry on working and meeting with her colleagues and the admin staff, knowing full well that many of them would be facing redundancy or the loss of some or all of their teaching load. She fought as best she could – she put up objections, offered alternative solutions, even begged. But Craig was unstoppable, and she watched his blatant takedown all but helplessly.

It was almost impossible to keep things secret, however, and many people had heard rumours. Many of the English department staff made allusions and dropped hints, hoping to get information out of her. A few asked directly, and she was forced to say that she was in discussions with the principal and the council about some proposed changes but that nothing was decided yet. This fanned the flames of panic, and she began to see clusters of people in corners, whispering. Rooms seemed to go quiet when she walked into them.

When she'd been offered the department headship, she had jumped at the chance. She could see no cons in taking it, only the pros of more money, a nice boost to her CV and a little more control over how things were done. Nothing much ever changed in a university, she had reasoned – it was merely a case of putting her hand on the rudder of a steady ship and steering it through calm waters for a few years. She hadn't reckoned on the icebergs of the hike in fees, the wobbly economy and the relentless march of progress.

When the time came to address the departmental meeting, Esther thought she might vomit from the stress. She gathered everyone from the English Department in a room in the

Engineering building. She wanted them as far as possible from prying eyes in the Drama Department. It was a hard-won concession – the right to address her own department alone for the last time. It had taken all her will to keep Craig out of it. Considering the sacrifices she had been forced to make, it was the least he owed her.

There was no point in sugar-coating it. Baldly, she laid out the university's case for uniting the two departments and explained that, as it was largely a cost-cutting measure, there was a price to be paid. 'There will be consultations on redundancies and changes to all of our terms of employment,' she said, keeping her voice as steady as she could. 'I have done my best to minimize the impact, but this isn't going to be an easy transition for any of us.' She looked around the room, at the faces of those good people. Friends, people she had worked with, many of them for decades. 'If your position is at risk, HR will be contacting you to discuss the consultation process. For everyone else, we will be talking to you about changes in your teaching commitments and your research and supervision roles.' She drew a long, shaky breath. 'I know this is a lot to take in. I believe, broadly, that the changes will ultimately be positive. Where they will be less than that, I can only say I am sorry, so sorry, that this happened on my watch.' She gave an involuntary hiccup, and then she was mortified to find that a tear was running down her cheek. How horribly unprofessional. 'I'm so sorry,' she said again, and turned away from the table to blow her nose.

There were questions. There was resentment, anger and even a little shouting. She had expected that. What she hadn't expected was the kindness, the solicitude from her colleagues, who seemed to sense the weight of the burden she had been carrying for weeks. She was crippled by this kindness. When Regina, whom she knew for a fact would be losing her job, came to hug her, she was unable to control the sobbing. She made it through the rest of the meeting and was left with a great to-do list of questions to be answered. She wanted them all to go. She felt wrung out, desperate. But as everyone stood up to leave, Regina addressed the meeting.

'Our colleagues back in the Humanities building know this meeting is going on,' she said. 'Many of them probably know what it's about, or they think they do. Let's not drift back in twos and threes, looking sad or angry. Let's go together.'

Professor Farrell, a young, handsome Shakespearean scholar, who would very probably lose his position to a Shakespearean expert from Drama, suddenly declaimed:

> 'But when the blast of war blows in our ears,
> Then imitate the action of the tiger;
> Stiffen the sinews, summon up the blood—'

And, as one, the crusty academics of the English Department shouted:

> 'Cry "God for Harry, England, and Saint George!"'

The united front and euphoric defiance lasted only as long as it took for the processes to begin. As soon as consultation letters started to arrive, the mood worsened, morale plummeted, and Esther found herself ostracized by many of her colleagues. Discussions began about moving what would be left of the department onto the floor where the Drama staff were housed, and this made people, especially the longer-serving members of staff, even more disgruntled and shaken.

Esther had to work closely with Regina on all of the logistical issues around the move and changes. Regina had received her redundancy letter early on and hadn't been at all surprised. She was sensible and knowledgeable enough about the university to anticipate how the cards would fall. Even though she knew her own days were numbered, she approached the necessary tasks with professionalism and dark humour. Her manner with Esther was as it had always been, friendly and straightforward, yet Esther sensed that Regina was applying a veneer of professionalism to their discussions that seemed somehow to hold her at arm's length; Esther could no longer imagine skiving off for coffee together to talk about her love life, for example. She hoped that she was imagining the growing distance between them, but as they sat poring over a class scheduling spreadsheet one day, Regina let the mask slip for a moment.

'Oh Lord,' said Esther, tracing down a column with a finger, 'Craig has proposed that Professor Knowles teach an introductory module in verse drama to the first years – Drama and English students combined. Knowles will have a coronary. She hasn't taught first years in a decade or more.'

'Yes, well,' said Regina, 'she'll just have to suck it up or go, won't she?'

Esther glanced at her, surprised. 'Everything okay?'

'Sorry,' said Regina curtly. 'Where were we? Verse drama? Can we not give the module to Farrell or Jones? An extra module to teach might make them look a little more indispensable.'

'Farrell's definitely going – he's had an offer to do some post-doc work in Edinburgh. And it's way outside Jones's area of interest.'

This time Regina just snorted. Then, without warning, she pushed her chair back from the desk and went to stand beside the window.

'Are you okay?' said Esther hesitantly.

'No, not really. I will be in a minute. I just wish...' Regina left the words hanging as she folded her arms tightly across her body. Esther could see that her broad shoulders were tense. 'I've been working with temperamental academics in this department for more than twenty years. Dealing with their foibles, their insistence that they won't go outside their comfort zone, and now...'

'Now...?'

'What about my comfort zone? What are my choices? The redundancy offer is shit – I'm sure you know that. Even though I've been here years. I'm not fifty yet, so taking early retirement would be financial suicide. I can't go out into the real world and look for a new job on the open market. I'm too old and too expensive. I know; I've looked. So my only option is to take something else on offer in the university. And do you know what's on offer? Assistant administrator in Electronic Engineering, or a job crunching numbers in the Admissions department. Less money, no contact with people, and I'd be working in areas in which I have no personal interest or investment. So, forgive me for being less than sympathetic that Prof Knowles might have to teach some first years.'

'I'm sorry.'

'It's not your fault,' said Regina, without turning from the window.

'It kind of is.'

Regina was silent. She clearly didn't have the energy for the platitudes she might once have produced. It was Esther's fault, and if anyone knew how Esther had dropped the ball in recent months, it was Regina. She stood by the window for a moment more, then returned to the desk, put on her glasses and continued with the job in hand, as professional and efficient as ever.

Esther had been so overwhelmed at what was happening to the department as a whole that she'd had little time to consider the impact on her own working life. But gradually it dawned on her that she would face as much change as anyone. She would no longer have her administrative duties and that, in a way, was a relief, but losing the position as head of department had financial implications too. She had earned well and been cautious with her money, so she was far from destitute, but she would definitely feel the drop in income. There were implications in terms of other funding too; she currently had the services of a PhD student to help her with some of her research, and this arrangement would fall away under the new regime. She also knew that her teaching load would increase; she would be taking on modules from staff members who were leaving but losing out on some postgraduate teaching work in modules that had been deemed not cost-effective. All in all, she would be teaching more of what she didn't like and a great deal less of what she did.

Like Regina, she considered the alternatives. Every evening, she found herself going over the possibilities in her head, fruitlessly looking through the websites where academic posts were advertised, and drinking glass after glass of wine. On a practical level, she didn't want to have to move institutions so late in her career. And, quite frankly, there weren't any opportunities at London universities that suited her. Moving further afield, with Lucie in her third year of secondary school, just wasn't an option. On top of that, she knew that abandoning what was left of her team for greener pastures would be cowardly and unscrupulous.

Michael was as kind and sympathetic as he could be but could offer no real solutions beyond suggesting that he move in with her sooner rather than later, so he could contribute to the mortgage and the running of the house. She knew he was doing it for the best and noblest of reasons and that it was a good and practical solution to her financial worries, but it made her feel pressured and desperate.

He let out his place in Surrey, put his furniture in storage and moved in. His ex-wife, Lisette, agreed to take his cat, as Esther was allergic. He brought all his clothes, boxes and boxes of books and a simply enormous television, which came with multiple speakers for cinema-style sound. It took him days to set it up in the living room, which was where Esther had her desk. As she tried to work in the evening, she had to contend with Michael clambering on the back of the sofa, rotating a speaker a millimetre to the left and then spending an age fiddling with buttons on a bewildering array of remote controls. She had no idea how any of it worked, or how she would operate it if she was ever inclined to see something on television.

There had been no time to refurbish or install additional storage, so she'd had to clear space in her wardrobes and drawers for Michael's things. Suddenly the house, which had always seemed quite big and airy for her and Lucie, felt cramped and over-full. She couldn't imagine how they would manage when Michael's sons came back from university.

She had a taste of what it might be like when they came to stay for a weekend shortly after Michael moved in. They were lovely boys – polite, charming and easy-going, and perfectly happy to sleep wherever they fell. She put one on the sofa and one on a fold-out bed that they had bought for Lucie's friends for sleepovers. But Luke and Oliver were just so *big*. Esther came down on Saturday morning to make tea and she was struck by a waft of funky, stale air from the living room as she opened the door. The floor was cluttered with the boys' possessions – clothes strewn around, kit bags gaping open, and their two large bodies sprawled under trailing duvets. One of Oliver's big bare feet hung over the edge of the sofa. She stood for a moment listening to their deep, sleepy breathing, and backed out. Tea could come later.

After an hour or so, they got up, and then the whole house seemed full of them – one toasting an unfeasibly large number of slices of bread in the kitchen, the other taking a long, loud shower upstairs. Then there was music blaring through the house, and all three men – Michael and both of his sons – settled themselves out on the deck, their long legs extended, chatting, laughing and dirtying more dishes. Esther told herself she didn't really mind. It was lovely to see Michael so happy in the company of his sons. They just took up rather a lot of room.

Lucie came downstairs and regarded them all with ill-disguised grumpiness. 'Urgh,' she said to Esther, who was in the kitchen trying to fit a few more cups into an already full dishwasher. 'There's too much man out there.'

'There is a lot of testosterone, isn't there?'

'They're all lovely,' said Lucie, trying to be charitable, 'it's just a bit much first thing. Can we go out?'

'Well, Sally did invite me for coffee this morning...' Esther began.

'Good, let's go. Sally's house is big and quiet and there are no smelly, hairy-legged boys there.'

They got to Sally's promptly at eleven, the appointed time, and Esther was surprised to see that Sally's car was missing from the driveway. Perhaps it had gone for repairs. She rang the doorbell, but there was no answer. She was walking back to her car, about to text and see if they had got the arrangement wrong, when Sally pulled up. She parked her car and hopped out, grinning broadly, wearing shorts and a bright-green shirt with a Macmillan Cancer Support logo on it. She rushed over and greeted Esther with a warm hug and a kiss on the cheek. It was the first time Esther had seen Sally since her revelation about helping Isabella to die. She had expected Sally to be reticent, perhaps, or awkward, but she seemed to be behaving in her usual cheerful way.

'You brought Lucie too! Fabulous! Sorry I'm late,' Sally said. She reached back into the car and brought out a shopping bag. 'I've got biccies though!'

'Where have you been?' Esther asked, as they went towards the house.

'I was just at Waitrose, but I've been at the race since six this morning.'

'Race? Did you run a race?'

'Heavens, no!' Sally laughed. 'No, I was a volunteer. Didn't I tell you?'

'No. A volunteer what?'

'Well, I've been thinking I wanted to do something worthwhile with my time, and so I looked up Macmillan on the internet. I knew I didn't want to be a charity-tin-shaking collection lady at Sainsbury's, but they have lots of other things you can do. I'm on a race support team. So I go along if there's a race, set up a tent for runners who are raising money for us, and offer them drinks and sweeties, and safety pins for their race numbers. Then I cheer them on as they cross the finish line.' Sally bustled around her kitchen, finding music on the iPod and setting it in its cradle on the speaker, then putting on the kettle and tipping chocolate digestives onto a plate as she talked. She'd let her hair grow a little longer and had scooped it back in a ponytail, which swung merrily as she moved.

'Sounds like fun,' said Lucie.

'It is! They're all such lovely people. And I get to look at lots of handsome young men in short shorts with very nice legs.'

'Yuck,' said Lucie. It was her default response to any suggestion that adults had sexual thoughts.

Esther was surprised to find her own eyebrows rising. It was the first time, as far as she could remember, that Sally had expressed an interest in a member of the opposite sex. Or in any sex, for that matter. There was no reason why she shouldn't – she was a single woman in her early forties, free to ogle, or date, or shag or marry as she pleased. But she had never mentioned it before. Esther realized that while she had observed Sally's outward transformation, she hadn't really considered how she might have changed inwardly – what might she want that she had never had? Had Sally ever had a boyfriend? Had sex? Esther had no idea.

'Did you see anything you liked?' she said calmly.

'Plenty!' Sally giggled. 'But they were all a bit young for me, I think.'

'What kind of race was it?'

'A ten-kilometre race in Richmond Park.'

'Ah. That will have attracted all the young bucks, trying to show how fast they are. Volunteer at a marathon, or a half-marathon next time. You want to find yourself an older fellow, someone with stamina who can keep going for a long time.'

'Mum!' gasped Lucie, horrified.

'Running! I meant one who can run for a long time,' said Esther innocently, and Lucie gazed at her balefully.

Sally and Esther glanced at one another and burst out laughing. 'Sorry, Lucie,' said Sally contritely. 'It's me making your mum behave badly.'

Lucie narrowed her eyes and glared at Sally with mock anger. 'You also made her laugh though, and I haven't heard her laugh for months, so I forgive you.'

They sat at Sally's kitchen table, eating biscuits and drinking tea, and Sally chattered happily about her volunteering, and the latest production by the amateur theatre group with which she was involved. She was even planning a holiday, she told them – a fortnight on a Greek island.

'I never got to travel when I was young,' she said. 'Not like Isabella did. I think now might just be my time.'

'Full of handsome, dark-eyed men, the Greek islands,' observed Esther. 'And they're rather fond of blonde ladies, I'm told.'

'Are they?' said Sally demurely. 'That hadn't crossed my mind!'

This time even Lucie giggled, although she was still obliged to say 'Eeeuw!' with pre-teen horror.

Esther leaned back in her chair and sipped her tea. Lucie was right, it was the first time she had smiled or laughed in a very long time. Throughout her life, Esther had been the serious one. She had grown up the gawky only child, had lost her heart to *A Tale of Two Cities* as soon as she was old enough to read it, and had found her sense of truth and reality between the pages of books ever since. She had been in awe of her mother's bright, creative spirit, and of Isabella's mercurial, magnetic personality. She had never learned the knack of lightness.

And yet here was Sally, once so awkward and dowdy, finding her own grace and sweetness. Sally laughed uproariously at something Lucie had said. How could she be so merry and frivolous? After all she'd been through? Sally had lost years of her life – the possibilities of a career, marriage, children – to the care of Isabella and her mother. And yet here she was, laughing and happy. Esther herself couldn't imagine a time when the darkness of Laura's death and the car-crash of her career would lift sufficiently for her to laugh like that. Was it possible that Sally just felt – less?

Sally got up to put the cups into the sink and wash up, and Esther was suddenly reminded of watching her wash up before – years before, in the last, awful days of Isabella's illness. She had gone round to see Isabella and found Sally in the kitchen, her face grey with exhaustion, standing at the sink mechanically washing up. Esther had offered to take over, but with an absent-minded 'No, no,' Sally had begun to scrub and rinse glasses, cups and plates. 'Isabella doesn't eat at all,' she said. 'But somehow we always seem to have a mountain of dirty dishes.'

'It's the visitors,' Esther had said, itching to get at the sink. 'Cups of tea and whatnot. You need to be less hospitable.'

'Well, there are fewer visitors than there were…' said Sally, and a cup slipped from her clumsy, tired fingers.

'Sally, please sit down and let me do it. It's bad enough that people come here and you have to entertain them on top of everything else. You shouldn't have to clean up as well.'

'If I sit down, I'll fall asleep,' said Sally.

'Then fall asleep. Isabella's sleeping now. If she wakes, I can do anything she needs.'

'She won't let you.'

'She bloody will. I'll make sure she does. You're about to drop. You've barely slept for weeks. Go. Rest.'

'She's due one of the big blue pills at two o'clock,' said Sally, stepping away from the sink reluctantly and drying her hands. 'Nothing more until six, I think. Except for the morphine, which she can have whenever, but I measured it out already and it's on her bedside table.' A look of alarm crossed her face. 'Oh, but if she needs moving, or any toilet things…'

'I'll call you. I promise. Now sleep.'

Sally went off to her bedroom and, to Esther's relief, shut the door. She knew Sally had been sleeping in fits and starts, getting up to Isabella ten or more times a night. She must be attuned to the slightest noise. With the door shut, Sally would at least have a chance of getting a couple of hours of uninterrupted sleep. Esther finished washing up as quickly and quietly as she could, then dried everything and packed it away behind the milky-white glass of Isabella's elegant kitchen cabinets. She poured herself a glass of water and, slipping off her shoes, went through to Isabella's room.

Isabella's king-size bed had been replaced with a high hospital one, and she lay, her head awkwardly tilted to one side, asleep. She was thin; that was to be expected. Esther had watched the flesh fall off her in the past six months until she was so tiny, so emaciated, that it seemed impossible for her body to support life at all. Esther had stopped seeing the thinness and looked instead at Isabella's eyes. Were they lively, or dulled by pain medication?

Right now, Isabella's eyes were half-open – Esther had noticed that the morphine tended to make her sleep like that. It was extremely disconcerting; it seemed she was watching you from below half-closed lids. But her regular breathing and the tiny, erratic movements of her fingers which lay on the bed covers told Esther she was indeed fast asleep.

Esther slipped into the chair which stood beside the bed and very quietly took out her diary and glasses. She needed to take a look at her timetable for the next few weeks and schedule in a few extra conferences with students who were working on their dissertations. With Isabella so ill, she also wanted to make sure there was plenty of leeway in her diary; she might need more time off to spend with her and, inevitably, for the funeral, and—

'Speccy four-eyes.' Esther jumped. Isabella's voice was gravelly and hoarse. She had turned her head on the pillow and lay looking at Esther. Her lips were dry and cracked, but her smile was wide and amused.

Esther snapped her diary shut and forced a smile herself. How could she be sitting beside Isabella's bed, trying to fit her funeral into a schedule?

'Could you pass me the water?' Isabella asked. There was a child's water bottle on the bedside table, one with a built-in bendy straw. Esther gave it to her, noting how Isabella's hands shook.

Isabella took a few sips. 'Thanks,' she said, passing back the bottle. 'I know it's not a champagne flute, but it stops me tipping water all over the sheets.'

'So, how're you doing?' Esther asked, slipping her diary back into her bag and taking off her glasses.

'Oh, yadda yadda, dying of cancer, you know. Much the same. More to the point, when did you start wearing spectacles?'

'I got them last week. I realized the other day that I couldn't read the instructions on my bottle of shampoo.'

'Wash, rinse, repeat. What's to read?'

'I was musing about whether the repeat was still required. Anyway, I realized I couldn't read a word, so I asked Stephen if they'd made the print smaller, but he could read it perfectly well. So I went for an eye test.'

'And they said…?'

'That I have elderly eyes. Nothing to be done. I just needed reading specs.'

'Elderly eyes? Bloody hell.'

Esther was glad to have made her smile. She noticed that Isabella's own eyes had big, dark shadows beneath them and were especially wide and staring. That was new, a change in the last few days. She looked as if she was gazing at something far away.

'How's work?' Isabella asked, and Esther told her a story about a colleague who had done something which had led to an argument about something inconsequential to do with student attendance. She had found herself storing up anecdotes about people Isabella didn't know, who had done things that were uncontroversial, so they could keep talking in their customary light, dry style.

Isabella dropped the occasional comment about her condition into conversation, but anytime Esther tried to discuss it with her, she became evasive, made jokes and changed the subject. She didn't want to talk about her prognosis. She didn't want to talk about anything serious, and she especially didn't want to be drawn into reminiscences. From long experience, Esther knew that the last thing Isabella would want would be a mawkish declaration of love and loyalty, as if the years of friendship they had shared could be summed up with platitudes. She didn't want that either.

She also knew that if she opened her heart, she would cry, and that if she started to cry at this screaming injustice, she would not be able to stop. And after all, it wasn't even her tragedy. She had her health, a husband, a child, a career, a future. Isabella had a bouquet of tumours that were eating her from the inside out.

'Did you bring the newspaper?' Isabella asked.

Esther had. Isabella often asked her to pick up a copy of the *Guardian* on her way over. She wasn't really up to reading herself, but she liked Esther to page through the paper and read her the headlines and the odd article. Esther usually skimmed over the political news and looked for celebrity gossip, of which there wasn't a great deal, but today Isabella asked her to turn back to the front page. There had been another shooting in America, this time in the Amish community. Esther sighed and made a passing comment about wishing Americans would see sense and tighten up their gun laws.

'Why?' said Isabella, and Esther looked up, surprised to hear her sounding so aggressive.

'Because things like this keep happening. These senseless shootings...'

'Americans have the right to bear arms enshrined in their constitution,' said Isabella hotly. 'They're a frontier people. It's in their blood. You are never, ever going to change that.'

'Perhaps not, but they're going to have to address the ongoing problem of mass shootings and gun violence.'

'That's very smug of you.' Isabella's tone was ugly. 'I'm sure they'd be thrilled to hear what some English lecturer in London, who's never held a gun and probably never even seen one, thinks about it.'

'Well, I...'

'What if you were in your home and some crack addict, some crazed lunatic broke in with a gun? Would you say, "Please hold on, my good sir, and let me inform you about how I believe in more stringent gun laws," while he gunned down Lucie and Stephen?'

'Why are you being so vile?'

'Why are you being such a left-wing pussy?'

Esther looked at Isabella, whose face was twisted into a snarl. She didn't understand what had just happened.

'Listen, just go, okay?' Isabella said. 'You make me sick. Just go. And don't come back. I don't want to see you.'

'Isabella...'

'Go. Fuck off with your lefty principles and your soft-on-crime stance. Just go.'

And Isabella turned her face to the window and refused to look at Esther at all.

Esther sat there for a moment, then carefully folded the newspaper, put it in her bag and walked out of the room. She walked down the long, white corridor that formed the spine of Isabella's beautiful home. It had a skylight that flooded the whole house with light. She found Sally in the kitchen, her hair mussed from sleep, painstakingly putting pills into little plastic containers.

'I heard shouting,' said Sally, without looking up.

'I'm so sorry we woke you. She picked a fight with me about gun control,' said Esther, bewildered. 'She came out with a tirade of right-wing, pro-gun views I didn't know she held.'

'And then she told you to go away and not come back.'

'Yes.'

'She's done it to everyone who's come in the last few days. Everyone important. Our mum, even.'

'Why?'

'I don't know. I think she wants people to stop coming. I think it's too hard for her.'

'Physically?'

'No. That's not it.'

'She doesn't know how to say goodbye,' said Esther, realizing.

'She's never been good at the soppy stuff. She's always said so.'

'She's been doing it to everyone?'

'Pretty much. Everyone she really loves. She lets the odd random person in and doesn't yell at them. No rhyme or reason, really. She's just dismissing people, it seems.'

'Except you.'

'Oh, she tells me to go away all the time. But she knows I have the drugs, so she doesn't really mean it.'

'Should I keep coming?'

'You can try, but she sent Mum away this morning without seeing her. I can't promise she'll let you in. She's making her choices. We have to respect them.'

'I suppose we do,' said Esther, not sure whether she wanted to cry or be sick. 'I just don't want the last time I see her to be... her telling me to fuck off.'

'I know. But it's Isabella. She's always told people to F off. Even when she wasn't dying.'

It wasn't the last time Esther saw her. She visited later the same week, but Isabella refused to see her. Then she returned the following week, and Isabella let her in, grudgingly. She dozed for 90 per cent of the time Esther was there. When Esther was certain Isabella was asleep, she stood up quietly to go. Isabella opened her eyes. 'This is the last time, old friend,' she whispered. 'For me. Don't come back. Please.'

Esther nodded. She didn't kiss or touch her. She walked out without looking back.

CHAPTER THIRTY-FIVE

The weekend after Esther and Lucie's visit to Sally's new house, Lucie went to stay with Stephen and Melissa. For the first time in weeks, or even months, the stress in Esther's life seemed to have abated slightly. She was experiencing a temporary lull at work – the short-term arrangements had all been made, and it was a case of waiting for the changes to take effect. Those who were leaving had yet to leave, but the plans were in place for them to do so, and while new timetables had been drawn up, they had not yet been put into practice.

Esther and Michael went out for a peaceful dinner at a local restaurant on the Friday evening, and Michael proposed a lie-in on the Saturday morning.

'But there's housework to do,' Esther protested, unenthusiastically.

'Indeed there is,' said Michael. 'And it'll still be there at lunchtime, when we get up. Come on. We haven't had a lazy morning in bed in forever.'

It did sound appealing – dozy lovemaking, maybe a little desultory reading, and an indulgent mid-morning nap. 'Well, if I must. Of course, I'd much rather be hoovering. But for you, I'll make the sacrifice.'

'Thank you, my love,' said Michael, taking her hand. 'You're so selfless.'

Knowing they'd be having a lazy morning, they stayed up late, sharing a couple of bottles of wine when they got home and talking until the early hours. When Esther's mobile rang at 6 a.m., she was so deeply asleep that it took thirty seconds or so for her to isolate the ringtone from her dreams. When she finally jerked awake, she sat up abruptly, her heart pounding, and grabbed the phone. She could see Lucie's number on the caller display. As she fumbled to answer it, the call cut out and her phone must have gone to voicemail. Why would Lucie be ringing at six in the morning? Something terrible must have gone wrong. She tried to ring back, but Lucie's phone went to voicemail too – she must be leaving a message. She was too worried to wait and listen to the message, so she just kept hitting redial. Blearily, Michael stirred next to her and turned over.

'Wha…?'

'Lucie,' she said, dialling again, her fingers shaking.

Michael glanced at the alarm clock on his side of the bed. 'Six in the morning? Must be the baby.'

The baby. Of course. On this attempt, finally, Lucie's phone rang and she answered immediately.

'Mum! Mum! She's here! We had to get up in the middle of the night because Melissa's waters broke at, like, ten last night. Dad wouldn't let me ring you till now. Anyway, she's here! We're at the hospital. I just held her. Mum, she's amazing! I've got a little sister!'

'Is Melissa all right? And the baby?'

'Melissa's fine, just tired. And Dad's so proud – he keeps crying, how lame is that? He's taken about a million pictures.'

'That's lovely, darling.' Esther tried not to think too much about Stephen's rather less enthusiastic reaction to Lucie's own birth. He'd been there, and he'd held her, but as a younger, deliberately cynical man, he'd felt the need to make sarcastic comments about how squashed and red she was. He certainly hadn't wept or taken photos. Clearly, as a fifty-year-old, he felt more able to be emotional and open. Well, good for Melissa for softening him up. 'Does the baby have a name yet?'

'Lyla. Isn't that lovely? They chose it to go with my name: Lyla and Lucie. She's got lots of black hair at the moment, but Melissa reckons that might fall out and she'll be blonde like her. And her hands and feet are so tiny...'

Michael was lying on his back, watching Esther, and she mouthed, 'A girl, all fine,' to him. He nodded and gave her the thumbs up.

Lucie was still chattering excitedly about the baby and how brilliant the nurses had been. Esther made a few encouraging murmurs, but then Lucie suddenly said, 'So, can I stay? Please?'

'What, sweetie?'

'Can I stay at Dad's next week? We're taking the baby home later today, and Melissa says she could really do with my help with bathing and nappies and things. Dad says he'll come past yours to pick up my school things. Can I stay? Till Wednesday or so?'

'Oh, Lucie, I don't know. School...'

'I've done all my homework. Dad says he'll drop me and collect me every day – he's not working for the next couple of weeks anyway. Please, Mum.'

How could she say no? Lucie's little sister — half-sister — had just been born. Of course she would want to be there.

Predictably, Wednesday got extended to Friday, and then Lucie begged to stay until the weekend, so, in the end, she didn't come home until the following Sunday. Esther tried not to mind; on a practical level, it made her working week easier, and she knew she should be glad that Stephen was again nearby and keeping Lucie involved, but she missed her, and she couldn't help nurturing a deep, ugly knot of resentment at the idea of them all snuggled up together like the perfect nuclear family — Stephen and his trio of girls.

Monday morning began well enough. Lucie, for once, was up bright and early. But it soon transpired that this was only because she wanted to Skype Melissa and see how little Lyla was doing. She sat at the kitchen counter with her laptop open, cooing at the screen as she watched Melissa changing Lyla's nappy. Esther, rushing around trying to get ready for the week, waved a distracted hello and tried to sound sweet and not hectoring as she reminded Lucie that she needed to get ready for school. Lucie ignored her, and Esther, busy with her own preparations, didn't keep too close an eye on the clock until, at 8.20, she realized that Lucie was not dressed, hadn't had breakfast, and was now going to be unconscionably late unless she herself made a detour and drove her to school.

'Lucie,' she said, quietly, and then, more sharply, 'Lucie! Look at the time.' When Lucie ignored her and continued to chat, she had no option but to lean in so Lucie's webcam showed her on screen and say, 'Melissa, so sorry, but Lucie has to get ready for school. She'll catch up with you later.'

Lucie signed off, but she was furious. 'That was so rude, Mum! How could you? I'm so embarrassed. Poor Melissa!'

There was no point in trying to talk sense into her, or argue. There simply wasn't time. She had to resort to barking instructions, just to get Lucie into the car. They left ten minutes later than she would have liked, and those crucial minutes dropped them bang in the middle of rush hour, adding forty-five minutes to her journey time to the university, making her half an hour late for a seminar. Naturally, the students had taken advantage of the university's staff lateness rule – they had waited the regulation fifteen minutes, then departed, reporting her absence to the department office.

It was the ammunition Craig had been waiting for. After she had rushed to the seminar room and made sure no students were there, she went back to her office to collect books and notes for her next class. She had to walk past Craig's office, with its open door ('I'm there for all of you, anytime, anytime at all,' he had announced expansively at the first joint departmental meeting). He glanced up as she passed and beckoned her in.

'Ah, Esther, my sweet,' he said, his voice warm and jovial. 'Come in! Come in!' Hesitantly, she did as she was asked. 'Sit down! Can I get you anything? Coffee?'

'No, thanks. I'm running a bit late, as it happens, and I need to get ready for a class.'

'Yes,' he said, his tone confiding and sympathetic. 'I did hear you didn't make it to your early seminar.'

Esther said nothing. She had no idea how he had heard, and so quickly. She certainly wasn't going to apologize or make excuses.

'You've been having a bit of a rough time, I believe.' Craig leaned back in his chair and pressed his fingertips together as if he was praying. 'A lot of absences, time away from the university. I took a look at your personnel file – I hope you don't mind.' His face was bland and friendly. She did mind, very much indeed. But she knew that as her boss, he now had the right to look at her file and she couldn't do a damned thing about it. 'We all know your mother died. I'm so sorry.' He didn't sound sorry. 'And then there was that little jaunt you took, without the principal's approval, you saucy minx. A naughty weekend in Venice with the new man, I heard.'

It was grotesque – a parody of intimate gossip. She felt certain he was going to click his fingers and call her 'girlfriend'. This wasn't the real him – he was faking it, pretending they were buddies as he dripped his poison, obliquely threatening her.

'You've been at the university how long?' he asked, smiling innocently.

'Twenty years,' she said flatly, knowing full well that if he had looked at her personnel file, he would know that.

'Wow, that's a long time. You must get tired, teaching year in, year out.' He paused for a long moment. 'After all those years, it would be such a pity if anyone had cause to doubt your... commitment, or to think you'd become complacent.'

She sat silently, her hands in her lap. She wasn't going to give him the satisfaction of a reply, let alone an argument.

He grinned broadly. 'Let's chat again soon,' he said, turning back towards his computer monitor. 'I'll keep an eye on how you're getting on and see if there aren't ways in which we, as a department, could help you.'

He began to type, quickly and efficiently, and Esther realized she had been dismissed. She got up, and with as much dignity as she could muster, left Craig's office without saying goodbye.

'It's verging on constructive dismissal,' Michael said, standing in the kitchen that evening as Esther viciously chopped tomatoes. 'He can't fire you or make you redundant, so he's going to make your life an absolute misery, to the point where you're forced to leave. He knows what he's doing as well, because he hasn't said or done anything that would be considered illegal if you went to tribunal. He's a clever little bastard.'

'So what do I do?'

'You have two choices. Stick it out, and make sure you're above reproach in everything you do, so you don't give him ammunition—'

'He'll manufacture ammunition if I don't give him any.'

'Possibly.'

'What's my other choice?'

'Leave.'

'And go where? I've looked around – there's nothing. It's not as if I have a rare area of expertise, or I've recently published some ground-breaking book. Craig's right. I have become complacent.'

'Why go anywhere?'

'What do you mean?'

'Take early retirement. Write. Why not?'

'Early retirement? I'm forty-eight! What would I live on? I've got years yet to pay into my pension.'

'But what if...' Michael hesitated. 'Well, I've got a lump sum, quite a big one, from selling the house when Lisette and I split up. What if we paid off the mortgage?'

'Wait... Hang on... You want to pay off my mortgage?'

'It's one possibility.'

'So I would be retired, with a very limited personal income, and you would own half my house? Are you completely insane?' Michael looked at her, eyebrows raised, and she realized she was shouting. She didn't stop. 'This is my only security,' she said harshly. 'This house, and my job. This is all I have for Lucie and me. I'm not about to give it up to be a *dependant*.' She spat out the last word angrily, and she saw Michael rear back slightly at her ugly tone.

'I'm sorry you see it that way,' he said. 'I thought the plan was that this would be our house, until we bought one together. I had this quaint notion that we were planning a future life together. A kind of... till-death-us-do-part arrangement, where we help each other when we can, through difficult times. I must have got it wrong.'

She wanted to shout some more, to rail against his tone of injured pride, but she knew, from years of battling Stephen, how it was all too easy to say things that could not then be unsaid. Not every point needed to be scored, not every fight needed to be won. With great effort, she said, 'I'm sorry.'

'Me too,' he said. 'I wasn't trying to swoop in and take over, really I wasn't. I wasn't offering a solution whereby you give up your independence and don a frilly apron to make my dinner. I was just offering a starting point. I wanted you to know that I'm here, that there are other options. If that's not the right one, maybe we can find a compromise. Who knows? I would say, "I'm only trying to help", but then I would fully understand if you threw a spatula at my head.'

She smiled weakly. 'I know you want to help,' she said. 'I'm sorry I flew off the handle.' She stepped into his arms and he held her, but there was something tentative in both of them, as if what was between them might have been bruised.

She turned away from him and went to the fridge to refill her wine glass. 'Do you want some?' she asked over her shoulder. He shook his head. She knew she was drinking a lot, more than she used to, and that Michael, conversely, seemed to be drinking less. But she didn't care. Alcohol seemed to be the only thing that quelled the over-the-top-of-the-rollercoaster feeling in her belly.

Luke and Oliver came to London again that weekend, arriving on the Friday afternoon when Esther was still at work. She had imagined that sleeping on sofas and floors would put them off visiting until there were better arrangements, but she was wrong. Her house was much closer to central London than Michael's Surrey home had been, and the boys had obviously worked out that it was a useful base for nights out in town.

When she got home on Friday evening, tired from a week of battling Craig and teaching great crowds of indifferent first years, all she wanted was to get a cold beer or two from the fridge and sit on the deck in the gathering dusk, listening to the birds. But Luke, Oliver and six of their friends had colonized the deck, and with it, all the beer. They were good boys, and as soon as she came in, Luke jumped up and apologized. 'I hope you don't mind,' he said. 'The guys just came round to say hi. We're on our way out in half an hour or so. Can I nip out and get in some more beer?'

There wasn't a shop nearby, not within easy walking distance anyway. She knew he didn't have a car, and even if he had, he'd been drinking. 'Of course not.' She smiled. 'Enjoy yourselves. I'll be inside with a glass of wine if you need anything.'

Luke grinned at her. He had Michael's sweet, heart-melting smile. He gave her a warm, one-armed hug. 'You're amazing, Esther,' he said. 'So, so cool.' He bounded back outside, where the boys were laughing loudly and singing along to a song blaring out of someone's phone.

And of course, she had to be cool. They were Michael's boys, and they were as sweet and considerate as two great, lunking six-foot boys could be in a small space not designed for them. They took up a lot of room, ate a lot and slept late. None of this was malicious or deliberately difficult. Nevertheless, as she loaded the dishwasher for what seemed to be the hundredth time, tripped over big trainers left beside the sofa, and opened the fridge to discover it was empty again, she found it incredibly hard not to be tight-lipped or judgemental.

Lucie seemed to hate them all. She snapped at Esther and was barely civil to Michael. She said she found Luke and Oliver embarrassing, and didn't want to invite her friends round when they were there. They were big and sporty and loud, she said, but Esther suspected that her resentment had more to do with the way Clara, Zoe and Rebecca turned giggly and silly in the presence of the older boys. Lucie seemed to find every aspect of their home life wanting. All she talked about was Lyla, her little sister, and how she wanted to be with her. She used every excuse to go over to Stephen and Melissa's house, and stayed there as much as she was allowed to. Esther found it impossible not to be infuriated with Lucie's behaviour. She was sulky, ungrateful and unhelpful. She resented any request that she participate in family life. At the same time, however, Esther knew that snapping at Lucie and demanding she pull her weight would only make things worse. If she ever asked Lucie to do something, Lucie would inevitably come back with 'I don't have to do that at Dad's,' or 'Melissa doesn't make me...' Esther tried to keep a tight rein on her patience when Lucie came out with comments like that, but frequently she lost the battle.

In contrast, Michael was boundlessly kind and tolerant with Lucie, and jolly and easy with his own sons. He always seemed to be defusing tense moments between Esther and the various children. He would come home to find her gazing angrily into an empty fridge and would laughingly blow her a kiss from the doorway and immediately turn around to go to the supermarket and restock. He cajoled Lucie out of her blacker moods and took over driving her to school to save Esther the stress of getting her daughter out of the house on time. And perversely, the better he was at managing the wrinkles of their new family life, the more she resented him.

As she said to Sally one evening, over a glass of wine on the deck, 'We're stuck in this good-cop/bad-cop routine. The kids do something impossible. I snarl. Michael makes light of my bad temper and fixes the problem. I look bitter, stiff and incompetent and he looks like a hero.'

'He is very patient,' said Sally. 'Is there such a thing as too patient?' She looked over the rim of her wine glass at Esther, and

Esther caught the twinkle in her eye. She laughed – for the first time in ages, it seemed.

'Oh, now I sound awful again,' she said. 'Disloyal and awful.'

'Nonsense. What you're doing is bloody difficult. Work, Michael moving in, all the kids... It's perfectly natural that you're feeling the strain. And when we do, we often take it out on the people closest to us. That's why they're the people closest to us. Because they can take it.'

'That was very profound.' Esther refilled their wine glasses. 'You should write it down.'

'It was, wasn't it? In days gone by, it would've been embroidered on a tea towel.'

'Now it would be an internet meme. Complete with a picture of a woman doing yoga on a beach.'

Esther marvelled at how she could still be light and funny and irreverent with Sally – she didn't seem able to achieve that with anyone else in her life. It helped that when Sally came over or she went to hers, there always seemed to be plenty of wine. And at least Sally didn't look at her quite so judgementally as Michael did when she filled her glass to the brim again.

Sally wasn't Isabella, not by any stretch of the imagination, and never would be. But somehow the long duration of their acquaintance and the history they shared made their interaction lighter and easier than her other relationships. Isabella had freed Esther to be silly, to be a little wild. Isabella had taken a serious, bookish, shy girl and led her to new places, daring her to be brave and funny. That first act of truancy the day they met, when she took Esther to hide in the school gymnasium, was the beginning of a relationship full of adventures and cajoling. Esther had flowered as Isabella's friend, and with Isabella's death, she had wondered whether that part of her would die too. But somehow, with Sally, she could find her again, that girl with the lighter touch. She could be, in Sally's eyes at least, what Isabella had once made her.

'All joking aside, Michael is a very good guy,' said Sally, interrupting Esther's reverie. 'One of the best. I'm sure many women wish they had one like him.'

Her tone was a little wistful, Esther thought. 'No one on the horizon for you, then?'

'No, yes… Well… Maybe,' said Sally hesitantly.

'What?' Esther asked excitedly. 'You mean you're seeing someone?'

'It's just been a couple of dates.'

'What? Dark horse. Tell me all!'

'Not much to tell. You were right. There were older, nice chaps at the longer races, when I started volunteering at them. And one of them asked me out for a drink after he finished running. Turns out he lives reasonably nearby, and we've been out a couple of times. He's a nice guy. I'm just… not in the market for anything long-term.'

She looked out of the window and Esther was struck once more by her ethereal prettiness. If anything, she'd got slightly too thin. And Esther had to admit, Sally had it all now. Her own home, substantial independent means, a busy, happy social life. It seemed odd that she wouldn't be looking to share that with someone. Maybe she had got too much in the habit of being on her own? Or maybe the man she was dating just wasn't the one.

CHAPTER THIRTY-SIX

Michael was away at a conference in Edinburgh, and Esther had had a particularly bloody week at work. She left the university late on the Friday and drove home feeling limp and bruised. It was a small mercy that Luke and Oliver wouldn't be coming to stay – they hadn't yet reached the point where they felt comfortable in Esther's house without their dad – so Esther was looking forward to a quiet weekend with Lucie. A chance to regroup, work on the garden and prepare herself for the trials of the week to come. The traffic was heavy, so it was almost six when she finally got home. As soon as she opened the door, she knew Lucie wasn't there. The house had the undisturbed quiet of a place no one had entered for many hours. She called out anyway, and listened to her own voice echo up the stairs. She looked around for a note and checked her mobile, but there were no messages. Frowning, she rang Lucie's mobile. Her daughter answered immediately, and before Esther could ask her where she was, she heard the wail of a baby in the background.

'You're at Dad's,' she said flatly.

'Oh, yeah,' said Lucie evasively. 'Didn't I say? I came after school. Can I stay?'

'No,' said Esther. 'No, you can't.'

'What?' Lucie's shriek was high with disbelief. 'I can't believe it, Mum! I just want to be with my little sister! How can you be so mean?' Her reaction was unnecessarily histrionic, and Esther knew the performance was as much for Stephen and Melissa's benefit as her own.

'You've been at Dad's place every weekend since Lyla was born,' said Esther as calmly as she could. 'You knew perfectly well that we were going to have this weekend together at home. You've gone over there without letting me know, hoping that I'll let you stay because you're there already. Well, I'm sorry, I don't like sneaky behaviour. Pack up your things and let Dad know I'm getting in the car and coming to get you.'

She hung up on Lucie's storm of protest, picked up her car keys and headed for the door. It was a no-win situation – she'd be dragging Lucie home, looking like the bad guy again, and she would now be spending the weekend with a child in the blackest of sulks. Nevertheless, she had to make a stand.

She hadn't been inside the house since Stephen had moved back to London – she usually only got as far as the doorstep, dropping Lucie off or picking her up. But this time when she rang the bell, Stephen answered the door, looking serious, and invited her in. She followed him into the living room, where Melissa sat on the sofa, breastfeeding little Lyla with Lucie nestled by her side. They looked the picture of contentment in the warm glow of a lamp – Melissa's blonde head and Lucie's dark one bent over the small, snuffling baby. Esther had met Melissa a few times in the past, but she hadn't seen her since the birth of the baby. She had sent a gift and card to congratulate them but had felt it wasn't appropriate to visit. Well, she was here now, looking at her husband's new wife, and at this child who shared half of Lucie's genes but none of hers.

Lucie looked up as she came into the room, and the happiness fell from her face like a shadow. She set her features in an expression of stony defiance. Esther felt so tired. There was no way she was going to get Lucie to come home with her willingly. She sat down on a chair facing the sofa and put her handbag gently on the floor. Stephen remained standing in the doorway behind her.

'I didn't come here to fight,' she said gently.

'No, just to drag me back to your place,' said Lucie coldly. Esther noted she didn't say 'home'.

'Lucie, you're thirteen years old. You came here without letting me know where you'd gone. It was dangerous, disobedient and just plain wrong. You know that. It's not that I want to keep you from Lyla...'

Lucie snorted and rolled her eyes. Melissa was watching Esther intently over the baby's head.

'... I just want to keep you safe,' Esther finished, rather lamely.

'We also want to keep her safe,' said Melissa, rather sharply. 'Safe and happy.'

Esther frowned and looked at her. 'Are you suggesting she's not happy?'

Melissa didn't say anything, but she raised her pretty eyebrows and glanced over at Lucie, who was slumped on the sofa, arms folded, glowering at her mother.

'Melissa...' said Stephen, with a note of warning in his voice. Then he turned to Esther. 'Esther, now seems a good time to talk about the... situation we have here.'

And in that moment, Esther realized she had walked straight into a set-up. They'd worked it all out. Stephen did the talking. Lucie added a few comments, speaking in an oddly polite, stilted and rehearsed way. Melissa, uncharacteristically, kept silent. They knew, Stephen said carefully, that Esther had been having a very difficult time, both at work and establishing her new home life with Michael and his boys. She was clearly under strain and very busy. Melissa was at home during the day and was happy to drive Lucie to school and collect her. Lucie loved being with her baby sister, and the room she had here in the Islington house was bigger than the one in Esther's house. Could she not make her weekday home with them in Islington, returning to Esther every second weekend? And in the holidays, of course?

Esther looked at Lucie's face. There was a sprinkling of acne on her high forehead, and she kept her lips tightly pursed over her slightly too big front teeth. Her features had been blurred by the changes of adolescence, but Esther could still see beneath them the perfect baby oval that had entranced her and stolen her heart. The pain was visceral and intense. 'I'll need some time to think about it,' she said, standing up suddenly. 'Lucie, perhaps I might collect you on Sunday afternoon and we could go for a walk and talk?'

She made her way to the door with all the dignity she could muster and said goodbye to Stephen without meeting his eye. She had asked for time to think, but in the instant Stephen made the proposal, she knew full well that there was only one possible answer. All she wanted to do now was get home, open a bottle of wine, drink the whole thing, forget and sleep.

She woke up early the next morning – before sunrise – and lay unmoving in the middle of her bed, staring up at the ceiling in the grey pre-dawn light. The house was unnaturally silent. She couldn't remember the last time she had woken up there completely alone. She knew she wasn't going to be able to get back to sleep, but she couldn't face getting up and wandering through the empty rooms. She took a book from her bedside table and tried to read, but she couldn't concentrate. In times gone by, she'd have got up and gone for a run, but she hadn't run for weeks now, and she could feel the result of that in her softening middle and sluggish lack of energy.

She could hear the silence in Lucie's room across the hall, like a presence. She'd have to live with that silence now, week in and week out. She sat up in bed and hugged her knees. It was five in the morning. Michael was asleep in his hotel room in Edinburgh. She had rung him the evening before and briefly told him what had transpired at Stephen's. He had been warmly sympathetic.

'I'm so sorry, my love,' he said. 'For what it's worth, Oliver went through a phase like that – pitting Lisette and me against each other, asking to live with the other one every time he was subject to a bit of discipline. Lucie may well find life with a tiny baby isn't as easy as she thinks and that she doesn't like the rules in Stephen's house either.'

He was right, of course, and in her calmer moments Esther knew that this phase would pass – must pass. But for so long it had been just her and Lucie, and she had imagined their bond to be inviolable and that Lucie's loyalty belonged to her, as hers belonged to Lucie. Somehow, without knowing how, she had failed as a mother. She smiled ruefully in the dawn light. She could chalk that one up on her board of failures, under her failure as a head of department, as a daughter, as a wife. It was only in her relationship with Michael that she seemed to be succeeding, and that was undoubtedly due to Michael's almost saintly forbearance, rather than through any action of hers.

The ensuing wave of self-pity drove her out of bed and into the shower. She had to do something. She dressed and went downstairs. In a brief fit of feverish activity, she cleaned the kitchen, put on a load of laundry and made a pot of coffee. She wouldn't sit and wallow. She fired up her computer and opened the folder which contained her long-neglected book chapter – the one on Austen that she should have delivered months ago. Still, no point in dwelling on what hadn't been done. She could only do what she could.

She read through what she had written already. It was completely foreign to her – she had no recollection at all of setting down those words, or indeed what argument she might have been advancing. She hesitated for a long moment, then selected the text and deleted it. She put her hands on the keyboard, looked at the blank page in front of her and began to type fast and fluently.

Hours must have passed – she had no idea how many. She got up from her desk only to refresh the coffee pot or to find a book for a reference. If she had stepped back to consider it, she might have marvelled that in this time of extreme insecurity, she was able to write with a courage and certainty she hadn't known since her undergraduate days. When the doorbell rang, making her jump, she glanced for the first time at the word count and the clock. She had written six thousand words, and it was 9 a.m.

It was Sally, clutching a steaming bag of warm croissants and a wrapped bunch of flowers. 'Breakfast?' she said, waving the bag aloft.

Esther ran her fingers through her unbrushed hair and swallowed. Her mouth tasted foul from all the coffee and she was suddenly starving.

'Hell, yes,' she said. 'Come in. Let me go and brush my hair and teeth. Can you pop the kettle on?'

As she headed up the stairs, she shouted down, 'Tea for me. I can't take any more coffee.'

When she came back down, there was a mug of tea and an almond croissant on a plate. Sally had found a vase and an outrageous tumble of sunflowers reflected a warm yellow light through the kitchen. She was humming at the sink, rinsing out the coffee pot. She came to sit at the kitchen counter with Esther and chatted amiably about the races at which she'd been volunteering and about her plan to drive to Warwickshire for a weekend away. It wasn't usual for her to talk so much about herself. It took a moment to dawn on Esther that Sally hadn't asked where everyone was. She didn't think she had told Sally that Michael would be away, and Sally would usually have asked after Lucie. She frowned a little suspiciously.

Sally caught her change of expression. 'Everything okay?' she asked.

'Why are you here?' said Esther. 'I ask this with all the love in the world, and I'm thrilled to see you. But is this just an impromptu Saturday morning visit?'

Sally sighed. 'I'm rubbish, aren't I? I'd never make a spy. Lucie rang me last night and said she was a bit worried that you might be upset. I said I'd pop round and see how you were.'

Esther put her head down on the kitchen counter and sobbed. The tears took her entirely by surprise – she knew it was a combination of exhaustion, stress and sheer surprise at Lucie's unexpected thoughtfulness. Sally patted her head and brought her squares of kitchen paper to blow her nose on. It was a brief, fierce storm of tears and soon wore itself out.

'What did she tell you?' she asked.

'Just that she said she wanted to stay at her dad's, and she thought that she had made you very upset.'

'Did she say why she decided to stay at Stephen's?'

'No, she mainly wanted to talk about you, make sure you were all right.'

'I don't know how we could have come to this,' said Esther, going to the sink to splash her swollen eyes with cold water.

'It has been a hard time for you both,' said Sally carefully. 'I'm sure it's just that she's so besotted with little Lyla. She always wanted a little sister or brother.'

'Did she? She never said anything to me about it.'

'Well, she knew you weren't going to have another, and—'

'Hang on.' Esther turned from the sink to face Sally. 'How do you know all of this?'

'Know all of what?'

'That Lucie wanted a sibling. That she knew I wasn't having any more.'

'Oh, I...' Sally looked stricken. 'I just know, I suppose.'

'Has Lucie been talking to you?'

'A little.'

'When? Here? At your place?' She tried to think of a time when Sally and Lucie had been alone together.

'Sometimes...' Sally said reluctantly.

Esther could see there was something she didn't want to say – a piece of information that, once divulged, she would never be able to claim back. Esther waited, staring at her.

'We chat sometimes,' Sally said eventually. 'On instant messenger.'

Esther nodded. 'Behind my back.'

Sally's cheeks went bright pink and she looked like she might cry. 'I... I did what I thought was best. She added me and seemed to want to talk. She begged me not to tell you we were speaking. But she needed an adult to talk to, and I thought at least this way she was talking to someone who cared for you, who had your best interests at heart.'

'Tell me,' said Esther coldly, 'how losing custody of my thirteen-year-old daughter is in my best interests?'

'She was unhappy at home. She struggled with all the changes that have happened in your life. She needed a little space. It seemed the best way to save your relationship in the long term...'

Esther walked past Sally to the front door. She opened it and gestured to Sally.

'Next time you think you know best and can decide how things should happen in my family, perhaps you might consider that Lucie is my daughter and you have no rights in her life. None at all. Get out.'

She went to see Lucie the next afternoon, and they walked to Highbury Fields in silence. Every now and then Esther glanced at Lucie. Her face was set and frozen, but not in sullen defiance as it had been before. There was something else there. Was it fear? She waited until they were in the park before she spoke. 'How's your weekend been?'

'Okay,' said Lucie carefully. 'How was yours?'

'Okay. I finished a first draft of that chapter for the Austen book. It's very late, but I hope they'll still want it.'

'Good. Well done.'

'Sally came to see me.'

'I know.'

'I thought you might.'

'She didn't ring me,' said Lucie, quickly and defensively. 'I messaged her. And she told me you were angry because I've been speaking to her.'

'I was. I was very hurt. Why couldn't you speak to me, Lucie?' Esther's voice was quiet and without recrimination. She and Lucie had both been talking in calm, subdued tones. She stopped now and took Lucie's shoulders, turning her towards her and looking into her eyes. Lucie suddenly and shockingly burst into tears. Passers-by stopped and looked as Esther drew her into her arms. She wept like a small child, and Esther was reminded of the time when Lucie, aged two, had thrown an uncharacteristic tantrum and had pushed a glass bowl off the kitchen table, causing it to smash spectacularly on the kitchen floor. She had wept then, as if she could not quite believe what she had done, and as if she knew it could not be undone.

When the sobs abated a little, Esther led her to a bench. They looked out over the picnickers in the park and the joggers and cyclists who passed by.

'I'm sorry, Mummy,' said Lucie eventually.

'So am I.'

'I didn't do it to hurt you.'

'I know.'

Lucie sat quietly for a long time, and then she said, 'Please, Mum. Please don't be cross with Sally. Please don't stop being her friend, it isn't her fault. None of it is. Please.'

Esther watched as a rollerblader swished past them. Her eyes followed the girl as she swung effortlessly and quickly up the path, moving with superhuman grace and speed.

'Please,' said Lucie again, her voice thick with misery and phlegm.

'Of course I won't stop being her friend,' said Esther. She was very tired.

CHAPTER THIRTY-SEVEN

She went home to the silent house and sat back down again at her computer to work. She turned on her desk lamp, which cast a small circle of light on her work area, leaving the rest of the living room in darkness. As she waited for her computer to boot up, she gazed at her reflection in the monitor. My God, she looked old. Worn by stress, marriage, childbirth, divorce, weight gain and weight loss, she was beginning to look very much her age. Unlike Isabella, of course. Who had not grown old, would never grow old. Always stylish and beautifully groomed, always slender, her figure and face were unchanged by excess, age or childbirth. At thirty-seven, before she got ill, she had looked pretty much as she had at eighteen. Esther shook her head and opened her email programme, looking at the new messages as they began to cascade into her inbox. There was so much to do. At least she had several uninterrupted hours to get on with it. It had not always been thus – and suddenly, unbidden, another memory of Isabella rushed to her. Thirteen or so years ago, when Lucie had been just six weeks old.

On that day, Esther had sat at home staring at her computer screen, tears blurring her vision. She couldn't. It just wasn't possible. She couldn't. There was a tiny grunting noise from her lap. Lucie lay on her stomach across Esther's knees. It was the only position that seemed to give her relief from the pains of colic. Even then, the respite was brief – she'd doze for thirty or forty minutes and then wake, crying and squirming. The mornings were all right, the afternoons an intensifying nightmare, and the nights endless and broken. Esther was beyond tired. She felt constantly on the verge of flu – shaky, achy, almost feverish. She knew it wasn't flu, because if Stephen took over for a few hours and let her sleep, the symptoms abated. It was sheer exhaustion. And here, on her screen, was an email from work. Apologetic, yes, full of understanding, yes. But the head of department needed her to write a short article, just a thousand words. Something to feature in some or other publication; it would be such a help for their research profile. It was on a subject she knew a lot about. She even knew where on her shelves the reference books might be found. But it was impossible. She was a thirty-five-year-old professional with years of education and experience, and she'd worked right up until the last days of her pregnancy, relentlessly efficient, determined to keep her identity and hold her life together. But this tiny, snuffling girl had robbed her of all of that in six short weeks.

She couldn't do it. And yet she couldn't not do it. She needed help. Stephen had used up all his holiday – they had taken a 'babymoon' break before Lucie was born, and after his two weeks of paternity leave, he had taken an additional week to help her. She knew he was playing catch-up at work anyway. Her mother?

She reached for the phone and rang Laura. But the phone rang and rang and she remembered that her mum and dad had gone away to the Isle of Wight for a few days.

Isabella. It would have to be Isabella. She felt curiously reluctant to ring her, however. Isabella had been coolly happy for her when she announced her pregnancy, and had asked all the right questions throughout. But she hadn't appeared truly engaged. It seemed she was academically interested, as one might be if a friend took up an alien but interesting hobby like taxidermy or sky-diving. She had come to see Esther and Lucie in the hospital, and had even held Lucie, but she hadn't gushed or cried. Isabella didn't judge Esther for wanting children or having Lucie, but she had no wish for one of her own. She was child-free by choice. She had known from adolescence that she didn't want to bear children, and although she wasn't hostile, she had no particular interest in the children of other people.

But there was no one else. Not no one – she had other friends, but none she would want to see her in the state she was in. She was, like so many new mothers, a mess. Stained clothing, rumpled, make-up-free face, tangled hair. Her house was a tip, and she was still liable to burst into tears at the slightest provocation.

The best thing about her oldest friend was that she needed so little information. She rang Isabella's mobile.

'I need your help,' she said.

'Now?'

'Tomorrow morning. For a few hours.'

'I'll be there at nine.'

And she was. She sailed in on a cloud of Issey Miyake, bearing takeaway coffees and fresh, warm croissants. 'I figured you probably weren't up to percolating,' she said, handing Esther a cup.

Esther paused for a moment, wondering about breastfeeding and the caffeine reaching Lucie. But the rich, dark smell filled her nostrils and, thinking of the brief artificial boost the coffee would give her, she took a grateful sip.

Isabella glanced around the house. 'Wow,' she said. 'Baby tsunami.'

'I know,' said Esther guiltily. 'But I didn't ask you round so I could do housework. I have to produce an article...'

'I don't mind what you need to do. If you want to hand the sprog over and sleep for six hours, that's fine. I'm here to help, all right?'

Esther's eyes filled with tears. 'Thank you.'

'Don't thank me. Just give her to me. And maybe start by having a quick shower. For all of our sakes, eh?'

Esther did as she was told, and when she emerged from the bathroom, feeling immeasurably better, she heard – nothing. Curious, she tiptoed downstairs. Isabella was in the kitchen, and for one heart-stopping moment, Esther had no idea where Lucie was. Then she saw the straps criss-crossed across Isabella's slim back. She'd found the baby-sling, a confusing item which Esther had tried but hadn't got on with. Isabella had obviously solved it though, as there was no sound from the baby, and she had both hands free to wash the dishes. The kitchen looked cleaner and tidier than it had in weeks. They seemed to be just fine without her.

It was one of the longest times Esther had spent without her baby in her arms. She felt the familiar cramp-and-gush of milk let-down in her breasts. Luckily her breast-pads would stop her from staining yet another shirt. She wasn't due to feed for another couple of hours. She steeled herself to turn away and go to her desk. She had piled the books she needed on the side table, and she forced herself to start work. It was difficult – so difficult – especially when Lucie woke up and she heard her crying.

Isabella popped her head around the door. 'The weather's

lovely. We girls are going to get a change of scenery,' she said, over Lucie's cries.

'Give her to me, let me feed her,' Esther pleaded.

'You told me she couldn't be hungry yet. If she keeps crying, I'll bring her back. Personally, I think she's just bored. I would be.' Isabella blew her a kiss and set off.

It was almost impossible to keep working after that, in the silent emptiness of the house, but Esther had to. She was constantly mindful of the fact that Isabella must have taken a half-day off work to help her, so she couldn't waste this precious time. In the end, she managed to scope out a rough first draft of the article. The hard work was done – the writing wasn't elegant, but an hour of intensive editing and it would be passable.

Isabella and Lucie still weren't back. She went to stand on the doorstep, nervously looking up the road. She was just about to go back in and ring Isabella's mobile, when she saw them coming around the corner. Isabella still had the baby in the sling on her front, and she had her head down, obviously chatting away to Lucie. Esther could hear Isabella's soft tones but nothing from Lucie, which meant, mercifully, she wasn't crying. Isabella looked up and saw her, and waved cheerily. Esther walked up the road to meet them. She was dying to get Lucie back in her arms. Isabella sensed this and unstrapped the sling as they got closer, passing the baby over practically on the move. Lucie's milky blue eyes looked up at Esther as she took her in her arms. Esther was so relieved to have her back, it took her a moment to notice the dummy in her mouth.

'Where did you get that?' she asked, shocked.

'Boots,' said Isabella.

'It's a dummy,' said Esther stupidly. 'I didn't want her to have a dummy. And it's not sterilized.'

'Well, it came straight out of the packet, so I'm sure it's clean. And look, she's not crying.'

She wasn't. Lucie was calm and relaxed in Esther's arms.

'I looked it up last night after you rang. Crying, colicky babies. Some people said a dummy helped. I thought it was worth a try.'

'I didn't want her to have a dummy,' Esther repeated, conscious that she was being stubborn.

'Why?' said Isabella, a little exasperated.

'I don't want her to be one of those four-year-olds, still sucking away. I think dummies are awful.'

'Firstly, she's five weeks old—'

'Six.'

'Six weeks old. Not four years old. And secondly, if it helps her with the pain, isn't that a good thing? It's not like I dipped it in gin.'

Esther managed a weak smile. 'I suppose so. As long as you left off the gin.'

'Nothing but champagne for my girl.' Isabella touched Lucie's tiny head lightly. 'Now, did you get your work done?' Esther nodded. 'Well, as you're dressed almost like a human being, why don't we take this little one out for lunch? She's been up and down the high street and she likes it. She's quite the little cosmopolitan.'

After that, Isabella would swoop in every few months and take Lucie away for a few hours. She liked to have her to herself and take her on little jaunts. She bought her beautiful outfits and toys, and even when Lucie was a plump eight-month-old, she liked to carry her in the sling.

At around that time, Laura, who was generally not one to lay down the law, said very firmly that she would like to see her granddaughter baptized. Esther and Stephen had no views either way but were happy to do it for Laura's sake. Rather hesitantly, Esther asked Isabella if she would like to be Lucie's godmother.

'An old atheist like me? Are you sure?'

'Well, this old atheist is asking. I know it's odd. We're doing this for my mum, really. Still, if anyone is going to be tied to Lucie for life, I'd like it to be you.'

'I'm not going anywhere,' said Isabella. 'But yes, I'd be honoured to do it.'

Neither she nor Esther were all that comfortable with the service – renouncing the devil and turning to Christ and so on – but Esther was still happy to see Isabella holding her beautiful daughter at the font. After the service, Isabella walked around the church with Lucie, pointing up at the stained-glass windows and explaining them to her. She always spoke to Lucie in a calm, adult tone. How Lucie would love her as she got older, thought Esther. Classy, elegant Isabella, bearer of cool gifts, purveyor of fascinating information, planner of astonishing outings. Isabella had painted Esther's life with great, bold swathes of colour, and she would do the same for Esther's daughter.

Except she didn't. Lucie was two when Isabella was diagnosed. It was another six months before Esther even knew – Isabella didn't tell anyone. And once the intense chemotherapy started, Isabella's immune system was destroyed. She couldn't risk spending time with a germ-ridden toddler – a sniffle or a cold could have put her in hospital with pneumonia. And so the reality was that Lucie had no memories of her godmother at all. All she had was a chewed and faded pink dummy, which Esther had tucked away in her baby memory box. And Esther had to go on alone.

CHAPTER THIRTY-EIGHT

Michael got back much later that evening. She had drunk three quarters of a bottle of wine by the time he came through the door. He was smiling and holding a tartan-printed tin of shortbread. 'Och aye!' he said, in an abysmal Scottish accent. 'Did ye long for me, lassie?'

She smiled lazily at him from her seat on the sofa. 'I did,' she said.

'You didn't ring me.' He sat on the sofa beside her, putting down the tin of shortbread and dropping his keys and phone beside it. 'How was your walk with Lucie?'

'Fine.' She opened her arms to him and kissed him hard, sliding her tongue between his teeth. Surprised, he leaned into her, and within minutes, she had pulled him on top of her. The sex was quick, desperate and strangely unsatisfying.

'Wow,' said Michael, withdrawing and flopping back into the

opposite corner of the sofa. He struggled to pull up his trousers and refasten his fly. 'Well, that was certainly a welcome.'

'I missed you,' she lied. She hadn't spoken to him since Friday night. Somehow, she hadn't been able to bear ringing to tell him about Lucie's secret conversations with Sally. She reached over and picked up her glass, which was empty. She refilled it, draining the last of the bottle into it. She saw him noticing, but he didn't say anything. Smiling, as if the idea had just occurred to her, she handed him the glass. 'I've had more than enough,' she said.

She drew his feet up onto the sofa and settled them in her lap, and as he sipped the wine, she began to rub them. He groaned with pleasure – she knew he loved it. He leaned back into the sofa cushions, drinking the wine in happy silence. She could see he was very tired. She kept massaging gently. The room was warm and quiet and dim and, sure enough, his eyelids started to droop. It took another five minutes before his breathing settled into the unmistakeable pattern of sleep. She slid his feet off her lap and sat quietly for another minute or so, but he didn't stir. Then, moving quickly and silently, she picked up her own mobile phone, which was an identical model to Michael's. She put it on the coffee table beside the tin of shortbread, swapping it for Michael's phone. She padded into the kitchen with his handset. If he woke and looked for his phone, he would assume it was still on the table. If he realized it was hers, she could say she'd picked up his in error.

Once in the kitchen, she immediately put the phone onto silent. She didn't want an unexpected call or text alert to wake him. Then she got a fresh glass and opened another bottle of wine, before sitting down at the counter. She worked methodically, starting with his text message folder, going back through all the messages from the last few weeks. Most of them were from her, with a few from Luke and Oliver, a couple of exchanges with work colleagues and friends, and a few from unidentified numbers. The content from the unsaved numbers was all innocuous – either spam advertising or work messages from people whose numbers he hadn't bothered to save. Then she opened his email folder. It took some careful searching because he was organized and kept all of his emails in different folders – work, personal, admin – but she found it eventually. A thread of emails between Michael and Sally.

She saw that Michael had also known of Lucie's plan to move out – Sally had told him, seeking his advice. He had said that they couldn't interfere and that Esther and Lucie would have to work it out themselves. He expressed concern about Esther's drinking, and Sally promised to try and get her to slow down. Now that she read this, she realized that of late Sally had been opting for coffee or fruit juice when they met, rather than wine. She had obviously been trying to lead by example.

Michael and Sally wrote about her as if she was some kind of invalid, someone who needed to be coddled and protected from herself. She was hot with fury. She wanted to storm back into the living room and wake him to confront him with his duplicity. But she knew that would just play into their narrative. Going through someone's mobile phone wasn't considered reasonable behaviour. She finished her glass of wine, poured another and drank it quickly, like medicine. She wasn't even tasting it anymore. This wasn't about Michael anyway. It wasn't him that she had doubts about. For all his emailing behind her back, she knew it came from genuine love and concern. Sally, on the other hand, she wasn't so sure about.

She took the bottle of wine with her and padded back into the living room. Michael was still fast asleep. She looked at him with pity and love, then replaced his phone on the table and retrieved her own. She went silently into the hallway, put on her shoes and got her keys and bag, then let herself out of the house. She stood for a while, in the dark street. She was swaying slightly, and she knew she was drunk. Way over the limit, she estimated. She had never before got behind the wheel having had more than a single glass of wine. Well, there was a first time for everything.

At first she drove aimlessly, heading out of town on a suburban road. It was quiet, just past ten o'clock, and there were relatively few cars about. She started to think back over the year or so since Joan had died and Sally had come back into her life. She thought about Sally's physical transformation and emergence into the world. She thought about how Sally had ingratiated herself first with Lucie, then with Michael. How she had made friends with Paul and Tim, and how she was now closer to them than Esther herself was. She thought about Sally at her birthday party, inviting herself to Laura's funeral and even to the burial, about her memories from their childhood, in which Esther seemed to figure so large. And now this clandestine communication with the two people closest to Esther. What was she trying to do? Did Sally want to be her? Own her? Take over her life? Or was it Isabella she was trying to be?

Esther slammed on her brakes and stopped, without checking behind her. She saw blinding lights in her rear-view mirror and heard the screech of brakes. A 4x4 swerved to pass her, its driver hooting, yelling and gesticulating. She waited for a second, checked the road was clear and then did a U-turn, heading back towards the northern suburbs of London. She felt nauseous and headachey as she pulled up outside Sally's house. She was very thirsty – she hadn't eaten anything all day. The half-empty bottle of wine lay on the passenger seat beside her, but she hadn't thought to bring any water or food, or, for that matter, a glass. No matter. She took a swig straight from the bottle and felt her headache abate slightly.

The house was dark, and Sally's car wasn't in the driveway. Sunday evening at eleven? Where could she be? Esther had a vague notion that the amateur dramatic society met on a Sunday evening. But surely they wouldn't still be at it at eleven o'clock? Some of them at least must have jobs to go to on a Monday morning. Still, it was the only clue she had to go on, so she turned her car around again, clumsily hitting her back bumper on a streetlight pole, then drove to the church where the group met.

The hall was locked up and the car park empty except for Sally's little car. She was around somewhere. Esther painstakingly backed her car into an alleyway opposite the car park, turned off the engine and the lights, and waited. The wine had made her dozy and ill, and it seemed like a very long time before she saw anything. The rather scruffy locale was all but deserted – even the corner shop was closed. A few people got off a bus and headed off to their homes, but apart from that, she saw no pedestrians. Then she saw Sally walking down the street. She was hand in hand with a tall man. This must be the person she'd been dating. Perhaps they'd been for a drink or to the man's home and he was now walking her back to her car. Esther leaned back in her seat, keeping her face in the shadows, and hoped they wouldn't glance her way. They seemed to be engrossed in one another, talking with their heads bent close together. The man was very tall, a full head taller than Sally, and slender, with a fit, athlete's build and sandy hair.

She knew, in the split second before he stepped into the glow of the streetlight beside Sally's car. She knew. It was Phil. Psycho, stalker Phil, who had called her a slut, told her no one would want to fuck her, who had scared and demeaned her. She watched him draw Sally into his arms and kiss her. She kissed him back, but not for long, then she withdrew, smiled and got into her car. In the yellowy light of the streetlamp, she looked frail, jaundiced, ethereal, almost. Then, as Phil watched, she buckled her seatbelt and drove away.

Phil smiled and waved, then turned to walk back to his home, which, Esther recalled from having seen him in the street, must be very nearby. As Sally drove out of sight, Esther watched the smile fall from his face as he assumed a grim, forbidding expression, lowering his head and walking quickly away.

CHAPTER THIRTY-NINE

She drove fast now. She was vaguely aware that she was very drunk, that she shouldn't be driving at all, and that she had no idea where she was going. But she also knew that she had to keep moving, and if she did, she might be able to drive away from the hurt and betrayal. She soon found herself in a part of London she didn't recognize. Harlesden? Willesden? Kensal Green? Somewhere like that. She was somewhere on the west side of town, she knew, and if she could just make it to the North Circular, she might be able to find the M1 and begin driving north – to where, she did not know. But she kept turning down a series of cul-de-sacs and blind alleys, which all seemed to end at a railway line. She was forever having to turn the car round and go the other way.

She was feeling more and more desperate, trapped and afraid. Eventually, she found what looked like an arterial road with signs suggesting that if she followed it, she might end up on the elusive North Circular. The road was empty, and she began to pick up speed. If she could just get out of London, she could clear her head, think about things, make some plans for the future. But as much as she tried to keep her thoughts on the problem at hand, she kept seeing Sally kissing Phil in the light of the yellow streetlamp, kept thinking how she had let this woman into her life, a woman who had calmly admitted to being an accessory in the death of Esther's closest friend. A woman who had cared for her own mother alone and under impossibly difficult circumstances for eight years. What had happened to Joan? People didn't actually die from dementia, did they?

The fox came from nowhere, streaking across the road in front of her. She hit the brakes, a fraction too late and much too hard, and felt the car begin to spin. It was very slow, very beautiful, and she watched the lights move in and out of her field of vision as the car described a 360-degree turn before drifting inexorably sideways and slamming into the central reservation. She heard the crunch but did not feel it. After that, everything was very quiet.

The engine had cut out and, after a moment, she shook herself lightly. She hadn't broken any bones and she seemed to be all right. Then she felt a small trickle of something warm and, glancing in the rear-view mirror, saw that she must have hit her head, just above the eyebrow, on the window. There was a small head wound, bleeding steadily. She scrabbled in her handbag for a tissue and pressed it to the cut. No doubt the side of the car was badly damaged, but she'd hit the barrier broadside on and she thought the engine, and hopefully the wheels, were probably all right. There were no other cars on the road ahead of her, and the fox was long gone. She should probably drive home and deal with the car and everything else in the morning. Cautiously she started the engine; it sounded all right. She turned the steering wheel, but even before she had attempted to pull off, she could feel the drag. She had clearly burst a tyre. She'd have to limp the car to the side of the road and ring for a cab. It was absolutely vital, however, to get away from the scene before... But it was too late. She saw the moving sweep of blue lights before she heard the car. They had come up behind her. She couldn't drive away now. She would just have to sit tight and accept what came next.

CHAPTER FORTY

There were two officers, one black and one white, both male, handsome and clean-cut, both young enough, Esther thought, to be her sons. They were polite and solicitous when they approached the car, and remained so, even when they got her out of the vehicle and saw how unsteady she was on her feet. Then one of them glanced at the passenger seat and saw the bottle of wine, and the other leaned in a little closer. He was still kind and polite, but Esther knew he could smell the alcohol on her breath and skin. They were still courteous and gentle when they asked her to breathe into their machine, still kind as they led her to their vehicle and put her in the back to drive her to the police station, still sympathetic when they had to stop and wrench open the door for her to be sick in the gutter. At the police station, they asked her to do two more breath samples, then a female officer took her to the bathroom to rinse out her mouth and wash the blood from her forehead, where it had dried. They politely asked her if she would accompany them into a cell, which she did, meekly. They asked if they could ring anyone for her, but she said no, she was all right.

She was no fool. The whole encounter had been handled with great civility, but she knew that this was only the beginning. She didn't know a lot about the law, but she did know she was in a great deal of trouble. She would lose her licence, for certain. For a year, perhaps? Maybe more. She would have a conviction. She might even have to go to prison. What Craig would make of that, she had no idea. What Michael would say, or Stephen, or... Lucie. Oh, Lucie... It didn't bear thinking about. She knew she should be worried, that she should have asked to ring Michael and get him to find her a solicitor, but she was just so horribly tired. She curled up on the narrow bunk and fell into a deep sleep.

She woke up feeling calm and surprisingly rested. She was very thirsty and could have done with a shower and a change of clothes, but other than that, she was perfectly all right. She touched her eyebrow carefully – the cut seemed to have closed up of its own accord. She thought through the events of the previous evening, and gradually, as she remembered what she had seen and what it had made her realize, she felt a bubble of excitement rising. It was the euphoria of discovery, the sense that she had solved a mystery and seen a truth. She sat on the edge of the bunk and waited. After a short while, a PC came along and unlocked the cell. She motioned for Esther to follow her, and took her to a desk where there was a stack of paperwork for her to read and sign.

The police station had the grim, stale air of a place that had seen people coming and going all night, and now the morning had finally edged in, grey and unpromising. The PC was pretty, in her mid-thirties and with round, apple cheeks. She looked tired; there were blue-grey shadows under her eyes and strands of mousy hair escaping from her ponytail. Her handwriting was neat and even, rounded, almost childlike, and she painstakingly filled out all of the forms and explained to Esther what would happen next. She was to be bailed, pending a court appearance, she was told. However traumatic the events of the previous night had been for her, and however much they would change her life, they were routine for the police. They seemed grateful that she was not troublesome, rude or argumentative and were happy to treat her with bureaucratic politeness. The sooner they could complete the necessary red tape, the sooner they could shunt her on to the next silo in the legal system.

She stared at the PC's pretty hands. They were white and smooth, and her nails were neatly shaped and varnished with clear polish. She wore no rings. Esther imagined her sitting on her sofa in pyjamas, filing and painting her nails. Perhaps chatting to a friend or a boyfriend? Watching television? What was her life like? The PC, whose name, according to her nametag, was Parker, pushed some papers across the desk for Esther to sign. She'd indicated the necessary places with a small, neat cross. Esther complied, and PC Parker smiled at her for the first time. She handed Esther a plastic carrier bag with her personal effects in it – her mobile phone and handbag, and a few bits and pieces that had been in her car, including an umbrella and a water bottle. She noted that the half-empty bottle of wine was not among the items.

'Your car has been towed to the police pound,' PC Parker explained, handing over a card. 'Here's the address. You'll have to settle the towing bill before you collect it. Mind you, I'm not sure it's driveable. You might just want your insurance company to send it straight to the repair shop.'

'Thank you,' Esther said, and turned her mobile phone over in her hand. Unsurprisingly, the battery had gone dead.

'Can we call you a taxi?'

'Er, yes. That would probably be best.' It was over, for now at least. She was going to have to go back out into the world.

PC Parker showed her to the front of the station. There was a man sitting on a plastic chair in the reception area. He looked grey and exhausted, as if he had been through a harrowing ordeal. It took Esther a split second to realize that it was Michael. He stood up when he saw her. 'I've rung every hospital, looking for you. And every police station in north London. Why didn't you get someone to call me?' She didn't say anything, just stood and looked at him, her belongings in their plastic bag dangling by her side. He sighed. 'Let's go,' he said, and turned to walk out to the car park. He hadn't touched her.

Esther remembered a biology class at school where a teacher had explained the process of ring-barking. You remove a strip of bark from all the way round the circumference of a tree trunk. It doesn't look like a radical thing to do, but it will kill the tree as certainly as if you had hacked it down with an axe. The tree will starve – all the vessels which feed it are in the bark, so everything above the line withers and dies. The tree may still be standing, just as it always has, but it is irretrievably, mortally wounded. Michael would stay, for a time at least. That was the kind of man he was – loyal and steadfast. But it was almost inevitable that the thing was broken. She had broken it.

CHAPTER FORTY-ONE

Craig was scared. It was really very funny when you thought about it. They were sitting in the principal's office, side by side, facing the principal across his big polished desk. The principal was scared too. In days gone by, Esther might well have lost her job for getting a drink-driving conviction, but now she could see them thinking how this might play out if it ever made it into the public eye. A university head of department, a woman of impeccable credentials and record, hounded out of her job, subjected to immense pressure by a colleague, losing custody of her daughter, crashing her car drunk. They were imagining spreads in the Daily Mail, constructive dismissal accusations at an employment tribunal, unwelcome scrutiny at a time when the university's reputation was shaky anyway.

She glanced across at Craig, who was sitting very upright, his hands folded across his small, barrel belly. There was a stiff smile on his face, and it looked as if his mouth was so dry, his top lip had adhered to his teeth. The principal was affecting a tone of grave, warm concern as he spoke.

'I don't think we realized,' he said very carefully, 'how difficult all this has been for you, with your bereavement and so on. We've held some discussions, and we felt we'd like to make you an offer.'

It was a cushy one and no mistake – a year-long sabbatical on full pay, to 'work on your research'. They didn't question whether she had a current research project, just made it clear that there were funds available should she have any travel expenses. Her court date was a week away, and she knew she was almost certain to lose her license for a year at least, so the break couldn't have come at a better time. Craig hadn't spoken at all during the meeting. Esther didn't think she had ever seen him at a loss for words before. It was refreshing. She thanked them both, stood and shook their hands, and left the principal's office. She walked to her courtesy car, a little blue hatchback. Her own car had been retrieved from the police pound and was in for repairs. At least it would look smart and new as it sat outside her house, undriveable, for a year or more.

She drove home and walked into the unnatural middle-of-the-day quiet of her living room. So there it was. Work, the last vestige of her old life, finally stripped away. Michael was still living with her and was treating her with kind carefulness, like an invalid. Oliver and Luke had stopped coming to stay at weekends. She suspected Michael had asked them not to. Michael himself was gentle as always – he had not reproached her for the night when she had crashed the car. She had not confronted him about his emails to Sally. Once or twice, when he was in the shower, she checked his phone, but there did not seem to have been any further communications from Sally, and nor had Michael contacted her to tell her about Esther's accident.

Michael was practical in his sympathy and insisted that she go to see her GP. She complied, and the harassed doctor had listened to what had happened, while keeping one eye on the clock. Then, with a rapid-fire burst of typing, he had issued a prescription for anti-depressants and sent her on her way. Esther showed the pills to Michael and put them in the bathroom cabinet. Every morning, she popped a tiny pill out of the packet and dropped it into the sink, washing it down the drain with a splash of water.

Of all the people in her life, Stephen was the most brutal. He was furious with her for the drink-driving incident, and told her so. She was perversely grateful to him for his censure. It was infinitely better than the careful tiptoeing everyone else was doing. He barked down the phone at her. 'For God's sake, how do you think this will look to Lucie?'

'Have you told her?'

'No. But you're going to lose your licence. She's bound to find out.'

'I suppose so. I don't want her to feel that she's… responsible in any way. She's not.'

'Of course she isn't!' said Stephen sharply. 'What an absurd thing to say. You're an adult and responsible for your own actions. You just need to pull yourself together.'

She laughed lightly, and he didn't ask why she found his comment amusing. Perversely, she rather liked his use of cliché, his stolid, British insistence that she could fix this by 'pulling herself together'. But the notion that she could, the idea that she could unshatter her life, unfragment herself, through an act of will was just… Well, it was funny.

CHAPTER FORTY-TWO

She was tired all the time. Although she wasn't working, she still found herself yawning by eight or nine in the evening, and she was usually in bed and asleep by ten. During the long, quiet days at home when Michael was at work, she often had an afternoon nap as well. Even when she was out and doing things – shopping, walking in the park with Paul and Tim, having lunch with Lucie or with friends – she would catch herself stifling yawns, and she would fantasize about the crisp, white bedclothes on her bed as she might once have fantasized about a lover. By the time Michael came to bed, she was usually asleep, and the sleep was deep and dreamless, almost drugged. Sex was the last thing on her mind, and even if he tentatively reached for her or stroked her, she couldn't rouse herself enough to turn to him and make love.

The date for her court case came round. Michael drove her to court and she stood before the judge, carefully and neatly dressed, and expressed abject remorse. Her good character and impeccable record were taken into account, and she offered to enrol in a drink-driving rehabilitation scheme to reduce the length of her ban. It all went as well as she could have hoped – a twelve-month ban, which would go down to eight months when she completed the course, and a fine, which she was able to pay from her savings.

One Saturday morning she woke to find herself alone in the bed. She lay for a while watching the breeze riffle the curtains. She could glimpse bright sunlight beyond them – the morning was well advanced. She reached for her phone to look at the time. After ten. She had been asleep for twelve solid hours. She felt quite able to roll over and sleep some more but knew that morally, responsibly, she really should get up. It was so hard to move, however. Eventually, the call of nature drove her out from under the duvet, and she stumbled, yawning, to the bathroom.

Now she was up, she realized she was both hungry and thirsty. A cup of tea and a slice of toast. That was what she needed. Maybe that would help her to shake this terrible lethargy. She pulled on her dressing gown and went downstairs. Michael was in the kitchen, standing with his back to her, ironing and listening to the radio. He was shirtless. He didn't turn – he clearly hadn't heard her come downstairs. She stopped in the doorway and looked at his back and strong legs. It reminded her of her first glimpse of him beside the pool at the conference centre. She had a sudden, intense memory of the first time they'd had sex, the taste of his skin, the mad swoop and rush of their falling in love. It seemed light years away now.

He must have sensed her presence because he turned, and she saw his jaw tighten for a split second before he mustered a warm smile. 'Coffee's on,' he said.

'Thanks.' She drifted over to sit at the kitchen table. He finished ironing his shirt and shrugged it on and buttoned it. He poured her a cup of coffee and brought it over to the table, sitting down opposite her.

'Listen,' he said hesitantly. 'I glanced at the calendar this morning.' He indicated the family organizer which hung beside the back door, and which, in the days when her life was full, Esther had used to keep track of Lucie's social life, and minutiae like dentist's appointments and birthdays. 'Tomorrow's the fourteenth,' he continued, and Esther looked at him blankly. 'Sally's housewarming party? We said yes to it months ago, but now... Well, I know you've not spoken to her for a while, and... Should I call her and cancel? Or would you rather—'

'We should go.' Esther surprised herself with the firmness of her tone. Michael raised his eyebrows. 'Yes,' she said. 'I can't drift around like a hermit forever. It'll be a good first step – getting out, going to see people – and Lucie said she'd come too. I'll ring her.' She smiled brightly at him, and she could see he was taken aback by her cheer and animation. 'I'd better find something to wear.' She picked up her coffee cup and stood. 'Or what the hell, maybe I'll go shopping!'

She did go shopping, choosing a calf-length navy dress which hung well, concealing the fact that she had got rather out of shape. She had no hope of getting an appointment with her usual hairdresser, but she popped into one on the high street and had the ragged ends of her hair trimmed, then bought an over-the-counter hair dye which covered the grey. At least she would go to the party looking like a normal human being rather than a mad bag lady or the spectre at the feast.

She went to a coffee shop and sat down, a cappuccino in front of her, and stared at her phone. She was finding it harder and harder to ring Lucie these days. Whenever she did, Lucie's voice was guarded and flat, and she answered in monosyllables, as if afraid even to give words away. Esther finished every phone call feeling sad and desperate. She wasn't sure how it was possible that she had lost her daughter so entirely in just a few short months. Where before she might have taken Lucie for a long walk or to a patisserie to share cakes and confidences, she could see no way to open a door now. The calls caused her such pain, she had taken to texting. She could at least pretend to ignore Lucie's shortness in written communication. She typed quickly. 'Sally's housewarming tomorrow lunchtime. Still up for it?' Then she sat for a couple of minutes, sipping her coffee slowly, hoping for an instant reply. Lucie must have seen the message. Whenever they were together, she was welded to her phone and would pause any conversation to reply to a message from a friend. But after fifteen minutes or so, Esther had to concede that the reply might take some time.

By that evening, she still hadn't heard from Lucie. She hesitated for a while, then fired off another quick text. 'Did you get my message about the housewarming? Please reply.'

Her phone beeped almost instantly. A single-word reply: 'Yes.'

Did she mean yes she had seen the message, or yes she was coming? This was the trouble with text messaging. It was easy to be imprecise. There was no alternative; she would have to ring Lucie. She dialled the number, but even though Lucie had replied to her text just seconds before, the phone rang and went to voicemail. As Esther listened to Lucie's perky voice giving her outgoing message, she felt a flash of deep anger. When the beep sounded and she began to speak, her voice was icy and clipped. 'I don't know why you aren't answering your phone. I know you've seen it's me and left it to ring. You're being rude. We will pick you up tomorrow at eleven for Sally's housewarming. Be ready.' She didn't expect Lucie to ring back, and indeed she didn't.

She didn't say anything to Michael about this exchange, or non-exchange. When he asked about plans for the next day, she just said, calmly, 'We'll pick Lucie up at eleven. Even with Sunday traffic, we should have ample time to get to Sally's.'

Esther was ready by 10.30, her hair drawn back in a tidy ponytail, make-up applied and accessories carefully chosen. She saw Michael watching her closely, clearly surprised. She smiled at him. 'I'm fine, really. This is just what I need. Bit of a knees-up.'

'It's a rather sedate housewarming luncheon party. I think you may be disappointed in the knees-up department.'

'Well, a party's what you make it,' she said. 'I helped Sally pick out the lampshades. It's only right I get to put one on my head and dance on the kitchen table.'

'Do we have a gift for her? I can stop and get a bottle of bubbly on the way over...' She heard the momentary hesitation in his voice. He still didn't know how to handle the issue of alcohol around her. She hadn't had a drink since the night she'd spent in the cells. It had seemed simplest.

'No, no, I have a gift,' she said. 'Sally asked me months ago if I had any pictures from when we were children. I dug some out ages ago and had them scanned and blown up and framed.'

'She'll love that.' Michael put an arm around Esther's shoulders, giving her a squeeze. 'Did I happen to tell you that you look beautiful today?'

'No, in fact you didn't.'

'Well, that was downright careless of me. You look lovely.' He dropped a careful, chaste kiss onto her hairline. 'Come on, let's go and fetch Lucie.'

The traffic on the way to Stephen's house was heinous, and even though they got there well after eleven, Lucie wasn't ready. They could hear raised voices through the front door as they walked up the path. When they got inside, it was clear that Melissa had been cajoling Lucie to get dressed. As soon as Esther came into the house, Melissa made a polite excuse and melted into her own bedroom, the baby in her arms. Stephen had retired to his garden office to work, and when he saw Esther and Michael in the kitchen, he waved at them through the window. He had no intention of getting involved. Lucie stalked off to her room without a word. Esther followed her. Michael hung back in the living room.

Lucie's room was in chaos; her hair was unbrushed and she was still in pyjamas. Esther could see they were in for a long haul or an ugly battle, so she went over and began to go through Lucie's wardrobe. 'How about this?' she asked, holding up a pretty yellow top. 'With jeans, or your white skirt, and a jacket?'

Lucie, slumped on the edge of the bed, curled her lip at this. 'I'm not seven, Mum.'

'Or this?' Esther held up a short skater dress, one she had initially resisted buying because she'd thought it too grown-up.

'I'll freeze.'

'It's warm enough outside. What about this?' She held up garment after garment. Lucie shook her head at the first few, and then just stared at the carpet, refusing to look at all.

Esther stood staring into the wardrobe, a space in a strange house packed with clothes she had chosen and paid for, and took three long, deep breaths. She turned to her daughter. 'Lucie...' she began.

'I'm not going. I don't want to go.'

'Oh, for heaven's sake,' Esther barked before she could stop herself. 'Michael and I spent an hour driving over here. You're being very inconsiderate.'

'I didn't say I was coming,' flared Lucie.

'And you didn't say you weren't.'

'Well, I'm saying it now.'

'Why? You love Sally.'

'It's all ruined. You ruined it!' Lucie's eyes filled with tears. 'If I go, and I talk to her, you'll be all staring and weird, wondering if we're talking about you. I don't speak to her at all now. Are you happy?'

Esther was a lot of things. Happy wasn't one of them. She arranged the dress she was holding more neatly on the hanger, slipped it back onto the rail and softly closed the wardrobe door. She turned and looked at her daughter sitting on the edge of the unmade bed. She smoothed her dress, tried to smile, failed, and walked out to the living room.

'She's not coming,' she said calmly to Michael. 'Let's go.'

Michael didn't ask why Lucie wasn't coming. He didn't express displeasure or comment that it was rude of her to have made them drive all the way to Islington when she had no intention of getting in the car. He just drove. It struck Esther that when your life was falling apart, it was notable how little people said to you – how much they accepted, how few questions they asked.

Sally's driveway was full of cars, and they had to find parking on the road. They didn't speak as they walked to the front door. Michael rang the doorbell, and as they waited for someone to answer, he took Esther's hand. Whether it was out of genuine affection, solidarity, or merely for show, she didn't know. She left her hand in his, although she didn't reciprocate the squeeze he gave as the door opened.

Paul answered the door, his face still bright from the merriment of the party, and for a split second he registered naked surprise. 'Esther!' he said, recovering instantly. 'We weren't sure you'd come!' He turned back into the house. 'Everyone!' he called. 'Esther and Michael are here!'

It was clear he was broadcasting a warning, and as they went through into the dining room, they could see that Sally had genuinely thought they weren't coming. Tim was up, getting everyone to move further round the table and drawing in two extra chairs, and Esther saw Sally disappearing into the kitchen, obviously rushing to get further place settings. There was a flurry of forced gaiety on their entrance, as everyone shuffled round, making room. The starters were already on the table, little individual salads. Esther imagined Sally in the kitchen, sweating and flustered, flinging rocket onto plates to make another two portions.

She was seated in a corner seat, with Michael wedged in on the diagonally opposite corner, as far away from her as he could be. She could see he was anxious about this, and she caught his warning glance as someone filled an enormous glass with red wine and placed it in front of her. She smiled sweetly at him, trying to reassure him that all would be well. She picked up the glass to take a sip and turned to thank the person on her right who had filled it for her. It was Phil.

Astonishingly, it hadn't crossed her mind that he would be there. She could have kicked herself. Of course he would be. He was dating Sally. She smiled, and lifted her glass slightly to him. 'Well, here you are,' she said.

'You've let yourself go,' he said, his tone even and conversational. 'You look like shit.' His face looked perfectly pleasant. Anyone else at the table would have assumed they were introducing themselves, making small talk.

'How did you manage to weasel your way in here?' she said. 'It seems a massive coincidence that you've managed to hook up with a friend of mine. Forgive me, but I don't really believe in coincidences.'

'I don't really care what you believe.' He said this with a warm but entirely artificial smile. 'It was a coincidence. Sally was volunteering at a half-marathon. I was running for Macmillan. We got chatting. Then we bumped into each other again because she goes to the theatre group which is near my flat. You might say it was meant to be.'

'Really?'

'Really. When she told me her full name, I remembered you'd mentioned some friends called Millais. It's an unusual name. I liked her, but the possibility that I might get to needle you a little was a delightful bonus.'

'Does Sally know you're a sad little stalker troll?' she said sweetly.

'Sally knows I'm a nice guy, which I am – to women who conduct themselves like ladies.'

'It'd be a pity if someone enlightened her about some of your past behaviour.' Esther took a large gulp of the wine.

'Go ahead,' said Phil, sipping his sparkling water. 'Why would she believe anything you say? The state of you. So how've you been? I heard you lost your job. And your kid moved out. And you've been hitting the bottle.' He glanced at her now half-empty glass. 'That sappy boyfriend of yours must be a saint. Or maybe he gets off on charity cases.'

Esther looked around the table. It was crammed with people. The only empty seat was the one at the head of the table, to her left, which was clearly Sally's place. There was no way she could move or swap seats without causing an enormous fuss. She was stuck next to this poisonous man.

Sally came out of the kitchen, carrying two small salad plates. She went over to Michael first, giving him his plate, apologizing and kissing his cheek. Her colour was high and the hair at her temples was wet with sweat. She came round to the head of the table and put the plate of salad down in front of Esther. She sat down in her seat and opened her arms, drawing Esther into a tight hug.

'I'm so, so glad you came,' she whispered into Esther's ear.

Esther could feel Sally's shoulder blades, like wings under her hands. She was small-boned, like Isabella had been. 'I said I was coming.'

'I know... but... well. We hadn't spoken for a while.' Sally drew back, and Esther saw there were tears in her eyes. 'I'm very happy to see you.'

'I'm sorry Lucie's not with us,' said Esther evenly. 'She's... well... You know how busy teenagers are.'

'No problem,' said Sally. 'Well, tuck in. Oh, I forgot... This is Phil.' She gestured to him.

'We introduced ourselves,' said Esther, not catching Phil's eye. Sally grinned at her, and she could see she was trying to telegraph that this was The Man. Esther managed a weak smile and started to play with the food on her plate.

The conversation, which had faltered on their entrance, picked up again. She looked around to see who was there. There were twenty people round the table – Paul and Tim, Sally and Phil, herself and Michael, and fourteen people she didn't know. Some she thought she recognized from the amateur theatre group, some were total strangers. They all seemed at home in Sally's home, an eclectic mix of friends such as one might expect to find around a north London Sunday lunch table. The room was flooded with wintry sunlight, the table laden with glasses, flowers and snacks, the garden bright and neat through the window. Music was playing, something light and jazzy. Esther looked around to see where it was coming from, and spotted the speakers set into the ceiling.

Sally saw her looking. 'I've had the most bonkers sound system installed,' she said. 'Speakers in every room. It should be crazy complicated, but I can actually make the whole thing work from my phone. Phil helped me set it up.'

Phil, neatly dissecting a tomato, gave Sally a warm smile. 'Well, you do love your music,' he said indulgently, as if Sally were a child. 'She shall have music wherever she goes.'

Sally giggled girlishly.

It seemed the only possible response to the situation was to keep drinking. By the time Sally, helped by Tim and Paul, had brought through the main course (roast chicken, lamb, and abundant vegetables), Esther was drunk. Phil kept staring disapprovingly at her rapidly emptying glass. She delighted in this, and kept topping it up. She was careful not to look up and catch Michael's eye, although she knew he would be watching her.

The meal passed in a blur. She must have eaten something, although she didn't really remember doing so. They decided to have a pause before dessert. The weather was unseasonably warm and sunny, so someone flung open the doors into the garden and a few of the party, including Michael, went outside. Esther stood, slightly unsteadily, and went through into the living room. Phil had taken up a position in the middle of the sofa, knees spread in what looked like a semblance of an alpha-male pose, and was holding forth to Tim about marathon running and nutrition. Tim, who Esther knew abhorred all kinds of exercise, had glazed over and was nodding politely.

Esther took herself off to sit in a patch of sunshine by the window. There was a small white wicker armchair in the alcove, and she curled up in it, enjoying the rays which slanted in and warmed her face. There were cushions in the chair, and she absent-mindedly ran her fingernail over the embroidery on one of them. She glanced at it and saw that it was a silk pillow with a hazy mist of wisteria stitched onto it. She recognized it. One day, months before, she and Sally had been shopping for cushions and curtains. They had paused for lunch, and Sally had spoken with wistful nostalgia about the wisteria which had blossomed over the door of Esther's childhood home. She herself had not thought of it in all the years since she had left that house, but she was touched by Sally's vivid recollection. She spent some hours that evening searching décor sites online until she found cushions covered in wisteria. She emailed Sally the link and thought no more about it. And here they were. She had brought a full glass of wine through from the lunch table, and she sipped it thoughtfully.

Sally came in with a big tray of cups of coffee and set it on the coffee table. People drifted in from the garden and served themselves. 'The desserts are all set out on the dining room table,' she said, smiling. 'Go through and help yourselves when you're ready.' Her smile was bright and rather forced, and her face was still a little shiny with sweat. It would just be the heat of the kitchen and the effort of hosting a party for twenty, but Esther couldn't help thinking she looked strained – and very, very thin. She had always had a peaches-and-cream complexion, but now her skin had a sallow tone, as if she'd been using a sun-bed. Maybe she had just caught some real sun or was experimenting with a different foundation. Either way, it looked a little strange.

A cheery-looking woman, whom Esther thought she recognized from the amateur dramatic group, came into the room with a large, wrapped parcel. 'Present time!' she trilled. 'Time to open all your housewarming goodies, Sally!'

Sally smiled. 'Oh, you shouldn't have... You really shouldn't. It's just so lovely to have all of you here...'

There was a flutter of reassurance, and people began to draw near, piling their gifts on the coffee table in front of Sally. Phil didn't move. Either he had given Sally her housewarming gift in private, or he hadn't got her one. Michael, who had come in from the garden, stood beside Esther's chair, resting his hand on her shoulder. 'Where did you leave the pictures?' he said quietly in her ear. 'Shall I fetch them?'

'They're in a bag in the hallway. But don't worry. I don't want to make a big deal about it. I'll give them to her when we go.'

'Come on,' said Michael. 'She's having such a ball opening things. Let's join in the fun.'

And indeed, Sally, who had taken her place on the sofa next to Phil, was exclaiming with delight over every pot-plant, tea towel and bottle of wine. Esther had a sudden flashback to the last 'party' she had attended that Sally had thrown – the lonely wake after Sally's mother's funeral. She would defy anyone to identify this laughing blonde, in her sumptuous living room and surrounded by friends, as the same person. But then who would recognize Esther herself as the person she had been that day?

Michael came back into the room carrying a gift bag. He put it on the table at Sally's elbow and she caught his hand, laughing up at him. His smile to her was warm and unguarded. When had he last smiled at Esther like that?

'I can't keep saying "you shouldn't have",' said Sally. 'But you really shouldn't.'

'I didn't,' said Michael. 'It was all Esther.'

Sally drew the three pictures out of the bag. Esther had folded each of them in tissue paper, and she carefully unwrapped them all, laying them down on the table in front of her. 'Oh,' she said, and there was something in her shocked and reverent tone that made the room go quiet.

Esther had chosen three images and had them enlarged, and she had put them in white-painted wooden frames that she knew would fit well with Sally's décor. They had been scanned from eighties snapshots, so they had the grainy, faded quality of moments long gone. The first featured Sally, aged four or so, celebrating a birthday. She was sitting at the Formica table in her childhood kitchen, and there was a cake with lit candles in front of her. She was squinting at the cake, her fat little cheeks puffed out as she prepared to blow. A dark shadow behind her could only have been Isabella.

The second picture showed Sally, Isabella and Esther in swimming costumes, playing under a garden sprinkler. This was in Laura's beautiful garden, and Esther supposed she must have taken the picture. Esther herself was off to one side, half out of the frame, chewing on a strand of her hair and glowering. Sally was standing square on to the camera, wearing a frilly bathing suit and positively bawling, her mouth a round, outraged, red 'O', her hair dripping wet. Behind her, Isabella was vaulting over the sprinkler. The camera had caught her movement as a blur, her long legs extended like a gazelle's, her dark hair streaming behind her.

'I remember that day,' said Sally, her voice so soft, it was almost a whisper. 'I hated getting my hair wet – I would scream and scream when Mum washed it. Isabella knew that, but she pushed me under the sprinkler anyway.'

The cheery lady who had begun the gift-giving laughed. 'Kids, eh?'

Sally turned to the third photograph. She wasn't in this one. Esther had had a print of this picture in her bedroom for years, although she had never shown it to Sally. It was a shot of Esther and Isabella. They were aged eleven or so. It was summer, and they were both barefoot, wearing shorts and very similar striped T-shirts. They were standing hand in hand, looking straight into the lens. Again, Esther's chin was lowered, and she stared at the camera distrustfully, but Isabella's head was thrown back, one hip cocked, the toes of one bare foot resting on the instep of the other.

'Twins!' said the cheery lady. 'Look at that!'

'They're not even sisters,' said Phil, and Esther was sure everyone must have heard the nastiness in his tone.

'Oh no,' said Sally. 'They were sisters. They were much more sisters than Isabella and I were.'

She looked up and caught Esther's eye.

If Esther could have found something to throw, she would have. An expensive knick-knack, something heavy and glass and damaging. She wanted to hurl an object with force at Sally's smug, pretty face. Sally, sitting on her expensive sofa in her expensive home, paid for with the money she had got from her dead sister and mother. Sally, who had achieved nothing in life but had everything. Sally, who had got to be with Isabella in the end, and with her mother, when Esther was the one who was sent away. Who wasn't good enough to look after anybody.

'Oh, she wasn't my sister at all,' Esther said, and her voice was very loud in the suddenly quiet living room. 'She was all yours. Right to the very end. So much all yours that you got to kill her, didn't you, Sally? Do all your smug friends and your psychotic boyfriend know that you fed your sister morphine and murdered her? It wouldn't surprise me at all if you knocked off your mother too, to speed up the whole process of inheritance. But it's all worked out fine for you hasn't it? Just look at you now!' She gestured, indicating the room with a sweep of her hand. Her wine glass went flying, spreading a pool of crimson on the cream carpet. 'Well, happy housewarming.'

She could hear the carriage clock on the mantelpiece ticking loudly in the silence. She counted five slow ticks before Michael's hand gripped her above the elbow. 'I'm so sorry, Sally,' he said evenly, as he dragged Esther to her feet. 'We'll go.'

CHAPTER FORTY-THREE

When they returned home from Sally's, she went straight upstairs and lay on the bed, fully clothed, staring at the wall. Her stomach roiled with wine and misery, and her head pounded painfully. She stayed there, without moving, for an hour or so. She could hear no sounds from downstairs, and she found herself hoping that Michael had just gone away and left her to her self-pity and shame.

Eventually, she had to get off the bed to go to the toilet. As she crossed the landing, she could see that the lights were on downstairs, and the smell of food – cottage pie, she thought, or bolognaise – floated up the stairwell to her. How was it possible that life was going on, normally, downstairs? She used the toilet and took a moment to wash her face and tidy her hair, then she went back into the bedroom and changed out of her crumpled dress and into jeans and a big, baggy jumper. She took a deep breath and walked slowly down the stairs. Michael was in the kitchen, stirring something in a saucepan. He had Radio 4 on, and she could hear a deep female voice murmuring quietly, although she could not distinguish the words. The sun was setting, and the kitchen was bathed in warm golden light. She drew out a chair and sat at the kitchen table.

He turned and gave her a small smile. 'Tea?' he said. 'Supper will be half an hour or so.'

She couldn't speak, so she just nodded, and he made a mug of tea which he placed in front of her. He went back to the stove, checked something in the oven and stirred another pan on the hob. Some music came on the radio and he hummed softly along with it. It seemed scarcely credible that he was still here, acting perfectly normally and seemingly not furious with her.

He finished what he was doing and, picking up his own mug of tea, came to sit beside her at the table. He took her hand and stroked the back of it lightly with his thumb. She snatched it away from him.

'Why are you doing this?'

'Doing what?' he asked.

'Being nice. Acting like nothing happened.'

'What's the alternative?'

Esther stared at him in disbelief.

'Seriously, what would you suggest I do? It's apparent that things are very bad for you right now. So should I yell at you? Storm out? Issue ultimatums? Treat you like a child? None of those seemed very helpful. So I thought I'd make something nourishing and comforting for dinner and see if you wanted to talk about it.'

'That's very grown-up of you. And very kind.'

'Well, it's also a little bit selfish. I live here now. I have nowhere to go. I can't just bail out. And I don't want to. I love you, and I can see you're in pain. You have been ever since your mother died, and I've watched you suffer, and have horrible things happen to you, and then do worse things to yourself. I want to help you. I want to make this stop.'

'So what do you suggest I do?'

He hesitated. 'Are you asking for sympathy or advice? I've got into trouble before for offering the second when what someone really wanted was the first.'

'Advice. Please. What do I do?'

'I think…' He paused. 'I think you need to knock the booze on the head. Totally. I think you need to work, even if it's just something voluntary. Or a proper research project with a real deadline. Leisure and introspection don't suit you. And you need to do something pro-active and definite to fix things between you and Lucie, because I can see that's killing you.'

'And what about Sally?'

'What about her?'

'I did something terrible. Unforgiveable.'

'It wasn't good,' he said quietly. 'But whether or not it's unforgivable… well, that's up to Sally, really.'

Dear Sally,

There is nothing I can say that makes up for my indefensible behaviour today at your lunch. I am so, so sorry. I do not wish to excuse my actions in any way. I lashed out to hurt someone who has never shown me anything but kindness, and I betrayed a confidence. I can only offer you a profound and sincere apology, and hope that, even though I do not deserve it, you can find it in your heart to forgive me.

All my love,

Esther

She wrote the letter by hand. It wasn't something that could be said in an email, or typed, and she certainly wasn't brave enough to try and say it over the phone or in person. She put it in an envelope, addressed it and stuck on a stamp. Then before she could overthink it, she walked to the post box on the corner and sent it on its way. She didn't expect a response. She didn't deserve one. But it had to be done.

CHAPTER FORTY-FOUR

It took Esther an hour and a half to walk from her house to Sally's place in Mill Hill. The morning had dawned rain-washed and sparkling, with a clear, azure sky. She had said nothing to Michael about her intentions. She had merely got up, made him coffee and kissed him, more warmly than usual, before waving him goodbye as he set off for work. Then she showered, dressed and began to walk. Walking, she noted, was much slower than running. At her fittest, she could run a mile in under nine minutes. Walking a mile took almost twice as long. She'd get there eventually, and she'd get fit again from the walking too. Or perhaps she could invest in a backpack and start running places.

It seemed right to be walking to Sally's, to be doing something that took a long time and used effort. Although she had ample time on the way, she did not think about what she was going to say when she got there. She walked with her head empty, watching the clouds scudding across the sky and observing the seasonal changes in the gardens she passed. It had been four months since she had posted the letter to Sally on the evening of the housewarming party. Unsurprisingly, until now, she'd had no response.

She had, however, taken all of Michael's advice to heart. She had stopped drinking completely and to her own amazement had not missed it at all. She was working on a research project about a previously unknown Victorian woman writer which she thought might make a reasonable book, and an academic publisher had already shown interest. She had agonized over what to do about Lucie, and eventually she'd tentatively asked her daughter if she would consider going to a family therapist together. To her immense surprise, Lucie jumped at the opportunity. They found a woman who worked from an upstairs room in her house in Golders Green. She was solid, Jewish, plain-speaking, and immensely warm. Lucie and Esther would meet at the Tube station once a week and go to see Leonora together. Progress was slow and fitful, but they were finding ways to spend time together. Lucie was beginning to grumble about the lack of space at Stephen's house, and how she had to keep quiet after the baby had been put to bed. Esther suspected she might ask to move home soon. With Michael's sons happily ensconced in the new summer house they'd had built in the garden, she thought Lucie might find the house a happier place. She hoped so.

She felt every step of the hill that took her up to Sally's front door. She stopped outside the neighbouring house and stood panting until she had her breath back. Then, self-consciously, she smoothed her hair and walked up to the door. With her hand hovering above the bell, she hesitated.

She didn't get to press it. While she was still hovering and thinking, she saw Sally's shadow through the frosted-glass panel; it moved slowly, and then the door opened.

'I saw you cross the driveway,' Sally said. She stood in the doorway looking at Esther. Her face was still and unsmiling but not angry. She kept one hand on the doorjamb, as if barring the entrance. Her appearance was markedly altered. She looked searchingly at Esther, and Esther could see that she was looking for a reaction. Esther knew that her face must register the shock she felt. It had been just a few months since she had last seen Sally. How could she have changed so much?

'Come in,' Sally said suddenly, and she turned and walked back down the passageway to the kitchen.

Esther followed, closing the front door softly behind her. Sally proceeded slowly, her steps small and careful, as if she was trying to move as few parts of her body as possible. They went into the kitchen, and Sally lowered herself gingerly into a chair. There was a pot of tea on the table, and a cup.

'There's still some in the pot, if you'd like some,' Sally said, as if this was a normal social visit. 'Cups are in the cupboard above the kettle, as you know. There might be biscuits too.'

Without comment, Esther fetched a mug and poured herself a cup of tea, sitting down opposite Sally. 'I'm not sure where to start,' she said hesitantly. 'Thank you for replying to my letter. I didn't expect you to. And thank you for inviting me here.'

'I know it took me a while,' said Sally. 'I was very angry with you. I needed to calm down.'

There was a cardboard folder on the kitchen table. Sally pushed it towards Esther.

'Open it,' she said.

Esther did. There were a number of papers in the file. The first was a letter in a spidery and unsteady hand, which she recognized immediately as Isabella's. In a few words, it laid out her intention to take an overdose of morphine with Sally's help but stated that Sally was in no way implicated or responsible.

'I don't need to see...' Esther began.

'There's more.' Sally gestured. Her tone made it clear that she would brook no argument.

Esther turned the page. There were copies of Joan's death certificate and a post-mortem report. Joan had died of natural causes – pneumonia.

'It's often the cause of death in dementia cases,' said Sally. 'I always knew someone would think I'd done Mum in – I just didn't think it would be you. I thought if you had doubts, especially after I told you about Isabella, well, I thought you'd just ask me. I wish you had. When Isabella asked me to... Well, she thought it was a good idea to make sure there was a clear record that it was her choice and doing, so I wouldn't get into trouble. When Mum went, I just added all the bits to the file. It seemed best.'

'I'm sorry,' said Esther.

'It's all right.' Sally managed a weak smile. 'Worse things happen at sea,' she said, and made a small sweeping gesture with her hand, indicating her own body.

'What...?' said Esther 'What's happening with you?'

Sally turned away from her then and looked out of the window. Her face, once plump and round, was skeletal, her top lip was drawn back, revealing her front teeth, and the flesh around her eyes had become sunken. Most worrying, though, was her colour. When Esther had seen Sally at the party, she'd thought the sallow tone of her skin was a faded fake tan, or bad make-up. But in the bright sunlight of Sally's kitchen she could see it was in her skin. She was actually yellow. The whites of her eyes were also tinged.

'Cancer, of course,' said Sally finally, almost cheerfully. 'Good old genetics, eh? I knew it would probably get me in the end. I just didn't think it would be so soon.'

'Cancer?'

'Pancreatic. Difficult to spot – no symptoms, really. Which is why they usually only catch it when it's too late. Like mine.'

'Too late?'

'Yup. Inoperable. I could do chemo and radiotherapy, but it's not going to give me much time at all.'

'Are you…?'

'In pain? Loads. It was the back pain that eventually sent me to the doctor. That and the weight loss. I went on a diet to lose some on purpose, but when I started eating normally, it just kept coming off. It got a bit alarming after a while. I… don't usually go to doctors. I've spent enough time dealing with medical things for other people. I tend to avoid them for myself, if I can. But the back pain got beyond a joke, so I went. He did an X-ray and couldn't see anything, so he sent me for some blood tests and a scan, and well… there you are.'

Esther sat and stared at her. This was a new Sally – blunt and plain-speaking; it was as if everything had been stripped away – her endless positivity, her sweet manner. She had neither the time nor the inclination to bother with niceties.

Esther decided that the best way to respond to Sally's frankness was to speak to her in the same way. 'How long have you got?'

'A couple of months, maybe less. The cancer's blocking my bile duct, hence my lovely colour. The tumour is quite big, so it's obstructing my stomach, which is why I can't eat much, and I keep losing weight. Not much fun, really.'

'And how do you feel?'

'Pissed off, actually.'

Her words came as quite a shock. Esther didn't think she'd ever heard her swear before. She laughed, involuntarily. 'You sounded just like Isabella then.'

'I feel like her. She was furious. She had so much to do, she said. And I feel the same. I just got my life, and now I'm losing it. There are so many things I've never done.'

'Like what?'

'Oh, you know, everything – had a career, been in love, had kids. Do you know, I've only had sex seven times in my whole life, and never in this millennium?' She managed a laugh. 'And in a hilarious twist of fate, when, at forty-two, I finally managed to meet a man I thought I might like, it turns out he only pursued me because he's obsessed with you.'

'Phil,' Esther said.

'It all came out when he realized I was ill. He panicked. He clearly wasn't going to go through being with a terminal cancer patient again... I suppose you knew about his wife.'

'I did.'

'He's gone now. He said some truly horrible things about you before he left, though. What a peach. I told him if he ever came near me or you again, I would call the police.'

'Thank you.'

'All the boys I used to bring home when I was a teenager were interested in me for about ten minutes until they saw Isabella. Then they were all in love with her. One or two still gave me a mercy shag, or at least I think that's what they call it.'

'I'm sure that's not true.'

'It is. It wasn't her fault. She couldn't help being what she was. She didn't do it on purpose. She couldn't help being fascinating and beautiful and charismatic. And anyway, she certainly wasn't interested in the weedy individuals I managed to drag home.'

Sally pulled the folder back towards her and looked at the letter in Isabella's handwriting.

'At the housewarming party, I said that she was more your sister than mine. I wasn't being... I don't know what you'd call it. I wasn't saying it to be nice. She loved you. She hated me.'

'Sally, of course she didn't.'

'No, you're right. Not hate. She was… indifferent to me. She thought I was worthless.'

'How can you say that? She asked you to care for her. You. She sent me away.'

'She asked me because she didn't care what I thought. Because if someone had to see her moaning in pain or lying in a pool of her own blood, it may as well be the one person whose opinion didn't matter. She was vile to me. Always. Right up until the end.'

Coming from anyone else, what Sally said might have sounded like self-pity, but she delivered the words with flat honesty and without drama. And looking into her eyes, Esther knew she was telling the truth. That Isabella would think like that. Do that.

'That must have been difficult for you.'

'Well, it was and it wasn't. She was never difficult to love, as you know. She just wasn't kind.'

'No, she wasn't.'

Sally smiled weakly, 'Well, it happens I suppose. Patterns get set when you're children, and they never change. People decide who you are, and no amount of evidence will change that opinion. Once the annoying little sister, always the annoying little sister. Not just to Isabella, to you too.'

'It wasn't that you were annoying, Esther said, 'we were just horrid girls. So wrapped up in ourselves. We kept pushing you away, torturing you, ignoring you…' She trailed off. Sally wasn't talking about their childhood. She was talking about their friendship now.

'I tried so hard to be a good friend to you,' Sally said, calmly and without recrimination, 'but for some reason, you distrusted that. Distrusted me.'

This wasn't the time for fervent denial. 'I did. I was suspicious,' Esther said.

'Of what?'

'I found your ability to remember disconcerting. The past was so vivid to you, and that seemed strange to me. I couldn't work out what you wanted from me, and I ended up suspecting you of the most dreadful things – of trying to monopolise my circle of friends, of trying to come between Lucie and me. I didn't know what you wanted from me.'

'I just wanted to be your friend. Through those years with my mum, when she was ill, remembering things became everything, really. I was alone with her so much of the time, and gradually she lost herself, and lost all memory of my dad, of Isabella, of who I was. All I had was what I recalled. I'm the last of my line, and the keeper of all the memories. But then you were there, and you remembered some of it too. And you were part of some of the stories. It meant a lot. You meant a lot. And I'm grateful to you, and to Lucie and Michael and Paul and Tim, for giving me a start, helping me make some new memories.'

'That's a much kinder interpretation of the past year or so than I deserve,' said Esther. 'I'm sorry.' She got up from the table and walked to the window. 'It seems that's all I have to say to you. Sorry.'

'You know...' Sally began, and then stopped. 'You know I'm going to need more from you than that.'

'I know.'

'Will you?'

'Of course. I am enormously grateful to be asked.'

They didn't hug, and they didn't say much more after that. Esther stayed and finished her tea, and they made a few practical plans. Then she left and walked back home.

When Michael came home that evening, she had her bags packed and ready in the hallway. She had prepared what she wanted to say, so she asked him to sit down in the living room.

'Michael, I love you,' she began, and he looked surprised. She realized what a very long time it had been since she had last said it aloud. 'I love you,' she said again. 'You are the single best thing, after Lucie, ever to have happened to me, and I've treated you appallingly. I have failed you in every possible way. I do not deserve your kindness and loyalty, and I am all too aware that I could have lost it forever.'

He opened his mouth to speak, but she touched his hand. 'Don't say anything yet,' she said. 'I need to tell you that Sally is dying. She has terminal, inoperable, pancreatic cancer.'

He looked horrified. 'I can't believe it. When did she find out?'

'Within the last few weeks. She's in quite a bit of pain, and she doesn't have a lot of time. I would like to go and live in her house and take care of her for as long as she has left.'

Michael nodded. 'If that's what she wants, then of course you must.'

'Thank you. And if you would be so kind as to stay here, to take care of our home...' She leaned lightly on the word 'our'. 'I would be so grateful.'

EPILOGUE

She'd been restlessly asleep for hours, her fingers plucking irregularly at the covers, her eyelids fluttering, her breathing rattly and noisy. Esther sat and watched her. She'd been told that these were all signs that the end was near. It was quite possible that she wouldn't wake again. Her breathing would slow and then stop, and that would be it. Esther leaned back in her chair. She hadn't slept for a long time and she was weary. She shut her eyes for a second, just to rest them.

The breathing stopped and her eyes flew open. The face on the pillow looked awake and alert, the eyes wide open and almost amused.

'Caught you napping.'

'Sorry,' Esther said. 'Can I get you anything?'

'No thanks.' She smiled, a genuinely warm, attentive and lovely smile. 'You must be knackered, sorry.'

'I'm fine,' said Esther. 'Honestly. How are you doing? Want more morphine?'

'No pain right now. But I tell you what, my feet are bloody freezing.'

'Your feet? Really?' The room was warm, and the bed was covered with a heavy, fluffy duvet.

'Yeah.'

'Can I get you some socks?'

'I don't think that'll work. I think my body's storing all the heat around what's left of my essential organs. I don't think I'm able to generate my own heat for my extremities. Maybe a hot water bottle... only I don't think I own one.'

'I don't think you do,' said Esther. She paused for a second. 'I read somewhere, although I suspect it's completely spurious, that when D. H. Lawrence was dying, he complained his feet were cold, and his wife, Frieda, put them in her bosom to warm them.'

'Her bosom?'

'I haven't got much of a bosom, but I do generate quite a bit of body heat.'

The chuckle from the bed sounded lively, warm, not at all like the chuckle of someone dying. 'Would you? Would you do that for me?'

'For you, Millais, anything.'

Esther folded back the duvet from the bottom of the bed and lay on her side. She lifted her shirt and drew Sally's cold feet to her, pressing them against her stomach, then drawing her jumper and the duvet down over them. 'Better?'

'Better. Thank you. Your belly is so soft. Squidgy.' A smile, silence, and eyes that closed slowly.

Esther lay still, breathing softly and watching, until she too fell asleep for a time.

If you enjoyed *After Isabella* you might like to read this exclusive extract from Rosie's new novel, *What She Left*

PROLOGUE

Helen brushed her hair and smoothed it away from her face, then used a hair tie to secure it. She combed the length of the ponytail until it lay smooth and shiny over her shoulder, split the hair into sections and plaited it neatly. She checked her reflection: light eye make-up and a becoming, pale pink lip-gloss. She went into the bedroom, where she had laid her dress out on the bed, a cotton maxi-dress, covered in big blue flowers. She slipped it over her head and slid her feet into flat white pumps. A spritz of her citrusy perfume and she was ready to go.

She went down to the kitchen. She'd cleaned up after breakfast, before she'd taken the girls to school. To an outsider, the kitchen would have appeared spotless, but Helen picked up a cloth and wiped quickly at a tiny smear on the otherwise pristine worktop. The washing machine hummed quietly, but other than that, the house was silent.

In the living room, her handbag, a large, soft leather one which matched the blue of the flowers of her dress, sat on the coffee table. She'd packed it carefully, as usual, but she checked through its contents one more time. Looking out of the window, she saw their next-door neighbour, Mrs Goode, leaving her house, Sainsbury's Bags for Life in hand.

Helen glanced around the living room, then took a quick tour round the downstairs to check that all the doors and windows were securely fastened before picking up her handbag and stepping out of her own front door. As she locked it, she called a cheery greeting to Mrs Goode, who was standing in her driveway, clearly waiting for a lift. Mrs Goode waved back, and Helen, dropping her key into her bag, headed off up the road on foot.

As was her habit, she set off at a brisk, focused pace. She imagined Mrs Goode watching her. She didn't look back. She walked quickly to the end of their quiet road, turned the corner, and disappeared.

CHAPTER ONE

Lara

Every middle-class London school has a Helen. Perhaps the Helen at your school has shining blonde hair or twinkling dark eyes. Perhaps she's called Sarah, or Rebecca or Shariza. The principle is the same. Our Helen had a clear, bell-like voice, and you had to speak to her for a little while before you picked up the slight twang and upward inflection that told of her Australian origins. She had a smooth, chestnut-brown ponytail, clear, pale skin and wide blue eyes. You would often see the ponytail swinging as she ran briskly through the park, half an hour before pick-up time. But more often than not, you'd see it swinging as she laughed among a bustling group of parents in the playground. She'd be there before school, after school, at every school event, at the school gate collecting for the summer fete that she'd organized. She'd be at the open day, merrily guiding a group of prospective parents from classroom

3

to classroom. She'd wink kindly at the harried mothers rushing in late, as her own demure girls, their smooth ponytails equally perfectly brushed, waited by her side. She produced perfect cakes for the cake sale, perfect costumes for the class assembly and perfect financial records after the astonishingly successful Christmas fayre. She was perfect.

And then she vanished.

It turned out that I was the first person at school to know she'd gone missing. Ella Barker did an interview with the *Daily Mail* and said she was the first 'because Helen was always at the school gates, so I noticed immediately when she wasn't there'. But that wasn't true. Ella was long gone when we realized, and so were all the other Year Three mothers. Ella didn't care if what she said wasn't true. The *Mail* sent a stylist and took a picture of her in her neat front garden, and said how much her house was worth, so she was thrilled.

Ella was gone, and the playground was all but deserted when I ran in, rattling the pushchair ahead of me, sweaty and out of breath. It's a long story, but not a very interesting one – any parent who has a toddler and a child at school knows it well. The toddler runs around like a lunatic, then spends some hours screaming blue murder, resisting their nap. Then they finally fall asleep fifteen minutes before school pick-up time. You end up stuffing them clumsily into the pushchair and running to school with a dozy, wailing, hot and miserable child. And, of course, you're late, and your eight-year-old is the last child left at the classroom door, next to the tight-lipped teacher who has several hours of planning ahead of her, delayed because of your poor time-keeping.

Except, on that muggy day in late May, Frances wasn't alone. Miranda was there too, her socks still spotlessly white and neatly pulled up and her hair tidy. Mrs Sinclair had a sharp crease between her eyebrows. She expected me to be late – it happened at least twice a week. But Helen was never late.

'Did you see Helen on your way in?' she asked as I hung Frances' rucksack on the handles of the pushchair and handed my daughter a brioche as an after-school snack. 'She's very late, it's most unlike her. Perhaps there were problems with parking.'

'The road's clear outside,' I said. 'And anyway, I think Helen walks. Did she leave a message with the office? Maybe Miranda was supposed to go on a play date with someone and forgot.'

Miranda regarded me with all the contempt an eight-year-old girl can summon.

'I didn't forget,' she said coldly. 'And anyway, my dad was supposed to pick us up today. He's supposed to come to my ballet class to see us perform, and now I'm going to be late.'

Mrs Sinclair looked at her, surprised. 'Your dad? Your dad never picks you up.'

'I know,' said Miranda. 'But he was supposed to do it today.'

At that moment, Marguerite's class teacher walked up, holding Marguerite's hand. Marguerite is six and in Year One, rounder and softer than Miranda, shy, but just as immaculately turned out. She had clearly been crying and her soft cheeks were puffy and wet. The teachers exchanged a glance and a quick word.

'She wants to be with her sister,' said the Year One teacher. 'Can I leave her with you, and I'll go to the office and see if they can't get hold of Helen or her husband?'

'I have Helen's number on my mobile,' I said quickly. Jonah, my two-year-old, had stopped wailing but was grizzling and twisting against the straps in the pushchair. I should just have taken Frances and left, but I wanted to help, if only to show Mrs Sinclair I wasn't a total dead loss as a parent. I pulled my phone from my pocket and dialled. Helen's phone went immediately to voicemail, so I left a message with my number. The two teachers and four children looked at me expectantly.

'Voicemail,' I said unnecessarily. 'Maybe she's stuck on the Tube or something. Or her battery's flat. Or she's lost her phone.'

None of these were likely. Helen's efficiency, forward planning and organization were legendary. Even I could hear how lame it sounded.

'I could take the girls home with me,' I heard myself saying.

Frances and Miranda weren't especially good friends. Helen had had Frances over for a play date, but only because she always conscientiously invited every little girl at least once during the course of each year. I'd meant to return the favour but never had. I'd been intimidated by the prospect of having those spotless little girls in my chaotic house, and I'd have had to clean for a week if Helen were coming to collect them and stay for a cup of tea. But now it was a case of needs must. I couldn't leave them at school.

'We can't release them to you without their guardian's authorization. I'll keep them in my classroom,' said Mrs Sinclair. 'Perhaps, Miss Jones, you could go to the office and get the family contact details? You might be able to get hold of the dad, if he's the one who's supposed to be picking them up.'

Miss Jones, a plump, self-satisfied woman, nodded. 'I'll go and call from the office.'

I would have left then, but as soon as Miss Jones walked away, Marguerite began to cry. My Frances went into full mummy mode and bustled over, taking Marguerite by the hand and leading her to the book corner in the Year Three classroom. Frances settled on a cushion and drew Marguerite on to her lap. She pulled a book out of the stack and began reading in a high, babyish voice, which she clearly thought was the way one spoke to six-year-olds. Miranda stood by coolly and watched as Frances cared for her sister. Jonah let out a roar of frustration. He'd tried to wriggle downwards out of his pushchair straps and had got himself stuck. I unstrapped him and straightened the straps, but when I tried to do them up again, he arched his back and let out a wail of pure fury. He shoved my hands away and climbed out, toddling over to Frances and Marguerite.

'I can't begin to think where she might be,' said Mrs Sinclair.

'Has something bad happened?' Miranda asked flatly.

'Of course not,' Mrs Sinclair and I said in unison.

'Miranda, love,' I said as sweetly as I could, 'are you sure your dad was supposed to pick you up today? Has there been some kind of a mix-up?'

Miranda looked at me coolly. 'Of course there's no mix-up. Dad wanted to come and see my dance show.'

'But wouldn't Helen—' I began, but Miranda cut me off.

'She's doing a course today. She said she would come along later,' she said.

That made sense and explained why Helen's phone was off.

'Do you know what sort of course? Or where?' Mrs Sinclair asked, but Miranda shook her head.

'It's just one of those things,' I said. 'I'm sure Helen or Sam will be along any minute.'

Miranda stared at me like I was some sort of idiot.

'I'll make some calls,' I said. 'Maybe she told one of the other mums where she was going.'

I ran through all the local families in my mind and decided to call Linda. She always asks a lot of questions and generally seems to know everything about everyone. She listened to my garbled account of what had happened. 'She didn't say anything this morning at drop-off,' she said, 'but I'll start a phone chain to see if anyone has heard from her.'

I felt better knowing someone as practical as Linda had taken charge. I glanced over to the children. Marguerite had stopped crying and was sitting happily on Frances' lap, sucking her two middle fingers as Frances read to her from a book of ancient Greek legends. It struck me that Marguerite was quite babyish for a child nearly in Year Two. But perhaps it wasn't fair to judge her in that rather stressful situation. Miranda stayed where she was, close by Mrs Sinclair's side, looking up into our faces. She's one of those wide-eyed, quiet children who listens intently to whatever adults say. 'Little bat ears,' Helen would often say when Miranda was nearby and we were chatting. 'Be careful what you say. She misses nothing.'

Miss Jones came back into the classroom. 'I spoke to Marguerite's dad,' she said. 'He was supposed to pick up the girls, but then he was called away unexpectedly to Manchester on a business trip. He sent a message to his wife and asked her to collect them, but clearly she somehow never got it. He's on his way back now, but it's going to take him some hours to get here. Lara, he asks if you could kindly take the girls with you. He has no idea why Helen isn't receiving his messages, but he says he'll keep trying to get hold of her. I left a message on her mobile saying that the girls would be going home with you. Perhaps you might send them both a text message with your address, if they don't have it?'

I nodded and did so, although I was sure Helen had the address of every child in the class in a perfectly annotated spreadsheet somewhere.

'Girls,' I said brightly, 'it looks like Helen's busy somewhere, and your dad's on his way. I've let him know you're coming home to my house.'

Marguerite managed a watery smile, and Miranda didn't say anything. I gathered their things and piled them into the pushchair. Jonah wouldn't get back into it without a fight anyway, so he'd have to walk, or rather be shepherded, home.

It took us twice as long as usual. Jonah was so excited to be free of the pushchair and to have two extra girls to show off to that he ran amok. Frances and Marguerite dawdled beside me, chatting, and Miranda walked slowly and reluctantly a few paces behind. She didn't say anything for a long time, and then, out of nowhere, she spoke. 'It's our ballet performance for the parents today,' she said. 'I was supposed to be a firefly. I've got a costume and everything. And now I'm going to miss it.'

I know how seriously Miranda takes her dancing – she and Frances were in the same class initially, but Miranda progressed much more quickly and is now in an advanced group. Even as a chubby five-year-old, she used to approach the class with fierce concentration. While the other girls were busy swinging their little pink skirts and giggling together, Miranda was focused on the teacher, pointing her toes and making pretty arms. I felt angry with Sam and Helen for letting her down so badly on this important day. I gave her narrow shoulder a pat. She stiffened slightly, and I took my hand away.

I got the kids back to my house and settled them at the table with cups of squash and a snack. I briefly considered taking Miranda to ballet myself, but her costume was at home, and as I don't drive, there was no way we could get to the ballet school in time, not with me wrangling four children on the bus. Someone had to let them know she wasn't coming though, and I was pretty sure Sam wouldn't think to do it. I managed to find the ballet teacher's number online and went into my bedroom to make the call. She was clipped and rude, as if it were my fault. When I turned round after I had hung up Miranda was standing in the door of my bedroom.

'I just remembered, Helen said she'd be back in time to watch the show,' Miranda said. 'She said she'd meet us at the dance school at four-thirty. It's four-thirty now. So where is she?'

Sam

I'd only just arrived in Manchester to take a short-notice brief from a brand-new client – a massive, multinational health-food company – when the school rang. I phoned the client as soon as I realized I would have to go back to London and told them there was an emergency with one of my children. That seemed serious enough that they might consent to reschedule. I couldn't say, 'My wife didn't get the message to pick the kids up from school and I don't know where she is.' What would they have thought?

I could only get a first-class seat on the train back to London, which was screamingly expensive, but at least it meant I could sit in relative quiet. I wanted to keep my phone free in case Helen rang, so I used email to cancel all my meetings. It didn't even bear thinking about what Chris, my boss, would say.

I know it sounds heartless when I put it like that – worrying about the cost of train tickets, worrying about what people would think. But at that point I honestly wasn't concerned about her. I was a little annoyed, actually. It just wasn't like her to let me down. I know she'd said she was on a course till after school pick-up time, and I had promised to leave work early and collect the kids, but then Chris told me I needed to go and take that brief. The account was worth a fortune and we'd been trying to get in with that company for ages.

I left a voice message, explaining what had happened. I figured Helen would have her phone on silent and would see my call and then listen to the message on her lunch break. She'd have to leave her course early to pick up the girls, but I knew she wouldn't mind.

I'd anticipated arriving in Manchester for the meeting, then calling Helen to say I'd be staying over. She was used to that – I often took the opportunity to spend an evening with clients. There are certain deals that only get done when the sun has gone down, the booze has flowed and the client in question feels he's got all the perks he deserves. I always kept a bag at work with a change of shirt and underwear and a toothbrush for days like that. Helen knew how unpredictable my work could be, and she always took the unexpected meetings and changes of plan in her stride. So this complete collapse of our arrangements really threw me.

This was Helen. Calm, capable Helen. Something had happened, that was for sure, and I didn't give much thought to what – a broken-down car, a lost phone. Something minor. I'd swallow my annoyance, because she was always so amazing, and it was actually slightly my fault for changing the plans at the last minute. By eight o'clock that evening, we'd all be sitting around the dinner table, laughing about it. She'd have sorted out whatever the problem was and smoothed things over. She'd even have dropped off a thank-you gift for Lara, the mum who'd taken Miranda and Marguerite home. I'd do my best to grovel to the man in Manchester and set everything up for another day.

Nevertheless, my phone stayed ominously silent for the whole journey. Shortly before the train pulled into Euston, I rang Lara. It was just after six o'clock. She'd heard nothing. Apparently Jilly, who lives in our road, had popped past our house to have a look. There had been no answer when she rang the doorbell. I knew, as I had dialled it intermittently, that Helen's mobile phone remained switched off. I think that was the moment I began to be concerned. Helen had said she'd be at the dance school by 4.30, and it was over an hour and a half past that now. She had a thing about 6 p.m. 'I like to have the girls home by then,' she'd say. 'Wherever we've been, six o'clock is home time – time to get homework done and baths ready.'

I wracked my brains, trying to remember what Helen had said about the course she was going on. Something about effective social media for small businesses? Had she said where it was? I didn't think so. I tried Helen's phone one more time, to no avail. I began to feel a little anxious then, and started to run. I'd planned to just get on the Tube, but I couldn't bear the idea of being stuck underground, even if it was for only twenty minutes, so I jogged to the taxi rank. Miracle of miracles, there was no queue and within seconds I was in a black cab and we were gliding through Camden on our way north.

Once I was in the taxi, I began to calm down. It had to be a misunderstanding. Maybe the course had gone on late. She did love her courses, I reminded myself. She was always doing them, learning about something new. She'd done several, one about starting a blog, and a few about search engine optimisation and basic computer coding.

Lara's house turned out to be quite near ours – maybe three or four minutes closer to the school. The front fence was unpainted and the little garden was a profusion of wild flowers. I kicked a football out of the way and rang the doorbell. Lara opened the door, a pretty woman with a narrow, freckled face and a tangle of red curls. I vaguely knew who she was and had heard Helen talk about her. She was a single parent, I recalled. She ushered me in and we went through to the back of the house where my girls and her two kids were eating around her big wooden kitchen table. An older woman, I assumed her mum, was sitting at the table, chatting to all the kids. She smiled kindly at me. They'd given the children what we would have called 'tea' when I was little – fish fingers and smiley-face oven chips, which Marguerite was enthusiastically dipping into a massive puddle of ketchup. Miranda was sitting up straight, cutting her fish fingers into neat squares with her knife and fork and eating as she'd been taught. The girls usually ate dinner with us a little later – proper, adult food served in the dining room. On any other day, this would have been considered quite a treat.

'Hey, girls!' I said, and my voice sounded bright and fake, like a children's television presenter. They both looked up.

'Daddy,' said Marguerite, in the babyish voice she uses when she's tired, and she jumped down from her chair and ran to me. I scooped her up and cuddled her. She curved into my arms, her plump arms and legs still soft. She's lovely to hold, and I took a moment to hug her and sniff her hair, which smelled of the strawberry shampoo Helen liked to use on the girls. Whenever I hug Miranda, which she will sometimes reluctantly allow, she's all sharp angles – pointy elbows and narrow, bony limbs. 'Finish up your food,' I said, gently putting Marguerite down, 'and we'll head home.'

The girls continued eating, and Lara drew me out of the kitchen and into the living room.

'Any news of Helen?' she asked.

'Nothing,' I said. 'But I'm sure there's a reasonable explanation. I'm absolutely certain she'll be at home when we get there.' I smiled at her, and she looked at me oddly. I suppose it must have seemed as if I were trying to reassure her. I didn't know what to say. 'Come on, girls,' I called. 'Let's get going!'

It took fifteen minutes of faffing to gather the girls' school bags, jumpers and shoes from the chaos of Lara's living room. We thanked her and her mum again and left the house to walk home. As we turned the corner out of Lara's road, a name came to me. Crystal Spectrum. They were the people who ran the internet courses Helen went on. I stopped in my tracks, ran a quick search on my phone and came up with a number for them. It was late, but there was a chance someone was still there.

Eventually a crisp-voiced woman picked up. I gave my name. 'My wife, Helen, was booked on to a course on social media today—' I began, but the woman cut me off.

'Helen Cooper? I know her well. She's attended a lot of courses here. I'm Diane, the director of Crystal Spectrum. Hang on a minute. . .' I could hear her typing, accessing records on her computer. 'Oh,' she said, and she sounded surprised. 'Yes, she was booked on the course this morning, but she was a no-show. That's not like her.'

'No,' I said. 'Are you sure?'

'Absolutely sure. There's even a note here that the trainer got our receptionist to ring her. There was no reply.'

'What time was she due to get there?'

'We started at eleven,' Diane said, and then she added hesitantly, 'I do hope everything's okay.'

So did I. I thanked her and rang off. So Helen could have gone missing as early as eleven that morning. What could have happened? The girls were looking up at me curiously, so I popped my phone in my pocket and walked us home.

I could see the girls were getting worried, so I tried to look and act cheerful. I chided myself for being a worrier and freaking them out. It was a beautiful, balmy evening, sunny and still, the kind of summer evening where Helen would serve dinner on the patio outside – grilled salmon, new potatoes and a salad with her homemade dressing. I imagined us walking into the house and seeing the patio doors flung wide, with music drifting from the kitchen radio; Helen, wearing her duck-egg blue skirt, feet bare and hair caught up in her trademark ponytail, would turn and smile as she carried the salad bowl outside.

We turned into our road, and I could see Helen's Prius parked in the driveway, just as it always was. I began to believe my own fantasy. I could practically smell the salmon. Helen might be a little annoyed that the girls had already eaten, but Marguerite at least would be up for a second meal.

I put my key in the door, but it refused to budge. Whenever

one of us was at home, we'd only use the Yale lock. We'd only lock the mortice if everyone was out. I took a deep breath and sorted through my keys to find the correct one, unlocked the mortice and then the Yale and the door swung open.

The moment I stepped inside, I knew she wasn't there. The air was dead and silent. There were no dinner smells and no music and the doors out to the patio were locked. There was no Helen to turn and smile, a dish in her hand and her blue skirt swishing round her smooth, tanned legs.

As if someone had forcibly punched me into another time, I was hurled back to that other night, five and a half years ago, when I stepped into an empty house for the first time. I couldn't help myself. My knees just gave way, and I found myself kneeling on the hall carpet in the dark, with my daughters standing beside me. Marguerite came to me and patted my shoulder, but, unexpectedly, it was Miranda who began to cry, in high, quick sobs.

'Daddy, get up!' she said sharply. 'Get up!'

I didn't get up. I fumbled in my pocket and brought out my phone. I dialled 999.

'Which emergency service do you require?' said a tinny voice on the other end. 'Police, ambulance or fire?'

'Police,' I said. 'Police. My wife is missing.' And then I began to cry.